THE RED MANOR

Rene Natan

PUBLISH AMERICA

PublishAmerica
Baltimore

ISBN: 1-60672-325-1
PUBLISHED BY PUBLISHAMERICA, LLLP
www.publishamerica.com
Baltimore

Printed in the United States of America

For Roberto with Love

Acknowledgments

The author gratefully acknowledges those who helped with the research and setting of this novel. They include Luisa Gargantini, Martin Strybosch and Damjana Bratuz.

Special thanks to Sharon Crawford and Harvey Stanbrough for the editing.

Main Personas

Lucio Maria **de' Vigentini**, Lord of the Red Manor
Christopher **Sandcroft**, Lucio's son
Mirko **Grogan**, an orphan from Croatia
Jim **Chagrain**, thief
Nozemni **Radic**, con artist
Poitr and Helena **Radic**, managers of the orphanage
Gabriele **Anzieri**, owner of Il Corsaro Rosso
Glen **Howard**, businessman
Vivian **Howard**, Glen's daughter
Lillian **Carrigan**, caregiver
Gideon **Wilson**, maintenance man
Kathy **Wilson**, housekeeper

PART 1

Settling in a New Country

CHAPTER 1

Boccascura di San Zenobio, Central Italy
Spring 2005

In the stillness of the night the church bells resounded once and then once again. Startled, Christopher Sandcroft stood still, waiting for the chimes to fade. He had been wandering in the main square of Boccascura for almost an hour, saying goodbye to the old town. Surrounded by buildings on all sides, Saint Zenobio Square measured about 150 by 80 metres. The slate roofs backlit by the moon, coupled with the square's emptiness at that time of night, gave it a spectral look.

Chris had come here in search of peace, trying to convince himself he was doing the right thing. He repeated his steps past the ice-cream parlour where his mother used to take him Thursday afternoons after violin lessons. On his right lay the bakery, which still smelled of chocolate cookies. He crossed the square; his steps made little noise on the old, cobbled pavement. He approached the church of Saint Zenobio and tugged at the ornate, heavy handle. The place was locked, of course. In this very same church his mother had come to pray, and often, too often, indeed, had come to cry.

Memories, memories…

Chris sighed. It was time to put everything behind him. With resolute strides he walked under the portico and out of the square, then took the steep road that would lead him to the ancestral castle: the Red Manor.

Everything was set for the big journey. Chris' father, Lucio Maria de' Vigentini, sat in a wheelchair near the entrance, a plaid blanket spread across his legs; the luggage was already in the limousine. Chris looked up when he heard a noise coming from above a balustrade where two imposing staircases joined in a landing. Marble columns, finely chiselled, with the same shape, but each a different colour, supported the handrails. An older man hurried down the right staircase. It was Salvatore Argento, his father's faithful servant of 55 years. He staggered, then descended farther, holding onto the handrail. He wore the trousers, shirt and vest of his butler outfit, with white shirt sleeves too long for his arms. Wrinkles covered his skin and his cheeks and nose were burnished. As he hurried to descend the last few steps, he stumbled and hugged the statue of an armoured knight to keep his balance. He then stood in front of Chris, heart-stricken, and with tears in his eyes.

"*Che cosa*, what…" His voice quivered. "What will I do without him?" he asked Chris.

Chris didn't know what to say. This departure was emotional enough for his father; he didn't want any aggravation. Then Salvatore rushed into his arms, his chest heaving with sobs, his small frame barely reaching Chris' shoulders. Chris glanced at his father. He had not turned his face; he had not said a word. Chris hugged Salvatore tightly, yet delicately, because his body was a small, frail assembly of bones.

"I'll send you a ticket and you'll come to see him," Chris said, in clear tones so the old man could hear. "Maybe you could stay with us for a while. Just give us time to settle." He repeated each word in Italian, to be sure Salvatore understood.

Salvatore let go and looked into Chris' eyes, relief on his face. "*È proprio vero? Is it a promise?"

Chris nodded, quickly hugged the man again, then pushed his father's wheelchair out through the door.

A vintage Boeing 767/300ER climbed into the air, entered a layer of soft clouds, and soon emerged into the blue sky. The Alps extended below, an immense arc of majestic snowy peaks glistening in the sun, their dark, steep, menacing cliffs reaching down for the valleys. They flew at only 7,000 metres above sea level because there wasn't much distance between Malpensa International Airport, the point of take-off, and the foot of the mountains. The aircraft kept climbing steadily and smoothly.

Chris lowered the back of his seat and stretched his long legs. One of the advantages of travelling first class was the ample space.

Finally his father turned to him. "Did you pack the Harlequin well?"

Chris nodded. They had decided to bring a few paintings from the family collection, and the Harlequin was a precious water painting by Federico Zandomeneghi, a Venetian impressionist who had refined his art in Paris.

"And the Model?" Lucio asked.

That was a large oil, dated 1900; it showed a smiling woman, the model of painter Cesare Tallone and the lost love of Lucio's grandfather.

"Yes, I took care of it personally," Chris said. "The frame is big, curved and very, very old, so I packed it well with lots of bubble wrap." He reached for his father's arm and squeezed it gently. "Relax. You'll find everything in order, even that gloomy picture of the Red Manor." He laughed. "I don't know why you want it with you; it's so scary. We should find a place to hide it." He hoped to get his father to lighten up.

"You would do that, wouldn't you?" His father feigned a look of reproach. "Just to get at me, right? You're still the mischievous little boy who hid in the suits of armour, moving their arms and making them clink when the servants passed by. You scared them."

"I never thought you noticed."

Chris had only a few memories of the time spent at the castle when he was a child; his mother had taken him away when he was barely six years old. Despite spending his vacations in his teens and twenties at the Red Manor, Chris' father remained a mystery. He glanced at Lucio. He wanted to prod him, get him to talk, ask him why Mother had left, why he had never come to Canada to see him, why he couldn't call him Dad anymore. But Lucio, his chin relaxed over his chest, had fallen asleep.

Chris slowly sipped the San Benedetto mineral water the flight attendant had deposited on his table. It was too late to have doubts and regrets, as the castle had already changed hands and there was no way to reverse the transaction. Yet, did he have the right to uproot his father and take him to a strange country? Lucio was 72 and no longer mobile. How much would his father miss his native land, and the ancient castle with the big tower at the front and turrets all around? How much would he miss sitting in the highest terrace of the Red Manor watching the sunset or going through the vineyards to check on the grapes?

It had been a big decision, one Chris wished he had never had to make.

Lucio was not asleep. He couldn't sleep; he was just pretending to avoid conversation. He was worried. Would he survive such a huge change, leaving his homeland behind? In his mind he bid farewell to his beloved castle, its image engraved in his memory forever.

Built on a highland, the Red Manor overlooked the convergence of two valleys, one on the north and one on the south, merging on the east. The massif of the Gran Sasso d'Italia sheltered the castle from the west. With its rows of 50 embrasures on the front wall and an equal number of slits spread out on the sides, the Red Manor had been known, in ancient times, as a fortress difficult to reach and almost impossible to storm. The village of Boccascura lay on a decline, protected by the castle's fortifications and reputation.

Lucio made an effort to chase away the images of the castle and village, both so dear to his heart. He began to take stock of his life, to think about what might lie ahead; he wondered whether the curse cast on the de' Vigentini family 500 years ago was still alive. It had already cost him a son, and he feared its spell continued to hold. That was why he hadn't vigorously opposed Deborah, his late wife, when she had taken Chris with her. Now, with the bond renewed between him and his son, he wondered whether Chris was at risk. His eyes semi-closed, Lucio changed position while peering at Chris, who was immersed in reading technical papers and making annotations as he went along. He definitely had a good-looking son. His large jaw and slightly arched nose gave him a masculine aspect; his tightly curled hair was cut very short. His hair and eye colour were the only features Chris had inherited from his father; they were both brown. Chris was slender, like his mother, and his personality reminded Lucio of Deborah: cheerful, kind, ready to help others.

He had met Deborah at the Toronto Art Gallery and watched her as she carefully packaged large prints for the visitors. Lucio had returned to the gallery that day at closing time and played the tourist lost in the big city. After their first date they had met every day for two weeks, at the end of which Lucio had begged her to follow him to Italy and spend some time at the Red Manor. He had fallen in love with a beautiful woman, who not only spoke his native tongue but also responded to his passion with equal intensity.

And he had lost her.

Lucio sighed, loud enough to attract Chris' attention.

"Are you okay?" Chris asked.

Lucio opened his eyes wide. "Yes, I'm fine."

"Good, you woke up just in time. They're serving dinner."

CHAPTER 2

At Pearson International Airport in Greater Toronto, two cars waited to receive Christopher Sandcroft and Lucio Maria de' Vigentini. Gideon and Kathy Wilson, who lived on Sandcroft's estate, had come to greet their employer and his father. They lugged the many suitcases and parcels into the trunks.

"Why don't you sit with your father?" Gideon asked, as Chris opened the door on the driver's side. "Kathy doesn't mind driving by herself."

Chris complied. Once they were on the road, Lucio became very alert and talkative, counting aloud the number of tires on the big trucks they passed, commenting on the large pieces of uncultivated land, and asking what was being planted in the fields so early in the year. Soy beans? He had never heard of them.

The trip from the airport to Harrisville lasted just over an hour and soon they crossed through the majestic cedar arch that marked the beginning of the Sandcroft property.

The GM Aurora stopped at the main entrance. Chris hurried out to flip open the trunk and unfolded the wheelchair. He helped his father out of the car and adjusted the blanket on Lucio's knees. The April air was chilly.

Lucio looked at the two-storey building. "*Ullalà!* Is this the residence of a bachelor?" He stared at the light-brown brick walls, the green shutters, and the mansard with two little windows. "Good structure." He nodded.

"It was built for two families; that's why it's so big. You'll enjoy the space, especially during the long winter days. It's only partially furnished. Some walls on the main floor are still bare." Chris looked at Lucio and winked. "Ready for all the paintings we took with us, and the many we've shipped." He tapped his father on the shoulder. "That gives you a chance to play interior decorator. Let's get inside now."

16

A second *ullalà*, louder than the first one, echoed through the entrance hall. "This is beautiful, Chris. Congratulations." Lucio marvelled at the big skylight that gave the entrance a diffused yet intense lighting.

Chris laughed. "I can't take credit for any of the house design. Grandpa did it all. I just moved in."

Lucio continued to gaze about the room. "A marble floor. I didn't expect this in Canada. And the staircase…the handrail is so elaborate, all wood, and the pattern is what? Grape leaves?"

"That's what they are. The house was designed for two families and has separate entrances and garages. There are two floors of apartments. They are almost the same. You get the first floor and I get the second. Come on; I'll show you."

He led his father further into the house, showing him the two main floor bedrooms, then the den, which he had turned into a family room and furnished with a new plasma HDTV set and a DVD player. Lucio stared at the far wall, covered with the awards Chris and his grandfather had collected over the years, then let out another *ullalà* when he turned and saw the expanse of backyard outside the patio door

"End of the tour," Chris said, and pushed the wheelchair back into the corridor. "Let's see what's ready for us in the kitchen."

"Oh, look what's on the table," Lucio said. "A nice snack."

Two coffee cups, sugar and cream were lined up along one side, and an angel food cake stood in the middle of the table in the breakfast nook. On the kitchen counter, the coffee maker displayed a green light, indicating that the coffee was ready to be served.

Chris pushed Lucio's chair close to the table, then called for Gideon and Kathy, as they finished unloading the luggage.

"Come in and have a bite to eat with us in the kitchen," he said. He turned back to Lucio. "Gideon takes care of the property and minor house repairs, and Kathy is my full-time housekeeper. They're wonderful, and you can depend on them in any circumstance. You'll like them."

*   *   *

"I'd love to join you guys, but I can't. Perhaps by the end of the month I'll be free to spend time down the river." Chris closed his cell phone.

For the third weekend in a row he had declined an invitation to go rafting, his favourite sport. He wanted to spend time with his father, show him the countryside, and introduce him to neighbours and friends of the family—making sure Lucio didn't feel neglected. So far things had been going better than he had expected. After two days' resting and dozing off because of the jetlag, Lucio had settled down. He seemed relaxed, as if a big load had been lifted off his shoulders. He inquired about the management of the household, and kept busy exploring the Sandcroft family's 40-acre estate. When weather permitted, he wheeled his way along the trails, some of which flanked the brook that meandered through the fields and emptied into a large pond at the property limits.

Chris brewed a cup of coffee. He wondered whether taking Lucio with him had been a good move. He really didn't know much about his father…

After his mother's death, Chris had visited his father every summer, staying two or three weeks at a time. His arrival at the Red Manor had been a big event, celebrated with a two-day party, and the festive atmosphere had lasted for his entire stay. He never had a boring moment, and everybody seemed to enjoy his presence. The hired help would bring him to the orchard to taste the first peaches, and Salvatore Argento would never miss a chance to show him the last antiques donated to the museum that had been carved out of the castle's dungeon. The older woman in charge of the kitchen, alarmed by Chris' slimness, had cooked sumptuous dishes that forced him to doze off for an hour after each meal. Families with children of the same age had taken him sailing in their cutters. His father had driven him around to visit the many people he knew, as if he were afraid of being alone with him.

Suddenly, the image of a red car flashed across his mind.

He had been barely 18 when a red Lamborghini waited for him in front of the castle. Speechless, Chris had moved to hug his father, but Lucio had turned away, mumbling, "I hope you like the colour." Those were the only words his father and he had exchanged about that magnificent gift. He had wondered then, and wondered now even more, whether he would ever manage to penetrate the emotional shield behind which his father hid.

Chris' gaze turned to Lucio, who had wheeled himself out of the house and into the garden. Today Chris would interview an applicant for the part-time position of caregiver. She would provide help and company for his father.

The sound of chimes broke Chris' musings. He quickly went to the main door and opened it to a young woman dressed in a light-green suit. She was medium height, with short blond hair and a scrubbed face with no makeup.

"Lillian Carrigan," she said in a soft tone. "I have an appointment with Mr. Christopher Sandcroft."

"That's me. Please come in." Chris escorted her into the family room at the back of the house. "On the phone we discussed the job, the hours and the pay." Chris gestured toward a leather chair near the window, and he sat in a companion chair opposite her. "So tell me a bit about yourself."

Lillian sat at the edge of the large chair, her knees close together, her hands in her lap. "Well, as I mentioned, I'm a social worker. I have my diploma with me…references too." She took a few sheets out of her purse and handed them to Chris. "For the last five years I worked with problem families, places where there is too much tension between parents and children or where elderly folks can't help themselves anymore. Sometimes it's a struggle to convince them to accept day nursing in their own home. It's even worse if they need permanent care." She paused. "When I saw your advertisement in the newspaper, I thought I might get a break. Dealing with just one person is going to be a breeze."

Lillian Carrigan had already scored several points in her favour. She had a positive attitude toward the job he was going to offer her, and she presented herself well. Chris glanced at the papers, then returned them to her.

"This is how I'd like to handle the situation," he said. "You come here from two to seven o'clock three days a week—you choose the days—and on the weekend from six o'clock to midnight. My father can help himself with pretty much everything; what he needs most is the company." He paused. "He comes from Italy, where people are warm. They easily chat with strangers wherever they go. He speaks the language, so there's no problem with that." Chris hesitated. He didn't need to justify what he had done, but since most of his friends had highly criticized him for having taken his father away from his home country, he wanted to be up front with Lillian. *If she even remotely shows disapproval, she isn't the right person for the job.* "For my father, coming to Canada has been a courageous and difficult decision. For me, too. I need somebody around who can help him buffer the blow of being uprooted so late in his life."

"He needs to be distracted from his thoughts…from his memories." She nodded. "Yes, I understand. He needs attention."

Chris laughed. "A *lot* of attention. Since we're in the good season, you should drive him around a bit. When the weather gets bad, there are the museums. He loves them. He can spend hours and hours looking at paintings, statues, archaeological findings, broken pieces of vases, amphorae…things that most people would never bother with and might even throw away. When at home, you can help him flip through the satellite channels to find a show he likes. He's a movie buff. He likes guy flicks, but also love stories. The mushier, the better. In the last two weeks he's watched one oldie after another late into the night."

"Seems simple. The job sounds interesting, even fun. Can I meet him?"

"Of course. He's picked up gardening, taking lessons from Gideon, the gardener." Chris glanced outside and saw that Lucio was holding a group of little plants in his hands. He was pointing at the flowers, and seemed to be asking Gideon to cut them before transplanting them. Chris smiled. "Well, taking lessons or maybe giving them…I don't know exactly."

Lillian rose and looked outside. "What's wrong with him?"

"He had a stroke three years ago. In spite of a lot of physio and all kinds of massages, he didn't regain the use of his legs. Nothing's wrong with his mind. The man is still sharp."

"I see." She turned toward Chris and flashed him a quick, happy smile. "Maybe it's a golden occasion for me to visit a museum and learn about plants and flowers. I never had time for any of that."

"For the work in the garden you might need different clothing." Chris glanced at the tailored suit that nicely outlined her full figure. "And oh, by the way, we have a spare room you can use. It's upstairs. You can keep some of your things there, if you like."

From the backyard Lucio turned to glance toward the house, waved at Chris, then followed Gideon to another flowerbed.

"Would you like to give it a try? Say two weeks? If my father likes you, and we're both happy with the arrangement, I'll ask my lawyer to draft a contract."

Lillian picked up the handbag she had deposited on the floor. "I have the feeling I'm going to *love* this job."

Chris opened the sliding patio door, stood sideways and beckoned Lillian outside.

A big Lab ran toward them and quickly directed a couple of sharp barks toward Lillian.

"Shush," Chris said. He glanced at Lillian. "This is Bertha, a six-month-old Lab. We hope she won't grow any bigger." Bertha sat on her haunches, and Chris bent down to fondle her ears. As soon as he stopped, Bertha began sniffing Lillian's shoes. "She's friendly but she needs to know you first. She feels she's in charge of the place, and she advertises the presence of strangers loud and clear."

Lillian extended her hands and let Bertha sniff them. "I'll be around, big lady. You'll see me often enough that we'll become good friends."

Chris' cell phone rang. It was a call from his office. He listened for a few seconds, then looked at Lillian.

"An important customer just dropped by," he said. "I have to leave. I'll introduce you to my father and then let you break the ice."

Later that evening Chris and Lucio were having supper in the kitchen. They sat close to the bay window at a small oval table set for two. The sunken lights in the ceiling supplied a uniform and suffuse illumination, very similar to natural daylight. The black and orange tiled floor offered a decorative backdrop to the ivory-coloured counter and the whitewashed kitchen cabinets. On the table lay two straw place mats, two large dinner plates, a bottle of wine, a floral design tureen and two ceramic mushrooms with perforated tops: tiny holes formed an S on the red one and a P on the brown.

Lucio had eaten the chicken noodle soup in silence and then had scooped an ossobuco with mashed potatoes onto his dish. Chris had done likewise.

"I like the girl. Lillian is her name?" Lucio asked.

"Yes, but she's hardly a girl; she is 42."

Lucio laughed. "From my point of view—or should I say from where I stand in age—she is a girl. How did you find her?"

"An ad in the Harrisville Dispatch. She likes the idea of taking you around for short trips. She thinks it's going to be fun." Chris grinned. "She doesn't know yet what a big complainer you can be."

Lucio brandished his knife at Chris in false reproach, then smiled. "We'll keep it a secret, then."

"Fine. For the time being we're going to be her only employer, so if we need her for some extra hours, she'll be available."

Lucio poured himself a glass of Barolo wine. "I don't think that will be necessary. I can entertain myself."

"I know. Just in case."

Lucio pushed away his empty dish. "The cooking is great and so is the wine. Nevertheless, it's just that I feel like I've been dropped onto a strange planet. That's how I feel. Everything is so different here."

Chris held his breath. If his father got homesick, there was nothing in the entire world he could do for him.

"What's so unusual?" he asked in an undertone. "Or what's *most* unusual, I should ask?"

"The people. They seem genuinely kind, not just because you're the boss. Take Gideon for instance. It's fun to be with him, and he's the only person about my age. I slow him down when he works, but he doesn't seem to mind."

Chris sighed with relief. *Thank God, he's focused on the present; he's adjusting.*

Lucio continued. "Gideon told me he plants a couple thousand little plants every year in the backyard. You have a big place!"

Chris laughed. "*I* have a big place? What about the Red Manor? Now *that* was a *big* place!"

"Yes…yes, I know what you mean. It was foolish to keep the castle open for so long—foolish and expensive—but that's how things are in the old country. The castle had been handed down from one generation to another for the last 600 years. Like others before me, I was afraid of change. There were people who depended on me for a job." Lucio stopped and stared into the distance. "Often for a job that didn't exist anymore."

Chris rose and served coffee.

"By the way, what did you do with the big picture of the Red Manor?"

"Well…."

"Spit it out, Chris."

"Temporarily, and I really mean temporarily, I hung it on the wall midway to the basement." He grinned. "It might deter a thief from going any further."

"But downstairs you have the games room, you told me—a pool table, table tennis and a small theatre. That's where you hold parties, right?"

Chris assented.

"Then everybody will see it!"

"But that's what you really want, right? You want people to know about the castle, about the history of the castle, about the Red Manor and you."

For a moment Lucio held his espresso cup midair, then set it onto the table. Without a word he wheeled himself away.

Chris was not surprised by his father's reaction. Lucio always hightailed it as soon as somebody guessed at his feelings, as he often pretended he didn't have any.

CHAPTER 3

"What a day," Chris said as he drove home from Vibratim Ltd., the company he owned and managed. He'd had to hire an extra engineer and two technicians to keep up with the manufacturing of the 20 portable Ultra-Low-Frequencies magnetometers, all due for consignment within three months. These instruments were capable of detecting the slightest telluric tremors, which often preceded a major earthquake. After the tsunami, the demand for the magnetometers had skyrocketed.

It was past two o'clock in the morning when he crossed the entrance of the Sandcroft property. He yawned. Lights were on all over the first floor. *Oh oh!* Neglecting Bertha's requests for attention, Chris rushed inside and found his father in the family room, sprawled sideways in his wheelchair. He knelt beside him and shook his arm.

Lucio woke up. "Oh, it's you!"

"What happened? Why aren't you in bed?"

"I got a call from Boccascura."

"And?"

"There was a fire. Salvatore Argento was inside. They took him to the hospital. Third-degree burns." Lucio's eyes and voice conveyed anxiety.

"Anybody else hurt?"

"No, just him."

"When did they call?"

"Around six."

Chris rose and looked at his wristwatch. "I'll get a cup of coffee, and then I'll wake up your lawyer in Italy, the one who's now the curator for the Red Manor. Arcibaldo...Arcibaldo what?"

"Arcibaldo Cortesi. You have the number?"

"Yes. Be right back with fresh news."

Chris didn't need this complication as Lucio had just started to settle down. Being reconnected with his former home would take him back emotionally, and knowing that his faithful servant had been injured could prove devastating. Chris quickly dialled the number.

Surprisingly, the lawyer answered at the first ring. "*Sapevo che eri tu,* I expected your call, Chris. Your father was so upset, I could hardly explain to him what really happened. Salvatore Argento insisted I call him and, to quiet Salvatore down, I did." He paused and cleared his throat. "I made Salvatore the curator's assistant—that is, my assistant. He was so happy, you can't believe it. He was there when the fireworks started. You know, in May we celebrate Boccascura's patron saint, Saint Zenobio."

Chris had met Arcibaldo Cortesi only a couple of times, and he remembered him as an old man. He didn't want to pressure him in any way, so he waited for the lawyer to continue on his own.

"As usual, it was a big feast, with young people dressed in local costumes and old wagons hauled by oxen. One of them carried a huge load of straw. Left unattended, the oxen wandered off. Apparently several sparks from the fireworks—" The lawyer stopped again, seemingly exhausted. Arcibaldo spoke English well, but it didn't come easy to him.

"Showered onto the wagon?" Chris asked.

"Yes, yes. That's what happened. The wagon caught fire. It was in the castle courtyard and the blaze reached the main entrance. Salvatore, *Dio lo benedica,* rushed inside to get one of those wall extinguishers, but it was too small. He could do nothing against the raging flames." Something rumbled deep in the lawyer's throat and he coughed. "When the firemen finally arrived they had to work hard to get him out."

"Is he okay?"

"He's in the hospital. His face was the most exposed. They think he's going to make it, but you never know. The man is fairly old, and he was in a state of shock. He asked me to call Mr. de' Vigentini, and then he passed out."

"I see. Nobody else got hurt?"

"No. He was the only one who noticed the wagon was burning and went after it. The Red Manor is insured, of course; an assessment of the damage will be done soon."

"Thank you very much, Mr. Cortesi. Please keep me posted."

"It will be done. Say hello to my old friend, Lucio."

Chris paused for a moment, the phone still in his hand. Then he went to report the latest news to his father.

Quickly retired to his bedroom, Lucio shifted from the wheelchair to the king-size bed, scrunched the pillows, put one on top of the other and lay down, still in his day clothes. Chris believed the accident at the Red Manor and Salvatore's injuries had distressed him, and he had done his best to let him believe so. Of course he was concerned about his old friend's health but the reason he was so distraught was another, far more serious matter of a different nature. It was the prophecy that had accompanied the Red Manor for hundreds of years—the prophecy that many considered a curse. *At the turn of each century the de' Vigentini family will lose one of its young male members, and at the turn of the millennium tragedy will strike: they will lose their ancient home and disgrace will descend on them, as one man will cause shame and harm to his own brother.*

The prophecy had been proclaimed by a monk who had been chased away from the castle by Riccardo de' Vigentini, Lord of the Manor and Lucio's most illustrious ancestor. During one of Riccardo's absences, the monk had lowered the drawbridge and let in a group of mercenaries. But before they had finished ransacking the valuables inside the mansion, Riccardo's guards had managed to kill them all. When he had returned, Riccardo had no hesitation in banishing the monk—only his religious habit saved him from summary execution. The story went on and on, describing the enraged, barefoot, long-hair monk genuflecting in the clearing before the castle, thundering his words of menace, his arms outstretched to hoist a large cross.

That was a long time ago, mused Lucio as he covered himself with the bedspread. And of course, between wars, diseases and accidents, the family had lost several of its young members at the turn of each century and during each century. But now…now the ancestral castle was gone and he had already lost one son. For years he knew he was hostage to death, and he didn't care. But what about Chris? Was he, too? Chris was so young, so full of life…Oh my, oh my…how much he would like to be inside his old, sweet home, able to wheel down to the magnificent chapel and lose himself in prayers…

CHAPTER 4

Not far from Chris Sandcroft's home, midway up a wooded hill, stood a white structure, four stories high and a hundred metres wide. It was a Catholic seminary, built a hundred years before, its size reflecting the hope of the missionary fathers who had founded it, its seclusion symbolizing the difficult life a priest would face in a country so far from the motherland. With a large refectory, a library, an infirmary and two chapels, it could house a hundred ordinands. The Don Bosco Seminary, as it was called, was home to Father Paul, the second in command at the institution. He spent more time on the road, visiting the sick or giving lectures, than at the seminary. Vocations were scarce and, since his call had been strong and unwavering throughout his life, he accepted any invitations, took any occasion to preach the beauty of His Word and the spiritual reward stemming from religious life. Father Paul belonged to a second generation of Italian immigrants, among which the hostility of the Anglo-Saxon dominated society was still felt strongly. Born in a family where the food was barely sufficient, Father Paul had learned, at an early age, that money was important and never hesitated to let people know that the church, and his seminary in particular, was in need of financial support as much as vocations. Only five years ago he had reluctantly obeyed the order of his superiors to abandon the black cassock and adopt a dark suit with the dog collar. The silver cross that his parents had given him the day he was ordained, however, never stopped glowing in the middle of his chest. It was more than a symbol; it was an open declaration of his mission and faith.

Father Paul's battered Toyota slowed down on the last curve at the bottom of the hill just before reaching the county road that crossed through the valley. Parked on the opposite shoulder was a black Aurora, the driver's window rolled down. Father Paul brought his car to a halt and crossed the road on foot.

"Can I be of help?" he asked the young woman behind the wheel.

"I was just looking at that big building up on the hill."

The elderly man seated beside her craned his neck. "We're curious. What is it?"

"A seminary. I'm Father Paul, the administrator."

The man nodded. "Lucio de' Vigentini, and this is Ms. Lillian Carrigan. A lot of students?"

"Unfortunately not. The seminary has become too large for our current needs. We could do with less than half the size. But the building is nice, with a big cloister in the middle that allows us to take small walks in the winter months." He paused as if trying to assess his interlocutor's interest. "We have visiting hours for the public, two days a week, Tuesdays and Thursdays, from two to four. Do come in when you have time."

"Thank you. I'll think about it. Father Paul, you said?" Lucio asked.

"Yes. I'm around those days. Just ask for me if you don't see me right away." Father Paul waved and returned to his car.

"Have you ever been there?" Lucio asked Chris that evening.

Chris was busy fighting a dish of spaghetti that the carbonara sauce made more slippery than usual. He tried to neatly wind it around his fork.

"Never. I hardly go that way. But I know it's a big place."

"You don't mind if Lillian takes me there one of these days?"

Chris shook his head. "It might be interesting."

Lucio hesitated. "Maybe you'd like to take me there."

"What days?"

"Tuesdays and Thursdays. From two to four."

Chris looked down at his plate as if trying to find an answer there. He swished around the remaining spaghetti and finished his meal in silence. Then he looked up at his father.

"I'd love to, but I have to be at the plant, Lucio. We're behind schedule with the production of the new compact seismographer we've just designed and tested. After the tsunami, the orders tripled. We're struggling to meet the demand. And I took plenty of holidays when I came to Italy and then stayed home with you for the first few weeks."

Lucio looked at him, genuinely curious. "Work. Work. Work. There are other things in life besides working. Your violin hangs on the wall, and I know you used to play it almost every day. Don't you do anything for fun? You don't have to put in these long hours. You already have plenty of money."

Chris reached across the table and gently squeezed Lucio's arm. "It's difficult for you to understand. Work is my life. It has been my life since Grandpa took me to work at Vibratim in my spare time. I was in junior high school then. My only vacations were when I came to see you in the summer." He paused, pensive. "After Mother died, Grandpa insisted I come see you and spend time with you."

"Your mother didn't want you to come?" Lucio's voice was a mere whisper.

"I don't know." Chris shrugged. "She never said a word about it. She never spoke about you, the Red Manor or the time she was with you." He scrutinized his father's face. Maybe this was the time to ask him the critical question: "Is it because of the way my brother died?"

Lucio looked at him blankly, drank the last of his wine and left for his room.

For a couple of days neither son nor father touched on the subject, each making sure to talk about the nothings of life. Chris promised himself he would avoid asking direct questions. It would take time to get Lucio to open up, to feel comfortable talking about the past.

Chris sat under the veranda, his eyes scouting the property around him. It was twilight and the trees at the back already appeared as black silhouettes. The only building visible was the Wilsons' cottage house. Donald Sandcroft, Chris' grandfather, had bought that property from the Wilsons 20 years ago when the price for a piece of land was incredibly low. The agreement was that the Wilsons could stay in their house as long as they wanted. In exchange for the maintenance of the cottage and the utilities paid by the Sandcrofts, Gideon would take care of the property. The arrangement had worked well for both parties, and now Lucio had found in Gideon a pal with whom to share activities.

Chris' mind began to wander as he thought about his future. At 32, he had no family of his own and, at the moment, did not even have a steady girlfriend. After the death of his grandfather, Donald Sandcroft, Chris became in charge of Vibratim Ltd., a medium-sized company his grandfather had started. Vibratim designed and built seismographs and other equipment capable of detecting even the smallest earth vibrations. Committed to bring the best to the market, the company had also been successful financially. Big oil companies involved in the exploration of offshore fields were among its clients.

Like his mother, Chris was a people person, who preferred working with others rather than sitting at a desk. However, from his father, Lucio Maria de' Vigentini, Chris had inherited determination and the desire to excel. Fascinated by the complicated machinery his grandfather worked with, he had made up his mind that he wanted, one day, to run the company. He studied hard and obtained an engineering degree. His schooling had provided him with the understanding of the earth's complex structure and movements; his apprenticeship under his grandfather's watchful eye had given him hands-on experience. When Donald, a widower of 20 years, had suddenly died five years ago in a car accident, Chris found himself overburdened with responsibility. He was only 27 year old.

The challenge ahead of him increased his commitment and energy. He was never tired, yet he slept little. Six months later, however, his girlfriend at the time declared that she found his lifestyle incompatible with a serious relationship. She left him without any further comment, and that was that.

The noise of a door opening behind him put an end to his remembrance. Chris turned his head. It was Kathy carrying a tray, followed by Lucio.

She laid a carafe and two tall glasses of iced tea on a small table, filled them to the rim, then hurried away, wishing Chris and Lucio a good night. They heard her close the front door and leave the house.

Lucio sipped his drink. "Do you think I can help around the house? Kathy has been very busy. The last two days she's had her nose immersed in a huge volume on Italian cuisine. I saw Gideon vacuuming and dusting yesterday."

"Help?" Chris laughed. "What is it you think you can do to help? You had an army of servants, Salvatore Argento was your valet—whatever that means—and you don't know the first thing about cooking. You only know about eating and savouring the food."

"You shouldn't discourage people who want to be useful. I'd have asked her directly, but every time I address her, her eyes becomes enormous, full of anxiety, as if she was scared of me."

"You'd scare anybody—dressed up in a dark suit in the middle of summer, and often with a tie. You look ready to go to a funeral."

"*Lo so, lo so,* I know, I know. I don't fit here. But I mean well, Chris; I really do."

Chris refilled Lucio's glass. "I'm just joking, Lucio. But I have to tell you something. Your coming here has created extra work, but also much-needed excitement. They can't believe the amount of mail you receive. After grandfather died, the Wilsons had little to do, except for a party once in a while—when I invite all the friends who regularly invite me. I never went out to look at the garden as you do, and I never praised Kathy for the way she arranges the knickknacks or the furniture. You've done all that. You're helping. It's enough of a beginning." He squeezed his father's arm. "By the way, I saw a letter from England. Was it from the Howards?"

"Yes. They don't know whether they're going to Italy this year."

"Why not?"

"They feel it won't be same. For 20 years they stayed at the Red Manor."

"Oh. They could come here, then."

"*You* would have to invite them. I'm sure they'd be delighted. A certain young woman would swim across the Atlantic to see you!"

"Vivian? Are you talking about Vivian?"

"Of course."

"That's unlikely. She can hardly swim. She plunges into the water like a brick, with goggles on and with a pin to keep her nostrils closed!"

"You know what I mean. She had a crush on you. She blushed every time she saw you."

"Blushing has to do with blood circulation; it has nothing to do with having a crush."

"Of course. You ignored her. You ignored a beautiful, well-bred woman who'll inherit a big estate in Scotland." As Chris remained silent, Lucio continued. "Didn't you like her?"

"Sure. Who wouldn't? I did regularly fetch her goggles, which she regularly lost in the water, didn't I?"

"You know what I mean. When we had the goodbye party for you last year, you didn't even dance with her once!"

As usual Chris had underestimated his father. Lucio played as if he didn't

31

notice anything, yet he noticed everything. He leaned close to his father's face.

"I need to let you in on a little secret of mine: I'm chicken. I stay away—very *far* away, I mean—from any potential trouble. I had a steady girlfriend at the time, and a jealous one."

"Oh, *now* you tell me. And how come she is not around?"

I can't tell you why she isn't around anymore, Chris thought. Since his first girlfriend had left him because of his busy—too busy—lifestyle, Chris had been very careful with Miriam, his second girlfriend. He made sure to spend time with her in activities they both enjoyed. Things had gone well until Chris mentioned he intended to bring his father to live with him. He made the case that the house had been built to accommodate two families, his grandfather's and his mother's, and that the two resulting households were totally independent of one another. With plenty of help, he reasoned, they could manage to take care of a man who had just one son he could depend on. The discussion on the subject had lasted one full weekend, and Chris had come to know the hard, dark side of the young woman he had planned to propose to. He didn't want to beg for something he was entitled to and he didn't want to fail his father. The solution came easily, as Miriam walked out of his house and his life, swearing like a construction worker.

"I don't want to go into the details about why she isn't around anymore," Chris said at length. "But I can tell you that I'm happy she is not. Let's just say I discovered she was not the woman for me."

Lucio's eyes brightened and his thick grey eyebrows arched. "Interesting."

"Oh, oh. Don't you get any ideas, now." Chris finished his tea. "You may be right after all; perhaps we need to find something for you to do. I don't want you to start playing matchmaker."

CHAPTER 5

As Lillian rounded the Sandcroft property to take the road leading to the Don Bosco Seminary, Lucio realized how little he'd ever known about his late wife's family. Clearly the Sandcrofts had money. When he had married Deborah he thought she came from a well-to-do family, but he never inquired about her financial status and Deborah never mentioned anything about being wealthy. They had fallen in love, oblivious to anything else.

Nostalgia washed over him as memories flooded his mind, vivid as yesterday.

How sweet and loving Deborah had been when she took over as the lady of the castle. She had infused her sunny personality into everything she did. Within months the old, decrepit castle had come alive.

She had remodelled the interior and had run from one government office to the next to obtain permission to give the ancient building a facelift. The Red Manor was, in fact, an historical site, which meant nothing could be altered without official approval.

After three years, the huge dungeon had been reclaimed to normal space, walls had been repaired and painted, and new flooring had been installed. Once a sombre place, the dungeon had become a museum where the interested visitor could look at tools, weapons and artifacts from the Middle Ages up to World War II. All the statues, oils and other works of art had been assembled on the first floor, with the second floor reserved exclusively for living quarters. His Red Manor. It was a place full of charm and history and it was the home of his ancestors. Likely he would never see it again...

Comfortably stretched out in his car seat with his eyes closed, Lucio didn't realize they had arrived at the Don Bosco Seminary.

Lillian stopped the car in front of the stairway and helped him get out. Lucio dismissed her. His new wheelchair was battery-powered, so he could easily climb the walkway for the handicapped.

He entered the seminary and stopped in the hallway. The ceiling, a cupola, was sustained by eight columns, and the marble floor was a delicate grey.

In no time Father Paul appeared from a side corridor.

"Mr. de' Vigentini, how nice to see you. I hoped you'd show up one of these days."

"Here I am, curious to see this place. It looks impressive from the outside."

"Wait until you see the interior. I'll take you on a tour myself. First of all, the cloister." He gestured broadly with his arms. "It's a beauty."

As he looked at the expanse, Lucio agreed that indeed it was. A columned opening led to a garden, and in the centre of the garden stood a brick well, a rope neatly wound around the shaft, a dark pail hanging at the end of the rope.

Father Paul bent to look into the well.

"Can you believe it's still working?" he asked. "Cool water even in the hottest day of summer. In good weather we say our evening Mass here before retiring for the night."

They toured the cloister, then Father Paul took Lucio inside.

"The cloister's walls are shared by the refectory, the library, the Rector's office and the reception room. The refectory and the library have large panes of regular glass, and the Rector's office and the reception room have high, narrow windows with stained glass portraying religious figures."

Father Paul opened the door of the library and turned on the light, but didn't enter. Tables and chairs of nondescript wood were arranged with no particular order in the room.

"You can come here any time you want," he said. "There is plenty to read, if you like memoirs of the early missionaries." He closed the door, then moved along a corridor. "Now I'll show you the pride of the seminary: the reception hall."

They entered a large room with red carpet and a big portrait of Don Bosco hanging on one wall. Oils of popes lined the others. An oval table with ivory inlay stood in the middle, surrounded by eight high-back chairs whose seats were covered with red velvet. A tray with small china cups sat on one side of the table, and on the other lay a thick album.

Father Paul opened it and pointed at a few pictures. "Look here. These are pictures of Pope John Paul II when he came to visit the seminary. It was a big event. He stayed with us two full days. It was an extraordinary experience, one we'll never forget."

Lucio leafed through the pictures and closed the album. He glanced around. On the fireplace mantel, statuettes of saints and ecclesiastic personalities vied for space. At the left of the fireplace a container almost disappeared behind a heap of chopped birch wood; at the right stood the fire irons, all bright brass.

"Any guest would be impressed by the display of so much ecclesiastic and religious content." Lucio paused. "How many students do you have?"

"This year, only 29. There are no new seminarians coming in for next year, and three of the current ones will be ordained soon." He hesitated. "That's one of our problems: lack of vocations. But let's talk about you." He sat in one of the high-back chairs, close to Lucio. "Through the grapevine I heard you came here only recently. Here to stay?"

"Yes. My only son is here and the household I lived in all my life was more a museum than a home. I couldn't take care of it properly anymore, and I was wise enough to realize I couldn't."

"Your son is Christopher Sandcroft, right?"

"Yes. You're wondering why he doesn't carry my name?"

Father Paul's vivid eyes expressed curiosity, but he kept silent.

"It was all my fault, Father. I married a beautiful woman, a loving woman. Deborah Sandcroft was her name." Lucio didn't want to reveal the truth. It was too painful. "I wasn't good to her. So she took Chris and returned to Canada." Perhaps he could say something about the malefic spell. "There was...a curse cast upon the Red Manor—the place I come from—that at the turn of the millennium a catastrophe would hit the de' Vigentini family."

Father Paul arched his eyebrows and his lower lip almost covered the top one. "But you don't believe in witchcraft, right? The church forbids it. And I assume you're a practicing Catholic."

"I really don't know whether I believe in it or not, Father, but I'm happy that Chris is here."

Father Paul's eyes expressed deep disapproval. "We should talk about it a bit more, Mr. de' Vigentini."

"Call me Lucio, please."

An ordinand entered the hall. "Coffee?" Father Paul asked Lucio. Lucio shook his head, and Father Paul gestured for one to the ordinand. "Tell me, Lucio, how are you going to spend your time?"

"I don't know yet. My son doesn't believe I can help around the house. He has given me a chauffeur, so I can go places. That's all for the moment."

Father Paul smiled. "Let's keep in touch, Lucio. I have a talent for finding work—volunteer work, I mean—for almost anybody."

Lucio laughed. For a priest, Father Paul was extremely candid.

"Great idea. Is your Sunday Mass open to the public?"

"Yes. The one at 11 o'clock."

"I'll be there. Thank you for your time." Lucio looked at his wristwatch. "I have to go. My chauffeur, Lillian, is probably already waiting for me."

CHAPTER 6

The dining room of the Trudeau Excelsior was extravagantly decorated with enormous, two-metre tall okra vases filled with plants and flowers that reached up to the ceiling. Sconces, installed in niches carved into the walls, spread a soft glow, and scented candles in the centre of each table lent the diner a touch of intimacy.

Chris and Lucio looked expectantly toward the entry.

Elisabeth and Glen Howard had arrived in town without notice. On their way to the west they had stopped in Harrisville to say hello to Lucio. Lucio and Glen had been long-time friends, sharing an interest in antiques of any kind and provenance, and good wine. Glen was in his late 60s, Elisabeth in her 50s. Glen, without offspring in spite of three previous marriages, had adopted Elisabeth's only child, Vivian, and given her his name.

"You mean to tell me the Howards showed up without any hint from you?" Chris asked. He twisted the white napkin until it almost resembled a thick rope.

"God's honest truth. Glen called me this afternoon; he was already here. He's on a business trip with his family, he said, and wanted to see me. It was nice of him. I talked to Elisabeth and Vivian too, answering the many questions they had about our town and lifestyle." Lucio helped himself to a second glass of Chablis. "Don't look at me as if I set you up. I'm innocent. But I think Glen stopped here with a purpose. I feel he has something to tell me. What that could be, I don't have the faintest idea—something important, though." He glanced around the big hall. "Let's admire the décor of this place. It's both grandiose and elegant."

"It is, and this is where I bring my potential customers. They know me well here, and I always get great service." Chris eyed the door, impatiently waiting for the Howards to appear.

37

He wondered about Vivian, the Howards' only daughter. He remembered her as a beautiful creature, gentle yet very much alive. Was she the same woman he had held in his arms years ago? He had been 22, she 19…

On a hot summer day he had gone with a group of friends to the beach. They had hoped for the afternoon wind to gain strength and offer the surfers a chance to ride the waves. Vivian and Chris had lingered longer than the others and had missed the last bus to Boccascura. They had started to make their way back on foot, at times climbing rocks or forcing their way through tall grass. Vivian had worn flip-flops, a pair of very short shorts and a top that wrapped around her waist and left most of her back bare. She had walked ahead of Chris, who helped her keep her balance every time she slipped.

Then her straw hat had flown away.

Chris ran after it. The hat whirled around a boulder and took off for the beach. After a zigzag chase, Chris managed to grab it. Vivian, standing on high ground, clapped her hands in admiration.

Chris waved the hat. "Want it back?"

Vivian smiled. "I wouldn't mind."

Chris hid the hat behind his back. "There's a price…a kiss."

He closed his eyes and Vivian pecked him on his cheek.

"Not good enough. Try again."

Vivian put her hands around his neck, leaned toward him and opened her lips against his. Chris let go of the hat and pulled her to him, but Vivian lost her balance, pushing him onto the ground and falling on top of him.

He grinned, whispering, "I only asked for a kiss."

He cleared a few strands of hair from Vivian's face. Her eyes held an intensity he had never seen before, and her heart-shaped lips were only an inch away from his. He pulled her completely on top of his body, put his arms around her, and kissed her hungrily as his hands caressed her bare back. Her skin felt smooth and soft; her breasts squeezed against his chest, and her heart pounded.

When finally Vivian lifted her head she tapped on his lips.

"Salty, very salty. We should clear up all this salt or you're going to have chapped lips." She bent to kiss him again…

"They're here." Lucio's baritone carried across the table.

The Howards stepped into the diner. With a brisk stride Glen reached out to shake hands with Lucio; Elisabeth and Vivian greeted Chris, then bent to kiss Lucio.

Glen was a large man with sandy hair and a rosy complexion. Elisabeth was fine-boned and medium height, with dark hair and big, brown eyes.

"Let me look at you," Glen said, then turned his head to inspect Lucio's face from both sides. "You're doing well, old boy. You seem relaxed, at ease. Good, good." He shook hands with Chris, then sat close to him. "I had to go to Calgary, so I said to my women, why don't you come along? Lucio will be happy to see us all."

"I surely am. Only a few weeks in this country and I already get a visit from one of my dear friends. It's wonderful. Thank you, Glen."

Vivian had taken a place close to Chris, and Elisabeth sat almost opposite him. As Lucio and Glen began discussing the latest news on the world scene, Chris offered wine to the ladies and asked about the weather in Edinburgh.

"Terrible," said Elisabeth. "We're well into the summer, and we still have the heat on in the house. And rain, rain and more rain."

"I don't mind the rain," Vivian said. "It gives me a lot of time to read." She looked at Chris. "How have you been? Busy with your father here?"

Vivian's red dress left her neck and arms bare, and a big bracelet set high on her forearm. Her brown eyes looked at him from under long eyelashes. When she gave him a tiny smile Chris' heart sank. Was it his turn to blush? He hoped not; his father would never stop teasing him.

"Yes, but things are slowing down now," he replied. "I surely will have time to show you around, if you'd like."

Vivian's eyes brightened. "I'd love that."

The waiter approached the table and distributed menus to the five customers, then quietly retreated.

"What do you suggest?" Vivian asked.

"The stuffed trout is excellent, the shrimp, too. Their garlic sauce is light but incredibly tasty. Fish is the specialty of this restaurant."

"Great. Are you choosing the trout?" As Chris assented, Vivian said, "Me, too." She closed her menu as the waiter returned to collect the orders.

Then with a powerful voice, Glen addressed his daughter.

"Show your ring, my dear!" Vivian didn't budge. "Well, show the ring!" Glen turned toward Lucio. "Vivian is always so shy—not like me—but this time she has something to be proud of: a three-karat engagement diamond."

Elisabeth took Vivian's left hand and stretched it out on the table. "Well, what happened to it?"

Vivian hesitated, then turned the ring up from underneath.

"Why didn't you tell us it was loose?" Glen's voice contained a veiled reproach. "That ring is made to be shown, not hidden!" Glen elbowed Lucio. "I made it. You remember that Texan with the big collection of coins? He never stopped talking about it! I'm in business with him now. He's Vivian's fiancé."

"Sincere congratulations," Lucio said, echoed by Chris. "Is this a business arrangement or real love? I mean, is she happy?"

Glen didn't give Vivian time to comment. "Of course she's happy. She's 29. It's time to get married, or I should say to *be married*, for heaven's sake! The social position of a woman depends on her husband's."

"Oh," said Lucio. "I didn't expect that you were so…so—" He turned to Chris. "What's the right word?"

"Sexist," Chris replied without hesitation.

"Eh, maybe that is the right word."

"Nothing to do with being sexist. It's the pure and simple truth, my friend: Vivian will never amount to anything if she doesn't marry a rich man."

On instinct, Chris put his hand on Vivian's and clutched it, and he was compensated with a long, grateful look.

"Well," Lucio said. "I always hoped—" He turned to look at Elisabeth and smiled one of his rare smiles at her. "Years ago I missed the opportunity to propose to Elisabeth. I thought maybe my son would repair my error by marrying her beautiful daughter." He paused and glanced around. "But that's all in the past." He raised his glass. "Let's toast, now. To Vivian's happiness!"

There was a tinkle of glasses and Chris admired the finesse with which his father had handled the situation.

"Anything else new and exciting?" Lucio asked a few minutes later.

"Yes. There is something I want to talk to you about. Something important."

"Fine. We'll have plenty of time tomorrow, since I'm lucky enough to have a chauffeur all for myself. Should I come to pick you up around, say, eleven o'clock? It'd give you time for a good rest."

Elisabeth looked at Lucio. "Glen can't wait to tell you the great news. He can't wait until tomorrow. Come on, Glen, tell him!"

Glen wriggled in his chair, as if taken by surprise. "I have with me two collector's items I bought from a friend of mine just a week ago. They look very much like the cups you've been missing for your collection. I want to show them to you."

"Oh." Lucio said. "That would be interesting. For generations my family has been looking for them."

Glen turned away from Lucio to explain to the others.

"The coronation of Matthias of Habsburg by Pope Paul V was planned to occur at the Red Manor. The Romanesque chapel that we all know had just been redecorated for the occasion. To honour his guests, Riccardo de' Vigentini had commissioned the creation of four drinking cups. Two of these remained at the Red Manor, but the other two were lost. Lucio and I wrote a note to the *Società Italiana di Archeologia e Storia dell'Arte* with a description of those cups and commented on the occasion for which they were manufactured. We wrote the note to record an historical fact, but also to stir up some curiosity and perhaps trace the two missing cups." Glen stopped and finished his glass of wine. He turned to Lucio. "It looks like we found them. Where do you keep the old ones?"

"I don't know where they are." Lucio hesitated, sneaking a glance at Chris. "They were my wedding gift to Deborah. She took them with her when she returned to Canada."

Glen turned to Chris who still held Vivian's hand. "Chris?" he asked, while flashing a disapproving look. "Do you know where these cups could be?"

Chris released Vivian's hand. "I don't have the faintest idea. In the old house they were on display in the entry parlour. The wall was panelled, dark wood with two niches carved in the middle. Those bowls had the place of honour, one on each shelf, with indirect lighting from the back. When we moved, Mother had just died, and Grandfather didn't know how she'd planned to arrange the furniture and all the knickknacks." He shrugged. "After a few months I didn't see them around anymore."

"They are antiques," Glen said in a pedantic tone. "Medieval people used them for drinking. They had no single glasses. They passed what you call a bowl, but it was really a cup, from one fellow guest to the next. The cup contained wine for six or seven people. So the container had to be big, yet manageable. The dimensions of the cups—" He stopped to take a sip from the glass the waiter had promptly refilled.

"They were 30 centimetres in diameter, and 25 tall," Lucio said.

"The cup was lifted with both hands since it had two flat handles, like a...well, think of it as a huge quaich."

"A what?" Chris asked.

"Of course you don't know what a quaich is," Glen said, his voice belying annoyance. "Again, it is an ancient Scottish cup that was used—"

"To check the quality and clarity of Scotch whisky," Lucio said. "I didn't see the cups either."

Glen flashed another look of reproach in Chris' direction, stronger this time. "Those cups are very valuable. They're collectibles of extreme historical importance." He looked at Lucio. "Lucio, don't you have anything to say to your obtuse son?"

"I don't control my children, Glen. I gave away those cups. They were a gift. If they got lost...well, too bad." As Glen didn't seem satisfied, Lucio continued. "We'll have plenty of time to talk about the old and new cups tomorrow. We don't want to bore the ladies with old folks' tales."

Glen was ready to reply when two waiters came with the orders, placed a dish in front of each person, then poured wine into the gold-trimmed glasses.

Dinner proceeded without any further hurdle as Elisabeth amiably talked to Lucio, often smiling flirtatiously.

It was ten o'clock when Glen said, "I'm tired." He turned to Elisabeth. "We've planned a full day tomorrow, so we'd better retire."

"A Drambuie for the road?" Lucio asked.

"Not tonight, my friend." He patted his stomach. "The calamari was excellent, and so was the shrimp. But I'm stuffed now more than the stuffed trout I ate. I don't have room even for a spot of tea." He rose, followed by the two women.

Chris opened the leather folder the waiter had inconspicuously deposited on the table, scribbled his name on the bill, then rose and slowly pushed Lucio's wheelchair toward the exit. He was about to say goodnight to his guests when Vivian looked at him.

"Oh, I forgot my purse," she said.

Chris engaged the brake of his father's chair and walked toward what had been their table; Vivian followed. He was looking around when Vivian quickly bent and lifted a purse from underneath her chair.

"Got it," she said, and stood there. "Is it true that you are not engaged anymore?"

When did that devil of a father find a way to trickle that information? "Yes. I'm free as a bird."

"Vivian!" Glen hollered.

Waving the red-bead purse at her father, she called back, "I found my bag." Without looking at Chris she said, "Pick me up at nine. My parents will still be asleep. I'd be very happy to spend some time with you, Chris."

For a while Lucio and Chris drove in silence.

"When did you tell Vivian I didn't have a girlfriend anymore?" Chris asked.

"I didn't say anything of the sort." Lucio sounded resentful. "Both Elisabeth and Vivian talked to me and asked a million questions. Was the house big enough for me after having lived all my life at the Red Manor? How was it? Old, modern, comfortable? A million questions, I tell you. When I said the house was very nice but maybe it lacked a woman's touch, Elisabeth asked me whether you were still going steady with a certain Miriam. It was then I said there was no Miriam or any other girls around." Lucio paused. "I'm perfectly innocent. I just described what I saw."

Chris laughed. "Innocent? Can't be. I never saw you flirting either. Did you really like Elisabeth?"

"Oh, yes, but when I met her I was still longing for your mother, even if she'd left me years before. Somehow I hoped she'd come back, and bring my little boy with her." Lucio's voice quivered.

"One day we'll have to talk about what happened between you and Mother. I've been waiting all my life to hear the truth…*all* the truth." He glanced at his father, who definitely seemed distressed. "Okay. I'll let it go for tonight."

"Good," Lucio whispered. "By the way, Elisabeth is the one with money. Glen and I became very close because he really knows about antiques; he has an antique shop. He can spot a fake from a long distance. Elisabeth brought in a lot of customers, wealthy people who buy from him on a regular basis."

"Interesting...and just think how rude he was to her and Vivian. Anyhow, I'll lift up Vivian's spirits tomorrow. It's all planned."

"With Glen around? He'll be on guard all the time."

Chris laughed again. "Nothing to worry about. When I helped Vivian rescue her purse, she told me to pick her up at nine. We'll be alone. It's up to you to keep Glen busy with old tales. If he carries on about those cups, let him search the house; in one word, keep him happy. I saw you at work last night. You're a very resourceful person."

"Thanks. I'll handle the Howards. Glen likes pushing everybody around, but he's more show than substance."

"Need a refresher course on courtship?" Lucio asked when they had almost arrived home.

Chris roared with laughter. "No need, no need at all. I'll count on my instincts and good genes."

CHAPTER 7

At half-past eight in the morning Chris parked his Camaro at the back of the Trudeau Excelsior and walked to the front entrance. He didn't know where to take Vivian; he didn't have a clue about her likes and dislikes. He pushed on the revolving door and entered the hotel. A carpeted floor covered the entire lobby and big armchairs were scattered around, interspaced with floral arrangements and low tables.

Vivian rose as she spotted him. She wore khaki shorts, a sleeveless top, and sneakers; a big duffel bag lay near her feet. She opened her lips in a warm, friendly smile.

"Hi, Chris. Like my new outfit?" She turned around twice.

Chris admired her slim waist and legs, her round buttocks and breasts. Her outfit was almost as revealing as the bikinis she had worn around the Red Manor's swimming pool. He could never figure out how those tiny strips of fabric stuck to her body.

"Nice," Chris said, then quickly changed the subject. "Did you have a good night's sleep?"

"Not bad, but I woke up early. Now look here. Do you like my head gear?" She laid a hat, which perfectly matched the outfit in style and colour, on her head, then pulled on two strings to fasten it in place. "Is it okay for canoeing?"

"Canoeing?"

"It's your favourite hobby, right?"

"Yes, but… *Oh my God! She wants to go canoeing…She'll probably fall into the water before getting into the boat.* He assessed her weight: about a hundred pounds, including the hardtop Saharan hat. No problem. He could fish her out of the water. "Sure, but I thought you might want to go to more civilized places."

45

"Oh no. I like the outdoors." She lifted the bag and tapped on it. It was so full it seemed the contents might burst out of the canvas. She smiled. "Sandwiches and drinks."

"Well, let's go then. I know of a park only a couple of hours from here. It has a nice river with no big rapids. It whirls around as it crosses the woods. You may see chipmunks, rabbits and, later in the day, even deer."

"Fantastic," Vivian said, and linked arms with him.

Taking no chances, Chris turned into a secondary leg of the river, where the water flowed slowly and smoothly. In front of him, Vivian paddled with expertise, each minute more pleasantly surprising Chris. He really didn't know what to think. The woman attracted him but she was engaged. A vague sense of honour told him he should just enjoy her company, nothing more. However...*however*...he also thought of an engagement as a trial period, a time when two people put themselves and their partners to the test. If so, he could court Vivian. It would be a good test for her. After all, she had invited him to spend time alone with her.

Two hours later, at about one o'clock in the afternoon, Vivian turned around to face him and said, "I'm getting hungry. What about you?"

She smiled. Her complexion was like that of a porcelain figurine. Her features were fine, her hair thick and lush, her neck slim, and her bearing aristocratic, a touch she had inherited from her mother. Her eyes—they were looking at him right now—were warm and full of *joi de vivre*, with a hint of mischief.

"Me too," he replied. "There's a clearing ahead, at the next turn. We can stop there."

They chose a spot underneath a big oak tree. From her bag Vivian took a plastic tablecloth, paper dishes and glasses. "I have bacon, tomato and lettuce sandwiches, and egg salad." She set two wrapped sandwiches on each plate. "I hope they're okay."

"They're fine." Chris opened two cans of ginger ale and gave one to Vivian. "Bon appetite," he said, and leaned back against the oak's trunk, his legs stretched out in front of him. For a while he observed his companion, trying to guess her feelings. Vivian was biting into her sandwich. She seemed relaxed and unconcerned about the strange situation she had created. It was time for an explanation.

"Where is your big ring?" Chris pointed at her hand.

"Oh, that. Last night Father made a big deal out of it. Max, our friend from Texas, gave me the ring and said, 'This is for you, so you'll think of me.'"

"He didn't propose?"

Vivian's mouth was full, so she just nodded. Then she said, "Yes, he did...but I told him I wasn't ready. Father—you know him, probably through your own father—is a little pushy. Max is an expert in ancient coins. He comes from Austin where he has a vast collection of coins from all over the world." She took a swig from her can. "He's a good friend of Father's. They talk for hours about old stuff, where and how to get it."

"I see. You don't plan to marry him?"

"No, even if I like him." She took a thermos bottle from her bag. "Coffee?" She poured some into two cups and offered one to Chris. "Max is almost double my age." She stretched out on the grass and propped her head on one elbow. "What about you? The last few times I was at the Red Manor you were engaged...not to the same girl, though."

Of course Lucio had kept Vivian informed of his son's romantic life.

He gave her a teasing smile. "I am not lucky in love."

"I see. What do you do wrong?"

"I don't know." He moved to lie very close to her. "Maybe you should tell me." He turned on one side, caressed her cheek and cleared away the crumbs the sandwich had left. "Maybe I don't kiss well."

Vivian giggled. "Oh, that's not what I remember!"

Chris jerked to sit up straight. "Do you still remember our first kiss on the beach?"

"I surely do...and more than the kissing. I always wondered whether you were going to make love to me."

"Isn't that what we were doing?" Chris asked, faking innocence.

"Well...I mean...oh, you know what I mean."

"No, tell me."

With a brisk movement she pushed him away. "You're playing dumb."

"I *am* dumb. Haven't you heard that most scientists are?"

He returned to his previous position, sitting close to her. She tried to push him away once more, but he resisted by holding onto her arms.

"You were only 19. Don't tell me you thought of something else...something more, I mean."

"Didn't *you?*" Vivian rolled her eyes. "It was written all over your face!"

"Well, yes…I had half an idea of going a little further, but then…then, that damn dune buggy came along and buried us in sand." Chris laughed and pulled her close. "Do you remember?"

She joined him in laughter. "Do I," she said. "Probably the only dune buggy in the entire country. But that wasn't the worst. Those two guys helped us brush off the sand, then insisted we accept a ride back to the Red Manor." She giggled, then sighed. "And that was the end of our romantic involvement. You left the day after, and I didn't see you until the next year." She tapped him on his nose. "I waited a full year to see you again, and then what do I find out? That you had a steady girlfriend. You hardly danced with me, and you ignored me most of the time."

"I'm the faithful type. I didn't let myself get close to you, but I noticed you and enjoyed looking at you."

Voices, at first just a faint garble, drifted through the trees, becoming louder and louder. Then there were screams and the noise of bodies plunging into the water. Both Chris and Vivian rose and approached the riverbank.

"Somebody's in trouble," they said in unison.

"They're behind the bend," Chris said. "Maybe I should see if I can help. Do you mind? If I go alone I can paddle faster."

"Sure," Vivian said. "But don't forget to come back!"

CHAPTER 8

When Chris arrived home at 2 a.m., there was light in the family room. He parked his Camaro in the garage and, instead of going directly to his bedroom upstairs, he tiptoed through the corridor on the main floor and cautiously opened the family room door. His father was there, leafing through an album of family pictures.

"How come you're still up?" Chris asked him.

Bertha lay stretched out at Lucio's feet. She rose immediately and claimed Chris' attention.

Lucio looked up. "Oh, hi, Chris. What a day I had! Glen was here until about an hour ago, pestering me about writing another note on those ancient cups. I wanted to relax for a moment, so I thought I'd look through this album. It contains a lot of pictures of a nice boy—my own little boy. I'll never tire of looking at him." He paused. "How was your excursion in the wilderness?"

"Perfect." As he talked he threw a toy toward the door and Bertha fetched it proudly. "Vivian dressed as if she was going on an African safari, but she proved herself to be quite a sport. She managed the canoe well. We had a lot of fun. I'm so late because we had to help out a family."

"Oh?"

"Two canoes tipped over close to where Vivian and I were having our picnic. A mother and a father with their two kids. They had no clue how to manoeuvre a canoe and the adults had no life vests. At that point the river makes a turn, not sharp, really, but the water flows faster on one side than on the other. I think they were taken by surprise, panicked and made some movements that tipped their canoe. Fortunately, the kids were wearing life vests. I fished them out first since they were moving toward the centre of the river; then I helped the parents. We got them all safely ashore. Then I went back to the park entrance to get their station wagon while Vivian calmed the kids. The only thing the parents were good at was shouting." Chris moved toward the bar, then stopped and turned around. "By the way, how did Glen take our escapade?"

"Not bad. As I told you, he's not the control freak he appears to be. I believe the two women keep him under check when it's necessary."

"Glad to hear that. Want a drink?"

"Just a little one. Grappa, if you still have some of that old Moschino."

"Of course I have." Chris poured a Crown Royal Whisky for himself and grappa for his father. "So the two cups Glen showed you are the missing ones?"

"I believe so, but the only way to know for sure is to find the ones I gave to your mother."

Chris sipped his drink. "I don't have a clue where they ended up. Did you ask Kathy? Did she help you search?"

"Yes, she did. But she's never seen them around either. We searched the house and couldn't find them. I find that strange."

Chris rocked the glass between his fingers, pensive. "No, it isn't strange. It means they disappeared about the time we moved from the old house, just after Mother passed away. Kathy started to work for us soon after that."

Lucio put his wheelchair in motion. "I'm going to bed. We have plenty of time to talk about those cups. The Howards leave tomorrow, but they plan to stop here on their return trip. By then we might have found them. Good night."

"'Night, Lucio."

Bertha quietly manoeuvred closer to Lucio's wheelchair, but Chris reached for her and held her by the collar. "No, my dear girl. You don't sneak into Lucio's bedroom. Your place is at the entrance, guarding the house."

* * *

"It was a nice Mass; Father Paul preaches well," Lucio said when they returned home from the Don Bosco Seminary.

"Yes, and the choir was fantastic, even with only five ordinands. The two solos were great. I also found out you sing well, something I didn't know. I thought I got my voice from Mother."

"You did. She was very musical, but I'm not bad either. It was a family tradition to play an instrument or learn an art, generally painting. I was terrible at drawing, so I took piano lessons and learned how to sing."

"Father Paul was also surprised. I thought he'd never stop congratulating you. For a moment he forgot about his mission in the world."

"Right, he forgot for a full five minutes. In general that's all he talks about."

Chris assented. "From his sermon I gathered that fighting poverty and ignorance is really more than a mission for him—it's almost a holy mandate—but of course, he belongs to the Salesians, a missionary group that has been very active all over the world, especially in Brazil."

"Ah, you know something about them. I'm surprised. I thought all you were interested in were earthquakes, vibrations and all those instruments that detect them."

"I'll tell you a secret, Lucio. I went on the Internet and educated myself right after your first visit to the seminary. I knew that, soon or later, but probably very soon, you would drag me there."

"Ah, it is so? Since you know so much about me, what am I going to do today?"

"You'll think about those cups and try to reconstruct where they've been placed…or misplaced, I should say. By the way, the entire affair is beginning to intrigue me, too." He smiled. "Besides, if you and Glen are busy investigating or writing a note for that journal you mentioned, Vivian will stick around."

"Another nice surprise," Lucio said.

"What surprise? You're responsible for at least half of what's happening between Vivian and me."

Lucio suppressed a grin and quickly moved toward the kitchen.

"Should we have lunch?" he asked. "I'm hungry. Kathy was busy in the kitchen this morning. I saw her working on a nice rice salad. It's waiting for us in the fridge."

An hour later Chris and Lucio were still sipping their coffee at the table.

"I have the feeling Glen has more than an historical interest in those cups, or am I mistaken?" Chris asked. "There's something you know and don't want to tell, or at least you don't want to tell Glen."

A Cheshire-cat smile appeared on Lucio's face. "*Hai fatto centro!*"

When he got excited Lucio often reverted to his mother language. Because he had promised Chris that, once in Canada, he would make an effort to speak English, he added, "Bingo! Those cups are very valuable."

Chris waited for an explanation but Lucio kept quiet, so he leaned toward him.

"We're alone in the house, and the walls don't have ears," he whispered. "Talk!"

Lucio laughed. "It's a long story."

"We have the entire afternoon."

"Well, as Glen said, in the olden days people had no individual glasses. They used cups and passed them from one person to the next. The coronation of an emperor was a big event, and one of our ancestors commissioned four beautiful cups from a local artist. Those were times of great political unrest. One sad day the Red Manor was put under siege for half a year. With great effort Riccardo de' Vigentini, our ancestor, managed to defeat the enemy. He pushed the attacker down into the valleys surrounding the castle and then farther away into the plains, but from time to time, mercenaries came from nearby towns, attempting to raid the place or, more seriously, to take over the fortified manor. Riccardo was a valiant warrior and also a wise man. He hid his valuables in two of those cups in case he had to flee. They were diamonds, pearls, rubies and other precious gems."

"But everybody could see them!"

"Oh, no. To create the perfect hiding place, the gems were set onto the external surface, then another cup of thin copper was built around the original, leaving the gems in between. The two surfaces were then soldered together along the rim and at the bottom. When you hold them in your hands you feel that they're too heavy to drink from. But of course, very few people are aware of their original use."

"I see. And you gave those cups to Mother? Was she aware of their value?"

"Yes. I told her they were insurance, in case something went drastically wrong for her. I didn't know her father was running a successful company. I discovered that only after I came to stay with you."

Chris remained silent for a while, then asked, "Is it possible that somebody discovered their value and stole them?"

Lucio shook his head. "Possible, but not likely. We have to trace what happened when you moved from the old house to the new house. Who supervised the operation?"

"Grandfather."

"Did he have a place somewhere—a hut or a shed—where he worked on his hobbies?"

"Not at the house." He paused, then snapped his fingers. "Maybe at Vibratim…he often spent his free time there. There's a big basement where he stocked all sorts of equipment and gadgets over the years. I never bothered to look at them or clean them up."

Lucio smiled and nodded. "That's where we should go search, then."

PART 2

The Odyssey of an Orphan

CHAPTER 9

Croatia, June 2005

On the other side of the Atlantic Ocean, Mirko Grogan was on the last leg of his journey from London to Zagreb in Croatia. He had dreamed of making that trip for years, planned it carefully for months and now, finally, it was reality. He hoped to find his roots in Croatia and he wasn't leaving until he did. His craving for knowledge had increased with the passing years, and his constant sense of estrangement had become unbearable. He needed to shake off these feelings. Maybe, but only maybe, he could also chase away the nightmare that haunted him. As night crept near, Mirko dreaded falling asleep and having the usual terrible visions. Even though he knew that those images were not real, the pain and anguish he suffered were real, and they lingered hours after he woke.

He was alone, floating in darkness, immersed in an element that was not air and not water: it was something fluid and sticky that barely allowed him to breathe. He tried to cry for help but no sound came out of his mouth; he tried to move his arms to part the curtain of darkness in front of him but nothing moved. It was like being swallowed by a strange blob many times over.

Mirko Grogan sighed. When he had left Toronto the day before, he had great hopes, but now he felt edgy, afraid of disappointment. Was the orphanage he had grown up in still there? In the 80s it had been run by Poitr and Helena Radic, two ex-gypsies living in the hills near Dubrovnik. He had made inquiries at the Croatian Embassy in Ottawa, with the Canadian representatives in Zagreb and at the municipality of Dubrovnik. None of them had produced any useful information. Were the Radics still alive? Once he had been adopted by the Grogans, an older Canadian couple who had lost a child about his age, Mirko had lost all contact with the Radics.

The adoption was the best thing that ever happened to him.

Back then, it had taken four long months of shuffling papers back and forth before the Radics took Mirko to the Canadian Consulate in Zagreb where they released their parental custody to Gladys and Gerald Grogan. At first, Mirko had felt nothing but exhilaration. *At last a break,* he had thought. He was Mirko Grogan; he had a real name and nobody would ever address him again as *Siroce,* a word that meant *orphan.*

For a while life had brightened. Gladys and Gerald Grogan were kind people, who tried to bond with him slowly, always gauging his reactions. They bought him plenty of pants and tops, and Gladys stripped his clothes off his body and threw them in the hamper whenever he wore them two days in a row. *And the food.* It was tasty and plentiful. He could ask for seconds and his dish would be instantly filled again.

And the house, what a surprise. He still vividly remembered the first day he had set foot in the Grogan's three-story house in Toronto. He spent the first day measuring the footage of the external walls, then that of the kitchen, of the living room and the bedrooms. When he went to look at the yard, he was amazed to see that the grass was actually green, and the flowerbeds burst with plants in bloom. But the best surprise was that he had a room all to himself. A small bookcase held colourful books and a huge poster with the Blue Jays baseball team covered one entire wall. A guitar hung on the back of the door and a dozen baseball caps, all too small for him, filled a rack. A baseball bat and a glove were in a corner, as if they were ready to be put into action.

For the first three months Mirko had lived in dreamland.

But things were not meant to last. At the first snowstorm of the season, his new parents, driving back from a party, crashed into a ditch.

They never came home.

For the years to come Mirko felt abandoned, almost betrayed as he experienced a succession of foster homes. Those places were not even worth the name of homes. He had to share transient parents with other kids, and never felt the closeness he craved. He was still grateful to the Grogans, though, because at the age of majority he came into money. Thanks to that inheritance he had been able to live comfortably without needing a steady job, something he would not have been able to do thanks to his emotional instability.

But even so, a big problem remained. He didn't belong anywhere; he never behaved like everybody else, and he never felt like anybody he knew. When he decided to fit into a group in order to be accepted, he faked smiles and gestures and pretended interest in what people were talking about. He had no roots, nothing to hang onto in the moments of sadness or despair. Would the trip to the country where he grew up reconnect him with a world he once knew? Would he find his soul?

When Mirko heard the landing gear being released he suddenly realized what a big test his trip was going to be. As the fortified walls of Dubrovnik appeared in all their imposing structure, memories of misery assaulted him in force, one after the other: first came the starving, then the beating, then the psychological abuse, and finally the despair of having no other place to go. They attacked him like ocean waves. One gave him a split second to lift his head and breathe; the next one was ready to submerge him. And of all his recollections, the day that was carved in his mind was May 27, 1985—a turning point in his life.

CHAPTER 10

Near Dubrovnik, 20 years earlier

Three small children, barefoot and in dirty clothes, sat on the parched ground in the orphanage courtyard. One pulled at a rubber duck with his teeth; another took a handful of dirt and brushed his lips with it, and a third sobbed timidly. Another young boy flew high on a swing, its seat made out of an old truck tire. Mirko Grogan, who at that time answered to the name *Siroce,* stood near the barbed-wired fence, nervously shifting a softball from one hand to the other. Another child lay asleep in a wheelchair.

A middle-aged woman appeared in the doorway of the courtyard. Her greying hair was folded in a knot at the back, and she had quick, dark eyes and high cheekbones. She swung a bell.

"Supper," she said. She approached each of the small children and kicked at their butts to get them up. The one on the swing rushed inside. The boy near the fence didn't budge.

"Siroce, if you don't come right now, you go to bed without eating."

She pushed the three small children inside, then came back and lifted the wheelchair up over the three steps that led into the house. The apron she wore over her faded polka-dot dress got trapped between one wheel and the last step. *Ne seri!* she cursed in her dialect, then lifted the wheelchair again. This time she made it to the top.

Slowly Siroce dragged himself inside.

The kitchen table was set with six small plates very close to each other. Noodles with red beans constituted the meagre meal. The woman woke up the child in the wheelchair and tried to spoon-feed him, but the child went back to sleep.

With a squeak of the hinges the door opened and a short, bulky man in working clothes and boots entered the kitchen.

"Are you finished here, Helena?" he asked. "I have something to tell you."

She looked up. "Got an adoption going?"

The man nodded, a big smile on his face.

"Which one? Tell me quickly and I'll give him a bath."

He neared the woman and whispered in her ear, "No need to rush. It isn't one of the little ones."

Helena stared at him.

"You won't believe this, but they want Siroce!"

Helena's eyes brightened with surprise and excitement. "It'll be great."

She scooped the sleeping child's leftovers onto Siroce's dish. She quickly moved to the pantry, got two cookies out of a glass jar and deposited them on the rim of Siroce's plate.

"Eat, then go wash up and come back here. I'll give you a haircut."

*   *   *

The gravel road first crossed a field where sheep grazed on the sparse grass, then skirted around the property of Poitr and Helena Radic and led into the hills. One big sign, *Radic Sirotište*, advised the place to the traveller. Poitr and Helena, born of generations of gypsies, had given up fortune telling and card reading for a more stable, profitable business: selling orphaned children on the black-market. They had remodelled a dilapidated one-story house they had bought after the collapse of Tito's regime and painted the stucco walls a soft beige. The façade, with four big windows and red shutters, now had a neat appearance. They conducted their business, however, in the Lubarda Hotel in downtown Dubrovnik, and they rarely took a potential customer to their house. Siroce was the oldest child of the orphanage. Twice he had been temporarily adopted and twice he had been returned to them with heavy complaints.

The first time the Radics had seen Siroce they were impressed: the kid was five or six years old, with curly hair that framed a beautiful face. At that time Poitr and Helena, forced to move from one place to another, made their living by stealing in any way they could, but with discretion. Often they used a well-trained child. A kid, especially a handsome one, could attract people's sympathy and get close to the victims without raising suspicion. Once the child had been instructed appropriately, the money he provided could be worth a day's food. But Siroce was a very special one. He spoke a bit of English, making it extremely easy for him to approach the wealthiest tourists of all, the Americans.

For a few years, Siroce had been a good source of income, especially in the summer. But one sombre day the police had caught him in the act. The kid had been sent away for six months, and the Radics had been heavily fined. After his return, Siroce was reluctant to work for them, and he resented both Poitr and Helena. It was then that they tried to find adoptive parents for him. The easier clients to deal with were the Italians, since an illegal, yet organized, trade of children existed between their countries. Although illegal, the adoption contract, however, contained a clause giving the potential parents two months' probation. Both Italian couples had sent Siroce back. Their complaint? The kid uttered hardly 10 words in a day.

Maybe this time it would work out…

Poitr sat outside in the darkness of the approaching night.

"What's the catch?" Helena asked. She placed two glasses with water on the wooden table, took off her apron and draped it over the back of a chair. Then she sat close to her husband.

"Only one, this time. I told them Siroce is our kid. This is a nice couple in their 50s. They just lost a kid the same age as Siroce. The mother is devastated." He paused. "You know the boy can be very nice, right?"

"Sometimes, when it pleases him."

Poitr nodded. "A week ago he offered them his services as a guide for the Dubrovnik's palace—all the guided tours were filled up. You know Siroce's fixation with that old building, the Rector's? He knows it inside out. So this couple was very pleased. They gave him $2. When I went to pick him up they asked me whether Siroce could give them a tour of the old city the next day. I said that was fine. Now they'd like to take him along for a week. They want to follow the Adriatic coast up to Rijeka then move inland, go into Ljubljana, then visit the Plitvice Lakes. You know all those places, right?"

Helena nodded. "We used to move from one to the other. We made good money on those foolish tourists."

Poitr took a long sip from his glass. "Well, I was there to pick Siroce up when this couple, Grogan is their name, asked me if they could hire him as a guide. We bargained about the price and we agreed on $60. I introduced him as my son."

"Why do you think they have any intention to adopt the kid?"

"Siroce heard them talking about it. He also gathered that they own a car dealership in Toronto. That spells money."

"Canadian, you said? They will never go for an illegal adoption."

"I know." He grinned, satisfaction painted all over his face. "That's why I told them Siroce was our kid."

"I don't understand." Helena shifted nervously in her chair.

Poitr stretched his legs on the bench in front of him, as if preparing for a difficult talk. "The couple will be back in a week, maybe 10 days. I'll talk to them…say we're very poor, and want a better life for our kid. An adoption would break our heart but we'd do it. Of course we'd need a bit of compensation, since we'd lose the son who'd provide for our old age. I'll keep playing that tune. I'll let them make me an offer—I count on a thousand." Poitr paused. "By that time our little Mirko will be dead. Siroce will take his place." He reached for Helena's hand and tapped on it. "Nothing's wrong with making a little money from our kid's death. He cost us a fortune with all those medications that didn't do *nothing* for him."

"They helped him with the pain." Helena tried to repress her sobbing, but tears raked her face.

Poitr dismissed the issue with a wave.

"The potion my grandmother used to make would have done the same. And stop crying. It bothers me." He slapped her hand. "We need to get rid of Siroce. He's growing into a man. A strong young man, too. I'm almost afraid of him now. Today, when I used the strap to beat him, he managed to grab it. He circled it over my head and said, 'Next time I'll use it on you!' That's what he said."

"I know, I know. I'm scared, too, when he looks at me with those dark eyes. I see hell in there. Yesterday I saw him playing target with a knife. He never missed the centre."

"Deal, then. Buy him some new clothes and a couple pairs of underwear. Ask your sister to take the other kids for a couple of weeks. I'll clean up the yard and repaint the entrance and the living room. You make sure the house is nice and clean."

"Why do all that work?"

"They may want to come down to see where Siroce—I mean Mirko—lives."

CHAPTER 11

Dubrovnik, June 2005

Absorbed in the recollection of the time he had spent at the Radics'
orphanage, Mirko Grogan didn't move when the aircraft touched down at
Zagreb Airport. After all the passengers had deplaned, a male flight attendant
tapped him on the shoulder.

"Sir?" he said. As Mirko didn't react, he repeated, "Sir?"

"Yes?" Mirko responded.

"We are in Dubrovnik." He looked concerned. "Anything wrong? Do
you need help?"

Mirko shook his head and glanced around, trying to get his bearings. Then
he rose slowly, took his carry-on from the overhead compartment and
stepped off the plane.

His journey into the past had begun.

The VW he had booked before leaving Toronto was ready for him at the
airport. He lugged his two bags into the trunk and, with a map spread on the
passenger's seat, he began driving.

When he arrived in Dubrovnik, he felt exhausted, so he quickly took
lodging at the Lubarda Hotel, a place he remembered well. It was a medium-
sized building in the historical part of town, with back and front entrances on
different levels. The best rooms contained little balconies where one could
look down and admire the many sailboats raking the blue waters. The lobby
had small booths where one could sit comfortably and have a drink or a chat.
The restaurant offered both local and international cuisine.

Mirko didn't bother with supper. He took a shower and then dove into
bed.

The following morning, well rested, he got up early and ordered breakfast. As he savoured the local pastry and sipped a Turkish coffee, he decided to momentarily put his quest on hold. He would first revisit the places that were once familiar to him.

He strolled leisurely along the old streets, surprised by the changes. The shop windows contained plenty of merchandise, including an incredible variety of clothing and an invasion of jeans. Everywhere the activity was frantic. Mirko descended to the harbour and watched commercial and private vessels come and go. For a good half-hour he observed the hydrofoil and marvelled at the way it lifted itself above the water. Helena and Poitr Radic had never wanted him to get close to the sea, probably afraid of an accident. He sauntered toward the two long piers where fishing boats engaged in unloading their night's catch. Several men busied themselves emptying the nets and filling crates of different sizes and shapes. Nearby a dwarf sat on the dock. He seemed oblivious to his surroundings.

"A tour with us, Mister?" a voice behind him asked.

He turned to face an elderly man leaning heavily on a cane, his face weather-beaten. Mirko shook his head.

"Maybe some other time," he said.

"Fifteen dollars for four hours of boating with my one-horsepower Zodiac. We can zigzag in and out of the little bays around here. Beautiful scenery. Or I can take you on my big boat with other tourists. Same tour, only $10."

"No time today," Mirko said. "But I'd be interested in going fishing at night to see how it's done."

Immediately the man offered him a business card. "This is my son's phone number; they go out every night. The catch is good this time of year."

Without saying a word, Mirko took the card and pocketed it.

He slowly returned the way he had come, got into his VW and followed the road that would lead him to the old orphanage, where, as far as he could remember, he had spent six or seven years. He should go see the Radics and get some answers to his most impelling questions. Had the government been involved in sending him to the orphanage? Even under Tito's regime there were rules and regulations. Or did the Radics act on their own and illegally? Did they know where he was born? He should be firm with them, and not let them get away with vague answers or lies.

The shriek of a horn made Mirko realize he was in the middle of the road. He quickly moved to the right and gave driving his full attention. The road wound left and right while cutting through the hills. Forty kilometres later he reached a clearing.

The board where the orphanage sign had once been pasted was still there, but the sign itself had been ripped off. Roof shingles lay on the ground and the shutters were missing. Mirko parked close to the entrance and knocked on the door. No answer. He tried the bell, but it didn't work. He listened attentively for any sound coming from inside the house. Nothing but silence. He rounded the corner of the house, jumped over the barbed-wired fence and tugged at the kitchen door handle. It wouldn't budge. He extracted his gunlock pick from the purse he carried around his waist and freed the lock.

He entered the kitchen and opened the drapes. The dust that spread all around made him cough a few times. Dirty dishes filled the sink and pieces of paper and dried banana peels littered the tiled floor. He opened the pantry. Rice, beans and noodles sat on the middle shelf; the other shelves were bare. He moved into the bedroom where he used to sleep. As before, it was clogged with bunks, thin mattresses rolled up on top of four beds and crinkled blankets lying across the others. *The Radics left in a hurry,* Mirko thought. He closed the door and proceeded to the room the Radics had kept carefully locked. Here, he thought, was where they hid their dark secrets. Once again he got his lock pick out and unlocked the door, then the desk. He found seven drawers filled with papers, envelopes, chains, watches, wallets, credit cards and driver licences—all with different names and all expired.

Mirko hurried back to his car, retrieved a pad and a pencil and went back inside. He sat in front of the desk. It was going to be a long afternoon.

*   *   *

"Are you sure?" Poitr Radic asked for the second time, his voice full of anxiety.

"Yes," Nozemni, the receptionist at the Lubarda Hotel, replied in a whisper. "The dwarf recognized him at once. He's tall now, more than six feet, but he has the same face with the same long hair. Sam offered him a boat tour. Your Siroce replied in Croatian. That's why I'm sure, Poitr."

"I see. Stop Sam from offering a boat tour. Mirko should be kept away from the water."

"Why?"

"Just do it!"

"But I have no way to tell Sam what to do. It's business for him."

"Well, try. Offer him the money he'd get from Mirko." He paused. "And another important thing…Ask our friend at the police station to forbid him to enter our house. I don't want him close to that either."

"I don't know if I can do that. Things are getting more and more legal here. It will cost you a lot of money."

"Nozemni, listen. Don't be afraid to put in a bit of money. I'll pay you back. Helena and I need to stay away only a couple more months or so. Then everything will go back to normal. Illegal adoptions will bring in a lot more money than before. They're going strong."

"Well, you know Interpol has been looking for you for a few weeks."

"Yes, I know, but the locals protect me. In awhile the Interpol people will go back where they came from and we can go back to our old business…like before…no, better than before."

"Ok, I'll try to do what you say." Nozemni didn't sound convinced. "I have to go now."

"One more thing. Mirko shouldn't find out where we're staying. Understood?" There was no reply. "I'll call you every other day until I hear that he's left town."

"Fine," Nozemni said, and clicked off.

*   *   *

It was getting dark and Mirko had almost finished examining the material accumulated in the Radics' desk. The most interesting thing was an accounting sheet with several rows and columns. The first column listed names; the second, birthdays; the third, the date a child entered the orphanage, and the fourth, the place of birth. *The list of the orphanage's guests,* mused Mirko. *A total of 38.* But the records were incomplete; in most cases they missed the date of birth, and in others, the location had a question mark. Mirko carefully copied all the information. He was, of course, interested in children about his age, anybody born between 1971 and 1975, because he didn't know his actual birth date. His birth certificate belonged to the Radics' real child. He couldn't find any record of a birthday within that range, and the name Siroce wasn't listed. He excluded about 15 names, either because he had come in contact with those children or because of their age. *I could be any of the remaining 23.* There was no way he would ever find out how the Radics had gotten hold of him, where he had come from, or if he had been abducted. He felt that somebody, if not the Radics, had snatched him from his real parents.

Disappointed, he put everything back in order and left the premises.

He was only a kilometre away from the house on his way back to Dubrovnik when he met a police car. He wondered where the cruiser was heading. As far as he remembered, that road terminated shortly after the orphanage. *Maybe there were new campgrounds ahead.* Along the coast campgrounds were very expensive, but in the interior a few dollars would assure a tourist a good night's accommodation.

Exhausted because of the long day and the emotions evoked from his childhood place, Mirko slumped into his bed as soon as he reached the Lubarda Hotel.

CHAPTER 12

Morning arrived too early for Mirko. He still felt tired, despite the long sleep. He should take time off and relax. He should control his craving for digging into his past. He was draining himself. He lingered in bed until noon, then rose, showered and dressed.

He descended the stairs to get something to eat. The meals were served in the garden at the front section of the hotel where colourful umbrellas, installed in the middle of iron tables, offered shelter from the sun. Mirko chose the table farthest away from the building, so he could admire the sea. He ordered coffee, fresh maize-and-bean soup, and patiently waited for his order to come. Finally the soup came, and he'd just begun savouring it when Sam neared his table.

Uninvited, Sam propped up his cane and sat opposite him. "I've good news. I talked to my son. He can take you on his fishing boat tonight. They leave early, around 7 p.m. They have to go about 30 kilometres southwest. That's the best fishing hole right now. Are you ready for that tour you were talking about?" Mirko didn't reply and Sam continued. "Twenty-five dollars. You'll be back tomorrow morning around eight." He smiled, showing yellow teeth. "Snacks and a drink are included."

Mirko looked at his wristwatch. It was past three. Maybe it wouldn't be such a bad idea to take a break from his compelling thoughts.

"What about the weather?" he asked. "It might rain, the clouds are so low."

"Not to worry. My son's boat has a 60-ton burden and a big motor left behind by the Germans. It can handle *any* sea."

"Fine." Mirko sipped his Turkish coffee slowly. "I'll come to the pier just before 7 p.m."

The *Rijeka* was docked at the end of the longest wharf. Dilapidated automobile tires hung around the boat to prevent it from damaging its hull against the dockside. The engine was running, spewing diesel fumes in the air. A small cabin was located near the bow and the gunwale was rusty, interrupted by scuppers to ease the launching of the fishing nets. Two men were loading crates and fishing nets when Sam and Mirko approached the gangway.

"Hi, Alesh," Sam said and then turned to Mirko. "That's my son. He's good at sea."

Alesh threw another net into the boat.

"Hello…we're almost finished loading," he said.

"This is Mirko, your passenger. He's already paid. Take good care of him." Sam waved that he was leaving and limped away, his cane resounding on the wooden dock.

"Jump in," Alesh said. "We're ready to take off. Most of the other fishing boats are already gone."

A big ship left the harbour at sustained speed, sending waves crashing against the stony walls protecting the harbour, the docks, and the anchored vessels. The *Rijeka* swayed from port to starboard and Mirko hesitated.

"One big hop," Alesh said, and stretched his arm toward him.

Mirko waited until the boat's side became lower than the pier, then leaped onto the deck. He turned to look at what he was leaving behind. Older folks and kids fished from the docks; some splashed their lures into the water with energy, hoping for a catch while others quietly waited for a bite. A dwarf sat on a rudimentary bench, watching the *Rijeka* leave.

As the vessel took to the sea, the piers and anchored boats became undistinguishable from the structures that clogged the harbour. Soon afterward, even the imposing walls of the old city lost their outline and became just a spot in the hills. Then the harbour's flickering light disappeared into the distance.

For an hour the *Rijeka* navigated smoothly with an alert Alesh at the helm. The waves had become more frequent, their height less than a metre. Two fishermen unfolded the nets and shoved them close to the scuppers. As darkness advanced, Alesh turned on a light at the bow. It was dim and Mirko wondered how far the *Rijeka* could be spotted.

"Check on the motor; it's losing beats," Alesh said.

A fisherman descended into the galley where an old stove and a 400-horse-power engine were located. He turned the motor off for a few minutes. It sputtered, then resumed its normal rhythm.

A lightning bolt appeared in the sky, followed by others.

"There's a bit of a storm behind us," Alesh said. "Nothing to worry about. We're ahead of it and we're moving away."

However, in the next half hour the wind gained strength and the height of the waves increased, their white caps almost invisible in the incipient darkness of night.

"The engine," Alesh yelled. "It stopped." He pointed to the seamen. "Go down in the hold and make it work."

The two fishermen rushed downstairs. For a while the motor rattled again, then went dead. The men returned to the deck and hurriedly approached Alesh, talking frantically.

Mirko's Blue Jays cap flew away. His jeans and turtleneck sweater were not protecting him from the blustering wind. He began shivering, not knowing whether it was because of the cold wind or because he was scared. He looked attentively at Alesh and his men. Only a few words reached him, but the tone of their voices and their gestures were frantic. He guessed at what they were saying: the boat had lost the power to control the sea.

A big wave swept the bridge, making the *Rijeka* lurch to one side. Alesh lost his balance but still hung onto the wheel.

"The life jackets! Get them! All of you!" he said.

Then the sea became enraged, bouncing the *Rijeka* like a toy in a bathtub. The wind reached gale force, and Alesh struggled to keep the boat level. Minutes later a second wave hit the boat sideways and the two fishermen clung to the railing. From the stern a third humongous wave washed over the vessel, submerging it momentarily. The *Rijeka* bucked like an infuriated horse as it emerged.

"Goddamn boat!" Alesh said after it levelled off. "We're losing plywood from the bow! We're going to take water!"

The wind subsided for a moment but the waves kept battering the old vessel. Alesh's voice hardly carried in the swirl of the howling wind.

"If things don't calm down soon we'll be smashed into a hundred pieces!"

A few moments later he yelled, "The flare guns! Fire them before it starts raining!"

It took what Mirko thought an eternity before he saw five arcs of light crack the darkness in a desperate appeal for rescue. More waves swept over the bridge, but Alesh seemed to be one with the helm. Then, as he turned the wheel to counteract the combined force of an incoming wave and the wind, the helm broke, sending Alesh's released body very near to the scuppers. A man rushed toward him and dragged him near the gunwale. They both clung there until the wave passed over them, then they staggered toward the cabin.

"We've got to stay together, here, close to the centre of the boat," Alesh said. "Pray for help to come."

With horrid fascination Mirko watched the scene unfold before his eyes, an eerie feeling of déjà vu permeating his mind. *That's what hell would look like,* he thought, *if there was one.*

CHAPTER 13

Aboard the luxury yacht *Il Corsaro Rosso* the party had wound down, partially because of the late hour and partially because of the sea conditions. Gabriele Anzieri and his four guests sprawled in lounge chairs listening to music. An ex-captain of the *Marina Mercantile*, Gabriele enjoyed being at sea in any weather or conditions. In the good season his yacht was his home. Accompanied by Sean Despen, an expert seaman, he moved from port to port, exploring new places, visiting friends or stocking his fridge and bar. His yacht had been custom-built at a legendary boatyard located in Piantedo. With its twin 715-horsepower engines, *Il Corsaro Rosso* could cruise at 30 knots.

The last CD had finished playing Dvorak's *The Bells of Zlonice* when a sudden change of course surprised everyone aboard, none more than Gabriele, who rose and walked briskly to the bridge. The motor had been forced to its maximum.

"What's up?" Gabriele asked Sean, the man at the helm.

"An SOS, Captain. I've veered 10 degrees east and aimed at the point where the flare lights came from."

"Sighting range?"

"I guess they were hand-held signals, so 5 kilometres, less than 3 nautical miles, something around that."

"Oh. The storm might have surprised more than one boat. I hope they'll repeat the signals, so we can pinpoint their position exactly. It isn't easy to spot anything in this kind of weather."

Sean glanced at the instruments neatly aligned in a glass case at his right. "At our current speed we can reach them in five minutes—assuming the sea doesn't get any rougher." He paused and patted at the helm. "This is a beauty of a ship. Listen to how well the motor responds." Sean was as in love with *Il Corsaro Rosso* as much as Gabriele was.

"What's our position?" Gabriele asked.

"About 60 kilometres from the Croatian coast, going north."

"I'll take the wheel, Sean. You go down and send the Mayday. Alert the Croatian and Italian coastguards."

Sean staggered as he left the bridge.

Five minutes elapsed but no more lights appeared in the sky. Gabriele smoothly reduced speed.

"All done," said Sean, back from the control room.

They both kept quiet, scrutinizing the sky for homing signals. None appeared.

"There was no forecast of bad weather," Gabriel said. "Maybe you should go listen to the marine radio. See if they've updated their bulletin."

Sean left again to return soon afterward.

"Waves of about two metres and winds of up to 50 knots. There's been a violent storm east of here. What we're getting is the tail of it. It shouldn't last much longer."

"Good. Please inform my guests of what happened. At daylight we'll need the cooperation of everybody to spot a wreck or men at sea."

Sean left and came back with two coffees. He placed one on the floor and gave the other to Gabriele.

"Let me take the wheel, Captain."

For the last five years Sean, Irish by birth, had followed Gabriele in his wanderings around the world. He was in his 50s, thin like a willow, his skin rugged from sun and wind. His curly, unruly red hair never quite made it inside his cap. Being at sea was his true passion—all that he wanted in life.

As the boat began circling around the presumed trouble spot, the wind subsided, but the sea remained rough. Sean and Gabriele worried. By now the boat that had sent the signals might have sunk.

At the crack of dawn everybody on the boat except the man at the wheel leaned over the gunwale, carefully looking for anything that wasn't water.

Then a large, dark object appeared on the crest of a big wave, to soon disappear in a swale. Gabriele immediately steered in that direction and soon he was able to identify the white script: *Rijeka*. People were lying on the wreckage, but there was no movement. He called for Sean.

"Radio to the Croatian coastguard and see whether they can tell us how many people were aboard the *Rijeka*," he said.

As they approached the wreckage, one arm lifted up from the floating wood and waved at them. Gabriele killed the engine while Sean lowered the rope stairway and released the inflatable lifeboat.

In no time Alesh and his two mates were lifted aboard *Il Corsaro Rosso* and taken to the galley. As soon as Alesh could talk, he turned to Gabriele, who had joined them.

"One of us is missing," he said. "The boat broke just under his feet. He was swept away. I yelled at him to hang on to a piece of wood. If he did, we should be able to find him."

"Another fisherman?" Gabriele asked.

"No, a tourist…Canadian, I believe, or at least that was what it looked like from his shirt."

"We'll keep looking," said Gabriele, and went back up to the bridge.

An hour later a narrow object appeared on the horizon, cutting through the sea like a powerful knife. The waters parted at its passage and created a continuous ruffle of white matter much higher than the waves. The Italian coastguard had arrived. The vessel stopped a couple hundred metres from the yacht. They were briefed by radio on the preliminary rescue and joined in the search for the fourth man.

It was noon when Gabriele spotted a small piece of debris, a yellow smudge on top of it. As they approached they could see a man prone on the floating wood, his feet and arms in the water. Once again they released the lifeboat.

Mirko was alive but only half-conscious. With a great effort he opened his eyes and looked around, first at the men who were wrapping a rope around his waist, then at the boat that swayed in front of him.

"Oh, no! Not again," he mumbled. He closed his eyes in an attempt to shake off the unwanted image that unfolded before him.

In no time Mirko was lifted aboard the yacht.

"Where am I?" His voice trailed off to a whisper.

"Among friends," Gabriele said, and knelt before him. "You're going to be all right. Welcome to my floating home, *Il Corsaro Rosso*."

"Oh, finally you came," Mirko said, and passed out.

Sean freed him of his wet clothes, dried his body with a towel and covered him with a thick blanket. He was about to take him down to one of the berths when two coast guardsmen boarded *Il Corsaro Rosso* carrying a stretcher. One, a paramedic, looked at Mirko.

"Severe hypothermia. We'll take him with us. He'll be in the hospital within the hour."

"Where are you taking him?" Gabriele asked.

"To the Perrino, the big hospital in Brindisi."

CHAPTER 14

Near Dubrovnik, Croatia

Holding tightly to the handrail, the dwarf descended the steep staircase that led to the Radics' hideout; his legs arched the full length to reach each step. He knocked at the door, one long knock followed by two short ones. He waited a couple of seconds, then knocked again using the same pattern.

The door opened and Poitr Radic let him in. Without saying a word, Poitr grabbed the Italian newspaper the dwarf held in his hands.

"Third page," the dwarf said. "It's all there. Two big columns."

Poitr opened *La Gazzetta del Mezzogiorno* and began reading as he crossed the big room to stop in front of the only window half-carved into the wall.

A bead curtain rolled back. Helena appeared and stood quietly for a moment. She then gestured for the dwarf to approach. From a nearby shelf she took a small object wrapped in greasy paper, unwrapped it and sliced off a piece of sausage.

"For you, Jos, it's the way you like it, dry and spicy."

"Easy on the food," Poitr said. "We're low on supplies."

"It's just a little piece," Helena said.

Poitr grunted. He sat at the table and continued reading.

"Bad news?" Helena asked.

"They've got our Mirko. An Italian boat fished him out of the water. He's in a hospital in Brindisi."

"Damn...oh." Helena slapped her hand against her mouth.

"There's a lot about the sinking of the *Rijeka* and the rescue. Not much about Mirko." He turned the remaining pages of the newspaper, looking for additional headlines. "It could be worse," he said after he was finished reading.

Jos munched quietly at his treat, then neared Poitr. "There's no point in watching the harbour or the Lubarda anymore, right?"

Poitr looked up. "Right. But I need you for a new job. Gather two good shovels, a wheelbarrow and a good gasoline lamp. Come back here with everything tomorrow at ten o'clock."

"Will I get paid?"

"You know I'll pay you," Poitr said, and went back to reading.

Jos didn't move; his eyes wandered between Poitr, Helena and the alcove where a bed lay.

"So get moving." Poitr glared at him.

"The word is out that you can't pay anymore."

Poitr threw the newspaper onto the bare concrete floor and jumped to his feet. Even though he was only five feet tall he could easily intimidate a dwarf.

"Do as I say." He gestured as if to hit Jos, who ran for the door, opened it and skittered away.

Jos' laboured steps were still audible when Helena asked, "What else was in the paper you didn't want Jos to know?"

"Mirko is unable to talk, which is good. But at the hospital they think it's a temporary thing. We may not have much time."

"What do you have in mind?"

"It's time we dig out the gold that the old German fellow buried in the grave. You know what I'm talking about." He pointed to the door. "Now go out and call Nozemni. Tell him to come here at once."

"Why don't you go out? It's always me who has to go out to get the food or whatever we need. They're looking for both of us."

Poitr raised his arm, ready to strike, but Helena made a beeline for the alcove.

"I'm the brain in this family," Poitr screamed after her. "If they catch *me*, you're done, too. Besides you can disguise yourself better than I can. Use that blond wig I gave you and the cane." As Helena was getting dressed slowly, Poitr yelled, "Move. It's urgent."

Five minutes later Helena was gone.

Poitr sat at the table, satisfied. He congratulated himself as he mentally reviewed his plan. It was the best scam he had ever thought of. What first had been a big worry—Mirko's going to sea and therefore having an occasion to remember about his past, had yielded the opposite result. Now Mirko didn't even remember about the present and had fallen back into one of his aphasia spells. Great. With Nozemni's help, he could clean up on whatever Mirko had left at the hotel—money, documents, clothes. And then, the icing on the cake. If he managed to get at the gold his father's friend had left him he could pay for Nozemni's cosmetic surgery. Nozemni could then go to Canada and clear out whatever wealth Mirko had accumulated over the years.

He had thought of that scheme non-stop for the last three days. It was a great plan.

Everything was falling into place. There was only one problem: they had to act fast.

*   *   *

"Hold that lamp high," Poitr said to Helena. "Higher."

Helena stretched her arm as high as she could.

Poitr and Nozemni had started digging in the backyard of an abandoned church just after midnight, and yet, two hours later, they still hadn't found the coffin they were looking for. The little cemetery had only a few dozen graves, but as a sepulchre in a holy ground had been discouraged for decades, a tomb often held more than one coffin, piled on top of each other. To make things more difficult, grass, climbing ivy and sand covered the commemorative stones, making it difficult to decipher any of the inscriptions.

Nozemni stopped and with a sharp move planted the shovel into the ground.

"*Ne seri!*" he swore in his dialect. "This isn't the spot. We have dug out eight graves. All so deep."

"This is the spot, I guarantee you. The instructions were very precise. Keep digging." Poitr jumped into the hole sending soil flying out of the grave.

For a while Nozemni complied.

"I'm tired," he said a short time later. "Can we not come back tomorrow?"

"No. And why are you complaining? You're stronger than me."

"Please, Poitr."

80

Shovel after shovel, Poitr kept throwing dirt out of an already wide and deep hole.

"It's too dangerous. It has to be done *tonight.* And call me 'Dad.'"

"You're not my dad. You're paid for feeding me, that's all."

"You were the last of our kids. You stayed at the orphanage 15 years and we treated you as our son. And I gave you my name."

"Sure, sure, but my real father paid you for that, too." He threw the shovel aside. "I have to stop. My right arm aches. I need to rest. Fifteen minutes."

"There's a bottle of water in my bag." Helena's voice was soft. "Drink some. You'll feel better."

Nozemni stepped aside, rummaged in the bag near Helena's feet, sat, and drank all of the water.

"So you already know of a surgeon who would do the operation?" he asked.

"Yes," Poitr said. "And he's here in Dubrovnik. It's going to cost us, but he can do it next week. For my plan to work we need to act fast."

He rested for a few seconds, then spit on his hands, and went back to digging. All of a sudden he stopped and used the spade to poke around the same spot, softly, probing. He knelt and brushed the dirt away with his hands.

"We've got it." Poitr reached toward Helena. "Give me the lamp." He placed the lamp at his feet and removed the soil from around a child's coffin. "My knife, Nozemni."

Nozemni rose and tossed the knife close to Poitr.

Alternating the use of his bare hands and the knife Poitr scraped and scraped, then set the lamp very close to the small coffin. He busted it open.

"It's here! It's here!" He lifted a canvas bag and exposed its contents to the lamp. "Gold coins." He opened a second bag, leather. "Big, solid pieces of gold, as the old man said I'd find." He reclosed both bags and, with some effort, threw them to Helena's feet.

"Who gave them to you?" Nozemni asked, his voice expressing incredulity mixed with suspect.

"A German who hid on our land for more than 60 years. My father saved his life. Before dying—he died two weeks ago—he gave the dwarf a piece of paper for me with the name of a church. I knew what it was all about, since he'd mentioned he'd hidden his treasure in the cemetery of an old church."

Poitr jumped out of the grave. "Nozemni, go to the Lubarda and get beer for all of us. Plenty of it. I want to get drunk tonight."

Nozemni turned around and was ready to leave.

"Wait," Poitr said. "Bring everything you can find in Mirko's room, then wipe out his record at the hotel. Make it as if Mirko Grogan had never been there."

"What about the car?"

"What car?"

"He rented a VW."

"Return it. And be sure you get back the deposit he must have paid for it."

*　*　*

The waiting room of the cosmetic surgeon had an attractive décor with upholstered armchairs grouped around a low table; on its centre stood a ceramic vase with plastic carnations and lilies; old and new magazines were artfully arranged around the vase; pictures with country scenes decorated the walls. The room exuded comfort, if not cheerfulness.

Nozemni waited only a few minutes. A doctor opened his office door and moved toward him.

"Dr. Karesi," he said with a conventional smile as he extended his hand. "Pleased to meet you, Nozemni."

"Good morning, Doctor," Nozemni replied. Since the age of 11, his face, disfigured by an explosion that had claimed part of his left cheek, had made him feel like a pariah among other children, even if he had an athletic physique. He had hoped and prayed for an occasion to have cosmetic surgery, and now, thanks to the deal he had struck with Poitr Radic, his dream was going to become true.

Nozemni had talked to Dr. Karesi twice on the phone. He had explained his long-term problem and received assurance that the reconstructive surgery he wanted was possible.

"Would you like to come into my office so that we can discuss the procedure?" He opened the door of a large room, and beckoned Nozemni in.

In the office, pedestals held model heads of adults and children, some complete, others just cutaways.

The doctor sat behind a wooden desk partially covered with medical journals. Two sets of folders were piled up in a corner and a telephone stood in the middle. Dr. Karesi gestured Nozemni to sit in a chair opposite him.

"Before I call for my assistant to update your medical record and get the imprints, I'll arrange for a CT scan. I'd also like to know if you have in mind some special facial features, some model we should consider."

The doctor looked at the right side of Nozemni's face, then the left, where part of the jaw was missing. The skin, tight on the superior part of the cheek, draped toward the chin. It wasn't a nice view. Nozemni had never become accustomed to it, and neither had the people around him. As a child, when he smiled, the kids ran away.

Nozemni hesitated at first.

"Actually, I do have something in mind," he said. "Nothing definite, but here it is." He removed a picture from his wallet and gave it to the doctor. "I wouldn't mind looking like this man."

The doctor's eyes flickered from Nozemni's face to the photo in his hands. "It wouldn't be that difficult. The structure of your jaw will allow shaping your face very close to this model." He pressed a button on his phone and called for his assistant. He looked over at Nozemni. "Should we begin? Are you ready?"

"Yes, doctor. I've been ready all my life."

CHAPTER 15

Brindisi, Southern Italy

In a room at the *Santa Rita*, the non-profit clinic where doctors at the hospital in Brindisi had transferred Mirko, Angelo Mariani, the chief medical doctor, looked once more at his patient.

"I can't understand what's happening," he said to the medical students accompanying him on his daily rounds. "He's still in shock. *Still* in shock after a full week." He turned to the nurse, who stood almost at attention beside him. "Am I right? It has been a full week?"

The nurse flipped a few sheets of the notepad she held in her hands. "Yes, sir. He was rescued exactly seven days ago."

The doctor stroked his goatee and pushed his eyeglasses up his nose. "He was dehydrated; that would give him convulsions, seizures perhaps? But these effects are temporary. They should have disappeared by now." He approached Mirko's bed and touched his forehead. "The fever is gone. He looks strong and healthy." Mirko didn't budge. The doctor then opened his eyelids.

Mirko jumped almost out of bed. "Mom, where are you?"

The doctor took a step back. "Your mom is not here, son. If you tell us a bit more about you, we can notify your family."

Mirko looked blankly at him, shivered and collapsed back onto the bed. He closed his eyes.

"Continue the IV. Make a note," the doctor said to the nurse. "I want an MRI to see if there is any damage to the brain. And ask administration to contact a Canadian consulate, assuming the information we got was correct. Something happened to this grown-up boy, in addition to having spent 12 hours floating on a piece of wood at sea. Try to find his next of kin. We need somebody here who knows him well."

*   *   *

Under Sean's attentive eye, *Il Corsaro Rosso* was getting a wash and a polish. Gabriele Anzieri jumped off the boat with a sports bag in his hands.

"I'll be back for supper," he said to Sean, and quickened his steps toward the marina's exit.

Gabriele had read in the newspaper about the state of mind of the young man they had rescued from the waters of the Adriatic Sea. Unfortunately, they only knew his name was Mirko or so the crew of the *Rijeka* called him. Since his rescue Mirko spoke only isolated words that didn't make sense to anybody. After three weeks he still lay in bed in an almost catatonic state. Gabriele decided to pay him a visit, attracted by curiosity and the recollection of his good looks.

He got a cab and 20 minutes later he received permission to visit Mirko. Mirko's room, medium size with pale green walls, had the usual sterile look of hospital rooms.

A young nurse accompanied him, her unruly mass of blond hair only slightly subdued in a ponytail. She lifted the Venetian blinds halfway, letting the afternoon sun filter inside.

"That's better," she said with a soft voice. "My name is Daniela." She pushed the over-the-bed table toward the window and pointed toward an easy chair in a corner. "You'll sit comfortably there, Captain."

"Is he talking now?"

"Not much, words here and there. When we ask him something about his family or the boat he was on, he smiles and says, 'I don't remember.'" The nurse fingered the pin on her lapel, clearly trying to find a reason to prolong her stay in the room.

Gabriele sat. "Thank you. If I need you I'll call you." He wasn't interested in women, not even pretty ones.

The nurse nodded and left the room.

Softly, Gabriele Anzieri dragged his chair close to Mirko's bed, took his hand and gently lifted it up in the air. Mirko's eyes followed the entire arc, then closed again. Gabriele released Mirko's hand onto the bed.

"Mirko?" he asked. "Mirko is your name, right?" There was no response. "Mirko, can you hear me?"

Mirko opened his eyes and looked at Gabriele blankly.

"We met on my boat, *Il Corsaro Rosso*," Gabriele said. He put his captain's hat on, rose and stood in front of Mirko. "Remember me?" He deliberately wore the same blue top with gold trim that he had worn the day he had rescued Mirko.

"Il Maniero Rosso," Mirko muttered without opening his eyes.

"That's what he repeats all the time," a feminine voice said behind him. Daniela had silently re-entered the room and was setting tea and cookies on the table. She pushed the table across Mirko's bed.

"Did you alert the Canadian consulate?" Gabriele asked.

"It has been done. They listened carefully but when we told them that the only evidence that Mirko was Canadian was his sweater with the maple leaf flag, they told us to contact the American consulate. Nowadays many Americans camouflage themselves as Canadians when they travel abroad, they've been told."

"It sounds like a lie to me. Government offices of any nation around the world find excuses not do their jobs. That's the trouble. So who pays the bill?"

"The Santa Rita so far; it's a charitable organization, but Dr. Mariani is concerned. Weeks of hospitalization, and Mirko is not even well enough to answer questions. He says this young man needs psychiatric help. But for this he needs to find some funds."

"Money, money, money. It all boils down to that. I'll talk to Dr. Mariani and see what can be arranged."

*   *   *

Il Corsaro Rosso was moored at the end of the wharf, almost immobile in the calm waters of the bay known as *La Scarpetta* because of the shape of a small shoe.

"I got butterflies in my stomach when you invited me for supper on your boat. To begin with I don't like to be bounced around when I eat, and then I remembered what a terrible cook you were when we were in college." Dr. Edoardo Santavecchia surveyed the sea and then the table set on the yacht's deck, carefully protected from the sun by a blue awning. "Well, there are absolutely no waves, and the food looks good." He helped himself to a salad of Belgian endive, raw artichokes and finely sliced calamari, then to a piece of smoked salmon. "Who prepared all this?"

"The deli shop across the harbour square." Gabriele quickly filled his plate. "And don't forget to taste their carpaccio. It's exquisite."

Dr. Santavecchia added a couple of bread sticks to his dish and sat opposite Gabriele.

"In all these years of wandering around the world did you manage to improve your cooking?" The two friends had shared an apartment for two years of college, after which Gabriele had decided to quit and enter the commercial navy.

"Somewhat, I got into desserts. A few recipes only. You'll taste my *crème plombière*. I'll serve it cold, suitable for a hot day like this."

"You're lucky. I'll probably be too full to want any dessert."

"Diffident, as usual. I should have known and saved myself the trouble of working a full hour in the kitchen."

For a while they ate in companionable silence.

"Tell me about this man you want me to help," the doctor said. "Tell me about the circumstances in which you met him, found him, I should say."

Gabriele filled the glasses in front of them with Verdicchio wine.

"I was cruising the Adriatic when a storm hit us from nowhere," he said. "No forecast, no warning on the marine radio, and little rain, just gusty winds and, of course, high waves. Flares were fired from a fishing boat, the *Rijeka*, minutes before breaking into pieces. We arrived at the scene and, after a few hours, we spotted a few isolated bits of wood close to our boat, then the remainder of what had been a rudimentary cabin, on which lay three men: the owner of the *Rijeka* and two fishermen. They were cold, scared and hungry but in reasonably good conditions. We took them aboard, gave them some dry clothes and fed them. But a fourth man—Mirko they called him—was missing." Gabriele paused to nibble at his salad. "We found him much later, floating on a small piece of wood, his arms and legs deep in the water. He didn't react much when we pulled him out; he just mumbled a few words." He sipped the wine and took another bite of food.

"Such as? What did he say? Those first words may be important."

"'Oh no, no! Not again!'"

"Hmm, was that in response to something you said?"

"No. When I welcomed him to my floating home, *Il Corsaro Rosso*, he said, 'Finally you came!'"

"Hmm, that's strange. He was never aboard your boat. I'll keep that in mind. Go on."

"The coastguard was circling around. We alerted them by radio and two paramedics came aboard. They diagnosed Mirko to be in a state of shock with severe hypothermia. They took him to a hospital in Brindisi. Later he was transferred to a small clinic—the name is—I know it, just a moment—well, it'll come to me sooner or later." Gabriele rose and set a few quichettes in front of his friend. "Try them, they are pretty good."

"No, I had enough food. My wife likes me slim." The doctor was short, with olive complexion and quick eyes that exuded vivacity of intellect even behind the thick lenses of his eyeglasses.

"Oh well, I know, I should watch out for myself since I noticed I'm growing a stomach. I should exercise more." He sat down. "This young man, around 30, wore a sweater with the Canadian insignia: the red maple leaf, the beaver and the words, *proud to be Canadian*. He had no documents with him and the men on the *Rijeka* were not much help in providing information, except that Mirko wanted to see how night fishing was done. They'd taken him aboard—for a fee, of course."

"No ID whatsoever?"

Gabriele shook his head. "He spoke English, however, and some words of Croatian. No idea if Mirko was on vacation or had gone to Dubrovnik for business."

"Not much to go on, I see. Was any Canadian consulate informed?"

"The one in Rome. They haven't taken any action so far. The clinic, now I remember, the Santa Rita, wants to discharge him: he's costing them money and nobody is there to pay the bill."

"I can see their point of view." Santavecchia took a swig of his wine and asked, "What's the interest you have in him?" He gave Gabriele a teasing, yet affectionate smile. "I heard you're alone again. Is he a new, how should I call him, a new candidate?"

"Suspicious as usual. I took an interest in this man because he's in trouble and nobody seems to care about him. It's a humanitarian case."

"Hmm, but he's good-looking, I bet."

Gabriele looked away. "It so happens that he is. Very handsome, slim and tall, dark curly hair, bright eyes, long eyelashes. Incredibly long eyelashes."

Nobody spoke and they both finished eating what was on their plates.

"Nice sunset," Gabriele said as he admired the sun dipping into the sea, leaving behind only golden reflections.

"Very nice, not a cloud in sight. So you'd like me to go see him, Mirko you said, right?"

"Yes, please. He needs help."

"I thought you didn't believe in my work, and in psychiatry in general."

Gabriele shrugged. "I think plenty of it is bogus—years back your church wanted to cure homosexuality. It was classified as a mental disorder. I think they did a lot of damage to young minds at that time."

"Any discipline progresses by leaps and bounds. Mistakes are made all the time."

"I suppose." Gabriele rose and began pacing in front of the table. "I'm leaving tomorrow for Dubrovnik. That's where Mirko boarded the *Rijeka*. Somebody must know something. I'll try to find out if anybody saw him at a camping ground or if he'd registered at a hotel. It might take some time but Sean, my second, will come with me. We'll share the work." Gabriele opened a bottle of Asti Spumante and poured the bubbling wine into two flutes.

"I've decided to taste your dessert." The doctor rose and took one of the cups filled with the *plombière* cream. "Some people show their courage by challenging the sea, others by tasting dishes made by everlasting bachelors." He took the first spoonful into his mouth. "But this is delicious, Gabriele. Really. Congratulations."

"Of course. I wouldn't dare to serve anything less than excellent to you." Gabriele stopped in front of the doctor. "So when do you plan to go see Mirko?"

"As soon as the hospital okays my visit. The case intrigues me. I always look for cases that seem out of the ordinary."

CHAPTER 16

Dubrovnik, Croatia

All the bandages on Nozemni's face had been reduced to a few inches of white gauze. Proud of his new look, he went to see the Radics. He brought a pork roast, fresh fruit and cold beer. It was time to celebrate.

At the conventional knocking Poitr opened the door. Without a word he grabbed the roast, still in the pot, and swivelled around towards the inside.

"Helena, set the table," he said. Then, he turned to Nozemni, "I don't complain because you brought food but it isn't dark enough to come here, you know that."

"Don't be such a prick. It's raining so hard I could barely see in front of me when I walked. Not a soul was around from the main road up to here. Relax, once, and for all." He left his umbrella outside the door.

Helena set three plates on the table, and a fork and a knife for each. Eagerly she cut the meat and dispensed two big slices to the men and took a small piece for herself. Poitr sat at the table and washed down half a bottle of beer while Nozemni and Helena quietly chewed on the roast.

"Did you manage to reach our old friend in Toronto?" Nozemni asked.

"Jim Chagrain? Yes. He's ready to give us a hand whenever we need him. He wanted to know the details of our operation but I didn't let out zilch. He could go ahead and do things himself."

Nozemni nodded and finished his meat. "We don't want that, right? We have to be careful." Everybody ate in silence for a while.

"Did you bring coffee?" Helena asked, as she lit the lamp and centred it on the table. "We have been out for almost a week."

Nozemni took a small bag out of his pocket. "I got some, but at the grocery store they asked me how come I wanted so much food for myself."

90

He gave Helena a smile. "I'll ask the dwarf to drop off some more tomorrow." Helena rose to put water on the stove, and Nozemni turned to Poitr. "So did you write down all the information I need when I'm there?"

"Yes. Everything is in order." He disappeared beyond the curtain. When he came back he gave Nozemni a few sheets. "Don't lose them." Poitr picked up the lamp from the table and moved it around the young man's head. "The doctor did a very good job. You look good. Very good."

A prolonged knock followed by two solid, short ones, repeated twice, woke Poitr. Alarmed, he rose and on silent feet he approached the entrance, then put his ear against the dilapidated door, trying to figure out who was standing outside. The police had been patrolling the area for the last few days.

"Open up!" Nozemni shouted. "It's me!"

Nozemni was scarcely over the threshold when Poitr lashed out at him.

"What are you doing here? I told you not to come. It's dangerous in the morning."

"Yeah, you're right. Things are getting worse by the minute. Wait until I tell you what happened." Nozemni walked towards the curtain. "Helena."

The bead curtain was pulled back and Helena wobbled into the middle of the room, her grey hair falling loose on her shoulders. There were two black crescents underneath her eyes and dried blood formed a crust around one corner of her lips. She reached the only table in the room and leaned on it.

"Yes?"

"Something to eat, and a coffee. Strong." Nozemni sat at the table.

Poitr stood behind him and held Nozemni's shoulder in a strong grip. "Talk," he said.

"They're all over town asking questions about Mirko. The police and two tourists. When did the man arrived in Dubrovnik, and how, by train, boat or car? Or did he fly in? Where was he staying? Who did he talk to?"

"Who told you?"

"Jos, the dwarf, of course. They offered him money, big money for information."

Helena busied herself at the stove and soon a smell of frying oil wafted into the room.

"The dwarf wants money to keep quiet," Nozemni said.

"The SOB! I paid him already!"

"He wants an extra thousand dollars."

Helena plunked a dish with a fried egg in front of Nozemni together with large pieces of dry bread. Staggering, she ambled toward the curtain and disappeared behind it.

"What happened to her?" Nozemni asked, pointing after Helena.

Poitr shrugged. "What happens to a woman when she talks back to her man."

"You shouldn't beat her. She is old; she looks sick. She worked hard with all the children you took home."

Poitr's reaction was immediate. His arm descended to strike Nozemni's face, but Nozemni captured it on the fly and twisted it.

"Don't try that with me. I'm much bigger than you." As Poitr didn't react, Nozemni gave Poitr's arm a second twist. "Understood?"

"Auch, auch. Let go."

"Understood?"

"Yes, yes," Poitr massaged his arm and went to sit opposite Nozemni. "I'll take care of the dwarf. I can scare him plenty. Leave it up to me. You must leave right away."

"My face isn't okay yet. The scar on the left cheek, close to my ear, doesn't want to heal. And see how tight the skin graft is?" He turned his face and lowered the collar of his turtle-neck top. "Ten more days, the doctor said." He took the last piece of bread, dipped it into the oil the eggs had been fried in, and chewed on it in big bites.

"Your face can heal in Toronto as well as here," Poitr said.

Nozemni finished eating.

"You have a point—a good point. I'll leave and put our plan into action. The sooner, the better." He rose, shouted "goodbye" in the direction of the curtain and quickened his steps to the door. Poitr followed him.

"Remember our agreement," Poitr said. "I get 50 per cent. If you don't stick to the agreement, I'll tip off the police."

Nozemni didn't turn around. He opened the heavy door, stepped out and slammed it closed.

Her hair in a knot now, Helena came out from her hiding place.

"Do you think he'll make it?" she asked.

"Oh yes. Nothing to it. Just a trip to Toronto and back. I bet it won't take Nozemni more than a couple of months to carry out the whole business. Jim Chagrain, our old friend, will show him the ropes. Nothing to worry about."

"Jim? Do we really need him? He's a cheat and a liar. Last time he was here my silver chain disappeared."

"We need him." Poitr shrugged. "Nozemni and Jim spent summers together getting money out of tourists, so they know each other well and know how to work as a team. Then Jim is a real Canadian, he knows the system over there. That's why we need him to carry out our little scam."

"I still think we'd be better to keep the money we just dug out for ourselves," she whispered.

"You don't understand, stupid woman. We cannot take those coins to a bank ourselves." Poitr shrugged. "First, we can't go anywhere for a while, second, they would ask a ton of questions."

"But—"

As Poitr was ready to strike her, she trotted away and disappeared behind the curtain.

*   *   *

Toronto, July 2005

What Jim Chagrain considered his greatest talent was that he could change his appearance quickly and effectively, an important asset for a person who made his living conning people. The son of a Canadian peacekeeping officer and a Croatian woman, he had taken more of his mother's physical characteristics than his father's. He was short; his cheekbones were pronounced; his complexion was dark, and his body was husky. His brown eyes, deep set, moved continually, as he kept his surroundings under surveillance. With his head shaved bald and a pair of lips that hardly parted into a smile, Chagrain looked tough and slimy.

He had spent most of his teenage years in Croatia, and had hightailed it to Canada only after the local police started looking for him. Because he spoke English he had no problem finding a job as a taxi driver once he arrived in Toronto. He considered it a temporary, yet useful, occupation, for it acquainted him with the city's topography.

Chagrain had no formal education, but he learned fast. One day he met the owner of a tourist office, The Skytrotter, who immediately hired him to help with planning itineraries for tourists interested in traveling to the Balkans, Greece, Turkey, and Italy in particular. It was then that Chagrain had become involved in the lucrative business of laundering money for his boss, using the exchange offices designed to help tourists convert their money into Canadian currency. After a few years, when he suspected that the police were after him, he changed jobs again and became active in the receiving and selling of stolen goods. This was not as risky as his previous job, especially as he dealt with rich clients who wanted to buy paintings or sculptures without bothering to check their provenance. One good sale could produce up to thirty thousand dollars. However, at the moment he couldn't put his hands on any items that his clients wanted. When he had discovered that Mirko Grogan owned an expensive house in an elegant quarter of Rosedale, Chagrain had agreed to help Poitr and Nozemni carry out their scam and assist them in stripping Mirko Grogan of his possessions. One big job like this and he could spend a few months in the Caribbean.

Wearing a polo shirt and blue jeans, and showing off a Rolex on his wrist, Chagrain now waited at Pearson Airport for Nozemni to arrive.

*   *   *

The tall, now somewhat handsome Nozemni shook hands with his old pal, Jim Chagrain. Chagrain, six inches shorter, looked at Nozemni and circled him.

"Boy, have they done a good job on your face. You look great."

"I *feel* great," Nozemni said, and smiled. "Now I'm ready to conquer the world. Finally women will look at me instead of running away."

"Look they will. But you have to behave. Do this; do that; open the door. It isn't the same as at home."

Nozemni shrugged. "I'll take what I like, believe me. I know what to do with women, never mind what they want." He paused. "You told Poitr that you've done some research. Results?"

"I gathered info on Mirko Grogan's assets, where he used to bank, neighbours' opinions, the works. The house is worth at least three million, I'm sure. It's been renovated recently and a brand new deck has been added at the back. The deck is 30 feet wide and 65 feet long, overlooking a ravine. I don't know what it can be used for, but it means the man had money to spare. For confidential information on his bank account, I'll need to bribe one of the employees. I need money. Do you have some of those gold coins we talked about on the phone?"

"Yes, but Poitr insists that we go together to cash them, you know, just to be on the level."

"Yeah, I know the man. He wants to be in control at all times."

"You got that right," Nozemni said, and followed his old pal to the airport parking lot.

PART 3

The Cups Attract Attention

Chapter 17

Harrisville, Fall 2005

Where's the summer gone? Chris Sandcroft asked himself as he left his office and quickly climbed into his Camaro. He had been very busy at Vibratim, but the time he had spent there had been rewarding. Old-model seismographers had been cleared out with a promotional sale; the others were in great demand, and the application for patenting a new, compact ULF magnetometer had just been filed. He was lucky he had been able to work the previous month without having to worry about Lucio.

In the summer his father had enjoyed helping Gideon in the garden. When the cold days had settled in, he had asked Gideon to help him hang the art shipped from Italy. They had filled the bare walls of the first floor with paintings and rearranged the knickknacks in the family and dining rooms. Lucio also visited the seminary regularly. The missionaries' diaries kept in the library fascinated him. Lillian had proved herself an invaluable companion. She took her job seriously and was always ready to take Lucio to any museum or gallery he wanted to visit.

Things have proceeded much better than I expected, Chris concluded as he drove underneath the cedar archway that demarked the boundary of his property. He looked up in the sky. Flocks of geese practised flying in the usual triangular formation as they prepared for their upcoming migration— an unmistakable sign of the approaching cold weather. *Fall and winter could be trouble,* Chris thought. The seclusion that would come with the cold months could have a negative impact on Lucio's spirit and mobility. Today was a taste of what was in store.

Rain had fallen steadily for a week, depriving the caduceus trees, which flanked the driveway, of most of their leaves. With the forecast of an early snowfall, Gideon had rushed to set up the snow fence to protect the outside area close to the house from a massive accumulation of snow. Bird feeders hung from the arms of the four mermaids, which formed the centrepiece of the bronze fountain, now bereft of its soft water jets. Soon myriad sparrows and a few cardinals and blue jays would populate not only the feeders, but also the large base of the fountain, where seeds would copiously fall.

Chris slowed down and opened the garage door with his remote. As the ceiling light appeared, he saw his father seated under the overhang, clearly waiting for him. He parked his car and joined him.

"How come you're here? I left a message I'd be late."

"I know. Kathy told me and she wanted me to go ahead and have supper, but I wasn't hungry. How was your day?"

"Busy. I got a new order for two seismographers just before I left." He pushed his father's wheelchair into the house. "We can have coffee or a drink together, with a snack, if you'd like. I ate with my client."

"Great. Let's have a hot chocolate. Kathy has baked some banana muffins. I've already tasted one. *Sono squisiti.*"

They moved into the kitchen and Chris turned on the electric kettle. "Anything new?"

"Yes."

"Ah ah! I thought so. Otherwise you'd be glued to the TV, watching a flick."

"You were always a know-it-all, even as a kid."

"So, tell me what happened."

"The Howards are coming in two days."

"I know. Vivian keeps me informed." He winked. "She calls me often."

"Happy for you, Chris. She's a real nice girl." He paused. "I talked with Glen for almost 40 minutes."

"So tell me."

"Glen asked whether I've found the cups, yada, yada."

"Oh, I wanted to talk to you about those cups. We wanted to go down to Vibratim and search the basement. Tomorrow is Saturday, right? Let's go there. Grandpa may have discovered something odd about the cups and planned to do some experiments with them."

"I hope he didn't ruin them."

"Well, what's done is done. We'll see tomorrow." He paused, looking concerned. "Something else...there's something else, right?"

"Well...I shouldn't bother you with the problem of the cups, I know."

"Bother? Lucio, the gems in those cups could be worth a quarter-million dollars, and Glen said a serious collector might pay half a million for the four cups. All together it's three times the salary I pay myself in one year."

"The problem is, Glen wants to write an article about the foursome in the lucky case that the new ones match the old pair."

"And?"

"The two—let's say the two in your possession—shouldn't have been taken out of the country."

"And why not? They were yours. You gave them to Mother and she took them with her."

"Yes, I'm not the guilty one. But the law in Italy forbids exporting any item of archaeological, artistic or historical value without permission."

"But they have more old rubbish they can take care of. And often oils lie in old, musty basements, where they get permanently damaged. Why not spread them around the world and let people enjoy them?"

"I know, but that's the way it is."

Chris added hot water to the instant cocoa in the two mugs and stirred vigorously. He set them on the kitchen table. "Watch out; they're hot." He blew on his drink and sipped it. "Well, it's too early to worry about our cups. First we have to find them. Let's have a good night's sleep. Tomorrow morning we'll hunt them down."

Once out of the car, Lucio engaged the wheelchair's brake and didn't move. He stared at the vision of the building that housed Vibratim's offices and plant. The double glass door opened and a guard came out to greet them.

"I'll go get an umbrella," the guard said.

"No need, Vicente," Chris said, and flipped off the wheelchair brake. "We're coming in." He leaned towards his father. "It's raining, in case you didn't notice."

The guard walked over to help push the chair toward the ramp beside the entrance, as Lucio hadn't turned on the power.

"Just a moment," Lucio said, restraining both Chris and the guard from moving him any further. "It's just drizzling. I wanted to see. This is my son's plant. Give me a minute to feel proud of his achievement." He looked up at the three-story structure and then around it. "*Ullalà!* It's a big building. Impressive."

Chris stopped for a second.

"Let's get inside," he said a few seconds later.

"How many people work here?"

"About thirty. Out of town there's another lab we use for testing."

The door closed behind them.

"Maybe we should take your father to the freight elevator that goes down to the basement," the guard said. "It'd be easier to manoeuvre with the chair."

Chris assented and they moved to the back of the building, where the loading dock was located.

"Thank you, Vicente," Chris said, and the guard turned to return to his dais.

At a snail's pace the elevator reached the basement and the doors parted.

"It might be messy," Chris said.

He turned on the fluorescent lights. Boxes, small tables full of papers, and a long counter attached to one of the walls gave the impression of a place that hadn't been looked after for ages. Dust blanketed everything. Spider webs created links from one object to the next.

"Hmm, it's going to be a big job. Lucio, why don't you start with the left half? It's the only side where a wheelchair can move around with ease. I'll take the right. We should start with the boxes. Look carefully in each of them. That's probably where Grandfather stored the cups, if they're here. Put things back in order, please. Later I'll ask one of my men to come down and make a list of what we have. And I'll get the caretaker to clean up the basement. It's badly needed."

They worked well past noon when Chris lifted his head from the latest box he was tackling.

"Should we take a break, Lucio?" he asked.

"If you want, but I'm not tired. Covered with dust, yes, but not tired."

And so they continued.

"There's something round inside this box," Chris said. "Something wrapped in old newspapers." He removed the paper, and in a jiffy he lifted a dark cup. He waved it toward Lucio. "Is this one of them?"

Lucio moved quickly to Chris' side, tipping over a couple of crates. "Yes. Tarnished and dirty, of course. Is it heavy?"

"Oh, yes, very."

"Good. Chances are the valuables are still inside. Look for the second one."

In no time the companion cup was in Chris' hands. He removed the paper inside.

"There's a note in Grandfather's handwriting." Chris moved under the fluorescent light and read, "Funny alloy. Take it to the chemist to be examined. It looks bronze or copper, but much heavier than either metal." Chris moved back and looked at the newspaper's date. "Grandfather set it up here just two days before he passed away. He had no time to talk to me about them, and even less to take them to the technician. We're lucky." He approached Lucio and put the two cups in his lap. "Got the treasure. Are you happy?"

Lucio turned one cup upside down. The inscription read, *To my beloved wife, Deborah.*

"They're the ones, Chris," he said. "Let's go home and compare them with those Glen Howard left with us. Then we have to decide what to do when he shows up at our door."

CHAPTER 18

Dinner at the Trudeau Excelsior was coming to an end. *Too soon*, thought Lucio as he hoped to avoid any serious discussion about the antique cups. Glen, however, had twisted in his chair for the entire meal. He had hardly touched his entrée and even refused to have a second drink.

"Do you mind if we go to your house, your son's house, I mean, and have another look at the cups?" Glen asked as they were finishing up with coffee.

"If you want, but the expert Chris has consulted dated them at approximately the same time, and the metal used for the interior is exactly the same." Lucio smiled. "They are the four originals, no doubt about it. I'll be indebted to you for life for having found the two missing ones."

"But the precious ones are yours."

"Chris, Glen…they belong to Chris."

"Okay, okay. What does he want to do with them? Keep them in a safe?"

"More or less. He'd prefer to do absolute nothing."

"But it's an exceptional find. The world has to know."

"Glen, those cups have an historical significance, I agree. But after all, as you and I well know, the coronation of Matthias of Habsburg didn't take place there, even if everything was ready to receive the emperor and the pope with all the pomp they expected, if not deserved. At the last moment the emperor changed his mind."

"Mere details."

"But important details. Not to mention that advertising the existence of the gems would give ideas to crooks."

Glen didn't acknowledge his friend's remark and continued.

"We could come out with a bit of history, show the cups as they are, show the craftsmanship used to insert the gems and create a second layer to hide them, then remove the gems." Glen threw his napkin onto the table. "What a hit!" Glen closed his eyes, enthralled. "I can see the small audience of invited guests comfortably seated in the easy chairs of a TV studio, wondering what those ancient cups might hide inside." He stopped and reopened his eyes. He waved his hand from left to right. "One camera takes pictures of the podium where the expert extracts the gems, another focuses on the audience." He glanced at Lucio. "Fabulous, my friend, incredibly fabulous. The show will reach thousands and thousands of viewers."

The usual boaster, thought Lucio. *He doesn't care about history or craftsmanship, just about getting publicity. His antique shop in Edinburgh will triple its business.*

"How about going home?" Lucio asked. "Maybe Chris is there. If so we can discuss the situation with him."

"Hmm, I doubt that son of yours will be home early. He looks a bit dumb, but he isn't so dumb, after all. He's out with Vivian, right?" Lucio nodded. "And Vivian is madly in love with him."

"Yes, I noticed." He grinned. "Chris doesn't stand a chance. I know how it happens. Among a dozen women there's one that makes you feel more of a man than any of the others. And then you're done, cooked, *finito!*" Glen sighed his agreement. "It must have happened to you too, Glen, since after three brief marriages, you've been with Elisabeth for some twenty plus years."

"True, true. It happens. I remember, when I met Elisabeth she'd been a widow for two years. Little Vivian, a miniscule reproduction of her mother, stuck to her like glue. I fell in love with both of them." He paused. "By the way, I like Chris. He's very dependable, something important if a relationship is to last."

"How true that is. I wasn't, and I lost Deborah because of it. I'm happy Chris is a responsible man. Handsome, too."

"Yeah, he was lucky to look like his mother. You're short and you were balding already at the age of 20."

"Eh, don't make it sound so bad. When the family artist painted my first portrait—the one in the main corridor—he said I had an interesting face, with vivid eyes, long eyelashes, a chiselled chin, and a sculptured nose."

"He couldn't find anything else." Glen laughed without mercy. "A chiselled chin? At a young age, everybody has a chiselled chin."

Lucio joined him in laughter. "I guess you're right. Still, Chris has my eyes and my cheekbones."

"Fortunately that's all he took from you."

Lucio shook his head and put his chair in motion, ready to leave.

Once home, Lucio complained of a sudden headache, and Glen looked longingly at the cups again, then left, saying he would be back tomorrow. Lucio retired to his room, pensive. Glen's idea sounded unorthodox and risky, and the last thing he wanted was to create work, or even worse, trouble, for his son.

When Lucio got up the following morning, Chris was nowhere in sight. First Lucio thought he hadn't come home, but a quick inspection showed his Camaro in the garage. It was Saturday and Kathy would normally make a brief appearance to see whether anything was needed for the day. But he found no sign of Kathy, and Bertha was nowhere to be found. Lucio made coffee and sat at the kitchen table near the bay window. Soon afterward an ambulance siren shrieked. Lucio wheeled himself to the main entrance and saw the vehicle entering the Sandcrofts' property and rushing toward the Wilsons' house. He waited, debating what to do.

Nothing, he finally decided. If there was an emergency he could only bring confusion. He was not mobile; he knew zilch about medicine, and he had no idea how the health system worked. He returned to the kitchen to sip his coffee, anxiously waiting for Chris to show up.

A half hour later he heard Bertha's cheerful barking, then Chris' steps in the hall.

Chris entered the kitchen, followed by Bertha.

"You heard the ambulance, eh?"

Lucio nodded.

"Kathy broke her leg, I'm afraid. While she was cleaning the windows she lost her balance. The stepladder tipped over and fell on top of her. Gideon was afraid to lift her up all by himself. It was then that he looked for me. I called for help instead of taking her directly to emergency. I thought it was wiser."

"How did it happen?"

"She was wearing her slippers. One got caught on a protruding nail. She leaned sideways and tumbled down." Chris plunked into a chair. "Gideon went with her to the hospital. He'll call us as soon as he talks to the doctor, but I'm afraid we'll be on our own for a while."

"I hope she's okay. Never mind about us. We'll manage." The coffeemaker gurgled and Chris turned toward it.

"You got coffee ready? I'll have a cup." He rose and filled a mug.

Lucio waited until Chris was seated with a bowl of cereal and his coffee in front of him.

"Sorry to bother you," Lucio said. "But Glen—"

"Oh, I forgot about him. Is he giving you problems?" Chris scooped corn flakes rapidly into his mouth.

"Yes and no. He has something in mind about the cups, but I told him clearly that the decision will rest with you."

"What does he want?"

"Publicity on the finding of the two matching cups. When we had dinner together last night he told me what his idea was all about. To have a live show on television, Harrisville Channel 9. It's one of the local stations, right?"

"Yes."

"He talked to the station director for about four hours. Together they'd like to mount a big show. First they'll do a short historical introduction about the Red Manor, then show the two pairs of cups, the ones recently found followed by ours…sorry, your two."

"Who will watch a show with such old stuff? This is a small town, only 100,000 people. And a blue-collar town. After a day of work people want to be entertained."

"Wait. Wait. After this brief introduction an expert will appear and try to separate the two surfaces with minimal damage to either side. Meanwhile the station will run a contest using phone and email, asking the viewers to guess what's hidden inside. One thousand dollars will go to the person who gets closest to the real stuff."

"Oh, I see. And then?"

"A couple of commercials, I believe."

"Of course. The station needs time to collect the answers."

"Exactly. Then the owner of Harrisville Jewellery will extract the gems, or whatever is between the two layers of metal. He'll clean them and give a rough appraisal right there in front of thousands of viewers."

Chris laughed. "What a terrible idea. It's almost offensive to an important discovery. It fits Glen, though. He likes to show off." Chris finished his cereal and took a long swallow of coffee. "How did Glen know about the gems?"

"I don't know. Maybe he gave Salvatore Argento the third degree. Salvatore knew."

"Oh, I see. It doesn't matter, really. By the way, how is Salvatore?"

"Not too good. Still in the hospital."

"Sorry to hear that." Chris paused, pondering Glen's idea. "When do they think they'll go on the air?"

"Monday, October 10."

"But that is Thanksgiving."

Lucio shrugged. "Apparently at the station they think the show could appeal to families."

"I don't think it will fly. But, what the heck. It means nothing to me and a lot to Glen." He looked at Lucio and grinned. "After all, he could become my father-in-law. If he's so hung up on having this show, let him have it. We keep the gems, right?"

"Oh yes. The gems are yours, Chris."

"Let's go ahead with it, then. The entire affair will keep Glen busy. Beside, people on this continent forget about what they see on television in a couple of days. They're bombarded with information."

CHAPTER 19

Not only Kathy's tibia but also the fibula of her left leg was fractured. If those injuries weren't enough, she had also sprained her right ankle. The doctors had operated on her, and now she had to spend three weeks in a special clinic for rehabilitation. From time-to-time, Gideon showed up to do some house cleaning, but he spent most of the day tending to his wife.

The situation was not the best, Chris mused as he jogged from the pond at the property limits back to his house. Suddenly, Bertha bounded away toward the bushes, tonguing as if she was tracking a wild animal. Chris kept running alone. When he was ready to open the house door Bertha came out of the woods with the speed of light and made a forceful stop just in front of him. He petted the dog and cleared her ears of all sorts of dirt she had picked up in the small marsh near the pond.

"You need a good bath, old girl," he said, and entered the house.

He refilled Bertha's dish with kibbles and proceeded to the kitchen. For a few seconds he stood before an almost empty fridge. Lillian approached him from behind.

"Would you like me to do some work for you?" she asked. "Shopping, fixing supper—I mean do whatever's necessary? I have time and could still take your father on outings."

Chris let the fridge's door go. "What a great idea. Kathy won't be able to work for a while. I find myself very busy with my father and my work…and of course, the Howards are still here. I don't think they're in a hurry to go back to the UK. They've rented an apartment downtown, Queen Street, I believe."

Lillian nodded. "I heard Mr. de' Vigentini talking about it. He was happy for the company, but worried about you getting tired of all the commotion."

"Well, I'm accustomed to a very simple life. Work during the week, going out on Saturday night, seeing friends on Sunday, back to work on Monday."

Lillian showed a sympathetic face. "I wondered how you've been coping. Let me help you. Five weeks, until Kathy is back in shape? I don't want to take her place. I know how much she enjoys working for the Sandcrofts."

"You're an angel, Lillian. Let me know the extra hours you put in every week. When can you start?"

"Right now. Scrambled eggs with toasted rye bread, right? And a glass of milk. Be ready in 10 minutes."

"Great. Just enough time for me to jump into the shower." He turned to leave.

"Mr. Sandcroft?" Lillian asked.

"Yes?"

"I heard of the show, a kind of reality show, that you and your father are going to have on television. About those old cups…I wonder…" Chris waited, but Lillian didn't continue.

"Yes?" Chris repeated. "What about the show?"

"Would you get me a couple of tickets? My boyfriend and I would love to go see it." Her eyes brimmed with excitement. "It doesn't often happen that I know important people who show up on television."

Oh, that's how it is. He had worked long hours with his grandfather to advance technology for the benefit of humanity, to detect tremors and identify critical regions likely subject to earthquakes, yet nobody ever asked to visit their laboratory. Now, here there was a show with trivia questions, betting and the like, a grand show with almost no substance, just a lot of talk and commotion, and people were anxious to be part of it.

"Sure," he replied, hiding his disappointment. "I'm sure Mr. Howard can find two tickets for you and your friend."

CHAPTER 20

Dubrovnik, Croatia

"I can't stand it here anymore," Helena said. "I want to go out, have some sun, have a bath." She kept her tone soft so as not to provoke a nasty reaction from her husband. "Jail would be better."

Poitr nodded. "There's a parade in town this afternoon. We could sneak out, have a good meal and a glass of wine. Maybe even a swim. The police will be busy with the traffic and with all the drunks in town."

"Great." Helena whirled around. "I'm going to get my bathing suit."

They reached a relatively deserted bay north of town and from a small rock plunged into the sea. The water was already cool, but neither seemed to notice. They swam, lay in the sun, then dipped again into the salt water. A couple hours later they were seated at a table at an inn close to a camping ground. Sausages and fried rice never tasted so good.

It was night when they started walking back to their hideout. Suddenly Poitr stopped, attracted by a newspaper lying on the ground. He picked it up and walked a little stretch until he came up to a street lamp. He began reading, Helena craning her neck to look at the same page.

"No seri!" He turned the page to read the next one. "Mirko is getting better. He's still in the hospital and mutters only a few words, but the doctors think he'll improve fast." They read the second column, then the third. "They're going to call in a shrink. Oh my God, they'll get all the facts out of Mirko! We're in trouble." He crumpled the newspaper and tossed it away. He pulled on Helena's arm. "Come. Come."

"Where to?"

"The Lubarda. I'll go through the rear of the hotel and use a pay phone. We have to alert Nozemni. He may be in danger. Us too, if they catch him."

"Do you have his number?"

"Yes. I got it with me."

Nozemni answered at the second ring.

"Bad news," Poitr said, and explained what he had learned. Then he listened and listened and listened, while Helena nervously paced back and forth. Fifteen minutes later Poitr said, "I don't know what we should be doing. I have to think about it. I'll call you tomorrow."

As a hotel guest lined up to use the same phone, Poitr rang off.

"Let's go," he said to Helena. "We have to disappear. It's late. People will be coming back to the hotel."

Back at their hideout, they tiptoed down the long stairway and entered the big room that had been their home for the last six months. Poitr lit the gasoline lamp and slumped in a chair.

"Trouble," he said in a quiet tone. "Big trouble."

Helena looked at him. "What?"

"Our Mirko had no big money."

"How come? The Grogans were well off. They had a fancy house when they adopted the boy, and Mr. Grogan had a luxury car dealership."

"Yea, but that was then. They died soon after they adopted the boy and Mirko went to some kind of home. Nozemni told me the name, but I can't remember. Grogan's house had two mortgages. Its sale produced only a few thousand dollars. Apparently Mirko never held a stable job; he worked here and there, got sick often—"

"Oh my God!"

"But that's not all of the bad news. Jim Chagrain helped Nozemni withdraw all the cash Mirko had—only $2,000 in his bank account."

"Dear God, no!" Helena sank into a chair.

"And there's more. It isn't easy to exchange the old coins even over there, and for the gold—ingots they call them—they have to wait about two months. Chagrain wants money."

"We could have kept those gold coins for ourselves. We could have gotten into the mountains and nobody would have ever looked for us again."

"Complaining doesn't help. I have to think about all this and find a way out."

CHAPTER 21

Harrisville, Ontario

In the shabby room of the Altavista Motel, Nozemni followed the show on Channel 9. The audience was small, about eighty people, mostly men dressed in suits and ties. The TV host told an old tale of popes, emperors and castles, stopping at times to show pictures of soldiers, armatures, and walls with turrets and high towers. Nozemni was ready to switch channels when the words, "precious gems," caught his ears. He didn't see any, but grasped that pearls and diamonds had been hidden in two big, rusty cups. He wondered how and whether the show was for real. But after the commercial, the presenter insisted that soon they would know whether two of those big cups did, in fact, hide something precious, and if so, what that was.

Nozemni tried to figure out how anybody would think of such a stupid hiding place but his attention was soon diverted by a man who deposited one cup on a red-velvet-covered table, then tilted it and used a flame to make an opening around the top rim. With his hands, he widened the breach and turned the cup upside down. Things fell onto the table; most were dark, but one sent out an unmistakable sparkle: it was a big diamond, four carats at least. If this show was for real and the cups were indeed very old, there was no doubt it was a fantastic stone. No synthetic gems existed at the time of emperors and castles. Nozemni hardly heard the big "wow" the audience emitted. His gaze followed a man who approached the table wearing a jeweller's loop over one eye.

The man took the gem in his hands and wiped it clean with a soft cloth, then looked at it intently in the midst of absolute silence.

"A crystal of magnificent lustre," he said a few minutes later, then returned the diamond to the presenter and went back to his seat.

The show went to commercial about a miracle drug that would enable people to lose weight without dieting, and then the program continued. This time new faces appeared on the screen. A man named Glen Howard took credit for having reunited the full collection of four cups; a person in a wheelchair was pushed in front of the cameras to spell out where and when the cups had been manufactured; the audience, impatient, began parading past the velvet-covered table to admire the gems, ask the TV host questions or chat among themselves.

Then the show changed tone. Five questions flashed on the screen, one after the other. Viewers had 10 minutes to provide the answers by phone or email. The five people who answered the most correctly would be invited to appear on television the following night and collect a cash prize.

But Nozemni's interest was centred on the valuables and the cups. His mind was already at work, wondering whether it would be easy to steal the gems. Security didn't appear to be tight at all. He would pay attention to see if they would mention where the cups and gems were going to be taken. The show now focused on the operators attending phones or computer monitors. The audience was in the background, still admiring the four cups and their content. Then the schedule of the upcoming games of the Toronto Maple Leafs filled the screen. Nozemni grabbed a beer from the case he had previously stocked in his room and patiently waited for the commercial to finish.

Then the presenter said, "Now we'd like to hear a few words from the owner of the two precious cups, Mr. Christopher Sandcroft."

Nozemni was glued to the monitor, hypnotized by what he was seeing, yet not a single word of what Sandcroft said ever entered his ears.

A few minutes later he was rushing to the television station in downtown Harrisville.

CHAPTER 22

Seated at a table near the glass wall of the French bistro, which was located across from the headquarter of Channel 9, Chris, Lucio, Vivian and Elisabeth watched Glen having his heyday. Cameras flashed and hands were shaken. Finally, still surrounded by a cloud of reporters, Glen made it inside the bistro. Standing near the table where his friends were sitting, he promised interviews. Flyers with the history of the Red Manor, the story of the missed coronation of the emperor as *defensor fidei*, and pictures of the four now-famous cups popped out of his briefcase like magic. Last but not least, he waved a poster of his Edinburgh shop together with a few antiques ready to be sold.

The man knows how to advertise, thought Lucio. *If I'd hired him as a PR liaison for my estate I wouldn't have had to unload the Red Manor.*

Half an hour later the crowd thinned and then vanished. Glen joined his friends at the table. He slumped in a chair and ordered a glass of water.

"What a night," he said. "Busy, busy, busy."

"It was a superb show, orchestrated and directed by a master," Lucio said. "Congratulations, Glen."

The waitress brought a huge glass of ice water for Glen and filled the flutes with the champagne Chris had ordered. The foursome raised their glasses in Glen's direction.

"Cheers," they said in unison.

"Thanks. A lot of work, but also a lot of fun. Everything worked like a charm. The station expects the ratings to go up, especially after they give out the prizes for the trivia questions. That's tomorrow. We're all invited."

Chris shook his head. "Don't count me in. I'm on a business trip for a couple of days."

"Of course, of course, you have to work." He stroked Chris' arm. "You should have taken advantage of the occasion to say something about your company. You could have increased your sales."

"Right now I'm swamped with orders. I don't need any more advertising." He winked at Glen. "I still make enough money to support a family."

"Good, good. See you on Saturday, then."

"Oh, no. Didn't Vivian tell you? We plan to take off early and go to Algonquin Park."

"Oh, yes," Vivian said. "I asked Chris to take me there. I heard that the fall colours are superb."

As Glen looked surprised, Chris said, "Not to worry. Lillian, the woman we hired to keep an eye on Lucio, volunteered to replace Kathy until Kathy comes back. From Saturday on she'll stay at the house and sleep in the room we have in the mansard. She's a good cook, too. You and Elisabeth can come to our house or ask Lucio to join you for whatever you have in mind. Full service is assured either way."

"No need for that, Chris. No need to take care of us. We'll pick up Lucio and take him back."

"As you prefer."

Glen was pensive for a moment. Then he asked Chris, "How did it work out with the insurance?"

"They issued me temporary coverage for $300,000. Once we get the stones appraised officially, they'll adjust coverage and premium accordingly."

"Fine. I can help you with that. I have great contacts." Glen tapped Chris on his shoulder. "Don't forget."

"I won't. Actually, I was counting on it."

"Fine, fine." Glen snacked on the hors d'oeuvre the waitress had brought to the table, then asked, "Where are you taking the valuables meanwhile?"

"We've done a quick inventory and the gems have been tagged by the jewellery shop in my presence. The shop is in charge of all of them for the time being since they have to appraise them. I took the four cups with me. They are safe here, in my sports bag." He tapped on the bag lying at his feet.

"But the cups are very valuable too," Glen remarked.

"I know, but my safe at Vibratim isn't big enough for all four. For the time being they have to stay at home." He glanced at Lucio. "Okay with you?"

116

"Sure. I think they're only valuable to a collector, and there aren't many around."

"I wouldn't be so sure," Glen said. "There's a black market for antiques, very lucrative indeed. I wouldn't be surprised if somebody pays half a million dollars for them."

"Half a million dollars?" Vivian and Elisabeth exclaimed together.

"Yes. Take my word for it."

"Shush, don't talk so loud." Lucio chuckled. "Chris would sell them right away. He has no use for them, he already told me."

"Young people are like that. No respect for tradition until they, in turn, come of age."

"Actually, once the dust settles I'd like to put Lucio in charge of the fate of the cups," Chris said.

Glen tapped Chris on his shoulder. "Good thinking, son, good thinking." He picked up the tab. "Should we call it a night? It's two o'clock in the morning."

"Agreed," Chris said, and they all rose and left the bistro.

Chris and Lucio drove in silence until they reached the entrance of the Sandcroft property.

"Everything went really well," Chris said. "Tired?"

"A bit, but pleased by the way everything fell into place. Where are you going to hide the cups?"

Chris chuckled. "It's a secret, but I'll tell you this: nobody will be able to find them."

Chris parked his Camaro, helped his father to his bedroom, and wished him good night. Then he checked on Bertha and slipped outside. He knew a place where it would be difficult to detect the presence of the cups.

*　*　*

Wearing a turban made from part of an Altavista Motel sheet and with a false moustache glued to his face, Nozemni remained seated at a table of the French bistro. He hadn't been able to follow the entire conversation about the four cups, but he had grasped that they were going to be taken to Chris Sandcroft's house. The solution was probably temporary; if he wanted to steal them, he had to act quickly. He ordered another cola and pondered the predicament the Radics had put him in.

He had smelled a rat the instant the Radics had called him and talked about that business of digging a treasure out of a grave. In principle, the coins and ingots should have provided about forty thousand dollars. But the problem was cashing them because the coins came from a German mint and the ingots were not easily exchangeable. No Croatian bank would trade them without asking questions—questions, clearly, that neither he nor the Radics wanted to answer.

Michael Karesi, the doctor who had done the cosmetic surgery on him, had been happy to be paid in gold. For everything else they had to depend on Jim Chagrain who, of course, was in business for himself.

After Nozemni had landed in Toronto he discovered that trading old coins and ingots wasn't a breeze in Canada either. In fact, Jim Chagrain, to avoid raising suspicion, had taken him from one gold-trading place to another, each time exchanging only a few gold coins or one ingot. When an employee asked a question, the answer was invariably that Chagrain had found a little treasure in his grandmother's old house. The process had been slow and cumbersome, not to mention that every time a transaction took place, Chagrain wanted a cut. And they had completed the sale of Mirko Grogan's house a week ago, only to discover that Mirko held two mortgages that took most of the money collected from the sale. They'd also paid $1,000 to an employee of Credits and Loans where Mirko banked to find out about Mirko's assets. That had resulted in another bad surprise. Like he had told Poitr on the phone, there was only a savings deposit with barely $2,000.

What a shitty idea Poitr had come up with. He was very angry at Poitr and Helena Radic, who had managed to involve him in an operation that was clearly a failure. Worst of all, Chagrain wanted the cash he had collected from Mirko's account and, under the threat of being exposed, Nozemni had complied.

The operation the Radics had mounted turned out to be a catastrophe. The only thing he had gained was his new looks. He didn't want to return to Croatia as a loser. He had to think of something else, an operation he could control from start to finish. And with that resolution Nozemni left the bistro and returned to his motel.

The following morning he called Jim Chagrain. He had decided. He would steal the four cups.

"I want to see you," he said. "I've got something in mind. Something big."

"Sure, sure. Like stealing from a poor man? I don't want to hear from you and your deals again."

"You'll get plenty of money this time; I guarantee you, if you listen to me and help me out."

After some hesitation, Chagrain said, "What do you want?"

"Come here and take me to a decent store where I can buy a good suit. As we drive, I'll explain my plan."

Twenty minutes later a white Buick stopped in front of Nozemni's motel room.

"This'd better be good, man," Chagrain said. "I have no time to waste, and I don't trust you or your parents. The Radics told me the last job would be a snap. Weeks I had to work for you. It took ages to sell the house with all the documents you had to sign—and you hadn't even bothered to practice Grogan's signature. Then we found out that most of the money had to go to the bank. And the bank account? The same story. If that wasn't my payoff, I'd have told you to go to hell. I've never worked so hard for two grand."

"Don't worry. I have something in mind that can't fail. You always brag about being one of the best fences in town. Is it true?"

"I am."

"Good. You're the man I need. This is big. Did you see the show on television, yesterday, the one about the old cups?"

"No. I don't think so. What station?"

"Harrisville Channel 9. They talked all evening about four old cups. They look like bowls to me and they are very old. I heard one of the owners say that some people would pay half a million dollars for them."

Chagrain became all ears. He had a wealthy customer who wanted museum pieces for his five-million dollar home in California. He hadn't been satisfied with the two little amphorae he had sold him recently.

"Fill me in," he said.

Nozemni told him what he had seen on television and what he had overheard at the French bistro.

"We can't lose. I just need a tiny bit of help, nothing more, but we have to act fast."

"You get half of what I get for the sale. Not one dollar more. Agreed?"

"But the risk is mine. I'm the one who is going to steal them."

"And what would you do with them? Eat your soup in them? Think about it. Half is all and it's final. You can get out of the car right now if you don't like the deal." As Nozemni kept quiet Chagrain stopped the car. "Deal or get out."

"Deal."

Chagrain resumed driving and reached the downtown area. He parked the car in an underground garage.

"Where do we go?" Nozemni asked.

"To the Bay. They've got good suits. You'll have no problem finding one that fits you. What are you? Size, I mean?"

"I don't know. I've never had a suit."

Jim Chagrain looked at him as they took the elevator up to the main level. "I'd say you're a 40, 42 at most. Long sleeves and long pants." He gave Nozemni a critical look. "Don't try to steal it. They have tags on each and every piece of clothing and detectors at the doors. They'd catch you before you have time to say 'oh'."

"Don't worry. I'm going to pay for it."

Two hours later they were back in the car with a chalk-striped suit, an off-white shirt and silver tie in a big plastic bag.

"Now what?" Chagrain asked.

"Let's drive back to Harrisville and find out where the Sandcrofts live. Then we'll look around, see what their security system looks like, if they have one."

CHAPTER 23

The wake-up call found Chris sound asleep. He fumbled to reach the alarm clock and turned it off. He rose and immediately peered out the window to check on the weather. The sky was lead grey and the clouds were low—not the best conditions for a long drive. He hoped Vivian wouldn't mind—probably not, as it had been her idea to go see the famous park. Maybe he should take the Aurora and leave the Camaro at home. The ride would be more comfortable and he could pack two sleeping bags in the trunk just in case they had to stop in the middle of nowhere. He moved into the shower, then quickly threw on jeans and a sweatshirt. He grabbed his leather coat and the bag he had packed the night before and descended to the main floor to get his morning coffee. He left a note for his father reminding him that he would be away until Sunday night. Satisfied that he had everything under control, he drove to the apartment the Howards had rented on Queen Street.

Wearing a parka over her tailored trousers, Vivian waited for him behind the revolving door. A suitcase stood near her feet. She grabbed the suitcase, slipped out, opened the passenger door, and tossed the suitcase onto the backseat before Chris could help her. She quickly entered the car.

"Good morning," Chris said. "I see you're dressed for the occasion."

Vivian gave him a peck on the cheek. "Nice to see you, Chris. Yesterday I looked at the weather forecast. A big change from last week. I had no warm clothes, so Mother and I went shopping. All day."

"So you missed the second big trivia show?"

"Don't worry. Father recorded everything. I felt like I was there."

"I was impressed with the way he organized the entire affair."

Vivian nodded. "He's good at those kinds of things." She opened her coat. "Any program for this morning?"

"A stop at Tim Hortons for brunch, then we shoot directly for the park. It's big, with a nice lake, called Surprise Lake."

"Surprise Lake? No. I don't want any surprises. We already had two— the dune buggy and the drowning family."

"Don't worry." Chris laughed and patted her on the knee. "This time we'll be alone and in peace. The park is an ideal place for people who want to find quiet and solitude."

As Vivian sniffed and coughed, Chris looked at her. "Are you okay? It's a bit of a drive. We can go somewhere else if you prefer."

"No. I'm looking forward to our weekend in the wilderness. And I came prepared. I have a collection of CDs—classical pieces for the violin player and rock music for me."

"How did you know I played the violin?"

"I have reliable sources."

"Lucio, of course."

She winked at him. "I don't disclose my sources, or they'll dry up quickly." She slid a disk into the CD player and let music fill the air.

Six hours later they branched off Highway 65 and eased onto Highway 60. Soon they arrived at the entrance to Algonquin Park. Vivian took out her camera and began shooting one frame after another. At times Chris stopped the car to give her a chance to play photographer from a stand still.

The recent rain had removed plenty of leaves from the trees, but the woods were still a palette of colours, ranging from delicate yellow to vivid orange and purple.

"We're getting close," he said, glancing at the Magellan fastened to the dashboard. "Only a kilometre to Kawawaymog Lake. Hungry?"

"Just a bit. And you?"

"Hungry, yes, but not for food." He gave her a mischievous look, then stopped near a chalet suite that had suddenly appeared in the middle of the forest. "This is our accommodation. I arranged to have the key left under a rock close to the door. It should be easy to find."

"Got it," Vivian said a few moments later and unlocked the cottage. She helped with the luggage, then stopped on the threshold. "Shouldn't you carry me in your arms?"

"Hmm…I don't know if I'm strong enough," Chris said from inside. "How much do you weigh?"

"About a hundred pounds." She stripped off her parka and threw it inside, showing her slim feminine body.

Chris circled her twice. "I can try, but what if I can't make it? I might drop you. Can you take the risk?"

Vivian nodded solemnly.

"If so…" He swept her off her feet, closed the door with his foot and rushed to the bed where he dropped her. "What a heavy job." He grinned and rolled close to her, his arms outstretched.

Vivian moved to the end of the bed and got on her knees. "You shouldn't be so impatient."

"But I am. When I see you, right away I get in the mood. And I feel that once I get started making love to you, I won't be able to stop." He reached for her, but she slipped away and disappeared into the bathroom. Chris rose, shook off his shoes and coat, and closed the drapes.

When Vivian came back she had a towel wrapped around her.

"That's a major improvement," Chris said as he moved behind her and caressed her naked arms and shoulders. He kissed her neck, then unfolded the white terrycloth to expose her entire body. "Look at you. You're so beautiful, so incredibly beautiful, Vivian. You can make a man crazy."

Vivian turned around to look deeply in his eyes. "I don't care about that. I want to make *you* crazy. Crazy about me." She stretched her arms onto his shoulders. "You know the first time I wanted to get your attention?"

Chris shook his head and caressed her arms. "Tell me."

"The first summer I spent at the Red Manor. It was Sunday morning. Your father, Salvatore Argento and all the guests had gathered in the chapel. I was seated in the first row. When the choir started the *Hymn to Joy*, you stepped in. I turned around to find out whom that beautiful, masculine voice belonged to. It made me vibrate inside as you held the tune with power, rising above all the other voices. At times you overcame even the organ." She paused. "I hadn't met you before, so I was going to ask your father, who was sitting beside me, who you were, but I didn't have to. He was snorting hard to hold his tears in check. Then I knew right away. His prodigal son had arrived."

"Lucio was always afraid to show his emotions. I had arrived a few days earlier and wanted to surprise him. I was just out of the cab when I heard the music, so I left my bag outside and rushed into the chapel." Chris pulled her close and smiled. "So it was my voice you fell for…and all this time I thought it was my looks."

"Oh no. The voice was only a pointer. I liked you right away. Being Lucio's son, I expected you to be short and husky. But the only things you two have in common are the eyes and maybe the jaw." Vivian caressed his cheek and turned his face sideways, examining it closely. "Yes, that's all. And what about you?"

"I remember when you came out of church that Sunday. You wore a light dress that outlined your body. You smiled and kept looking at me while Lucio introduced us. I always had a liking for dark eyes and petite girls. I wanted to hold you in my arms that very same moment." He lifted her and laid her on the bed. "Enough talking," he said and jerked his sweatshirt over his head as Vivian struggled with his belt and the cell phone attached to it.

"Oh, just a moment. Better take some precautions." He jumped off the bed, muted his cell phone and took the hook off the phone lying on the night table. Then he went back to lie close to Vivian. "This time I won't allow anything to come between us. It hasn't been easy to find a way to be alone, with all the commotion we've had in the house." His hands moved easily, hungrily over her body.

"I know," Vivian murmured. "Oh, I wanted so much to get together, and for so long…"

Chris smothered her words with a kiss. When he let go minutes later, he looked into her eyes. "You don't know how much I've wanted to touch you." He caressed her forehead, then her hair. "Every time you walked by me, I felt like sweeping you off your feet and taking you to a secluded place."

Vivian fervently finished undressing him. "After our canoe trip I couldn't think of anything else—just how we could get together." She closed her eyes and reclined.

"Finally, here we are." Chris bent to kiss her again, then stopped abruptly.

Vivian opened her eyes, worry on her face. "Any problem?"

"Hmm, not really, but yes, there is a something—"

"What is it?" As Chris didn't respond, she shook his shoulders slightly. "Tell me, sweetheart."

"Hmm, I was thinking…before we start, we'd better decide whether we should use some protection," Chris whispered.

"Do you want to?"

"It's up to you."

Vivian didn't respond right away. Finally she said, "There is no other man I'd like to have a child with but you."

Chris bent to kiss her, then arched over her, kissing the hollow of her throat. He moved down to suck on each of her nipples. His hands caressed her hips and legs, feeling the smoothness of her skin.

"Kiss me again," Vivian said. She closed her eyes, her body quivering. She reached for his hardness and slowly guided him inside her, locking her legs around his hips.

Chris gasped, then murmured, "Oh lord, Vivian, you're wonderful! You make me feel so alive, so wanted." And he sank into her, thrusting deeper and deeper.

CHAPTER 24

Early in the afternoon on Sunday Chris and Vivian packed their luggage and started back to Harrisville. They had seen little of the park, but much of each other.

"That was the best weekend of my life," Chris said, more relaxed than ever.

"Mine too."

They had been driving for three hours when Chris realized Vivian had become strangely quiet.

"Something wrong?" he asked.

She took a spray out of her purse and inhaled deeply. "It's my asthma. It's acting up again. I already used the spray twice this morning."

"Is it serious?"

"Yes…no, not right now…It could be, I mean."

"Let me know what I can do. Keep in mind that it's Sunday and we're in the middle of nowhere. Most pharmacies are closed."

Vivian leaned her head on the headrest and closed her eyes.

A drizzle wet the windshield at first, then big drops hammered it without mercy. Even with the windshield wipers going at maximum speed, visibility was poor. Dark clouds formed a curtain that seemed to part only a few centimetres in front of them, and the rain soon changed into snow. Chris concentrated on driving, making sure to stay in the middle of the right lane. As the road bent sharply, a squall enveloped the car. Chris let off the accelerator and steered cautiously into the turn.

Vivian wiggled in her seat. "Isn't it dangerous, driving in these conditions?" she asked softly.

"Nah, it's our usual winter weather. It just came early." He looked at Vivian, who was hanging tightly to the armrest. "Are you scared?"

"Ah, hmm…a bit, yes."

"If it gets bad, the police close the road. Until they do that, it's safe to move on."

The snow squalls persisted as Chris proceeded slowly and in silence. All of a sudden, a set of amber lights pierced the white wall in front of them, and Chris pumped on the brake to bring the car to a halt.

"What happened?" Vivian asked, shaking.

"Don't know…oh, look, somebody drove into the ditch. Those flashing lights belong to a tow truck. I'll go see what happened."

The tow truck driver was brief and to the point as he got ready to climb into his cab.

"A couple of flurries and people fly into the ditch," he said. "It always happens at the beginning of the season. It's not even slippery. Nothing serious, fortunately." He gave Chris an attentive look. "Drive safely."

Chris waved, then walked back to the Aurora. Vivian was pale and didn't seem at ease.

"How are you?" he asked. Her breathing was irregular and laborious. "Maybe we'd better stop at the next town. Rest a bit, have something to drink."

"I'm sorry. I don't want to be a bother."

"Don't worry. We're together, right? That was the whole purpose of our trip."

"Okay, let's stop for a while."

And so they did.

In the coffee shop an older man was standing behind the counter, drying a few glasses.

"I didn't think I'd get anymore customers," he said. "What's your pleasure?"

Chris eyed the slices of cheesecake in a plastic container. He pointed to them. "I wouldn't mind one of those with a coffee. And you, Vivian?"

"Just a tea, an herbal tea if you have any."

"Sure I have it; cinnamon okay?"

"Fine," replied Vivian, and she sat at a table, followed by Chris.

"It will take just a moment," the older man said. "Awful weather we're having, so early in the season."

"Yeah," Chris said. "It sure isn't fun driving in these conditions."

Vivian sipped her drink slowly, then got her spray out and inhaled deeply.

Chris waited until Vivian had finished drinking her tea.

"Feeling better?" he asked.

"Yes, much better."

Chris looked at his watch. It was seven o'clock.

"Ready to go?" he asked.

"Yes," Vivian replied, and rose.

Chris wanted to take her home quickly, but the darkness of night coupled with snow squalls made him proceed cautiously.

They weren't on the road for long when suddenly Vivian began rummaging in her purse.

"My spray! I can't find it!" Her movements became frantic as she emptied the contents of her purse into her lap. "I know now. I left it in the coffee shop where we had our snack. I put it on the chair beside me."

"Do you need it right now? We'll be home in about an hour, maybe less."

"Oh yes. Please, Chris. My chest feels tight. I'd better have it. I don't have one at home."

A 50-kilometre sign appeared, indicating that they were entering a populated area.

"I'll go back right away, Vivian. Meanwhile let's look for signs. I'm sure we can find a quiet place where you can stay until I return. Take the cell with you and call 911 if things get worse." A few moments later he eased off the road and stopped in front of a gas station with a convenience store adjoining it.

"That's great. I'll go to the restroom and let the hot water run. The steam may improve my breathing. Thanks, Chris." Holding her hood tight to her face, Vivian took shelter inside the station.

The northwest wind blew without mercy, and the snow fell so fast and thick that the few vehicles on the road didn't seem to leave any tracks. The driving was far more treacherous now than when Chris had driven in the opposite direction. He guessed more than saw the post carrying the luminous sign of the coffee shop. There were no lights on inside the building. He stopped in front of it and knocked at the door. Nobody answered. He searched for a pay phone. There wasn't one. He looped around the building in the faint hope that a window could be lifted from the outside, but no such luck. He returned to his car, pondering the situation. There was nothing else he could do, but go back to the gas station where he had left Vivian. He put the car in gear and began driving, hoping to find her in better shape. Maybe driving in such a poor weather had contributed to her asthma attack. After all, she had never seen a blizzard.

When he stopped at the gas station, well after ten o'clock, Vivian was sipping a cup of steaming tea, both hands holding the mug. She looked much better than when he had left her.

"Am I happy to see you." She rose and hugged him tightly. "I was afraid something had happened to you."

"It took forever to get there. At times I guessed at the road more than saw it. I'm sorry about your spray. Everything was closed up and nobody was around."

Vivian smiled broadly. "It's okay. I feel better now. Let's go home." She thanked the station's owner and linked arms with Chris. "Are you tired?"

"Tired? No, I'm okay. We'll be home before midnight."

CHAPTER 25

As he rounded the last bend leading to his property Chris was troubled. He thought of his father, of the commotion recently created by the TV show and the long-term hardship of having been uprooted from familiar surroundings. Is he paying the toll for all this? He looked cheerful, at times happy to be with his son, but was Lucio's attitude just make-believe? Was he struggling with his feelings? Suddenly Chris felt guilty about having been away for the full weekend. He quickly glanced at Vivian, asleep, her head reclined to one side. He tugged on her parka sleeve.

"Vivian?" he called. "Vivian?"

She woke up and smiled at him. "Yes, love?"

"We're home…to my place, I mean."

The house was alight from the mansard to the basement. As he passed the archway, the silhouettes of several cars drifted into sight. He recognized the Lexus, the Howards' rental from Hertz, but neither of the other two.

"What the hell? What's happened here?"

Vivian raised the back of her seat, slid back the window and leaned out to get a better view.

"I hope it isn't anything to do with your father."

Chris stopped the car in the driveway and rushed toward the entrance door. Gideon was the first to approach him.

"It's Lillian," he said to Chris.

A policeman pushed Gideon aside.

"Mr. Christopher Sandcroft?" he asked.

"Yes. What's happening here?"

"Lillian was injured, badly," Gideon said. "They took her to the hospital."

Another officer then grabbed him and took him aside.

130

"Oh." Chris tried to hide the relief in his voice. Lillian was important, of course, but not as important as his father.

"Let's go inside," the man who seemed to be in charge said. "I've got a few questions to ask you. I'm Constable Ethan McClosky."

"Can I first go and see if my father's okay?"

"He's okay. Nothing's wrong with him."

Chris towered over the man by a full head. "I want to see my father." With decisive strides he entered the house, followed by Vivian and the officer.

In the family room Glen and Elisabeth sat on the sofa, and Lucio, close to the walnut desk, unworriedly leafed through one of the family albums.

"Hi Chris," he said, his voice even. "Nice to see you made it back in one piece."

"Mr. Sandcroft," McClosky said. "I don't want you to talk to anybody here before I have a chance to ask you a few questions."

Chris turned brusquely toward him. "Am I a suspect of some kind?"

"As a matter of fact you could be, sir." His tone became mellower. "Of course, you have nothing to be concerned about if you're innocent."

"Innocent? Of course I am. I've done nothing wrong."

"No need to shout." McClosky took his arm. "Let's go to the kitchen, where we can talk without being disturbed."

Moments later, Chris leaned his elbows on the kitchen table and crossed his fingers.

"So what seems to be the big problem here, constable?"

Another officer entered the kitchen, then closed the door and stood by it.

"Where were you from eight to eleven o'clock tonight?"

Chris made some mental calculations. "On the road—mostly with my companion, except for a short time. Vivian, the young woman who was with me, needed her spray. She has asthma. She'd left it in the coffee shop where we'd stopped to have a drink. I went back to get it."

"Alone?"

"Yes. She was sick so I left her at a gas station."

"How long did it take?"

Chris thought again. "Coming and going…let's say an hour and fifty minutes, maybe two hours. The road was bad."

"How far from here?"

"Fifty-five kilometres, give or take."

"I see. You don't mind if we take you in for a simple test?"

"Test? What test? You haven't even told me what this is all about!" McClosky rose.

"Ms. Lillian Carrigan was brutalized," he said. "She's being treated in the hospital. She was in shock, and she kept repeating your name." He stopped for effect. "It happened during the time frame you just gave me."

CHAPTER 26

It was 7 a.m. when the police finally released Chris. It had been a long night, spent in rooms with hard chairs, mainly waiting for a brief interview, in which Chris repeated what he had said when he was in the house. Then there was half an hour spent at the lab for a swab of saliva. When Chris was ready to call his lawyer, McClosky had released him, a sneaky smile on his face.

Chris was just out of the cab when he saw his father coming from the Wilsons' cottage and wheeling himself toward the house. He had a blanket across his knees and wore a fur hat that covered half of his face. The wheels had hardly any grip on the path, which was already covered with a couple of centimetres of snow. Chris went to meet him and vigorously pushed the wheelchair.

"What are you doing out in this weather? Your cough will get worse!"

"I was gathering important information."

Chris helped him into the house and tossed Lucio's blanket and hat onto the hanger.

"I need strong coffee," he said. "I'm exhausted."

"Espresso coming up, Chris. I'll make it. You sit." Lucio made coffee quickly, then reached into the fridge and set a platter with cheese and grapes on the table. "Vivian prepared it last night. She thought you'd be back soon." Lucio coughed, that insistent, raking cough that he had developed in the last few weeks.

"Oh, so where are the Howards?"

"At home." Lucio laughed softly. "I thought Glen would end up in jail, but at three o'clock in the morning a lawyer popped up from nowhere and replaced Glen in a goliath's fight with the policeman McClosky had left behind. The lawyer is Jeremy Weldon, sent here through the British Embassy in Ottawa." He laughed more loudly. "The man has connections, I tell you!"

133

"What happened?" Chris drank his coffee.

"Glen wanted to keep you from going to police headquarters, but he didn't have a chance to talk to you. But with Vivian it was another story. She'd said only a few words when he stepped in and forbade her to say any more. The policeman, a young fellow, even threatened Glen, but Glen didn't give in. Vivian is expected at headquarters this morning. Mr. Weldon, who lives in Aurora, will pick her up and accompany her to the station."

"Why in the world would Lillian accuse me of raping her?" He stroked his hair in a compulsive gesture.

"She was mistaken, evidently." They both nibbled at the food in silence. "I talked to Gideon. He was the one who heard Lillian screaming for help and rushed to the house. A man was coming out of the main door. He was about your height."

"Hmm...but why didn't the alarm system work? And Bertha should have spotted him! Why didn't she make any noise? She rumbles and growls and barks at every stranger."

"Apparently she didn't or Gideon didn't hear her."

Chris finished his second helping of grapes.

"I'm going to bed. I need a few hours of sleep. Tomorrow I'll check with the company that installed our security system. Why didn't the alarm sound off? They owe me some answers. And I'll call my lawyer." He paused. "I never thought it would become necessary, but I think I should replace the cedar hedge around the property with something more secure."

"Oh no. The hedge is so beautiful: I've never seen a Greek fret so nicely done, following the ups and downs of the terrain."

"Yeah. Grandfather worked on it four times every year. He trimmed it with the gas saw like a sculptor uses a chisel, with precision and accuracy." Chris was silent for a while and then continued. "It isn't safe, though. The city is moving this way, with more houses, more people, and more troubles." He sighed. "We need a brick wall, and the beautiful archway that now welcomes people at the entrance should be replaced with a gate that closes and opens with a remote."

CHAPTER 27

It's the lucky break I've always dreamed of, Constable Ethan McClosky thought as he drove to police headquarters. He knew Chris Sandcroft was guilty. The man didn't fool him a bit with his air of superiority, throwing fancy words around and treating him like he was crazy. He knew the type. Sandcroft was the boss of an important company where the employees danced to his music. He owned a fancy house with two housekeepers and a gardener. Ridiculous. And at 32 he hadn't married even once. *The man isn't normal. It's a simple as that.* McClosky had read a lot about profiling criminals:; he knew their need to be different. He could easily guess what had happened. Out for a weekend of fun and pleasure, the girl had rejected him, faking an asthma attack. When he couldn't take it anymore, he had dropped her at some gas station close to home, driven to his house where Lillian Carrigan was, and forced his way on her. *This is the simple truth, and I will prove it!*

The lab had run the PCR. It was more economical than a DNA test, he was told. He hoped it would prove Sandroft's guilt. Then that SOB would spend years in jail.

And that little friend of his with the funny accent? Guilty about the situation she had created, she would probably testify in his favour. Rich people always stuck together. He would get her, too. Today he planned to have fun with her. He would grill her on every detail of her return trip with Mr. Sandcroft.

Proud of his deductions and satisfied with his plan of action, McClosky now sat in the interview room upstairs at the police station. This time he would conduct the interview instead of being stuck next door in the monitor room looking at the two video screens. His moment had finally come. At 39, he was still a constable after 12 years of service. But now, with his boss in the hospital, he was in charge. The department was looking for an acting chief, but once he had charged Sandcroft, there would be no need to search any further. Everybody, especially those clowns in the squad room, would realize he was the man for the job.

He let Vivian Howard wait for an hour before inviting her in. To his surprise, a large man with long white hair and dressed in black with a blue tie walked in with her.

"I'm Mr. Jeremy Weldon, *doctor juris*—that's attorney at law." He took a chair from the corner and sat close to Vivian. "I want to know why Ms. Howard has been summoned."

McClosky wiggled in his chair. "Summoned? That's not the right word. I just asked her to come to the station, that's all…to have a friendly chat." He didn't think Weldon had any business being present when he questioned the woman, but he wasn't sure. With all the authority he could muster, he said, "A crime has been committed at the residence of Mr. Sandcroft. I'm the investigating officer."

Weldon looked straight into the policeman's eyes. "So let's get on with it."

"I want to ask Ms. Howard a few questions." Inconspicuously, McClosky turned on one of the video recorders, cleared his throat and looked down at his notes. He addressed Vivian. "Where were you last Sunday from 5 p.m. to midnight?"

"You know very well that my client *does not* have to answer any questions," Weldon said.

"You both have to understand that Ms. Howard's testimony can clear Mr. Sandcroft, and so spare him further unpleasant inquiries." That's how his boss had handled this kind of situation many times over. He tried a smile. "All I want to know is how she spent Sunday afternoon and evening, and with whom."

"I'd like to answer," Vivian said softly, but clearly. "Mr. Sandcroft and I left Algonquin Park early in the afternoon, maybe two o'clock. We stopped for coffee around 6:30. Then we stopped again when my asthma acted up."

"Were you with him all the time?"

"Well, not completely, actually."

"Why not?"

"I had forgotten my spray at the coffee shop, so Chris went back to fetch it."

Weldon put a hand on Vivian's arm, clearly trying to stop her, but Vivian glanced at him with surprise.

It was time for McClosky to praise Ms. Howard. "That's good, very good." He paused and wrote down Vivian's answers. He should try to spread an atmosphere of concern. "Did you have a good time at the park?"

"Oh yes. We had a wonderful time."

Of course, that was the standard answer due to the circumstances.

"Would you remember how long it took Mr. Sandcroft to go to the coffee shop and back?"

"An hour and three-quarters, two hours? Something like that."

McClosky feigned writing notes. This was the time his boss would drop in a *red herring*—something designed to catch a lie in the witness' testimony—but he couldn't think of anything suited to the circumstance. He looked at the ceiling, trying to gain time, hoping something would come to mind. Then he turned a couple pages of his pad and scribbled down the lawyer's name.

Ten minutes passed.

"You seem to be busy, Mr. McClosky, so I guess we're free to go." Weldon rose, followed by Vivian.

Taken by surprise, McClosky didn't know what to do. "Yes. You're free to go," he whispered, but Weldon and Vivian were already out of the room.

Never mind. This was only an interview. The real interrogation will follow later. He would have plenty of time to ask more questions and find contradictions during the woman's deposition.

In Weldon's car Vivian kept quiet for a moment, then turned to Weldon.

"I didn't have to answer any of those questions?" she asked.

"Not really. Just your name and address."

"Would it have been better if I hadn't answered? Mr. McClosky said I could help Chris—"

"My dear girl, policemen are trained to use tricks to get the so-called truth out of people. I can tell you the exact page in which this is spelled out in one of their law enforcement handbooks."

"I didn't know. I think it's awful."

"In fact it is, but it's the way the system works. By the way, you weren't informed that the interview was going to be taped. I saw McClosky turn on the system. That's a flaw on his part."

"I didn't see a camera."

"One was in the ceiling, near the smoke detector." Weldon stopped the car in front of a building on Queen Street. "This is where I picked you up this morning, I believe."

"Yes. Thank you, Mr. Weldon."

"Oh, by the way, did Chris find your spray?"

"No. The coffee shop was already closed for the day."

"I see. Don't volunteer that information. Answer with the truth if you're asked, but don't fill in the gaps."

Vivian had already opened the car door. She wheeled around.

"Gaps? What gaps?" she asked.

"Well, here's the situation. Since McClosky was the senior member available at the Harrisville police department at the time the 911 call came in, he took on the case. He isn't the smartest man in the world. He's filling in for the real McCoy. He doesn't know how to handle a case. The crucial point of the questioning would have been to ask you whether Chris gave you back the spray. Since he didn't hand it back to you, Chris has no alibi for that period of time."

Lucio was busy around the stove when he heard a knock on the kitchen window. He wheeled across the room to see who it was. When he saw Weldon's face peering through the sheers, he waved at him and went to meet him at the patio door.

"Sorry I'm late. Ms. Howard and I waited at the police station for over an hour."

"No problem. Chris isn't home yet."

"Where's your dog?" Weldon stood still, looking around suspiciously.

"In the hallway near the main entrance. I took her in there when you told me you were coming. Sorry about yesterday." The day before Bertha had tugged at Weldon's trousers as soon as the lawyer had stepped into the family room.

"Oh, good." He followed Lucio into the kitchen. "Anything new concerning the injured woman?" Weldon asked.

"She was taken to surgery. We'll know tomorrow. Care to stay for supper? It's just a one-course meal, though."

"Might as well, thanks. Glen Howard insisted I talk to your son."

"Yes, I appreciate that. But I know more than my son does, since I talked to Gideon, our gardener. He rushed over here when he heard the commotion coming from our house."

"And?"

Lucio turned off the stove and offered Weldon a drink. He took a bottle of mineral water from the fridge and set it in front of the lawyer.

"You see, Lillian Carrigan was temporarily staying in the guest room upstairs, filling in for Gideon's wife, my son's regular housekeeper. When Gideon checked on the house Sunday evening, she was having her boyfriend over. Gideon heard voices, laughing...that sort of thing. He went back to the house to watch a movie. It was well past ten o'clock when he heard screaming and a call for help. As he arrived at the house, he saw a tall man running away from the main entrance, and a car crossing the archway, probably to pick him up. He didn't see what kind of car it was. Then he entered the house and went upstairs. Lillian was on the floor, half-naked and bleeding. He called for an ambulance and tried to stop the bleeding. Lillian didn't mutter another word until the paramedics came and took her away."

"So why did the police think she identified Chris Sandcroft as her assailant?"

"I don't know."

"Did they question Gideon?"

"No, not yet."

The sound of an engine grew louder and louder.

"My son is home," Lucio said.

Lucio set the table, manoeuvring between the kitchen equipment and the furniture with surprising dexterity.

"Mr. Weldon," Chris said as he entered. "Pleased to meet you." As Weldon started to rise, he added, "Please, don't."

"You look tired," Lucio said.

"I am, a bit at least. I spent the night at the station, as you know."

"Yes. Mr. Howard keeps me informed of what's going on down to the smallest detail."

"I'm grateful for that. The lawyer we use for Vibratim is a corporate lawyer. He'll refer me to a friend of his. He'll probably call tonight. I gather Mr. Weldon cannot represent both of us—Vivian and me."

Weldon nodded. "Right, not if charges are laid. But I can advise you if you have any questions."

"I'm sure I'll have several, if not today, tomorrow for sure. But first let's have something to eat. I haven't eaten since breakfast."

Silently, Lucio set a tureen in the middle of the table and lifted its lid. A wonderful, zesty aroma spread all around.

"What is it?" Chris asked, and sniffed it. "Chili? Since when did you learn how to cook chili?"

Lucio made a dignified, almost offended face. "Since Kathy taught me, one step at a time, patiently, over the phone. For almost an hour. She said you liked her chili."

"Oh, yes, I do." Chris invited Weldon to help himself. "It's safe, Mr. Weldon. Help yourself."

Weldon complimented the entrée and slowly finished his water.

"The police took all the photographs and gathered all the evidence they wanted last night," he said. "When they left I asked if they were finished and they answered positively. So Chris, you should look to see whether anything is missing. We have to establish whether, by any chance, the perpetrator was also a thief. This could give police something extra to work on."

Chris nodded. "I'll conduct a thorough search tomorrow." He paused, perplexed. "I can't understand why the alarm wasn't activated. It's supposed to ring at the company that monitors our house, which, in turn, calls me on my cell."

"Since Lillian was expecting her boyfriend, maybe she turned it off," Lucio whispered.

"But why?"

"She's the only one who knows. I can only guess. Suppose that the boyfriend went out to buy something they wanted, and that he was expected to re-enter the house very soon." Lucio hesitated, then added, "Maybe she was already in her room, undressed."

"Ms. Carrigan's boyfriend—" Weldon said. "Does anybody know anything about him?"

"We met him once at a recent TV show. He was in the audience, and he looked like a nice guy," Chris said.

"Hmm, he was around earlier, from what the gardener said. I wonder why he isn't suspect number one?"

Chris nodded. "That's what I keep asking myself. Why suspect me and not the one who had been lingering around the house? Or maybe McClosky doesn't know about him?"

"It wouldn't surprise me if he doesn't," Weldon said with a grave tone. "McClosky doesn't know much about anything. He shouldn't even be conducting the investigation. I got a few tips on his progression through the ranks. He directed traffic until last year, and for more than a decade. However, we're stuck with him, for the time being." He addressed Chris. "Tell me how it worked out with McClosky last night."

"He kept me waiting most of the night, then he asked me about my weekend and the trip back. Over and over. I told him that I was with Vivian all the time except when I went back to the coffee shop to get her spray."

"Anything else?"

"He said that Lillian has identified me. I'm sure he's mistaken or Lillian is mistaken."

"I see," Weldon replied, his tone uncommitted.

They finished their meal in silence. After they'd had coffee Weldon stood up.

"It's getting late and I need some rest," he said. "I should be going." He handed a card to Chris. "Here's my phone number. Call me if you think of anything important." He turned to Lucio. "Thanks for supper, Mr. de' Vigentini."

Chris rose and shook hands with him. He was ready to accompany Weldon to his car.

"Did they ask you for a DNA sample?" Weldon asked.

"Yes. They took me to their lab downtown. The technician told me they'll run a PCR, a sub-sampling of the DNA test. It'll clear me for sure."

He opened the sliding patio door. "Only identical twins have the same DNA."

CHAPTER 28

The last words of the conversation between Chris and the lawyer resounded gravely in Lucio's ears.

He quietly wheeled into his bedroom, his heart in turmoil. *The curse...the curse is taking effect...slowly, inconspicuously, inexorably.* The events had started to unfold and he wouldn't be able to stop them. He shouldn't have come to stay with his son and endanger his life, but he had longed so much to be with Chris, to see him every day, to witness his success that he hadn't been able to resist. So he had followed him to Canada and taken the curse with him. Chris would be the victim of somebody else's crime and suffer all his life because of it. No doubt all these events were written in the stars. Everything was falling into place.

Chris' twin brother, Rick, the one he thought had been dead for years, had found a way to bring harm and shame to the de' Vigentini family. There wouldn't be any escape. The terrible moment he had feared for years had arrived.

He bowed his head and tried to mutter a prayer, but no words came to him. He felt guilty for what he had done, and for having hidden the truth from Chris.

Images from the past began unrolling in his mind, as vivid as yesterday...

It was a beautiful summer day. Chris was in bed with the mumps and little Rick had been banned from his room. Rick was sad, very sad: he couldn't play with his two-hour older brother and leader, and he couldn't visit with his mom, who was taking care of Chris in an isolated wing of the castle. So against Deborah's advice, Lucio had taken little Rick aboard his new yacht. Rick was too young to be on a big boat without adequate supervision, Deborah had stated firmly. But Lucio had dismissed her concerns, saying that she, like most mothers, was overprotective.

Intimidated by the boat's size and its unfamiliar layout, at first Rick hung onto his father's trousers and didn't say a word as Lucio showed him around and introduced him to the crew. But that didn't last long. When finally the boat moved out of the harbour, Rick became free, alive, running up and down the deck.

"Want to be the skipper?" Lucio asked. "The skipper is the boss around here, the one who tells the boat where to go."

Little Rick nodded, his eyes sparkling with excitement. Lucio took him to the bridge, told him to stand on a stool, and put Rick's hands on the helm. Of course, he couldn't hold it as his hands spanned only one third of the wheel's diameter. Together Lucio and Rick happily navigated the calm waters of the Adriatic Sea for the entire afternoon.

Then night came…that terrible night…

"Are you doing okay, Lucio?" Chris shouted from outside the bedroom door.

Lucio was brusquely brought back to reality. He didn't answer right away.

"Are you okay?" Chris repeated. "I'm coming in."

"No. Yes, I'm okay. Just praying." Tears raked Lucio's cheeks every time the recollection of that fatal night surfaced. "Good night, Chris. Sleep tight." He hoped his voice didn't betray his emotions.

Levering himself on his arms, he rose out of the chair and dropped into bed.

When Lucio got up the following morning Chris had already left, leaving a note that he would be back around noon. Lucio went from room to room to see whether anything was out of place. Over the last few months he had become familiar with the furniture and the accessories spread all over the first floor. He was wandering in the family room when the house phone rang. At first, background noise didn't allow him to identify the caller, but then he recognized the voice of Arcibaldo Cortesi, his former Italian lawyer and current curator of the Red Manor. Lucio listened attentively.

"Arcibaldo, ma cosa mi dici?" It couldn't be true!

"È così, Lucio mio. Salvatore Argento ci ha lasciati. Ieri notte. E' morto nel sonno, tranquillamente."

Lucio hung up. Salvatore Argento, the person with whom he had shared the vicissitudes of the Red Manor during his long life, had left him. Forever. He felt a pang in his heart. He wanted to leave, to go back where he belonged. He wanted to see his old friend one last time.

His senior by eight years, Salvatore had played babysitter to him, played ball with him, and several times rescued him from the moat that surrounded the castle. During World War II, he had stayed with the de' Vigentinis, hiding in the dungeon with the rest of the family while bombs fell like confetti onto the castle. After the war was over, Salvatore had helped his father lay one tile after another to repair the roof of the living quarters first, and then the roof of the art gallery. There was a shortage of construction material, and they often had to resort to solidified mud to build the embankment around the brook. When all the major repairs were done, they learned how to swab smoke from the paintings; in the most damaged cases they replaced the back of the old canvas with new material. Salvatore had never married, considering the de' Vigentinis his own family.

When the Red Manor was sold—oh did Lucio remember the tears Salvatore had shed. Salvatore had felt betrayed even if he was allowed to remain in the castle, first, as a custodian, and later, as the assistant to the curator.

And then…then, there had been that terrible fire at the castle during the celebration of Saint Zenobio, the protector of Boccascura. Salvatore had been the only one who had patrolled around the Red Manor and discovered that the flames had invaded the entire main floor. And that ultimate act of love had cost him his life. Hospitalized because of multiple burns, Salvatore had never recovered.

Yesterday his frail body had given up.

His companion and friend had left him, leaving a great void in his heart.

Lucio wheeled himself close to the patio door. Outside a blanket of snow covered the flowerbeds, the fountain and the stony path leading to Gideon's house. The sky, a blanket of lead, added more desolation to the sight.

Nothing was left for him, except waiting for fate to take its course. He reclined his head; he felt distraught.

"Lucio, Lucio!" Chris' voice filtered through Lucio's semiconscious state.

"*Eh, che cosa?* What?" He opened his eyes. Chris was tugging at his sleeve and Bertha was going from Chris to Lucio to see who would pet her first.

"You're sleeping. It's too early for a nap. It's just 12:30, time for lunch."

"Oh. I'm sorry. I didn't think about fixing anything."

"No problem." He winked at his father. "I thought your cooking spree would be short-lived." Without another word he pushed Lucio's chair into the kitchen. "I stopped at Pizza Hut and got a vegetarian pizza. It'll do for today." He gave Lucio a critical look. "You look pale. Are you taking your medications?"

"*Sì, sì.* I am! Blood thinner in the morning, and cholesterol pill at night." He patted the bag that hung from the armrest. "And in here is Benylin for my cough." He tried to smile at Chris. "Everything is okay. Stop worrying."

Chris took two glasses from the china cabinet and set a bottle of Barolo on the table. He opened the carton with the pizza and pulled a slice free.

"No dishes and no fuss—the bachelor's way. Help yourself, Lucio, while the pizza is still warm."

Lucio slowly complied, his mind elsewhere.

"Busy at the office?" he asked.

Chris nodded and took a second slice. "I organized things so that I can take off all the time I need for this week. By then I hope everything will be cleared up." He took a swig of wine. "I'm going to look around and see whether I can spot misplaced objects or whether something is missing."

"Don't forget to check on the cups—wherever you've hidden them."

With a piece of pizza hanging from his mouth Chris nodded. He stalked out of the kitchen, followed by Bertha.

CHAPTER 29

Little sleep and plenty of worries were taking their toll on Chris' spirit. He had put up a brave face for his father's sake, and avoided showing how he really felt. The truth was, he was numbed by hurt and shocked by the recent events. His word had been doubted, his name tinged with crime, his intimacy violated, and his girlfriend questioned by police and treated like a criminal's accomplice. What was happening? The world he knew had crumbled.

At last alone in the family room, he stretched out in the recliner, wanting to relax. The door opened and Lucio wheeled himself in.

"I need to go talk to Father Paul," Lucio said.

Chris shot him a curious look. "At this hour? It's nine o'clock."

"It's a must. My soul may be in trouble."

In recent days his father had become dramatic.

"And was it not in trouble this morning? It would've been a more reasonable time to contact Father Paul."

Lucio wheeled close to Chris' recliner.

"Please," he said

"You can't be serious—going to the seminary this hour of night?"

He pulled his chair straight and tried to look at his father's face. He switched on the floor lamp to have a clearer view. Lucio looked stressed; his cheeks were red and his hands trembled.

"I called him. He'll talk to me. It's just that…that he cannot leave. Somebody has to take me over there."

"Lucio, do you know what I've been through this last past week? I'm lucky my name hasn't been disclosed. That's the only good part of it."

"I know, I know. But still, I need to talk to Father Paul. Now!"

Chris rubbed his forehead. "Can you not talk to him on the phone?"

"I also need to confess."

"Confess? You go to the seminary twice a month. You've had plenty of time to confess."

Lucio dismissed Chris' statement. "When I go there I help Father Paul reorganize the library. That's what I've been doing the last few times."

"I see. Can you tell me what's so urgent?"

"No. But trust me, it's something important, something that came to my mind just a while ago."

"And something you don't want to share with me, obviously."

Lucio grinned. "Of course not. I've never heard of a father confiding in a son. Too inexperienced."

Chris sighed deeply. Maybe a change of scenery would be good for him, too. Father Paul had become a good friend of Lucio's.

"Let's go, then." He rose and followed his father out of the room.

They arrived at the seminary to find Father Paul standing at the bottom of the outside stairway, which was illuminated by two tall halogen lamps. Clearly he shared Lucio's opinion that the meeting was urgent. Immediately the priest helped Lucio out of the car and followed his battery-powered wheelchair along the slope flanking the wide staircase. As soon as they entered the building, Father Paul extended his hand to Chris.

"We met at a Sunday mass, right? In the spring. Thank you for bringing your father here." He gestured to an ordinand standing in the hallway to come close. "Fernando, show Mr. Sandcroft around while I take Mr. de' Vigentini to my office." He smiled at Chris. "The seminary is beautiful, and well lit at night. See you in half an hour or so." He was almost out of sight, following Lucio's wheelchair, when he turned around. "There's coffee in the cafeteria. I just put on a fresh pot."

"Thank you," Chris called back, and the two men were out of sight.

The ordinand bowed slightly. "My name is Fernando. I come from Campo Grande, in the wetlands of Brazil."

"Chris Sandcroft. I hope it isn't too much trouble to show me around. I could go to the cafeteria and wait there for my father."

"Oh no. We're expected to answer any call our superiors make. Follow me, please." He walked briskly into the reception hall.

Half an hour later, with the tour finished, Chris and Fernando sat at a metal table in the cafeteria, a mug before each of them.

"Where will you be going when you're finished with the seminary?" Chris asked.

"Wherever they send me. But I hope to become a missionary. Brazil is my first choice, of course. Don Bosco did a lot of good down there, in the Amazon region in particular."

"I'm sure your people will be happy to have you back."

"I hope so."

A grandfather clock had just finished chiming ten when a little red light on the wall began to flicker. An insistent beep sounded loudly in the almost empty cafeteria.

"Somebody's sick," Fernando said, rose and quickened his steps out.

Chris, recovering from the surprise, followed the ordinand, murmuring, "It could be my father; he didn't look well when we came in."

Immediately the seminary became alive, as half a dozen people gathered in the corridor. Fernando opened the door of Father Paul's office.

Kneeling near Lucio was Father Paul, busy talking into his cell phone. Chris rushed to his father's side and bent over him.

"Is he alive?"

Father Paul shut off his phone. "Yes, yes. I just gave him CPR, then called for help. They should be here in minutes." He rose and tapped Chris on the shoulder. "Let's not lose any time. Let's put him on the standard stretcher we keep in here. Then the paramedics can load him into the ambulance right away. We can take him to the garage and wait there."

Chris didn't move. He caressed his father's thin grey hair. "Hang in there. You're going to be all right," he murmured. With relief he watched his father's chest move up and down, though irregularly. Was he responsible for Lucio's troubles? A sense of guilt invaded his mind and heart.

"Chris?" Father Paul called. "Chris. Let's get moving."

Reluctantly Chris rose.

"What was the urgent issue Lucio had to discuss with you?" he asked.

"He didn't manage to speak about it. As soon as we were in my office he knelt in front of me, took my hand and said, 'Oh Father, oh Father! What have I done?' Tears gushed out of his eyes. I tried to lift him up, put him at ease, asked him to sit—but he wouldn't. Then, among strong sobs, he said, 'It's him! It's him! I know it's him!' Seconds later he collapsed onto the floor." Father Paul paused. "I have no idea what he was talking about."

148

The wail of an approaching ambulance became stronger and stronger. Father Paul and Chris lifted the stretcher and took it to the garage entrance. The ambulance roared into the driveway and stopped before the garage. Two paramedics hopped out of the vehicle and opened the rear door of the ambulance. They loaded the stretcher while Father Paul exchanged a few words with them.

For a moment Chris was shocked by what was happening. He felt like he was reliving a scene from the past. Just like this his mother had been taken away.

"Sorry I can't come with you," Father Paul said.

The rear door of the ambulance was going to close, when Chris jumped into the vehicle. He sat on the floor in a corner as the ambulance whistled its way to Victoria Hospital.

A paramedic checked Lucio's vital signs and put an oxygen mask over his mouth.

Moments ticked away as more thoughts of guilt tormented Chris' heart. Was he the cause, even the remote cause, of Lucio's heart attack? Coming to a strange country, losing contact with the people he knew, witnessing his son being accused of assault—had all this been too much for him? Did he unknowingly create too much distress for Lucio's troubled soul?

PART 4

The Curse of the Red Manor

CHAPTER 30

Harrisville, November 2005

For two days Lucio de' Vigentini lay on a bed in the Intensive Care Unit, his vital signs monitored each minute of the day. He had survived a heart attack, but he was very weak. Then his doctor transferred him from Intensive Care to a private room but he had to remain in the hospital until the extent of the infarct could be determined.

Chris entered Lucio's room and tiptoed close to the bed. His father now slept. An oxygen tube was inserted in his nostrils and leads connected his body to a monitor set high on a pedestal. Chris raised the blinds halfway and sat on the only chair available. He was worried. Who would take care of Lucio once the hospital dismissed him? Would he need nursing assistance day and night? He sighed deeply.

Lucio stirred. "Is it you, Chris?" he asked, without opening his eyes.

Chris rose and drew close to the bed. "Yes, it's me. How are you?"

"Weak." He opened his eyes and searched for Chris' hand. "This old man gives you problems. I'm sorry."

Chris squeezed his father's hand. "Don't think about that. The important thing is that you're okay now."

"They won't let me out, not yet, they said."

"No. They want to evaluate the extent of your heart damage. They're also concerned about your lungs and have to run some tests. Then they'll decide what to do next and what medications to give you. Probably the same as you're taking now, they said, but a higher dose."

Lucio swallowed, coughed and adjusted the tubes in his nostrils.

"I'd like to go home. Being in the hospital is depressing."

"I understand, but it'll be only a few days more." Lillian being gone was going to be a big concern, but Chris didn't want his father to worry about it. "You have to come back soon, or Gideon will die of boredom. He's waiting for you to work in the greenhouse."

"Nice fellow, Gideon. He's such good company for me. I like Kathy, too."

Chris nodded. He pulled the chair close to the bed and sat in it.

"Father Paul wants to know if you'd like to see him sometime this week."

"Oh, yes. I remember now." He gave Chris the shadow of a smile. "We went to see him at the seminary. I wanted to talk to him. I felt he also should hear my confession."

"Some old big sin you couldn't wait to tell him about."

"Sure, sure, make fun of me. You're almost a non-believer. You don't believe in confession, penance and the like."

Chris shrugged. "We're punished for the wrong we do—I believe that— but I don't think God waits until we're dead. He does it right here, on this earth."

"You may be right, Chris, you may just be right." Suddenly a deep cough shook Lucio's chest.

Chris filled a spoon with the syrup lying on the side table, waited for Lucio's cough to subside, and then gave the cough medicine to his father. He was worried about Lucio's condition and hoped that he would soon have the test results back. Lucio slowly swallowed the syrup and then closed his eyes, exhausted.

"Time for me to go. Rest well, Lucio. I'll tell Father Paul he can come visit."

He bent to kiss Lucio on the forehead and quietly left the room, but not before looking back at his father, so small and frail.

"I'm here for a quick hello and a quick goodbye," Glen Howard said as he strode into Lucio's room at Victoria Hospital the following day. "I'm on my way to Edinburgh. My business needs my attention." He set a floral arrangement beside a vase with yellow roses on the windowsill.

Lucio opened his eyes. "Oh, hello, Glen."

"I wanted to see you, and tell you not to worry. Our lawyer, Jeremy Weldon, thinks there is no cause for concern. The police have questioned

Lillian's boyfriend and they're searching for a third man." He eased his massive body onto the chair close to Lucio's bed. "I'm leaving in three hours. I'll stay in Scotland a week or so, and then I'll hightail it back here. Elisabeth and Vivian will stay put."

"I see. Thank you for being so close to us."

Glen waved off Lucio's thanks. "What are friends for? I have to tell you this, though; I've already gotten three email requests for the cups—and they aren't even mine."

"I believe you. Your TV show was quite an event."

"Yes, it went really well. Some of my customers want reproductions, since they know they can't afford the real thing. But we'll discuss everything when I come back."

Lucio nodded. "Thanks for the flowers. They're beautiful." He closed his eyes.

"I see you're tired. I should be going." He lifted up Lucio's hand and held it between his two. "'Bye, Lucio. Get better soon."

CHAPTER 31

"Mr. de' Vigentini? It's Father Paul."

Lucio opened his eyes. "Hello, Father. Come in; come in. It's nice to see you."

"I was told you're recovering and will be home pretty soon." Father Paul approached the bed and shook the hand Lucio extended. "Have you been up yet?"

"Oh yes, and I've been outside already. It was nice to breathe the fresh air." He gestured toward the chair in the corner. "Do sit, please."

"The night you got sick you wanted to talk to me. Urgently. You said it was important."

Lucio turned his face away. "I'm a fool…an old fool."

Father Paul laughed. "That much, I've guessed."

Lucio looked at him. "Yeah, laugh…laugh at a poor old man with a bad ticker. That's compassion."

"Maybe when you tell me what that urgency was all about, I'll get serious."

Lucio pressed the button to lift up the headrest and adjusted the pillow behind his head. His face was grave.

"Remember the curse I mentioned?" As Father Paul frowned, Lucio raised his hand to prevent any interruptions. "Listen, Father, listen for a moment before you start preaching. It was something one generation told the next. It was more of a prophecy than a curse. At the turn of the millennium the de' Vigentini dynasty would cease to exist as one brother would turn against the other."

"So?"

"I had two sons, Father. The day they were born I began to worry."

"Two sons? Chris has a brother?"

156

"*Had* a brother." Lucio closed his eyes and the two men kept silent for a long moment.

"What happened to this phantom son?"

"He drowned, or so I believed until recently."

"Drowned? Where? How?"

Lucio inhaled deeply and then began. "That day my wife, Deborah, didn't want me to take Rick—that was my other son's name—she didn't want me to take Rick on the boat. She was home with Chris, who was down with the mumps. The boys were lively. They were a handful. They'd try anything, at least once. One of Rick's favourite games was to hide in the dungeon, and another was to climb the 40 steps of the tower, which was a small replica of the famous *Filarete.* He'd turn on the switch to unleash the big bells, disturbing the peace of the entire neighbourhood. Chris' specialty was jumping off the turrets. Chris was walking around with a cast before he was six."

"From the turrets? Weren't they very high?"

"Not really. In the 1800s their use as defence against enemy warfare became obsolete; they were restructured to form architectonic motifs around the imposing mass of the castle. In our case they enclosed the huge terrace on top of the dungeon, which our kids and their little friends used for roller-skating and basketball." Lucio stopped and coughed. "This cough doesn't want to leave me. I have lung problems, they told me. It goes back to when I was a smoker. Anyway…what was I saying? Ah, about the castle. The turrets weren't high enough that the kids could get seriously injured when they jumped off." Lucio paused, fatigued. "The boys tried anything. They kept their mother and a few other people at the castle very busy." Lucio stopped and added in a contrite tone, "They took after me."

"Their misfortune." Father Paul smiled.

"So Rick had no playmate that weekend. He loved to be at sea and wanted to come with me. I took him." Lucio stopped, clearly distraught.

"And Rick fell overboard," Father Paul said in a quiet, soft tone.

Lucio nodded. "When I retired that night, I carried Rick to my berth. The boy was sound asleep. I stripped off his life jacket and put him in bed with me, then lay close to him." Lucio couldn't hold back his tears. "When I woke up, he was nowhere to be found."

Father Paul rose, picked up a tissue from the nearby table and gave it to Lucio.

"Did you search for him?"

"Yes, of course. The rubber boat used for emergencies was missing. We gathered that Rick had released it, and that both boat and boy had ended up in the water. The sea was rough. The coastguard was called in. We searched and searched and searched. We alerted all the harbours on the Italian and Yugoslavian coasts. Nothing. No Rick, no boat." Lucio dried his eyes, pain washing over him. "Deborah, my wife, never talked to me again. A year later she divorced me and took Chris with her."

"A pretty tough lady, if you ask me. There was sorrow on both sides, not only on hers. A poor way of acting from a Christian point of view." Father Paul's eyebrows crinkled, his look stern.

"That's the way it went. I always felt guilty for that night on the yacht."

A nurse entered the room carrying two cups of tea.

For a while Father Paul and Lucio sipped their drinks in silence.

"It was a mistake, Lucio. You made a mistake, that's all; you didn't commit a sin. You don't need absolution for that. You've suffered enough for what happened."

"Did I suffer! Deborah was the light of my life. I have known many women, loved some of them, but my Deborah was somebody special. She was beautiful, it's true, but that wasn't all. When she looked at me…it was like I was part of her. I felt that close to her. Silly, eh?" Lucio finished his tea. "But what I told you is not the only thing that troubles me."

"What do you mean?"

"I came to believe in the prophecy, that our family was going to be wiped out one way or the other."

The door opened and the nurse re-entered the room. "Time for a nice stroll in the park. The sun is high, and it's almost 18 degrees. Another extraordinary day for November." She opened the metal closet and pulled out a pair of trousers, a flannel shirt and a sweater.

"Thank you," Lucio said, and extended his hand to get hold of his clothes. "I can take care of myself." With difficulty, Lucio rose from his semi-sitting position and swung his feet to the floor. As the nurse stood there, ready to help, Lucio dismissed her. "I'll dress myself."

"I'll look after him," Father Paul said. "And I'll take him down for a bit of fresh air."

The nurse gave him an inquisitive look. "Do you know how to operate the wheelchair safely?"

"I'm an expert, nurse." Father Paul smiled.

The nurse looked satisfied and left.

In no time Father Paul and Lucio were out in the open, following a path that meandered alongside a creek.

"I know this park," Father Paul said. "It's a beauty. A hundred kinds of different trees and shrubs. It's a show in its own right when spring comes."

They soon reached a clearing surrounded by tall blue spruces. Father Paul sat on a wooden bench, and turned Lucio's wheelchair to face him. Lucio remained quiet.

"Believing in witchcraft is a sin and I understand you want to repent," Father Paul said. "I can see to it, but later. I feel there is more to your story about Rick. Something so serious that you had to talk it over with somebody you could trust."

"Yes," Lucio whispered. "That's why I wanted to see you that night."

"So tell me."

Lucio closed his eyes, immersed in his recollection. "When we couldn't find Rick anywhere I went to see a clairvoyant—*Filomena la Veggente*—she was famous for finding lost people."

"Regrettable action," Father Paul said.

"You've never had children." Lucio scowled. "You don't know what it means to lose one. They're part of you, the best of you." He swallowed hard. "Filomena told me I wouldn't find Rick, that he'd been abducted by bad people. I was numb with pain. I was there, and I believed in her powers, so I told her of the curse as it had been passed on from my ancestors to me." Lucio paused, exhausted. "She consulted her tarot cards, then told me that she saw a thick, black cloud around Rick, but that she couldn't tell what it was. She said I should come back the next day and bring another piece of Rick's clothes. I had already given her one of his T-shirts."

"I see. You listened to one fabrication after the other. She probably also told you to come back with more money!"

Lucio opened his eyes wide, a small laugh shaking his shoulders.

"Yes, but what can I say? One grasps at straws when there is nothing else to hang on to. And I'd done all the searching that could be done." Father Paul kept quiet, and Lucio continued, "So the day after, Filomena told me she could see two Ricks, one good, the other bad." Pearls of perspiration raked Lucio's forehead and Father Paul dried them with a tissue. "You have to know that I hadn't told her that Rick had a twin brother."

"Hmm, she may have read the newspapers and…"

"Will you listen or not?"

"Fine. Go on."

"She confirmed the curse, then added that the bad one would find the de' Vigentini family and attempt to bring harm to the good one."

Father Paul kept silent for a few minutes.

"I understand you and your wife were distraught," he said. "You went outside the Church to find comfort." He quickly pronounced the ritual words of absolution. "Do you feel better now?"

"Yes and no. There is more."

"More?"

"Yes. Much more. You know of Chris being suspected of Lillian's rape, don't you?"

"Yes, Chris told me. But if he's innocent, as he says he is, he has nothing to worry about."

When Lucio talked, his voice wasn't more than a whisper.

"I think Rick is alive. The man who raped Lillian is Rick."

CHAPTER 32

Chris conducted a quick search of his home. He couldn't find anything missing, but he would have to wait for Kathy to return and go through the house more thoroughly. Only she could determine for sure whether any of the silver, knickknacks or décor items was missing.

He looked at the four reproductions of the ancient cups that the lab at Vibratim had recently made. They were nicely tarnished so that they looked antique. Making the replicas had been Glen's idea. If somebody asked to see what kind of cups were used in the Middle Ages, the facsimile would be more than adequate, provided the reproduction was accurate. Chris wrapped them in a plastic bag and set them in his mother's old hope chest.

The sound of an approaching vehicle with a noisy muffler invaded the quiet of his house. He wondered who could be arriving that early in the morning: it was only seven o'clock. He glanced out through the window. He couldn't be mistaken: it had to be Father Paul. Only Father Paul would drive such an old, battered car. He descended to the main floor and opened the door before the priest was out of the car.

"Coming to share breakfast with me, Father?" Chris asked.

"I wouldn't mind. The novice in charge of our kitchen doesn't even know how to fry an egg, not to mention baking. Yes, I'd definitely like to have breakfast with you, son."

Chris stood sideways and let Father Paul enter.

"Keep going. The kitchen is at your right, third door." He followed him and gestured that he should sit at the table. "Coffee, scrambled eggs and toasted raisin bread sound okay?"

"Sounds terrific."

Seemingly from nowhere Gideon showed up and gave the priest a critical look.

"I just came back from a walk with Bertha. Everything okay with you, Mr. Sandcroft?"

"Yes, thank you, Gideon."

Gideon glanced at the table, set two plates on it together with a creamer and the sugar. Then he poured two glasses of orange juice and stood there, almost on guard.

"You can go, Gideon. Father Paul is a friend. Don't worry."

"I'll be outside if you need me." He turned toward Father Paul. "Have a nice day, Father."

"Thank you. The same to you, Gideon."

As Gideon left, Chris turned to Father Paul.

"After what happened, Gideon is checking on the house and me, with one excuse or another, and since his wife can't work until next week he does most of the chores."

"I see." Father Paul shifted in his chair, put cream and sugar into his coffee and stirred it slowly. "Yesterday afternoon I was at the hospital to see your father." He paused and drank some coffee, then looked intently at Chris. "Your father told me something I need to check with you."

"Be my guest. I've nothing to hide."

"Did you have a brother?" As Chris' bread slice lingered in the air, he added, "A twin brother?"

"Yes, yes, I did, but it's a big secret, at least as far as Lucio is concerned. He doesn't want him mentioned—ever. I'm surprised he talked to you about him. His name was Rick; he died when he was five. He drowned, I was told, but I never got a grasp of what actually happened. I feel there is much more to it." Chris rested the untouched slice of bread on his plate, focusing his attention on the priest. "You know, there was a big mystery in my family, something my parents didn't want me to know. After my mother died and I went to spend my summer holidays at the Red Manor, my father didn't want me to call him dad or father, as if he was unworthy of that name. Can you imagine anything more strange? Like abdicating from a status. And the relationship between my mother and my father was a foggy area. Apparently they loved each other, but then why split? My mother was no better than Lucio. She never said a word about her life at the manor."

"You never asked your father?"

"I tried, several times, but Lucio would close up like a clam, going into a mute spell or changing the subject. That topic was taboo. I learned to accept that. I know Lucio loves and trusts me, and that's enough."

"And why did he come to stay with you at such a late stage of his life?"

"After he had a stroke I went to see him. He could still manage his affairs, but he couldn't move around. There was no elevator in the castle, and the hired help was no help at all. The old folks were unable to help him effectively, and the young folks didn't give a damn. Excuse my expression, Father, but that's only an understatement of what was pure and simple abuse." Chris stared into the distance. "I gave the situation serious thought, and then asked Lucio if he wanted to come to Canada and stay with me. You should have seen how happy he was. I couldn't believe it. At first he asked me whether I was serious, whether he wouldn't be much trouble, things like that. When I assured him that my offer was real, he called his lawyer and put the sale of the castle into action."

"It must have taken time," Father Paul said.

"Three months total—less than the time it took me to get the papers ready and sponsor him into the country. He came with 30 million euros and insisted on depositing them in a joint account." Chris paused. "He had already invested about the same amount in my company after my grandfather died. I never asked for anything. That tells you something about Lucio's personality, and his reluctance to be in the spotlight."

For a while there was silence, interrupted only by Bertha's joyful barking coming from the outside. Father Paul broke the silence.

"There is more...something you may not be aware of. Yesterday your father told me he believes your brother is alive."

"Alive?" Chris shifted in his chair. "And doing what? Where?"

"Around here." As Chris stared at him, Father Paul muttered, "It may not be true. Do you think your father may have invented something like that to...to—" He stopped, uncertain.

"To exonerate me from the accusation of rape? Is that what you mean?" Only the tone of Chris' voice betrayed the hurt he felt inside. As Father Paul didn't react, Chris shook his head. "No. Lucio wouldn't do that...for several reasons, but mainly because he knows I would never do anything of the sort. And he believes in my word. If I say I didn't, that is enough for him."

Father Paul looked at Chris with sincere admiration. He buttered his slice of raisin bread and savoured it. "So it could be a fib only if your father's mind is out of whack?"

Chris nodded and sipped his orange juice. "I'm curious about this story. Very curious. Did you gather anything else?"

"Yes, that your twin brother, Rick, may have been lost at sea and picked up by some unscrupulous people. You were sick in bed at the time and your mother didn't want your father to take Rick with him aboard his yacht." Father gave Chris a teasing look. "You were both pesky kids, apparently." Chris made a condescending gesture and Father Paul continued. "Your mother never forgave Lucio for failing to supervise the boy. She left him because of that."

Chris sighed. "My mother, as I remember her, was always sad. She never opened any letters that came from the Red Manor, never accepted a call from my father. She never laughed, and hardly ever smiled. She ambled through the house like a robot, took care of the household but seldom went out. She never joined Grandpa and I when we went to Marineland or Disney World. My grandfather wanted her to get help, but she always refused. I played more with my grandfather than with her. At nighttime, when she tucked me in, she'd hug me so tight I couldn't breathe. She never talked about my brother. Not one single word."

"We'll have to do more digging." Father Paul looked at his wristwatch. "Some other time, though. I have to be going. Be careful when you talk to your father. Yesterday, after he opened up to me he got sick. The doctor issued a strict order of no stress." He rose and Chris motioned to do the same. "Don't get up, please. I know the way. Eat your breakfast."

CHAPTER 33

Harrisville, November 2005

As soon as he entered his motel room Nozemni took the chalk-stripe suit he had picked up from the dry cleaners out of the plastic bag and hung it in the closet next to the other one. Even if the fabric was not of the same quality, the two suits looked quite alike.

He then sat on the bed and placed a call to the Lubarda Hotel. Having worked there for two years, he had no problem talking with somebody who knew him well and was ready to do him a favour. He left a message and asked the desk clerk to forward it to the dwarf as soon as possible.

Two hours later Poitr Radic was on the phone, his tone worried and hurried.

"What's so urgent?" he asked. "You know Helena and I still have to hide. Not only the police but also strangers were in town asking questions about Mirko. The police have questioned the dwarf. Hurry up and come back. It's getting more dangerous by the hour."

"Hold your horses. We cleaned up on all of Mirko's money—all the money we knew of, of course—but as I told you before, there's very little left for us. Something came up that could make us a bundle. Chagrain and I have been working on it. Actually we already gave it a try, but things didn't work out. But before we give it another go, I need more information."

"You know everything I know!" Poitr said. "There's nothing more I can tell you."

"Yes, there is. I want to know how you got Mirko."

"Mirko? He's my own son."

"Don't give me that bullshit! I know enough to realize Mirko was kidnapped." There was silence on the line, and Nozemni pushed ahead. "I want to know where you got him and when."

165

"Why do you want to know?"

"A very important reason. It may be very dangerous to walk around with his ID in my pocket."

"And why?"

"Later, Poitr. I may tell you about that later. Now, the date and location where you got Mirko. And the names of everybody else involved."

"Will you cut me in the new deal? I want $20,000. I was the one who came up with the gold, after all. The new look you got—it's all because I gave you the money."

"Five. I'll give you ten. Now talk or you get the police knocking at your door."

"Mirko—I don't know his real name—was washed ashore on a rubber boat. He was sick, with sunburns on his face, arms and feet. Two fishermen rescued him; they lived in a village close to where our gypsy camp was. I got wind of the situation and went there. The boy was in shock. He mumbled in English and Italian, only a few words, but that was enough to convince me I could train him to approach the tourists." Poitr's voice became almost inaudible.

"Not enough. Where was he found? And speak louder, I can hardly hear you."

"I can't talk loud. There're people working around here. The Lubarda Hotel kicked me out. I can't use their pay phone anymore." He paused. "The rubber boat was found about 50 kilometres north of Dubrovnik."

"You don't know his real name?"

"No. The boy muttered, but he didn't speak. We couldn't even grasp what his real name was. We still don't know."

"Why do I feel you're not telling me the whole story? They must have searched for the boy. Speak up."

"I think so, but at that time we were moving very quickly from one place to another. Later on I heard they were inquiring about an Italian boy, but by then I could do nothing. They'd have accused me of kidnapping."

"Did he have family? Brothers?"

"I don't know. I really don't know, Nozemni. You have to believe me." A whistle signalled that the call was paid for only a few remaining seconds.

"Okay. That's all for now," Nozemni said, but the line had already been cut off.

*   *   *

The CN Tower restaurant revolved slowly, letting the patrons admire the traffic on Toronto Island. Small planes landed and others took off, circling in the sky before disappearing in different directions. Nozemni and Jim Chagrain had chosen a table away from the few other guests. It was too late for lunch and too early for supper. They indulged in their second Bloody Marys and waited to order a meal.

"This is our last meeting in public, do you understand?" Nozemni said with an authoritative tone.

"Nobody knows you. This is Toronto. Over two million people live here. Don't you know that?"

"We shouldn't be seen together; it's dangerous."

Chagrain shrugged. "I just wanted a fancy meal in a fancy restaurant. Your place is a dump."

"The motel is a temporary arrangement."

"That's what you said two weeks ago. Did you bring what I asked? I'd like to have another look at those things you call cups. To me they look like bowls."

Nozemni slid a piece of paper toward Jim. "This is a picture cut out of the Harrisville Dispatch. It's the best I could find."

After a careful look, Chagrain pocketed the piece of paper. "Before we talk any further, I want to know *exactly* what went wrong last Sunday when I took you to the Sandcroft house."

"How many times do I have to tell you?" Nozemni banged his fist on the table. "Somebody came into the house while I was still searching. I had to run."

"But in the meantime you had time to change clothes. Explain, damnit!"

Nozemni hesitated. "Mine got dirty with oil when I searched the basement. There were boxes there, so I moved them around and opened them, and I spilled a can of Pennzoil; that's what happened. I went upstairs and found a closet, changed, and put my dirty clothes in the garbage bag you saw me carrying." He paused to sip his cocktail. "We have to case the place better than we did last time. Who comes, who goes, when, how many times. Everything has to be recorded precisely."

Chagrain rolled his eyes. "Hmm, and you don't have a clue where the cups could be?"

"No. They weren't in the basement. Not last Sunday, at least. You can exclude the first floor too. I searched every corner and every piece of furniture on that floor."

There was something Nozemni wasn't telling him, and it was important to know what problems he had encountered, if it was his turn to break in.

"It's easy to enter the house with one excuse or another," Chagrain said. "But searching? You speak of 8,000 square feet."

"Only half that. The second floor and the guest's quarters. There is a mansard with a mini-apartment carved in."

"But there are people in and out all the time. Why don't you go there once more? At least you're familiar with the layout; I'm not."

"I can't. Surely not now. The person who came in may recognize me." Nozemni leaned toward Chagrain and bore his eyes into him. "That's all."

"You haven't told me the entire story," Chagrain said.

Nozemni threw the white napkin to the table, hitting his glass. Red liquid spilled onto the immaculate tablecloth. "Enough whining."

"Calm down. I have to know as much as possible. And I want to know why you aren't interested in the gems."

"What are you? Crazy? They're at the jewellery store. I wouldn't dare get close to it. You wouldn't either. It has the newest and fanciest security system, made by SL, the Silent Guardian. My Howler wouldn't work on it."

"What about the one at the house? Did you have any problems with it?"

"No. There was one, but it wasn't on. I just walked in through the patio door. It was ajar."

"I see."

Chagrain was not satisfied with Nozemni's answers. The more they talked, the more the operation appeared cumbersome. He kept quiet. He felt like refusing to go along, but unfortunately his best client had heard of the four cups and had offered him a nice half-million. He had to get them, and once he did, he would get rid of Nozemni. He was becoming a nuisance.

Nozemni exploded. "Now, are you going to do it or not?" he asked.

"Okay, okay, I'll do it."

"Good. Maybe you should see if the Sandcrofts need a handyman. It'd be a good way to stick around and observe the people who live there and their schedule. Find some excuse to get close, for heaven's sake! Perhaps the maintenance man needs help. By the way, I found out his name: Gideon Wilson."

CHAPTER 34

Once again Jim Chagrain focused his binoculars on the Sandcroft residence. On the pad on his lap he had recorded a list of the people he saw coming in and going out. He needed to find a way to spend a few hours inside the place. What he believed to be the maintenance man resided in a cottage 300 metres away from the main house. He fiddled around the Sandcroft house without a schedule, his duties apparently varied and unpredictable. At the moment—it was nine o'clock in the morning—he was standing in front of the fountain, refilling the birdfeeders. The only person with fairly regular habits was the owner, Chris Sandcroft. He left around 7:30 and was back by suppertime. But what puzzled him the most was the absence of the older man. Where was he? Cooped up in the house? Last time, when he had run the first surveillance, he was in a wheelchair, exploring his surroundings. Chagrain wouldn't be surprised if he had a gun hidden in one of the bags underneath the chair armrests. Now there was no sign of him. If he was in the house, no way would Chagrain attempt to break in.

A cleaning company van had stopped by the house yesterday, so he assumed they would be back at the same time next week.

He had hoped the weekend would be quiet. Instead, the Sandcrofts had a sort of meeting, with three cars parked in the driveway and people coming and going.

How could he ever find those stupid cups? Snatching them would be a breeze once he got an idea where to look. He refocused the binoculars on the house, hoping to spot places that needed repairs. Maybe some shingles were missing or the shutters were discoloured. Maybe the driveway's pavement required resurfacing. He looked and panned. From where he hid, however, halfway in the middle of the thick cedar hedge surrounding the property, he couldn't see a single spot of the Sandcroft house that required urgent repair work. Playing a construction man was not going to work.

After all, Nozemni could be right: to conduct a fruitful surveillance, he needed to be hired by the Sandcrofts in one capacity or another.

Time for action, he thought. He left his post and drove home. He placed a call to Gideon Wilson, offering his services. He changed clothes, got his previous work references, mostly false, and drove toward the cottage house at the end of the Sandcroft property. He banged the brass handle against the door a couple of times. Before long, he heard steps coming to the door.

"Who is it?"

"Jim Chagrain. I'm the handyman who just called you."

"Come in."

A woman was sitting on a sofa watching television. "Sorry," Chagrain said with a contrite voice. "I didn't mean to disturb you."

Gideon invited him in. "It's okay. We're the Wilsons: Kathy and Gideon. So tell me about yourself."

"Not much to tell. I'm out of work. I heard, but maybe I'm wrong, that there's a job available here. I'm interested in knowing what it is." Outside, under a protective roof, he had seen a tractor, a lawn mower and a one-ton truck. "I'm a good mechanic too."

"Hmm, I take care of all the repairs normally, but I've been very busy lately since my wife has been in physiotherapy." He paused and gave Kathy an affectionate look. "She still has to take it easy for another couple of weeks. That is why I'd be interested in getting some help, as I told you on the phone." He turned to Chagrain and seemed to assess him. "Sit down. What did you say your name was?"

"Jim...Jim Chagrain."

"How come you're out of work?"

"I've just been laid off. I worked at an RV factory in North York, The Busy Beaver. They let everybody go. Not enough new orders for campers. The lot's full, more than enough for next summer." He smiled at Kathy, who was watching him carefully.

"Hmm...in general this is the time I overhaul all the equipment so it's in order for the spring, but I've had no time do to anything this fall." He paused. "Tell you what: if you leave me some references, I'll take them to the owner and see what he thinks about getting some extra help. This is his place. We just live here. Maybe you can work on the equipment, so I can spend more time around the Sandcroft house."

That was not what Chagrain wanted, but it could be a way to get closer to the cups. "Great," he said, and extracted from his pocket a few crumbled sheets. "Here they are. My phone number is written on the top page." He forced a friendly smile. "Hope to hear from you soon." He tipped his baseball cap and jogged off.

*   *   *

Nozemni was growing impatient. He needed to get at the cups, be present when Chagrain sold them to his customer, receive his share of the money and disappear. He could feel the heat mounting despite the newspapers had reported that a sexual assault had occurred in Harrisville but had omitted the names. The police hadn't disclosed any details to protect the innocent. The acting chief of police, who had been sent expeditiously from the Ontario Provincial Police to Harrisville, had taken over the investigation. He had declared that he needed a couple of days to collect all the relevant facts. Initially there were two suspects, he had said, but new evidence had emerged that pointed to a third person, not yet identified.

Hoping to get good news about the cups, Nozemni called Chagrain and asked him for an update on his surveillance of the Sandcroft place.

"Got a three-day job for overhauling equipment: a tractor, a small and a big lawn mower, and an edger. An outdoor job, they told me. They spelled out they don't want me to enter the cottage or the main house. They were very suspicious, but they needed help. So I started this morning." Chagrain emitted a long-suffering sigh. "I got my hands and the coveralls all dirty. When I came home I had to spend an hour in the shower and I still smell of oil and grease. What a job!"

"So—"

"Gideon, the maintenance man, wasn't around or he'd discover I know zilch about mechanics."

"So get to the point. What did you find out?"

"Nothing good. The man in the wheelchair is in the hospital—so no problems with him—but the housekeeper, Kathy Wilson, the wife of the man who hired me, will start to work again at the Sandcroft residence on Monday."

"Shit. The weekend is out of the question—too many people—and today is already Tuesday."

"I know. We have to move on Friday night at the latest. It's our best choice. Actually it's our only possibility, since we need time to get ready."

"Friday night then. I'll take you there and wait for you." Nozemni paused. "Another problem popped up, Jim. I need a passport."

"A passport? For what? You have Mirko Grogan's. It's still valid for a few weeks."

"Yes, I know, but just in case, I want a Croatian passport with my real name on it, Nozemni Radic."

"It's going to cost you since it must be computer readable." Chagrain paused for a few seconds. "Probably a couple thousand."

"Two thousand dollars? That's crazy!"

"I have to depend on other people. I don't do it myself."

Nozemni pondered his predicament. If he had to flee the country in a hurry, he would need that piece of paper.

"Okay. Order it," he said.

CHAPTER 35

Ethan McClosky had tried everything to avoid serving his new assignment. Yesterday he had called in sick, hoping somebody else would do his work. But the acting chief at the station, Terrence Villard, an annoying and arrogant young man just out of the Police Academy, had waited for him to come back. *Why are people with no experience and no seniority given the authority to boss around qualified people like me? What's the world coming to?* McClosky thought.

Villard had left him no choice. He had waved the five-page complaint that Jerome Weldon had filed against the station.

"Remember," Villard had said. "No siren and no speeding. You aren't in a hot pursuit. You're just going to deliver a message...*my* message."

Villard had typed what he had to say and had also given him a piece of paper with his instructions, as if he were the village idiot. *If it weren't for the good pension I'll get at the end of my service I'd change jobs. The police department isn't run well; that's why there's so much crime. And to think I had to call ahead to find out when this hot shot Mr. Sandcroft was going to be home so I could fit my visit into his schedule. Unheard of. And all because of that lawyer Weldon stirring up problems at the station, complaining about how I had conducted the interrogation. Weldon probably invented this phantom third suspect they're talking about. Lawyers like to muddy the water to collect a big fee.*

McClosky stomped to his cruiser, stepped inside and slammed the door.

He was still grumbling when he passed through the Sandcroft's archway. He parked the car close to the main entry and rang the bell. A furious barking was the first response. Then Chris Sandcroft, holding the dog by the collar, bade him come in. He didn't want to enter because the dog had a mean look and kept growling. Finally he slithered in and waited for Sandcroft to close the door behind him.

"Be good, Bertha," Sandcroft said, "Sit." He pointed to the floor. The dog sat. "Stay."

McClosky passed through a second door and stopped, speechless. The marble floor, green with white and black venations, was as shiny as if it had been polished that very same morning. A huge skylight brightened the entire room. The stairway, to the left, had an ornate wood railing. Two antique chairs and a console, to the right, gave the entrance hall the final touch of class. *These people have money; that's why they're treated so special.*

"What's the reason for your visit?" Chris asked.

McClosky took off his hat and glanced at the sheet his boss had given him.

"The officer currently in charge of the investigation of Ms. Carrigan's assault wants you to know—" He stopped and cleared his throat. This was harder than he had anticipated. "He wants you to know—"

"Yes?"

"That you aren't a suspect anymore." He felt like hightailing it out of there, but the instructions were precise. He had to continue. "The PCR test was negative."

"Of course," Chris said.

"When Ms. Carrigan was taken to the hospital she was mumbling inco…incohe…rently. Later she made a formal statement, saying that her assailant *looked* like Mr. Sandcroft, but that she was sure he wasn't him."

"Good. I knew there'd been a mistake."

McClosky stared at Sandcroft. The man was arrogant. He'd better get out quickly. He opened the door behind him and was ready to go when Bertha sunk her teeth into his pants. He tried to shake her off but Bertha stuck to his uniform trousers until he reached the car door. He opened it as fast as he could and dove into his cruiser.

From the front door Chris watched the scene, and only after McClosky had left, did he whistle to call Bertha back. He didn't feel proud of himself when he realized that he'd fully enjoyed the scene.

He was ready to re-enter the house when the shriek of brakes startled him. He waited outside to see who was coming. A Lexus approached the house, slowed down and stopped.

Vivian got out of the car.

"Can you believe it?" she said. "That police cruiser almost hit me. It was driving in the middle of the road. I had to brake hard and swerve to avoid it."

Chris held her in his arms. "I believe it. It was McClosky, sent over to offer some kind of apology on behalf of the station. It was the condition Jeremy Weldon had posed in order to withdraw the complain." He put a hand on her chest. "I can feel your heart, racing. Come, love. Come inside and let me take care of you."

*   *   *

They were lying on the white-and-gold striped chesterfield, oblivious of the outside world. Bertha, in the hallway, kept whining. When people were home, she didn't like to be shut out from the centre of action. Chris rose and let her enter the family room. She vigorously wagged her tail, then squatted on her haunches, waiting for a good petting.

Chris kneaded Bertha's ears while addressing Vivian. "So your father went back to Scotland alone? Your mother stayed here?"

"Yes. Father gave her some homework. She has to type two articles, one about the cups and another about our shop in Edinburgh. My father thinks he can increase sales significantly, both directly and through the Internet. He says one has to exploit the momentum created by the show."

Chris laughed. "He tried to get my lab to go into full production of replicas. I told him he'd have to find a specialized company."

"I know." She turned to face him. "Any agenda for tonight?"

"What about going out? They just opened a new nightclub, *Le Montmartre*—good wine and good music."

"Great," Vivian rose. "Just give me an hour to clean up and get ready."

"Take your time. I'm going for a walk with Bertha."

CHAPTER 36

Hidden behind the fountain, Jim Chagrain listened to Chris' and Vivian's conversation. The reception was poor because the spying device he had attached underneath Bertha's collar was only a short-range transmitter. It was good enough, however, to let him grasp most of the words.

In the afternoon, while he was changing the oil in the lawn mower, he had a lucky break. Gideon had joined him to give Bertha a bath and had tossed Bertha's collar onto the ground close to him. Chagrain had quickly gone to his car and grabbed the transmitter. Bertha's bath turned out to be a lengthy enterprise, as the dog kept trying to sneak out of the old tub Gideon had set in the backyard. Water splashed all over as Gideon poured liquid soap on her back and then started brushing her. Chagrain had plenty of time to attach the spying chip underneath the collar. He had then offered to help with the drying and put the collar around Bertha's neck.

Now Chagrain, crouched behind the fountain, was impatient to move into action. *So the lovebirds are getting out of the house and the Wilsons have their noses stuck to the TV. The timing couldn't be better.* When he saw the Camaro back out of the garage he called Nozemni, who was parked in the bushes half a kilometre away.

"I'm going in," he said.

"What about the dog?" Nozemni asked.

"She should be asleep by now, with that juicy piece of meat I seasoned for her. It's the alarm system I'm worried about. I'm planning to enter through the window in the mansard. My guess is that the pane isn't wired to trigger the alarm. I measured my portable stepladder. I should make it up there without any trouble."

"I'll be ready."

"Great. If you hear the alarm go off, come immediately to get me. *Immediately.*"

"Got it."

As the rear lights of the Camaro disappeared in the darkness Chagrain moved out of his hideout, wearing a tool belt and carrying a toolbox and a folding stepladder. He drew near the wall underneath the mansard, unfolded the ladder to its full extension and positioned it against the brick wall. In no time he was in front of the guest room. He removed the outside screen and tugged at the window. No alarm sounded. He tried to force the window open, hoping the mechanism that blocked it shut would give. It didn't. From his belt he extracted a penlight, a suction cup and a glass cutter. He set the suction cup onto the windowpane and traced a disk around it. Then he tapped on the glass to free the disk from the pane. He extended his hand inside and unlocked the window.

He had succeeded in penetrating the house. He sighed with relief.

The metal detector didn't reveal the presence of any metal, but as he had no previous experience with the device, Chagrain didn't trust it completely. He began a search of the guest room, starting with a closet that occupied an entire wall. He moved the clothes aside and peered behind and underneath them. No cups. Moving to the stand-alone cabinet located in a corner, he opened it and pawed its contents. Only linen and bed sheets. He quickly checked under the bed and in the small bathroom, and then descended one floor. From the landing he entered a corridor with several doors. He temporarily skipped over any small rooms and marched directly into the master bedroom. The detector blinked. Immediately Chagrain circled his penlight. A silver basso-rilievo, representing a Madonna with Child, was responsible for the detector's reaction. He neared it and quickly appraised its value. *I should take it; it could bring in a few extra dollars,* he thought. But first he had to get the cups because his buyer was growing impatient. He peered into the walk-in closet. Nothing there. He opened the only big drawer of the triple dresser and then looked under the bed. No cups.

He started when the house phone rang. *Are the people living here deaf?* The message was soon redirected to a voice mail.

His heart still pounding, Chagrain slowly moved around until he almost stumbled on the threshold of a big room. The detector began blinking again, so he stepped inside. There was only casual furniture: a rocking chair, an old desk, a huge floor lamp and a sofa. He glanced around and was stunned by the number of pictures hanging on the walls. It was like an art gallery. Then he noticed a chest lying under the bay window. Guided by the detector, he rushed there and opened it. Bingo! Inside a bag, he found the four cups, wrapped in tissue paper and neatly nested inside each other. He couldn't believe his luck. Satisfied, he glanced at his watch. He had found the treasure in less than 12 minutes. He opened his cell phone.

"Get ready, Nozemni. I'll lower the cups, then I'm going back for a few other items."

"Other stuff? Is it wise?"

"What a question to ask to a thief. You should ask whether it's worthy. And the answer is yes, yes, yes!"

The Buick stopped just underneath the broken window and Chagrain lowered the bag with the cups. He retraced his steps and stopped on the landing to admire a beautiful picture of a smiling woman dressed in black veils. Unfortunately, it was too big to fit through the small window frame and he didn't want to try the main door. Even if he trusted the sleeping drug he had given to the dog, he didn't want to put it to the test. *Better leave that painting alone.* He quickened his steps to the last room, lifted five pictures from the wall and tied them together. In no time he was lowering them into Nozemni's hands.

"Let's go," Nozemni whispered.

"No way! One more!"

Chagrain walked back to the master bedroom. Minutes later he was carrying a picture carefully folded in a towel. He cautiously descended the stepladder and gave it to Nozemni.

"This will bring in big money. It was hanging on the master bedroom wall above the bed. It's a basso-rilievo, all in silver, and it's heavy. I'll bet it weighs at least three kilograms." He climbed into the car. "Let's go. We'll take our treasure to my house and call for a couple of broads to come over. Time to celebrate!"

*   *   *

Toronto

The party at the Go Fridays club was in full swing. A young crowd danced frantically to the hip-hop rhythm. Nozemni was restless, trying to attract the attention of a waitress who moved skilfully among the tables and guests.

"Let's go upstairs, to the rooftop," Chagrain said. "They have a heated swimming pool."

"I didn't come here to swim! I'm staying here until I latch onto one of the girls."

"It's late, Nozemni. Most women who came here to get laid have found what they were looking for."

"What about the waitresses? They bounce around with those enormous boobs and have only a strip of material around their hips. They're advertising."

"They're for looks only. I told you that before we came here. It's part of the show. You're supposed to find yourself a woman who wants you, one who's in the mood. You aren't here to grab one and force yourself onto her. Got it?"

"That's what you said, but I know better."

"Don't get us in trouble, not now that we've gotten our cups and a handful of valuable paintings. We're ready to cash in."

"*Ne seri!* You always want to boss me around." He imitated Chagrain's shrieking voice. "Take a shower…shave…wear this and not that…" He finished his draught beer. "You said you had a couple of broads coming to your house tonight. Instead, zilch!"

"They were busy. I called them after our job was done. It was well past midnight. And don't shout."

Nozemni raised his empty glass and a waitress, dressed in a red top and a white mini-skirt, glided to the table. As he ordered another beer he slightly stroked her behind. The waitress gave him a dirty look and retreated. A quarter of an hour later another waitress approached their table and placed a beer in front of Nozemni. When he caressed her legs, she didn't keep quiet.

"Bastard! Get your hands off me!" She kicked him in the leg.

Her loud cry attracted a big man, his black T-shirt showing massive shoulders and very muscular biceps. From behind he grabbed Nozemni by the shirt collar and lifted him from his seat.

"Out! Now!"

Chagrain was taken by surprise. He hastily set a couple of twenty-dollar bills on the table.

"I'll take care of him, Rocky."

Then he helped the bouncer drag a kicking Nozemni out of the nightclub. Nozemni ended up on the curb outside.

"Why did you help that fucking man?" Nozemni asked. "I wanted to punch him in the face!"

"Yeah, sure. He's one of the bouncers. I know him. He's an ex-wrestler. Your face would have ended up worse than before the surgery. You're an asshole, Nozemni, a big one, too. You look for trouble. Lucky for you I knew Rocky." He moved decisively toward his car. "Get moving or I'll leave you here."

Once in the car Chagrain turned to Nozemni.

"I can't get through to you, can I? I told you, you can't go around touching the girls' bodies. I told you that a thousand times."

"But why do they dress with everything hanging out?"

"That's their business. It's just part of the uniform for their job. Do you promise not to get into trouble anymore?"

As Nozemni didn't answer Chagrain stepped on the brakes, slamming the car to a sudden halt. Nozemni, who hadn't fastened his seat belt, flew against the windshield.

"What are you doing? Trying to kill me?"

"It's tempting, believe me. Now, have you got it?"

"Yes. Just take me to your house."

"Only until we've sold the cups. Then you go your way."

"Not only the cups. I want a percentage on the pictures, too."

"You didn't even want me to take them."

"But I helped you carry them out. And don't forget that you got into the Sandcroft residence on *my* information. I deserve half of the total sale."

CHAPTER 37

Dancing had been fun, but his knees were sore. Chris hadn't danced so much since the last summer he had spent at the Red Manor. He had taken Vivian home, and now all he wanted to do was dive into bed and sleep to his heart's content. When he entered the house Bertha didn't attempt to follow him, so he quickly walked upstairs. On the night table the phone blinked and signalled the number of messages: one. He felt like ignoring it, but it might be a message from Victoria Hospital, where Lucio was still hospitalized. He lifted the receiver and listened to the message. It was from Lucio's Italian lawyer, Arcibaldo Cortesi.

Oh my God! Oh my God! Why in the world didn't Lucio tell me? He knew Salvatore Argento had died. That explained why he was so upset when he went to see Father Paul at the seminary! Chris replayed the message. There was something else, something the lawyer wanted to talk about with Chris. It could be important, the lawyer had added.

Chris looked at his wristwatch. *Maybe it's too early to get an old man like Arcibaldo Cortesi out of bed. I'll get a few hours sleep and then ring him up.* Chris kicked his shoes off and, still fully dressed, lay in bed.

When he woke up in the morning, it was six o'clock. He dialled Arcibaldo Cortesi's number and, after exchanging a few words with the lawyer's wife, he got Arcibaldo on the phone.

"Oh, Chris, what a tragedy, Salvatore Argento is gone. You can't imagine how much we'll miss him. With Salvatore disappears part of the Red Manor's history. The entire village of Boccascura mourns him. I still can't get over the tremendous loss. I can't begin to explain what it means…*una perdita tremenda!*"

Italian people tend to be melodramatic, Chris knew, but Arcibaldo Cortesi had a penchant for tragedy.

"I just learned of Salvatore's departure a few hours ago. Lucio didn't tell me about your previous call; it was the same day he got sick. My father had a heart attack and he's still in the hospital."

"Serious?"

"Fairly. He'll have to take it easy from now on."

"I see." There was a pause. "Hmm. Maybe you should be careful in telling him what I found out just two days ago."

"What did you find out?" *Why doesn't he spell out what he has to say?*

"There was an article in a newspaper asking information about a boat called *Il Maniero Rosso*, the Red Manor."

Chris patiently waited for the lawyer to continue.

"Some months ago—it was summer—they fished a young man out of the sea. He was traumatized from having spent several hours floating in rough waters. He lost his memory—temporary amnesia due to trauma."

"And?"

"The man's name is Mirko, Mirko Siroce. I'd like to ask Lucio whether that name rings a bell."

"I see. I'll ask him when I see him."

"Well, no. No, no, it's better not to." The lawyer paused. "You see, there could be a connection. It could be dangerous to talk to your father in his condition."

"*Signor Cortesi*," Chris said in a firm but kind tone. "*Veniamo al nocciolo della questione.* Please spell out what the problem is."

"Well, the newspaper had a story on Mirko, how they found him, that he couldn't talk for weeks and then that he mentioned the name of a boat, *Il Maniero Rosso.*" Cortesi paused. "You see, there is a *legame di un certo genere,* a link, I feel."

"A link? A link with what? He was mentioning a boat with that name, not a castle. Can you be a bit more explicit or do I have to stay on the phone all day?"

When Cortesi replied, his voice trembled. "*Il Maniero Rosso*—the Red Manor—was also the name of your father's brand new yacht." He paused as if afraid to continue. "It was the yacht from which your brother disappeared."

CHAPTER 38

Near Brindisi, Southern Italy

The picnic table lay under an umbrella pine tree, its branches providing good shade even at midday. Gabriele Anzieri had joined his friend, Dr. Edoardo Santavecchia, in the country house located 40 kilometres inland from Brindisi off Road SS605. At lunchtime, the children's constant chatter, the poodle's insistent whining to claim scraps from the table, and the barking of the German shepherd pursuing a tabby cat in a vicious circle had made it impossible to hold a serious conversation. But it was peaceful now since Fedora, Santavecchia's wife, had taken the kids and dogs for a walk.

"They're still looking into the naval registry for a boat with the name that Mirko is obsessed with," Gabriele said. "These registers are old, not computerized yet, so the search is slow and painstaking."

"Keep them under pressure. Call them every week. The more information we gather, the easier it will be for us to help Mirko. By the way, both Dr. Mariani and I feel we should wait awhile before trying to talk to him about his past. There's been a regression since I hypnotized him last time. He doesn't even want to get up."

"Is it serious?"

"We don't know. He may come around. We just have to be patient." Santavecchia rose. "Let's have a drink. I have some good scotch in the house."

They took the kitchen entrance into the one-floor stucco house. It was a low-ceilinged large room, sparsely furnished, with a big stove in the middle and tarnished pots hanging on one wall. Santavecchia opened a cupboard and, from behind the dishes, rescued a bottle of Grant.

"I forgot to tell you, Dr. Mariani said thank you for picking up Mirko's tab. He was in a tight spot, he said, wanting to help the young man, yet trying to balance the clinic budget." He poured whisky into two tumblers.

Gabriele just wetted his lips with the drink. "I really want to help Mirko. I feel sorry for him. Nobody even came around looking for the poor guy. He must be a very lonely fellow."

Santavecchia nodded and clinked his glass with Gabriele's. "To us, our families and to Mirko's recovery," he said and downed his drink.

Two weeks elapsed before Dr. Santavecchia returned to Brindisi, still very much perplexed and doubtful. *"It's a lost cause, a total waste of time,"* he thought as he reached the Santa Rita clinic. He had hypnotized Mirko three times and all he had gathered was that his name was Mirko Siroce; he loved the sea one moment and hated it the next, and he was scared of big waves. He also kept mentioning a boat called *Il Maniero Rosso*, probably confusing it with his friend's yacht. If Gabriele weren't his dearest friend he would close the case without hesitation. But Gabriele had taken Mirko's situation seriously. He would visit Mirko once more.

When he entered the hospital room the atmosphere was completely different from his previous visits. Dressed in jeans and a sweatshirt and wearing a pair of tasselled loafers, Mirko stood looking out of the window. With the Venetian blinds raised to the top, the afternoon sun brightened the entire room. Dr. Santavecchia was pleasantly surprised. Any change was a good sign. Mirko was reacting to his environment. Santavecchia laid his briefcase on the floor and tried to project a cheerful image.

"Hi, Mirko. You look good. I'll bet you're ready to talk to me."

Mirko turned and nodded as the corners of his lips bent into a smile.

Could this be the day? Will I be able to break through the wall of numbness that had surrounded Mirko for weeks? He took a new tape from his briefcase, installed it into his machine and dictated into it the place, time and date, then the identification of the patient. He gestured to the recliner.

"First of all, make yourself comfortable. I think today you're going to tell me a lot of interesting things, I can feel it." He smiled at Mirko as a sign of encouragement. "Simple things, things that come to your mind. I already know you're Mirko and that you love to be at sea, but not during a storm."

He paused, waiting for a reaction. When it didn't come, he continued. "I understand that, of course. Waves higher than a metre frighten me too."

Silently Mirko sat on the recliner, then stretched out in it.

"Anything else you want to tell me right away?"

Mirko shook his head. They were communicating, even if only at a very low level.

"Would you like to look at my locket again?"

Mirko nodded, and Dr. Santavecchia extracted a yellow locket from his pocket and began swinging it before Mirko's face. "Your feet, they're starting to feel light...very light." He paused. "And now your hands: they feel light, too, as if they don't belong to you."

Mirko didn't respond. He just kept looking at the object swaying in front of him. The session progressed in similar steps for a few minutes.

"Are you ready to remember what happened when the *Rijeka* broke under your feet?" the psychiatrist asked. "You fell into the water, right? It was dark, and there were big waves—"

Mirko jerked, but kept looking at the round-shaped object.

"What did you think at that precise moment?"

Mirko recoiled into himself, and when he spoke his remote voice was that of a frightened child.

"I didn't mean to press on the red button, I swear. I know I shouldn't. It just happened. It hit me, and I went down with it." He jerked again, turning on the opposite side. "Dad! Dad, help me!"

The doctor stopped swinging the locket. "What button, Mirko? What hit you?"

"The one on the left. It releases the lifeboat, the dinghy." Mirko hesitated. "The boat hit me in the face and threw me into the sea." Mirko seemed to be swimming in the water, moving his arms frantically to try to keep his head above the water. He used the present tense to describe something happening right now. "I call...I call, but nobody comes. Nobody hears me."

"And then?" Santavecchia asked. He had to keep Mirko going. His recollection was precise and, of course, very enlightening. "And then?" he repeated.

Some of Mirko's words were garbled. He cried, then said, "I swim...I cry...I call...It's dark. Then a wave makes the dinghy tip over me." Mirko stopped for a moment, his chest shaking with convulsions. "I'm scared…but I grab the rope attached to the boat rim and turn the Zodiac over. I pull myself up…lie in it." Mirko stretched again in the recliner, clearly relieved. He opened his eyes and pointed in front of him. "I see it…*Il Maniero Rosso*…it's far away…all the lights are on…it goes fast, going farther away from me. Nobody, nobody looks for little Riccardo." He began shaking from head to toe.

"Riccardo?" Santavecchia asked, surprised. "Who is Riccardo?" As Mirko kept quiet, Santavecchia asked, "Are you Riccardo?"

Mirko nodded. "Mom calls me Rick." He paused. "My dad is gone…gone away on the boat…My mom is home…both far, far away…I don't see them." Tears ran down his cheeks.

The doctor bent over him and caressed his hair. "Sleep, my child…sleep."

Santavecchia turned off the recorder. He couldn't believe it. Finally he had a lead into what had happened to Mirko Siroce.

The nurse, Daniela, entered the room and quietly placed a Styrofoam cup with black coffee on the over-the-bed table. Santavecchia thanked her with a nod and sipped on the coffee while debating whether to terminate the session. Mirko solved the problem for him.

"No! No!" Mirko thrashed in the recliner. "I don't want to go with you! I want my mom and dad! Go away! *Go away!*" His frightened voice carried a strong tone, and Daniela was right back.

"Do you need anything, doctor?" she whispered.

Santavecchia shook his head. "It's all right," he murmured. "But thanks."

The head of the hospital, Dr. Mariani, entered the room soon afterward. He pressed his hand onto Santavecchia's shoulder.

"What happened?" he whispered.

"The best we could hope for. Mirko has unlocked his frightening memories." He turned to face Mariani. "Mirko almost drowned when he was a kid. He fell from his father's boat and was never reunited with him. His parents never found him, but somebody else did, I guess." He waved the tape he had extracted from the cassette. "It's all here."

CHAPTER 39

As he drove back to his country home, Santavecchia pulled out his cell phone and called Gabriele in Dubrovnik. He left a message for him.

"Great news. Mirko was lost at sea when he was a child. This has created a trauma that he relived when the *Rijeka* sunk. When you come back, go to a library where they keep records of old newspapers…still on microfiche, probably. Search for an accident that occurred about 25 years ago, involving a yacht called *Il Maniero Rosso*. See what you can find."

He hadn't reached home yet when Gabriele called back.

"I knew you'd do it! *I knew!*"

"Not so fast, Gabriele. It's only the beginning. I didn't get a great deal out of him."

"But he'll talk again, right? And he'll tell you more?"

"Maybe, but when I left the hospital they had to give him a sedative. After he snapped out of the hypnosis he became very agitated. We'll have to leave him alone for a while."

"I see. I drew a blank here in Dubrovnik and in the surrounding areas. I'll come back soon and look for the newspapers, as you suggested. I don't remember having seen any news about a kid lost at sea. But of course, I was a teenager at that time."

"Same here."

* * *

"We can't proceed any faster," Dr. Santavecchia told Gabriele a week later. "Mirko or Rick or whoever he is suffers from Delayed Post-Traumatic Stress Disorder. It will take time and a lot of care to help him live a normal life."

188

"I see. But he doesn't need to be hospitalized, right?"

"No, but if we don't want to lose what we've gained so far, he has to see me at least once every two weeks." Seated around an iron table at the little outdoor café of the Bellavista Restaurant, they sipped their vermouths in silence. "And I suggest you don't take him aboard your boat. We need to keep him away from any kind of water."

"That's a problem. I don't have an apartment anymore, and I'd like to take him with me."

Dr. Santavecchia kept quiet and appeared to be thinking it through.

"I'll tell you what," he said. "It's late fall now, and Fedora normally closes our country home. I could ask her if she'd let you stay there for the time being. It's not a luxury accommodation, though."

Gabriele almost jumped out of his seat. "That would be great." From his wallet he pulled 20 euros and deposited them on the table. "Let me know if it works out with Fedora." He rose and waited for his friend to do the same.

"Gabriele?"

"Yes?"

"Don't get your hopes too high. Mirko or Riccardo or whoever he is has an eye on Daniela."

Gabriele replied with a blank look.

"Well, it's just a hunch, you know…but I saw how he reacted every time she popped into his room with one excuse or another."

"I noticed that, too. At first I thought Daniela came in for me—my big ego, you know—but then…well, things became clear when I found her in Mirko's room on her days off." Gabriele sighed. "In any case I want to help the guy, at least until we find out what happened to him. It'll be my good deed for the year."

With a car full of groceries and other everyday necessities, Gabriele drove to Molino di Sant'Anna, where Santavecchias' country house was located. Sean, his skipper, had complained about giving up cruising for a full month, but Gabriele had managed to appease him. "Just one month, for a good cause," he had said, and Sean, though grumbling, had agreed to spend time with him and Mirko in the country house.

Gabriele unloaded his buys and looked for Mirko.

"Behind the house, Captain," Sean called from the side of the house. Sean was doing some repair work on the picket fence. "Last time I checked on him he was in a lounge chair, playing with the cat."

Fortunately the Santavecchias had taken the two dogs with them. The cat could come and go, roaming in peace.

"Did he talk?" Gabriele asked.

"Yes. He asked me if this was my place. He smiled, and walked too, a bit around here. Then he ventured to the neighbour's house, which is quite far away. I could hardly see him from here. He lingered there and then came back."

"I'll go see him. I have some newspapers, two in English. I hope to interest him in some reading."

Gabriele waited a few minutes, then joined Mirko at the back of the house.

"Hi," he said. "Do you enjoy sitting in the sun?"

Mirko assented and kept petting the cat. "It's nice here."

Gabriele dragged a chair over the gravel pavement and sat close to him. He tossed the English newspapers onto the iron table, crossed his legs and opened *La Gazzetta del Mezzogiorno*. That newspaper carried Mirko's story—at least what Santavecchia and he knew about him—and contained a specific call for help. Anybody who knew of a boy lost at sea in the late 70s or of an old vessel named *Il Maniero Rosso* was invited to call the newspaper office. Gabriele, who had been interviewed at length for the article, checked to see whether his words had been transcribed accurately. From the corner of his eye he saw Mirko picking up one of the other newspapers. *Good.* He continued reading.

Silently Mirko exchanged the New York Times for the Toronto Star and leafed through it.

Inconspicuously, Gabriele followed the little movements Mirko made, trying to see whether he was actually reading. *Yes*, he concluded. Mirko had folded the paper in quarters to better focus on the top, left columns.

With a tray in his hand, Sean approached the group and set two rustic mugs on the table.

"Green tea, the only sort I could find." He offered one mug to Mirko, who lowered the newspaper and looked at Sean.

"Tea? No, thanks." He returned to his reading.

Gabriele took the mug. "Great. I love green tea." He grinned and looked at Sean. "Thank you for the impeccable service."

Sean rolled his eyes. "What a qualified skipper has to do to make a living!" He took back the mug Mirko had refused and quickly rounded the corner of the house.

It was then that Gabriele heard a voice, Mirko's voice, saying softly but clearly, "I want to go home."

PART 5

The Pull of the Homeland

CHAPTER 40

Harrisville, end of November 2005

Numb with pain and hurt, Lillian Carrigan entered her little apartment and put her duffle bag in the entrance closet. Her bruises were not yet healed and her shoulder, which had received surgery, still ached. The hurt, however, was not only physical. While in the hospital, her solitary support had come from her former co-workers at the Ministry of Community and Social Services. Not one day had passed without somebody from work visiting her with a flower arrangement, chocolates or candies, or even new nail polish or lipstick of the fall variety. But all that didn't make up for the sad reality: her boyfriend had dumped her. At least that's how she interpreted his reluctance to visit her first at the hospital and later at the rehab centre.

She slid open the glass door of the shower and turned on the taps, revelling in the soothing, warm water. She stepped inside and stayed under the powerful jets a long time. She then dried herself and began styling her hair. This was the first time she'd been able to lift her right arm high enough to do the job. She dressed in a jumpsuit and made herself a cup of tea. With her pocketbook in her hand, she stepped into the living room. There were a number of calls she wanted to make. She knew the police were still looking for her assailant, but she needed more answers than the authorities had given her.

She sat on the couch and reached for the phone lying on the side table. She unwound the cord to extend it to its full length, then leaned against the back of the couch and called the Wilsons.

Kathy answered, and right away they exchanged a few pleasantries.

"This is my second week home," Kathy said. "It feels good to be on your own turf. Don't you feel the same?"

"Yes. You said it right. I feel reborn."

"Gideon and I were planning to visit you at the re-hab centre, but since you're back home, what if we drop by sometime today?"

"That'd be great. I can use some company."

"Tell you what. We'll come around five and bring supper. Let me think: what about a spinach salad, shepherd's pie and brownies? Shepherd's pie is my specialty. Gideon thinks it's the best in the whole country."

"That's kind of you. I'll dig out some wine to go with it." She paused. "Thank you."

Lillian put down the phone and then rang Chris Sandcroft. She wondered why he hadn't found the time for a quick visit—not even a call. She let the phone ring a few times, but didn't leave a message. She wanted to talk to him in person.

In a nook carved out of the kitchen, near the window, a table was set for three, with straw place mats, plates of a rich turquoise colour and a little vase with pink lilies.

Lillian welcomed her guests warmly as Kathy set the dishes she had prepared at home on the table. Dinner proceeded smoothly and Lillian spared no compliments on Kathy's cooking. Supper was almost over when Lillian turned to Gideon.

"I want to thank you again for coming to my rescue that terrible night. I don't know what would've happened to me if you hadn't come."

"It was a strange situation. I did what I could. Everything was normal when I checked the house around eight o'clock. I saw your boyfriend's car parked outside the family room. When I heard you scream later in the night, I came right away. There was light in the den, and your boyfriend's car was gone."

"He'd gone to buy…" She blushed, then continued, "Some stuff. Maybe he left the light on."

"Probably."

"That guy—the rapist—first threw me to the floor. Then, when I tried to scramble away, he hit me. He took off his tie and shoved it into my mouth, then ran me into the bed's footboard. It's solid oak, you know. It hurt like hell. That's how I injured my right shoulder." Lillian paused, distressed.

"After he raped me I tried to get up and run, but he grabbed me by the ankles and began bouncing me around as if he was going to throw me against the wall. The tie he used to gag me got loose and I screamed with all the wind I had in my lungs. But I screamed only one time because he quickly gagged me again." Lillian's face was red, and she fought to hold back her tears.

"I rushed there as fast as I could," Gideon said. "I heard the sound of a car engine and I saw a man leaving the main entrance, but I couldn't describe him to the police."

"But I did. The man was the same height as Mr. Sandcroft and wore Chris' suit—the same one he had on the day he appeared on TV, a chalk-stripe. Even the tie was the same—that silver-looking tie in raw silk Vivian bought him—and he had on Chris' cologne. At first, when he entered my room, I thought it was him. That's why I didn't scream right away."

"That would also explain why Bertha let him go without a hitch." Gideon added, "And that's also why they took Mr. Sandcroft to the police station and kept him there the entire night."

"They did *what?*" Lillian asked.

"They treated him like a suspect," Gideon replied in a low voice.

"But that was absurd. I told the police right away that the rapist looked like Mr. Sandcroft, but that it was *not* him!" Lillian's cheeks were on fire and her hands were trembling. She set her wine glass on the table.

Kathy tapped her on the left shoulder. "Well, the truth came out, even if only weeks later. The chief of the Harrisville police had an accident that night and was taken to the hospital. The police officer who came to the crime scene that Sunday night was...was—"

"An idiot," Gideon cut in. "A plain and simple idiot."

"I see. Mr. Sandcroft must have been terribly upset."

"He was," Kathy said, "but he immediately stated there'd been a mistake. Fortunately, the media reported the crime, but left out the names."

"That explains why I haven't heard from him," Lillian murmured. She rose and filled everybody's cup with coffee.

"That isn't the only reason. I see you don't know the latest. Mr. de' Vigentini had a heart attack."

Lillian jerked forward, holding the coffee pot in mid-air. "Sorry to hear that. How is he now?"

"So-so. He'll come home on Monday. Anyway, Mr. Sandcroft was busy with him, the installation of video cameras to monitor who comes and goes, and ordering a solid fence around the property. He also had little help around the house—just me."

"How do you think that man entered the house?" Lillian asked.

"After you were taken to the hospital I checked all the doors. The patio door was unlocked. I think he just walked in. No alarm and no dog to stop him."

Lillian's face turned red. She turned to Kathy. "Was the man a thief? Was anything missing in the house?"

"Nothing Mr. Sandcroft could see first-hand. But on Monday I'll start to work over there again and I'll go through every room, closet and drawer. I'll also look for the suit you mentioned."

CHAPTER 41

"I feel sorry for Lillian," Kathy said to Gideon on their way home.

"Yeah, a sad story. I think she's lost her job."

"Oh, Chris wouldn't fire her. Not now."

"Well, she had a contract for six months. I doubt Chris would rehire her."

"But she needs to work, and what she was doing for Lucio didn't require physical strength. She has to take it easy for another couple of months, the doctor has told her."

Gideon shook his head. "I know Chris. He's kind and all that, but he's been under terrific pressure since Lucio came to stay. He can cope with only so much. Lillian ended up being a liability instead of a help."

"But it wasn't Lillian's fault that creep raped her."

"No, surely not. But to start with, it wasn't wise to invite her boyfriend in. She has her own apartment for that sort of thing. And she must have been the one who turned off the alarm when her boyfriend left to do some shopping. She expected him back soon, so she didn't bother to turn the alarm back on. It goes on automatically at 10. That's how the creep entered the house undisturbed."

When they reached the Sandcroft property they saw a police cruiser parked in the driveway.

"What the hell?" Gideon said. "I hope it isn't McClosky." He stopped in the driveway. "Go home, dear. I'll go see what the problem is."

Two officers, one with a notepad in his hand, came out of the house as Gideon walked in.

"What happened?" Gideon asked Chris.

Chris threw his hands up. "One problem after another. I've been robbed. They cleaned up on several oils." He waved a list in front of Gideon. "The ones listed here are the items I could see missing. I'll wait for Kathy to come over and see if there are more."

"How did they enter?"

"Through the window of the guest room, the only one that isn't wired to sound the alarm. The cameras that were just installed took some pictures of the thief. He wore a ski mask and gloves so there won't be any fingerprints. There were two of them, judging from the footprints left near the outside wall."

"Any other valuables taken?"

"Six small oils and the silver basso-rilievo of the Madonna that hung above my bed."

"The cups?" Gideon asked.

"Ah! They got the fake ones, not the originals. We fooled them."

"Good," Gideon said. "I'm sorry you've got more troubles. I'll tell Kathy to come over and see if she has to add other items to your list."

"Great."

Gideon was almost outside when Chris called him back.

"Gideon? The paintings that were stolen were all on the second floor. I don't want my father to know about the robbery just yet. He comes back on Monday. For the first couple of days I want him to think everything is back to normal. I'll break the news to him slowly, when I feel he can take it."

"That's wise," Gideon said, and quickened his steps to his house.

"The old cups..." Chris murmured as soon as he was alone. *The thieves were after the antiques. The television show did too much of a good job in advertising them. Well, they didn't get them. In their hands they have four well-made reproductions, but still four fakes. When they try to sell them, they'll have a surprise.*

Chris drove to the hospital and visited Lucio, then continued on to the police station. It was time to exact the credit he had with the Harrisville police department. He knew they owed him one for all the trouble regarding Lillian's assault.

It was past five o'clock when he parked his car in the space reserved for visitors. The two-storey building was brand new, with red brick at the front and a ramp for the handicapped beside the three steps leading to the main door. He entered the station, introduced himself and asked for Terrence Villard. He was told to take a seat, and Chris complied.

The place teemed with people, some in uniform, others in plainclothes. He was surprised to see how busy the station was at such a late hour. He waited only a few minutes.

A man, exuding energy from every cell of his body, approached him, his hand extended. "Mr. Sandcroft, what can I do for you? I'm Terrence Villard, Acting Chief."

"Pleased to meet you, sir." He accepted his hand, noting Villard's firm shake.

"Come to my office. There's too much noise around here."

He escorted Chris to a medium-sized room furnished with a metal desk, three chairs, and computer equipment. A stand with a scanner, a DVD player and a TV set took a full corner of the room. Books and hardcover binders lined one wall and file cabinets lined another. He gestured for Chris to sit in one of the chairs, then took his place in the one closest to him.

"Sorry to hear about the robbery," he said.

"Yeah, seems like it's one thing after another. Anyway, that's what I came to talk to you about. I wonder whether your office could withhold the news of the theft. As I told the officers on the scene, the cups were only a reproduction of the real thing. A friend of mine, who deals with antiques, could help me recover the goods by acting like a buyer and exposing the thieves."

For a moment the room was filled with silence.

"You have to understand, Mr. Sandcroft, that we have a duty to inform the public. We could withhold that information for awhile, but only for a while." He paused. "And how do you plan to recover your valuables? You lost me there."

"Well, I was going to ask you if I could get the list of people suspected of fencing in the Toronto area. I'm sure you've built a thick file over the years."

"That's information we can't divulge," Villard answered.

"I see." Scowling in disappointment, Chris rose.

"Wait," Villard said.

"Yes?"

"I'd like to help you. It's just that—"

"I know…you can't." Chris walked to the door and opened it. He turned around and mumbled, "Thanks for your time." He had not quite reached the front door of the station when an officer called his name.

"Mr. Sandcroft."

"Yes?"

"Come with me, please."

Chris followed him into a big room with a dozen desks. The officer neared one of them and opened a side drawer. He extracted a stack of computer printouts.

"From time to time we fish out our suspects by posting some ads." He gave Chris the papers. "Something like the ones you can find in here. We either use the lost and found section or the section on buying and selling." As Chris took the sheets, the man continued. "If you're successful in setting up a deal or even only establishing a contact, Chief Villard expects you to inform us immediately. Don't act alone. It can be dangerous, as I'm sure you know."

Chris nodded. "I'll let you know if my friend and I decide to go that route, and if so, what the results are." He thanked the officer and strode away.

A half-hour later he was back home, not completely satisfied with what he had obtained from Villard, but not disappointed either. As soon as Glen was back from his trip, he would ask him to advertise his intention to buy antiques.

Now it was time to relax. He entered the family room and reached for his violin, a Quercetani from a famed luthier in Parma. He blew the dust off the instrument and tuned it. When that was done, he sat on a stool and began to play his favourite piece, "Spring," from Vivaldi's Four Seasons.

Chapter 42

"I've got it, I've got it! No need to shout! Nine o'clock, Pearson Airport, short-term parking lot, Terminal 3." Chagrain listened to the person on the other end of the telephone line. "Can you explain again why Mr. De Bruyin didn't call me? I've always dealt with him personally. I don't know you." He listened again. "Hmm, okay, we'll be there. You get the money ready. Remember, twenty-dollar bills or fifties—nothing bigger." There was a pause. "Never mind if it'll take time to count them. There are two of us; we'll split the work." He listened again, longer this time. "Then make it earlier. Eight o'clock. You'll have enough time to catch your plane."

Chagrain closed his cell. "I don't like it. Why did Mr. De Bruyin change the arrangement? He was supposed to pick up the cups at my house, very discreetly. That's what he did in the past." Chagrain tugged on his shirt collar. "I've already had to come down to $400,000 to conclude the deal, and now this!"

"Think he has something up his sleeve?" Nozemni asked.

"I don't know how he made his money—he's filthy rich—but I've never heard anything bad about him."

"Things change."

"Yeah, that's true. So far he's kept everything I sold him. He never tried to make money on it. He couldn't do it, probably, with the price I charged." Chagrain pondered the situation. "They told us that something urgent came up and De Bruyin has to leave earlier. That's fine. But with a commercial flight? De Bruyin has his own plane." Chagrain paused. "We're lucky there's no news of the theft yet."

"So what do you make of his story?"

Chagrain tugged at his collar again. "It sounds risky boarding a commercial plane with the four cups." He went to the desk in the living room, opened the main drawer with a key, and got out a Mauser and a PX4 Beretta. "Better be careful." He fastened the Beretta in the shoulder holster under his coat and tossed the old Mauser C-96 to Nozemni. "For you, just in case. Don't forget the ammo."

Nozemni shook his head. "I don't want any part of this."

"Don't be stupid. If De Bruyin or his men intend to play games, we have to be ready." He looked at his wristwatch. "Time to go. It'll take us at least 45 minutes to get to the airport."

They were just on the road when the low, thick clouds released their burden of water. Rain seemed to come from all angles as the wind whirled, picking up old leaves from the ground and breaking branches from the trees.

"*Ne seri!* Where are all these clouds and rain coming from?" Nozemni asked.

"It's the lake effect. They aren't frozen yet, so when cold air moves over the water, the moisture gets dumped on land. That's why we get heavy precipitation. We're lucky it isn't snow."

Nozemni leaned toward the windshield. "Can you see where we're going?"

"Yes. Don't be a nervous wreck."

An hour later they entered the parking lot of Terminal 3. Chagrain spotted De Bruyin's brown Cadillac and turned his car around so that no manoeuvring would be required when leaving.

"Carry the cups with your left hand," Chagrain said. "At all times keep the right arm free, ready to handle the gun."

He ambled along, scanning the environment in case a quick getaway became necessary. The place was almost deserted and the Cadillac was parked near the exit. A troubled feeling began to settle in Chagrain's stomach as they approached the Cadillac. Chagrain knocked on the tinted passenger side window. The door unlocked. He looked into the car as Nozemni took a seat in the back. There was another man in addition to the driver, and neither was Mr. De Bruyin. Chagrain leaned inside.

"Mr. De Bruyin?" he asked. "Where is he?"

"He had to leave," said the man in front. "He sent us to take care of business. Get in."

Chagrain hesitated. "My friend here has two of the cups. I want to count the money before handing you the other two." He sat in the passenger seat and waited.

"Mr. De Bruyin told me to show you the money when you showed us all *four* cups."

"Yes, but Mr. De Bruyin isn't here, is he? So I can't deal with him. I have to deal with you, and frankly, I don't like you. You can't have the cups before I've counted the money—*all* the money."

The man in the driver seat turned to face his companion, seated in the back. "Show him."

A briefcase sprung open. It had currency on the surface, but the man kept it away from Nozemni's reach.

Chagrain opened the door and looked at Nozemni. "Let's go. These people don't understand English."

"Wait, what's the rush?" the man behind the wheel asked.

"You told your man to show us the money. We want to count it. Split it in half. Toss half the bills onto my seat and the other into my friend's lap."

The man seated at the back didn't move, so Chagrain got out and slammed the passenger door as Nozemni jumped out of the car.

"Run, and take the wheel" Chagrain said, and pulled his gun.

From the Cadillac, now backing up, two shots were fired at the Buick's tires. Nozemni had already put the car in gear and was driving. Chagrain, crouched behind the car and running to match the car's speed, emerged to discharge his gun against the Cadillac.

"Don't stop at the exit!" he said as he dove inside the Buick. "Take down the bar, then rush to the small ramp and stay to the right. We'll be on the 427 in no time."

Nozemni followed instructions. "You don't think they'll follow us?"

"We'll see. Follow the signs for the 401 west. We can go 120 here."

"The speed limit says a hundred."

"Never mind what it says. Keep up the speed."

"Why don't *you* drive?"

Sheets of rain obscured Nozemni's vision in spite of the windshield wipers, which sent a periodic swish through the car.

"Don't be an idiot. We can't exchange places right now."

They hadn't been on the road for more than five minutes when the brown Cadillac appeared in the rear-view mirror.

"They're coming up fast," Chagrain said, keeping his head turned to monitor the movements of the pursuing car. "There's an exit coming up soon—Highway 10. Go for it, but don't put on the blinker. It must come as a surprise to them. Move to the right only at the last moment."

"I've never done anything like that."

"Time you learn. When I say *go*, swing to the right and exit down the ramp." Minutes full of tension ticked by and Chagrain said, "I don't see the car anymore. Too much rain. Good thing is, they can't see us either."

"Highway 10 coming up," Nozemni said, his voice trembling.

"Don't move. Not yet." Fifteen seconds elapsed. "Go! Now!" Chagrain said.

Nozemni negotiated the rapid change of lane and the branching-off skilfully. As they exited the 401, the brown car continued west.

"We made it," Chagrain said.

"What now?"

"Pull over and I'll drive for awhile. We'll go home. I'll call Mr. De Bruyin's main residence in California to see whether I get an answer. Something went wrong. Hopefully we'll find out what."

From a distance Chagrain spotted a flashlight zigzagging through the main floor of his house. He turned off the car lights and stopped.

"What's the problem?" Nozemni asked.

"Somebody's in my house."

"But it isn't possible. We came here at full speed, and they were stranded on Highway 401."

"Have you ever heard of phones? Clearly whoever was in the Cadillac sent a message to some of his friends. They're waiting for us."

"What do we do?"

"We can't call the police—not directly, I mean, with all the merchandise stocked in my house. They'd immediately get suspicious. Let's have a look at their car. I assume it's the one parked on the shoulder under those trees."

"I don't see a car."

"Look more closely. Light is reflecting from the wheel's metal rings. It's barely visible, but it's there."

Chagrain charged out and, flanking the grove of trees, reached the parked car, followed by Nozemni. He tugged at the driver's door. It wasn't locked. He extracted his penlight and circled the interior of the car. The case of a huge automatic rifle lay open on the back seat, and two magazines lay on the passenger's seat.

"Great," Chagrain said. "We've *got* them!"

"How?"

"First we cut their tires." In no time Chagrain pulled a Swiss knife out of his pocket and inflicted a deep cut in each of the four tires. "Let's see what licence plate they've got."

Nozemni followed him around the car. "And then?"

"Simple. I'll call 911 and report a suspicious car parked on the shoulder of the road with slashed tires and weapons inside." He gestured for Nozemni to follow him back to the Buick. "Then we'll draw them out. You just follow me."

He drove for a little stretch and parked the car about 30 metres from the driveway. Chagrain put a tissue over his mouth and placed a call to the police. Then he got out and, followed by Nozemni, hid in the woods flanking the road. He called De Bruyin's Canadian number and let it ring. Finally somebody picked it up.

"This is Chagrain," he said, without waiting to hear a voice from the other side. "I know your men are in my house. I'm parked on the road and I'm going to wait for them. Instruct them to come out without playing any tricks if they don't want any troubles."

Fifteen minutes passed without any movement. Then two shadowy figures came out of the garage's side door, their flashlight pointed intermittently at the road. They looked left and right, then slinked toward Chagrain's Buick.

"Come with me," Chagrain whispered. "We'll reach my house from the back. We'll be inside in no time."

"What if there are others?"

"We'll take care of them, that's all."

Chagrain had just punched in the digits that unlocked the back door when the wail of a police car resounded in the calm of night. "Let's enjoy the scene," he said as he walked toward the front of the house, moving skilfully to avoid the furniture, crates and boxes clogging the place.

The two strangers rushed to their car and turned the engine on. However, there wasn't enough traction to bring the vehicle onto the driving lane. Headlights on, one cruiser stopped in front of their vehicle while another rushed in to position itself behind it.

In a flash, the two men jumped out of their car and took for the woods.

"They can't go far," Chagrain said, and laughed. "There's a steep slope, and then a brook that makes its way through high trees. They won't see it until it's too late. They'll get a cold dip for sure." He turned to Nozemni. "Let's have a drink and turn on the light. We'll play the honest citizens awakened by an unpleasant disturbance."

Thirty minutes later two dripping silhouettes were packed into one of the police cars.

"End of the show," Chagrain said, and closed the drapes. "Now let's see if I can contact De Bruyin and find out what happened."

Chapter 43

Chris couldn't wake up. He felt as if he had just fallen asleep a moment ago. He could hear familiar voices and Bertha's joyful barking but they seemed to come from a great distance. He sensed a commotion, but couldn't tell if it was real or belonged in a dream. Finally, he opened his eyes and glanced at the clock. It was 11 a.m. He walked to the bedroom window, lifted a corner of the heavy velvet curtains and peeked outside.

On top of a scaffold Gideon was finishing adorning the windows of the upper floor with Christmas decorations, while Kathy and Vivian watched from below. *Excellent*, Chris thought as he moved quickly to take a shower. They had anticipated setting up the decorations to welcome Lucio back home. For sure, his father would enjoy seeing them and probably would marvel at the abundance and variety of garlands and lights.

Chris dried himself, dressed in a pair of jeans and a turtleneck sweater, and walked outside.

"Hello everybody," he said, skirting Bertha, who was ready to greet him. "Bertha, you have to wait." Then he approached Vivian. "First I have to hug my girl." He gave Vivian a full embrace and a kiss on the cheek. Then he went to hug Kathy and welcomed her back to the house. Finally he bent to fondle Bertha's ears.

"Sorry we woke you up," Gideon said as he descended from the scaffold. "We're finished now."

"It was about time I got up; it's almost time for lunch. But first let's go around and look at the work of art Gideon has created this year." He took Vivian by the arm and together they drew near the fountain.

"Wait, wait," Gideon said, and rushed to turn on the lights. Ancient lanterns hung from the necks of the four mermaids and spread bright red light.

209

"Kathy and I bought them at the Christmas shop in Frankenmuth. They were on sale and my wife couldn't pass up such a chance."

"They look great. I always thought the bronze fountain looked kind of bare in the winter," Chris said, then moved away, taking Vivian to admire the four pine trees where light bulbs formed colourful spirals through the branches.

"I like those lights on the brick walls," Vivian said as they circled the house.

The top of each door and the first floor windows were decorated with tiny white bulbs that looked like icicles. They stopped in front of the patio door where three deer stood, majestic, each set at a different height.

"These deer light up one after the other," Chris said. "At night one gets the perception of one big buck jumping higher and higher, rushing to disappear into the woods. It's a beautiful show."

"I've never seen anything like that. You must spend a lot of money just for the outside. What do you do inside?"

"Since Grandpa died, not much. A small Christmas tree, normally, that Kathy decorates, but this year I'll set up the crèche Lucio brought from Italy. Little wooden figurines, animals and singing angels, all sculpted by hand." He looked at Vivian. "By the way, are you going to be around at Christmas?"

"I'd love to, but I have to wait and see what my parents want to do."

"Of course." He pulled her close and kissed her on the lips.

Strong applause came from Gideon and Kathy.

"We'll leave you alone," Gideon said. "We'll come back when your father arrives."

Vivian glanced at her watch, then at Chris. "When will we be going to get your father?"

"Two o'clock." Chris caressed her shiny shag and pulled her close, his dark eyes looking intensely at her. "You have a choice: lunch or..."

Vivian giggled. "I'm going to choose the second one, even if I don't know what that is." She took his hand and together they ran into the house.

*   *   *

The homecoming party had been superb, celebrated with Kathy's baking and plenty of bubbling wine. It was seven o'clock in the evening when Father Paul, the last of the guests, got up to leave.

"You really have to go?" Lucio asked.

"Unfortunately, yes," Father Paul replied. "I'll leave you with Chris. I suspect you and your son have a lot of things to talk about." He bent over Lucio. "I'll see you next week." He smiled at him and kept Lucio's hand between his. "Make an effort not to get into much trouble—if at all possible." He dispensed his Christian blessing to father and son and put his hand up to stop Chris from showing him out. Then he bustled off, his firm steps pounding on the carpeted corridor that led to the main door.

With Vivian gone to pick up her father at the airport, Chris sensed that Lucio wasn't at ease being alone with him. There were many, many things to discuss, but they could all wait. He approached Lucio and tapped him on the shoulder.

"What about a movie? I bet TMC is showing one of those oldies you're so fond of. We could watch it together."

Lucio didn't respond right away, his head down. "I have to go back," he finally murmured. "I want to go back to my country. I belong there."

"What did you say?"

"I want to go back to Italy."

For a moment Chris was numbed with hurt. He sat in an armchair opposite Lucio, crossed his legs, leaned back and closed his eyes.

He had surrounded his father with things familiar to him and had been happy when the Howards had stopped by for a short visit. He was even happier when they had decided, later on, to stay for a longer period of time. He had tried to smooth the enormous difference of culture and habits Lucio had to face. Unfortunately, some of the plans he had put in motion or agreed upon, mainly for Lucio's sake, had backfired. The old cups had attracted crime into his own house, and the assault on Lillian had brought hardship to them all. Then—something nobody could foresee or avoid—the fire at the Red Manor, and the death of Salvatore Argento, the last close link his father had with his beloved castle. Clearly, all this had dragged Lucio's morale down.

He remembered the doubts and thoughts that had tormented him the night he spent wandering in the main square of Boccascura, the day before he had taken Lucio to Canada. He kept searching his soul as he realized that the only possibility to take care of his father was to uproot him. His father would have to leave behind people dear to him and things he cherished. He wondered then, and wondered now even more, whether he'd done the right thing. For the first few months the novelty of a new place, his own presence and the affection surrounding Lucio had minimized the losses his father had suffered. It had been a truce, Chris realized, not the permanent overcoming of difficulties. Now, after weeks in the hospital, Lucio had begun to feel the wound created by severing himself from the people and things that had surrounded him all his life.

Chris felt a pang in his heart. Lucio's words contained what he had feared the most that night in Saint Zenobio Square. It was the possibility of Lucio becoming homesick that had tortured him and made him wander for hours, and this same feeling distressed him now.

To steady his heartbeat, Chris took deep breaths and remained silent.

It was Lucio who finally spoke. "I want to go pray on Salvatore's tomb, see what remains of the manor. I want to die there. I'm nothing but trouble to you."

Oh my God! Chris thought as he reopened his eyes. *Things are worse than I suspected.* He tried to read Lucio's body language. He had lost his usual erect posture and was bending forward, looking at the floor. *This is trouble...real trouble.*

He would try an emotional appeal. He rose and knelt close to his father.

"Don't I mean anything to you? You waited so long to be part of my life, and so did I. Now we're here, together. Why do you want to change all that?"

Lucio's eyes were moist. "So many things came to my mind. All the things I did wrong in my life. I bring bad luck, and then there is the old curse—"

"The curse? I never thought you could believe in that lie after so many centuries."

"I never believed in it, it's true. When I was young I kidded everybody who mentioned it. I started to consider its veracity when I lost your brother. And then, when you were accused...I thought my other son was still alive and had come to harm you. I couldn't get that thought out of my mind."

"I know that, but everything is fine now. The misunderstanding has been cleared up, totally and completely. Father Paul made a special trip to the hospital to tell you that I'd been cleared only minutes after I was informed. We thought it was important to put your mind at ease. So that part of the so-called curse has been voided, invalidated, totally nullified. Don't you see that?"

Lucio gave him a faraway smile. "Yes, but half of the Red Manor was destroyed. That was also part of the curse."

Chris shrugged. "Only the first floor was damaged. The *Ministero per i Beni e le Attività Culturali* plans to rebuild the castle as it was before. So what's really changed? The prophesy said the manor would be totally destroyed, *raso a zero*, right? There's a big difference." Chris rose and tapped his father's shoulder. "Let's talk about all this tomorrow."

Lucio assented, but only faintly. "Maybe I should retire now. I'm exhausted." Without looking at his son he wheeled out of the family room.

Engulfed in misery, Chris stood motionless, his father's words wafting over him. *Does he really want to return to Boccascura? Who could possibly take care of him? Does he realize he can't go back to the Red Manor, that it's changed hands? Does he realize it would take a massive effort to help him settle in another place, and that it would probably be an institution?* Chris wondered what had triggered Lucio's sudden desire to move back to the old country. Had it been just a recent thought or had it lurked at the back of his mind for some time? *Did I delude myself that my presence would compensate him for what he left behind?*

There was no way he could go to sleep. As many times in his life, Chris knew he could find peace and refuge in his work. He grabbed his coat and went to Vibratim. His incoming tray was probably overflowing with papers.

Chapter 44

Chris returned home early in the morning, satisfied with the productive time he had spent at the lab analyzing a project for reducing the weight and bulk of ULF magnetometers. He would have a couple of hours rest later in the afternoon. He made himself a cup of coffee, grabbed a couple of cookies and walked into the family room, his favourite place in the house. It was still fairly dark, but he opened the blinds. It was then that he saw the lights of an approaching car. *Who would come to visit at such an early hour?*

Vivian got out of the car, Glen at her heels. She waved at him and Chris immediately opened the sliding door, a sudden bracing draft invading the room.

"Come in, come in," he said and welcomed them both. "What a nice surprise. What brings you here?"

"Father has news, and plenty of it. He wanted to tell you right away. We came directly from the airport. His plane had a 12-hour delay. Can you imagine that?"

"I can, I can. I've travelled enough to have experienced every kind of delay."

Vivian shook off her faux fur coat, tossed it on the floor and threw her arms around Chris.

"Easy, easy…people are watching," Glen said, and draped his coat on a chair back. "Hi Chris. I could use a drink. I need to relax. First a long wait at the airport, then poor weather—a lot of bouncing around. They didn't serve any food or drink." He eyed the bar that occupied an entire corner of the room.

"Scotch coming up," Chris said, and let go of Vivian. "And what about you, Vivian?" He pulled out a few bottles from the lacquered cabinet underneath the counter and examined their contents. "There's rye, brandy, a bit of sambuca, grappa, Grand Marnier, Drambuie. What would you like?"

"*Sambuca colla mosca*."

"Sambuca it will be."

Chris poured a scotch for Glen, then took a small glass and emptied the bottle with the anise-flavoured liqueur into it. He sprinkled the drink with four coffee beans, put the glass on a silver coaster with a little spoon, and handed it to Vivian.

She sipped on her drink and chewed on the coffee beans. "I like the bitterness of coffee combined with the sweetness of the anise." She sat on the sofa and adjusted an accent pillow behind her back.

"So how is your Edinburgh store doing?" Chris asked Glen.

"Wonderful. Sales are up. I had to hire two new people just for the shop. My second in command has designed a new web page with pictures of all the items we have in stock. We get orders from all over the world." He paused and took a long swig from his glass. "I'm also trying to buy the rights from Channel 9 so that I can post the digital version of the TV show on my Web site. Then I'll get even more exposure. I already get plenty of emails requesting information about the famous cups. I could sell reproductions as décor items by the dozens."

"I'm glad you're raking in money. At least some good came out of all the commotion created by the cups." Glen was always upbeat, and Chris was glad to have him around. Maybe he'll have a positive influence on Lucio. "You should talk it over with Lucio. If he doesn't mind seeing fakes floating all around, I personally don't care, provided you don't ask my lab to work on it. I'm very, very busy at the moment."

Glen waved off the issue. "I already know of a small shop around here that can do the job." He winked. "I'm always prepared." He slumped into an easy chair and slowly savoured his drink. "You very busy?"

"Oh, yes. I beefed up the security system with more hidden cameras in the house and hired a contractor to build a wall around the property. There will be a gate at the entrance that opens with a transponder or by punching in the right code."

"That'll cost you a fortune," Glen said, circling the glass in his hand.

Chris smiled. "It's only money," he said, waiting for Glen's reaction.

"I know, I know…some people were born rich and never care much about a dollar here or there."

"I see that you don't know the latest." Chris lowered his voice. "I didn't tell Vivian either. The house was burglarized, so fencing the property isn't a luxury anymore. It's a must."

Glen sprang up to sit straight in his chair. "The cups?" His brows arched and his eyes opened wide, betraying just how worried he was.

"The *fake* cups…and a few valuables."

"That famous picture your father loved so much, what's it called? The Model?"

Chris shook his head. "No, only pictures that hung in the big room at the end of the second floor and Raffaello's Madonna, the one in sterling silver above my bed."

"Oh, that's terrible. It was so beautiful," Vivian said. "I've never seen such a beautiful engraving of the Madonna with the Goldfinch."

Chris went to sit close to Vivian and, keeping his voice down, said, "I didn't tell Father about the theft yet." He paused, trying to find the right words. "Yesterday Lucio came home from the hospital. We had a little party for him, as Vivian probably told you. After everybody left he became very upset."

"About what?" Glen asked.

"I don't know exactly what triggered his reaction. He told me he wants to go back to Italy. Visit Salvatore's tomb and die there. Those were almost his exact words."

Glen jumped out of his armchair, spilling what little liquid was still in his tumbler. "What? He must be crazy!"

"Crazy or not, I won't be able to keep him here if he doesn't want to stay."

Glen exchanged a terse look with Vivian. "Then we shouldn't tell him what I got from a friend of mine."

Chris glanced at him. "What's that?"

As he spoke Glen reached into one of his coat pockets and pulled out a newspaper. "There's a young man stranded near Brindisi—you know where that is, right? About 350 kilometres southeast of Boccascura—talking insistently about a yacht called *Il Maniero Rosso*."

Chris nodded. "Lucio's lawyer, Mr. Cortesi, told me about it."

"He did? And you told your father?"

"Not yet. I wanted to know more before arousing old memories in his mind."

Glen opened the newspaper to the middle. "You should read this. It's the story of Mirko Siroce, who was lost at sea when he was a child and was raised in an orphanage near Dubrovnik. A few months ago he was lost at sea again. When they fished him out a day later, he didn't talk and couldn't remember anything. Only a couple of weeks ago he began recovering. He mumbles in Croatian, English and Italian. The author asks for anybody who might remember anything about that yacht to come forward."

Chris hid his face in his hands, shuddering at the implications of what he had just heard.

"Oh God. No. Not now. I won't be able to keep Lucio here if there is even the slightest possibility that this Mirko is his lost son."

Vivian knelt before him and took his wrists in her hands. She shook him. "Chris, Chris. Don't do that."

Chris opened his hands and caressed Vivian's face, sighing deeply. "You know what I feel like doing?" He paused. "I feel like taking off and disappearing into the woods."

"And leaving me?"

Chris forced a tiny smile. "I could take you with me—"

Vivian sat close to him. "That's already better. I understand how you feel, Chris, but you're not alone. We're here to help. First we have to find out what this is all about."

Without a great sense of conviction, Chris nodded.

Glen moved closer to them. "We need a plan. Tomorrow morning we'll call the newspaper. We'll leak a little and try to find out what they know. I can handle the situation, Chris, if you'll let me."

Still distraught, Chris assented.

CHAPTER 45

Glen Howard introduced himself to the switchboard of *La Gazzetta del Mezzogiorno* and asked for Mr. Gino Gavezzani, the reporter who had crafted a feature article on Mirko Siroce. Minutes went by before Gavezzani came to the phone.

"*Parla italiano?*" he asked.

"*Solo un poco,*" Glen answered.

"*Dobbiamo farlo bastare. A me non piace parlare inglese. Veniamo al dunque: cosa ne sa del bambino che naufragò nel '78?*"

"*Mi permetta di spiegare,*" Glen replied. The conversation hadn't started the way he had envisioned, as his Italian was very limited. He wanted to establish an atmosphere of trust and understanding, but Gavezzani didn't seem to give him a chance. "*Quello che mi interessa è il nome dello yacht: Il Maniero Rosso, vero? È da lì—*" He stopped and continued in English. "It's from that yacht that the child, Mirko Siroce, fell into the water, right?"

Gavezzani hesitated. "Yes. But why are you interested in the boat's name?"

The reporter understood English, and he spoke it too. The man either had reasons to be very cautious or he was plain difficult.

"I thought maybe you knew the owner of that boat," Glen said.

"Mr. Howard, listen to me: I'm not here to provide information. To you or anybody else. We ran that story to help Mirko Siroce. If you don't know anything about him, I don't see any reason for talking to you."

"Wait, wait, please. It's just that if the owner's name is what I think it is, this might be a clue to determine who Mirko is." He paused for effect. "Can you put me in contact with somebody who spoke recently with Mirko Siroce?" He waited for an answer that didn't come. "I understand the young man had a temporary memory loss, but that he's coming around with more information every day."

218

"Mister, since you don't have any information about the boy, I'm not interested in talking to you." He clicked off.

Glen was still upset about the conversation with Gavezzani when he, Elisabeth and Vivian met with Chris for supper the following evening.

"You can't believe how rude that reporter was. And he wasn't even interested in finding out the name of *Il Maniero Rosso's* owner. I can't understand it. From a journalistic point of view, a follow-up on Mirko Siroce's story could be a good scoop. Anything that can be added to the first piece should be an asset."

"Maybe he thought you wanted to pump him. Maybe he thought you were a reporter, too," Elisabeth said.

"But I introduced myself."

"That's a minor point. A reporter poses as anybody these days just to find out what he wants to know. They have their tricks."

"That might be true." As Chris had been silent for the entire meal, Glen asked him, "Your father? How was he today?"

"Lucio didn't come out of his room. He only exchanged a few words with Kathy and me. He spent most of the time in bed. He felt tired. On top of a damaged heart, they found out that he has COPD, a lung disease. Lucio was a heavy smoker. He stopped smoking only after he had a stroke."

"Is it serious?" Glen inquired.

"In his condition, it surely is. The lungs don't provide enough oxygen; the heart should pump stronger but it can't—so a person is always short of breath."

When Kathy stepped into the dining room to say goodbye for the day, Chris barely complimented her for the excellent pork roast with potatoes and Brussels sprouts, something unusual for him. He exhaled deeply, raking his fingers through his thick hair.

"What were you saying about the reporter?" he asked Glen. "I lost you there."

"I got nowhere with him. Frustrating."

"Thanks for trying, but don't worry. I think I have something that will enable us to get more information before saying anything to Lucio."

"You do?" Vivian said. "That's great."

Chris nodded. "I went through the Italian newspaper that you left with me and read every line carefully. They mentioned that Mirko Siroce had been hospitalized at the Santa Rita in Brindisi. It so happened that I sold them one of my seismographs—exactly four years ago."

Vivian looked at him, a big smile on her face. "Excellent."

"We sell a lot of our equipment in Italy. As you know, that region is singled out as having a high probability of earthquakes. In general, I go there personally to demonstrate how the equipment should be installed and how to operate it, since I'm the only one at Vibratim who speaks Italian. When I was in Brindisi, the director took me to his home and treated me like a VIP. I think I'll give him a call early tomorrow morning. Maybe he remembers me."

"Oh, that's a major breakthrough," Glen said.

"I wouldn't call it that. But it might work." He paused and pushed his half full dish toward the middle of the table. "Should we all go to see how Lucio is? I'm sure he'll find a bit of energy to smile at Elisabeth." He winked at Glen. "She can get his attention. Never fails."

The Howards left soon afterward because Glen was anxious to prepare a juicy ad for the *Toronto Star*.

Chris watched the CBC National, vaguely following what Peter Mansbridge had to say. He wondered whether he should contact Lillian Carrigan and hire her back. Would it improve the situation or would Lucio just see it as a manoeuvre to pressure him to stay? *Hard to say*, Chris concluded.

And as if he had nothing else to worry about, there was also this story about Mirko Siroce. He should investigate the entire situation carefully and be sure Mirko wasn't an impostor. His father hadn't recovered yet, and a clever impostor could inflict incredible damage to Lucio's emotional status. He toyed with the idea of hiring a PI, but quickly dismissed it. It would be cumbersome to deal with one out of the country.

He yawned. It was time to get some rest. Tonight he would sleep until morning in one long, beneficial stretch. He was sure of that.

CHAPTER 46

It took some time to get connected to Dr. Mariani, but the wait had been worthwhile because the director of the Santa Rita recognized Chris immediately.

Eager to help, Dr. Mariani gave him plenty of information on how and when Mirko Siroce had been rescued. Then, without going into detail, he told Chris how the young man, who had suffered from amnesia for months, was now recovering in a country house as a guest of the man who had rescued him, Gabriele Anzieri.

After an exchange of courtesies Chris was transferred to the clinic switchboard that gave him Anzieri's phone number.

Anzieri answered at the first ring. "Who is it?"

"My name is Chris Sandcroft. Mr. Gabriele Anzieri?"

"This is he."

"I got your phone number from Dr. Mariani." Chris quickly explained the circumstances under which he had met the clinic's director and gave him a brief account of what he was doing for a living.

"I see. I met Dr. Mariani only recently because I often visited one of the patients he was treating at the Santa Rita. What can I do for you?"

Chris hesitated a moment, uncertain of how he should start to tell him about the Red Manor. "I spent my childhood, or part of it, at the Red Manor, *Il Maniero Rosso*, a castle about 350 kilometres northwest of Brindisi. I'm curious to know how the young man mentioned in the article of *La Gazzetta del Mezzogiorno* got hold of that precise name."

"Oh…he kept mentioning it as the name of a boat."

"A boat? He never mentioned a castle called *Il Maniero Rosso*?"

"No. Just the boat."

"Dr. Mariani told me you rescued Mirko Siroce. Did you get to know him well?"

"Not really. He didn't talk at all for weeks, and then, when he finally decided to tell us what happened when he got lost at sea, he told us of a similar experience he had when he was a child. That's how that boat's name surfaced." He paused. "May I ask the reason of your call?"

"Curiosity, mainly. I was also a bit puzzled why there was no picture with the story. Since the paper was looking for information, a photo could have been of help, don't you think?"

"We tried, but Mirko put his hands in front of his face as soon as he spotted the camera. And we didn't want to take his picture without his consent."

"Of course. Mirko is your guest, Dr. Mariani told me. Can I talk to him?"

Gabriele uttered a long, suffered sigh. "Unfortunately not. Yesterday Mirko disappeared. We've searched all over. We have no clue where he might have gone. Even the police are out looking for him."

For a split second Chris was tempted to give Gabriele his phone number, but then changed his mind. The more information people gathered on him and his family, the easier it would be for an impostor to make up a believable profile.

"I'm sorry to hear that," he said. "Thank you very much, Mr. Anzieri. You've been very helpful. I really appreciate you talking to me. I'll keep in touch." He rang off.

CHAPTER 47

Molino di Sant' Anna, Southern Italy

Something was tickling his nose, then one of his ears. In his sleep Mirko tried several times to brush it away. Finally he woke up and looked around, surprised. Where was he? He shook the straw wisps from his face, hair, sweatshirt and jeans, and sat up. Now he remembered.

Yesterday, after having read the *Toronto Star* again—column after column, page after page—he realized how familiar he was with much of the information contained in that newspaper: the Maple Leafs, the Raptors, the Toronto Stock Exchange and the news from Queen's Park, in particular, evoked memories by the dozen. Now he knew where he had been for years, and to where he wanted to return. He needed time to put together his reminiscences; he needed time to get his bearings.

He wanted to be alone with his thoughts, so he'd walked along SS605 and then skirted that road to follow a trail that cut through an old cornfield. He had stopped near an abandoned barn and sat in front of it to admire the sun disappearing behind the hills as the sky tinted from yellow to purple. His recollections were like clouds twisted and dissolved by the wind, each recollection changing shape and intensity as he tried to concentrate on it.

He had spent the evening and part of the night forcing himself to remember everything he could until, surprised by darkness and cold, he had found shelter in the barn.

Mirko rose, stretched, and walked outside to breathe some fresh air. He circled the barn and looked around. He knew the way he had come and would be able to retrace his steps. But before he went back, he wanted to remember more. He wanted to put together the hundreds of fragments that had popped up in his mind for the last week vaguely, and yesterday, forcefully.

He tried to establish a time line, or at least to separate what came earlier from what happened later. What did he remember about his childhood? That he had fallen from a boat and almost drowned. And then? He had spent years in a horrible place with little food, dirt all around and two shady characters shouting and fighting...*It was an orphanage! Radic was their name.* They'd used the strap on the children, even the little ones...*What a dreadful place!* That part was vivid in his memory.

He was doing well, very well. *What do I remember from when I was a teenager?* Slowly, some scenes of the past took form. He had lived in a nice home with two kind people. *The name...the name was...*"Grogan!" he shouted. "Gladys and Gerald Grogan." But that was also his name. *Sure, Mirko Grogan.*

Satisfied so far, Mirko began pacing in front of the barn, at times kicking the rotten cobs left behind by the combine or the dead branches that the wind had recently accumulated. *What happened next?* Yesterday, when he'd looked at the quotations of the Toronto Stock Exchange, some of those tables seemed familiar...*Maybe I was an accountant of some sort, or somebody who took care of the sales.* At the moment he couldn't add anything else.

Then he had been lost at sea and had been rescued by the man who was now hosting him, Gabriele. Those events—the rescue, the hospital stay and the care that Gabriele had given him—these were recent memories, and quite detailed.

Pleased with his achievements, Mirko decided to go back, but as he walked through the cornfield, he became afraid. *Why wasn't I taken to a Canadian consulate? Who is Gabriele, and what's his interest in helping me? Should I trust him or should I try to run away?*

When he reached the main road, he was still uncertain what to do. The problem was that he didn't know his location and he didn't have any documents or money. Whatever the reasons Gabriele had to take him in, he had to go back there, talk to him and find out more.

Mirko was on road SS605 for only a short stretch when a police car stopped near him and lowered the window. "Mirko?" one of the officers called out. "Are you Mirko?"

Puzzled, Mirko stopped and looked at the man. *Why are they looking for me?*

"Mr. Gabriele Anzieri was worried about you. He gave us your description and asked us to keep an eye on this road. We've been looking for you since yesterday. Mirko Siroce, right?"

Mirko nodded, as the name *Siroce* filled another gap in his memory. *Siroce...orphan...I'm an orphan!*

The policeman seated on the passenger's side reached over the seat and opened the back door.

"Hop in and we'll take you to Molino di Sant'Anna; that's where Mr. Anzieri is staying."

Alerted by phone, Gabriele stepped out of the house as the police cruiser stopped in front of the property. He opened the gate in the white picket fence and welcomed Mirko.

"You're cold," he said as he touched Mirko's hands. He quickly thanked the policemen and took Mirko inside.

Sean Despen rose from the kitchen table and extended his hand. "What a scare you gave my boss. He thought you'd had an accident or something like that." He quickly moved to make some coffee.

Mirko smiled. "No need to worry. I'm okay."

"Okay but cold," Gabriele said. "Care for some breakfast?"

Mirko nodded. "Bacon and eggs?"

"Sure. I can fix that in a hurry. Coffee is in the making."

"Good. I'd love a warm cup of coffee."

Gabriele busied himself around the stove.

Mirko hesitated for a few moments then inched up to Gabriele. "I know who I am. I'm Mirko Grogan, from Toronto." He paused. "Yesterday I started to remember a few things about my life, and then more and more. I can't put it all together, not yet, but I think I'll make it with time."

Gabriele turned to look at him. "You said Mirko *Grogan*? I thought your last name was Siroce!"

"No. Siroce was the name the people at the orphanage gave me. It means *orphan*."

The smell of burning bacon called Gabriele back to his chef's duties. He replaced some of the burnt slices with fresh ones. "Are you sure your name is Mirko Grogan?"

"Yes. And if it isn't too much trouble, I'd like to be taken to a Canadian consulate."

Silence reigned in the room, interrupted only by the gurgle of the coffee machine.

Gabriele scooped bacon and eggs onto a plate and laid it on the table near a steaming mug of coffee. "Eat, Mirko." He fetched two pieces of toast and put them on Mirko's plate. "I can take you to any consulate you want." His mouth full, Mirko nodded. "What else do you remember?"

"Snapshots of my life: that I was in an orphanage with abusive people; that somehow a nice couple took me to Canada; that I worked there—I kept the books for a grocery store."

"How did you end up on that decrepit boat, the *Rijeka*?"

Mirko arched his eyebrows. "I don't know yet." He smiled. "But I know I have a lot to thank you for, including this meal." He wiped his mouth with a paper napkin. "It was excellent."

Gabriele dismissed the issue. "You know Dr. Santavecchia, right?"

"Yes, the man with the locket. He made me talk. I remember him."

"Would you like to see him before I take you to the consulate?"

Mirko laughed. "You don't believe me, do you? You don't trust me."

Gabriele blushed. "I do, I do, but…everything came out so fast and—"

"I can talk to the doctor if you want." He paused. "I am in Italy, right?"

"Yes."

"I thought so when the policeman talked to you on the phone, from the car."

Within a couple of hours Dr. Santavecchia was at Gabriele's.

"Where is he?" he asked.

"Sleeping. He spent last night in a barn. He was cold and hungry when the police picked him up. After a good breakfast he went to his room and fell asleep."

"Do you believe what he told you?"

"Oh, yes. Things fit together. When we fished him out of the sea he was wearing a sweatshirt with Canadian symbols on, and he chose a Canadian newspaper over an American. Yes, I believe his memory is back, even if there are huge holes between events."

"What worries me most is that you found no trace of Mirko in Dubrovnik. Nobody seemed to have noticed him, except when he boarded the *Rijeka*. No hotel records either."

"He could have camped."

"Hmm…true. Let's wake him up then. I have only a half hour. I'm on duty in the afternoon."

Mirko appeared in the kitchen, rubbing his eyes. "Hi, doctor," he said. "I remember your yellow locket. Do you still have it?" He shook the hand the doctor proffered.

"Yes, I do, but Gabriele here tells me you won't be needing it anymore." He scrutinized Mirko. "Your colour is good, and you have a relaxed, yet alert aspect. Excellent. Want to sit down?"

Mirko took a chair at the kitchen table and sat between Gabriele and the doctor.

"Shoot, doctor," he said.

"Why were you in Croatia? Were you on a trip?"

Mirko closed his eyes. "I don't know exactly. I guess because that is where the orphanage was."

"Tell me what you remember after Gabriele and his men rescued you." These were facts that the doctor or Gabriele could easily verify.

"I was exhausted when they took me aboard *Il Corsaro Rosso*. Then I remember being taken to a hospital, then to another. The room was nice, with pale green walls. Gabriele came to visit me often, and you came three or four times and made me look at your gadget." Mirko opened his eyes, his gaze shifting from Gabriele to the doctor. "There was a very beautiful nurse…Daniela. She had nice blue eyes. She came to visit me on her days off and brought me candies."

"Yes, I know," Gabriele said. "Somebody tipped me off."

Santavecchia tapped his friend on the shoulder, waved at Mirko and rose. "I have to go. Let me know how you make out at the consulate."

"Sure," Gabriele said, and saw his friend to the gate. When he got back Sean was bending over a huge telephone book. "What are you looking for?"

"The list of Canadian consulates. I had a friend who lost his passport. He had to shop around to find one that wasn't too busy. It isn't as straightforward as in the past to get a new one." He copied down some numbers. "I'll make a few calls and find out where it's best to go." He took Gabriele's phone and disappeared into his bedroom.

CHAPTER 48

Milan, Northern Italy, December 2005

In spite of the afternoon hour, the fog had not lifted. They were too early for the meeting with the Canadian General Consulate, so Mirko, Gabriele and Sean lingered in downtown Milan. They lined up to enter the Duomo as four army officers checked all bags, packages and cameras. Once inside, they admired the immense stained-glass windows and the rose window with the Madonna and Child; then they circled the apse and stopped in front of the cordoned-off steps leading to the altar, marvelling at the inlays of pink and grey marble. Because it was too foggy to ascend to the church's multi-layer roof and have a view of the city from there, they walked out and took a stroll.

"The meeting is for four o'clock?" Mirko asked. "That's almost two hours from now, isn't it?"

"Yes, so we have time to look around a bit more," Gabriele said as they leisurely ambled through the pedestrian zone of via Dante. "We can look at the shops, maybe stop for a cappuccino, something like that."

"Why don't we do some *serious* sightseeing? When I toured the Vatican Museums I saw one of Van Gogh's Pietas. It's an incredibly expressive small oil. I was told it recreated the set-up of the Pietà Rondanini, Michelangelo's latest Madonna. Should we go see the Rondanini? It's at the Castello Sforzesco." Sean looked at Gabriele for approval. "Since we're here—"

"Great. Okay with you, Mirko?"

"Sure."

They quickened their steps toward Piazza Castello as the fog gave way to a light haze. They had just crossed the square when Mirko stopped and looked up.

"Wow! What a big tower!"

"It's known as the *Filarete,* a last century addition to the old castle," Gabriele said.

Mirko didn't move, as the others proceeded farther.

"Wait, wait! I've seen that before," he said.

Gabriele retraced his steps and grabbed Mirko's arm. "Where, Mirko? Where?" As Mirko didn't respond, Gabriele shook his arm. "Where? What do you remember of a tower like that?"

Mirko jerked his head toward Gabriele and then looked up straight at the tower again. "It *can't* be…"

"What can't be?" Gabriele pressed.

"The one I know wasn't that big…maybe half that tall, but the shape was the same. Two square towers, one on top of the other, and then a—"

"A loggia. That's a loggia that you see." In his mind, Gabriele replayed the call he had received from Chris Sandcroft. This could be important for tracing Mirko's childhood. "Do you remember anything about this tower of yours?"

"Yes!" Mirko raised his arms in victory. "*Yes, yes!* It stood at the entrance of our castle, *Il Maniero Rosso.*"

*　*　*

Exhausted, Mirko covered his faces with his hands. For a few seconds, nobody said a word. It was seven o'clock in the evening and the meeting at the consulate had started punctually at four. Three employees had alternated at the desk in front of Mirko, trying to gather enough information to allow them to repatriate him. At the end, however, they had concluded that the situation was very unusual and they needed time to ponder what to do.

Now Gabriele addressed Mirko. "Are you okay?"

Twice he had explained to the government employees what Mirko's condition was and showed the articles that had appeared in the newspapers, reporting the salvage first, and then the almost catatonic state into which Mirko had plunged.

"This young man needs help," Gabriele said. "And he needs it *now.* At least he needs to know what steps you're going to take to help him."

"Steps? We don't even know whether he is a Canadian citizen!"

"So you plan to do nothing?"

"We'll think about the case."

"My friend is not a *case*."

"Of course, of course…I understand his predicament and sympathize with him," said the chief immigration officer, his tone and demeanour showing the opposite of his words. "But we don't have a date of birth, address, bank account, credit card, or person who can testify for him. We have nothing." He paused. "We have to be careful these days."

To that Mirko murmured, "I'll never be able to go back."

Gabriele patted his shoulders. "Of course you will. What we need is a lawyer." He rose resolutely, followed by Sean and Mirko.

The immigration officer seemed perplexed. "Wait…wait. What's the rush?"

"Rush? Who is rushing? We've been here three hours, and what did you accomplish all this time? You and your employees keep asking question after question, the same questions that my friend, due to his condition, can't answer."

"What good would a lawyer do you?"

Gabriele bore his eyes into those of the chief immigration officer. "He'll write letters to Canadian newspapers so more information on Mirko Grogan will be gathered. Then he'll package it all in a ton of paper and he'll bury you in it." He took Mirko's arm. "Let's get out of here."

"Wait, wait! Tell you what. I'll put out a search under his name. It'll take time, though—"

"How long?" Gabriele asked.

"A few weeks. You have to understand, we're close to Christmas."

Gabriele gave them a look of contempt and left, followed by his friends. Outside, he let off more steam.

"It's a case of simple memory loss. There are hundreds of cases a year of transient or permanent amnesia, and the police are quite familiar with this issue, Canadian police as well as any police in the western world. The employees of the immigration office have to do some work, but like most bureaucrats, they're primarily interested in their salaries and their positions."

"So what do we do now?" Sean asked.

"Relax. I'll take you out for a great meal and then, if Mirko isn't too tired, we'll go home. I like to drive at night since there's much less traffic than in the daytime."

"You have something in mind. I can tell," said Sean.

"You bet I have. I want to trace back the man who called me from Canada, asking whether Mirko ever mentioned a castle."

"And you told him?" Mirko interjected, anxiously.

"That you never did. Then he asked if he could talk to you, but you'd disappeared."

"He's the link," Sean and Mirko said in unison.

"Did he leave a phone number?" Sean asked.

"No, but we have a common acquaintance: Dr. Mariani."

CHAPTER 49

Toronto, Chagrain's house

No answers at De Bruyin's phone. Feeling on edge, Chagrain tried one more time to call De Bruyin at his residence in California. A voice came on, "This number is not in service." *Damn! The deal is off. I can't unload the cups.* Clearly, something had happened to De Bruyin and there was no way to find out what it was or why it had happened. He could no longer reach his best customer. He had to find another buyer for the cups, and soon, because he wanted to get rid of Nozemni.

After the sinister encounter in the airport parking lot, Nozemni had cleared out of the motel in a hurry and set up camp at his house. Sprawled on the living room sofa, he was now watching a boxing match.

With one whack on Nozemni's feet, Chagrain sent him rolling onto the floor.

"*Ne seri!* What's the problem, man?" Nozemni asked.

"No shoes in here. I've told you a hundred times. No munching in the living room either. I can't have anybody coming in to clean the house. I have to do it myself. Go eat in the kitchen."

"But there's no television in the kitchen."

Chagrain lifted the Yellow Pages from the coffee table and was ready to throw it, when Nozemni picked up his beer and a bag of potato chips and disappeared from sight.

Chagrain turned the television off and sat in front of his laptop. Having acquired a reputation as one of the best fences in Ontario, he didn't normally need to contact people—they contacted him. His modus operandi was simple. On a web page dedicated to promote art awareness, he announced his new products and waited for customers to come forward. He had reported the availability of "artistic antique vases" a week ago, but nothing had happened despite no news appearing in the media about any theft at the Sandcroft residence. That was unusual.

Minutes ticked by as Chagrain considered what could have happened. *Is it possible the robbery hasn't been discovered due to the commotion created by the return of the older man? Hmm…possible but unlikely.* He reasoned that even if nobody had entered the room on the second floor where he had stolen all the art pieces, it would have been virtually impossible for Chris Sandcroft not to notice the empty space above his bed. *Maybe he sleeps on a couch downstairs?* Chagrain felt the urge to unload all of the stolen goods, the cups first of all. He had a funny feeling about them. *They're so old. Is it possible they're bad luck?*

He opened a spreadsheet with the names of his past customers, their addresses and phone numbers, what they had purchased from him, and the price. He wondered whether any of them would be interested in the cups. Contacting them was a possibility. He opened another file that contained the names of art merchants and shops selling or buying antiques. These were legitimate businesses, although he knew that, from time to time, they had purchased items of unknown provenance. Maybe he should try some small shops out of the country. That was another option. Just to be thorough, he surfed the Internet looking for companies that traded art items or antiques.

There was a posting from a shop in Scotland, showing an interest in buying old or new basso-rilievi in silver. It was a long shot, but maybe he could unload the Madonna. Once in contact, he could mention that other merchandise was available. The price wouldn't be as good as trading directly with a private customer, but there was a possibility of bargaining. He wrote down the phone number, then checked his electronic mail. There were no important messages. Finally he put his laptop on standby and went to fetch a copy of the *Toronto Star*.

In the *Classified* section, under *Merchandise*, he found the advertisement of an Australian operator claiming to be in North America to enrich his collection of antiques. He would consider any item and promised to make reasonable offers. He gave his phone number at the Four Seasons Hotel, and introduced himself as Alain Front.

Interesting, but risky, Chagrain thought. He had narrowly avoided falling into a trap a few weeks ago; he didn't want to walk into another. His phone rang and he answered it promptly.

It was Poitr Radic. "Jim? What's happening over there? Where is Nozemni? I haven't heard from you guys in weeks."

"Everything's fine. We just have to find a proper buyer."

"I thought you already had one."

"Something happened to him. He disappeared."

"I have problems here. I need money. Jos, the dwarf, wants money and now there's another problem…Alesh, the owner of the *Rijeka*, is inquiring about Mirko. He'd been promised 5,000 euros by an Italian fellow. Alesh wasn't insured, so he's after that money. The search is becoming bigger and bigger."

"Let them search."

"There's more. I've seen the headlines of a magazine here in town. Mirko has recovered."

"Oh?"

"Yes. He remembers. He's not in a hospital anymore. We're in danger." He paused to clear his throat. "The dwarf wants 3,000 now."

"Euros?"

"No, dollars. American. He's old fashioned. I have to have it. I can't keep him quiet."

Suddenly Nozemni was standing on the threshold of the door. "Who is it?"

Chagrain covered the mouthpiece. "It's Poitr. He wants money. Now. The dwarf is blackmailing him."

"How much?" Nozemni asked.

Chagrain made the sign of a three followed by three zeros while he said into the phone, "Call back in a couple of days, same time, Poitr." He closed his cell. "Shit. Mirko is recovering fast. We have to act."

"Act? What do you mean?"

"Two things: first, we can't wait for the ingots or a large amount of coins to be changed into cash. We have to unload the cups. And second…" Chagrain walked to the cupboard below the TV set and took out a bottle of vodka. He took a swig directly from the bottle, then another. "Second, Mirko has to disappear—for good, this time."

"What do you mean *disappear?*" Nozemni asked, alarm in his voice.

Chagrain grabbed Nozemni's shirt. "Are you stupid? Can't you understand that Mirko can send us both to jail? We robbed him of everything he had."

"He had almost nothing," Nozemni said.

"That's immaterial. He can't come back here. We have to act, and fast." Chagrain picked up the *Toronto Star* and extracted the pen he always carried in his shirt pocket. He circled the phone number of the Aussie operator staying at the Four Seasons Hotel. "This man is interested in antiques. I'm going to contact him and get an appointment. This time we show only a picture of the cups, and then get a second appointment."

"Why?"

"I want to do some checking. Find out from the hotel receptionist whether he was staying at the hotel when the show went on the air. If not, I'll tell him about *two* cups. After I meet him, you'll follow him for a day or so to see where he goes and what he does. We ought to be careful."

Nozemni looked at him. "And then?"

"Once he's paid for the two cups, we'll offer him the other two. There has been no news about the theft."

Chagrain was ready to dial the number when Nozemni put a hand on his cell phone. "Wait. I want to know what you plan to do with Mirko."

"Are you fucking deaf? We have to go to Italy and take care of him, *permanently!*" As Nozemni looked at him blankly, he shouted, "*We have to kill him!*"

CHAPTER 50

Nozemni stared at Chagrain. "What in the hell are you doing to your foot?"

"I'm putting some tape around one side of my ankle and underneath my heel so I won't be able to walk straight. If Mr. Alain Fort ever describes me to the police, they'll have a hard time recognizing me."

Chagrain slipped on a pair of old linen trousers. A loose coat over a white shirt and a blue scarf around his neck conferred on him the appearance of an artist. A wig with medium-length grey hair, almost buried under a fishing hat, made him look 20 years older. Finally, he put on a pair of shoes usually worn by a person with a clubfoot, and stood in front of Nozemni.

"What do you think?"

"Incredible. A perfect...perfect—"

"Camouflage. Nobody would be able to recognize me, not even people who have known me for ages. I'm a pro at this kind of stuff. Ready to get the ball rolling?"

"Sure. I know the part. I have to sit in the lobby with a newspaper open in front of me and wait for you. When you're finished with Mr. Fort, you'll approach me and show me some pictures. We'll make it look as if we're talking business. I'll give you the parcel with the change of clothes." Nozemni closed his eyes, then recited, "You'll go to the Men's room and change. You'll be yourself again and nobody will associate you with the person who had a business meeting with Mr. Fort." A crooked smiled appeared on Nozemni's face as he opened his eyes. "That's smart. Then we'll wait until Mr. Fort comes down so you can point him out to me. I'll follow him to see where he goes."

"Good. Let's get moving then."

*   *   *

In a room on the fourth floor of the Four Seasons Hotel, Glen Howard took his time to peruse the photos Chagrain showed him. He refrained from scratching his upper lip where a false moustache tickled his lip and nose. The moustache was reddish, the same colour of the hair he had just shampooed with a dose of Grecian Formula. He hoped that the dark green hoodie with the City Hall Towers sketched white on the front would give him the unmistakable appearance of a tourist and that his turtle-rimmed eyeglasses would give him the serious, committed look of a collector.

Glen continued looking at the pictures Chagrain showed him and nonchalantly asked about the provenance of the cups. When Chagrain told him they had been in his family since he could remember, he looked satisfied and offered him $20,000 dollars apiece.

Chagrain jumped to his feet. "Not even for *twice* that amount," he said.

Glen opened his arms, showing dismay. "I see that they're valuable, but that's all I can offer without having seen them." His tone was even, his face unruffled, despite the effort he made to imitate an Aussie accent.

"But they're extremely valuable, unique antiques. My great-grandfather brought them back from Italy. He got them from a museum. I know they're worth a lot of money."

Glen shuffled the four pictures in his hands. "Maybe you should show me the real thing. Then I'd be able to assess their value properly. Pictures don't say much."

"I won't make another trip if we can't agree on the price. I want a hundred thousand each. And I won't sell them separately. They're a pair. If you aren't prepared to spend that amount of money, forget it." He grabbed the photographs Glen had laid on the glass table and put them in his pocket.

"Hmm...the price is steep. I ought to think about it. Do you have a phone where I can reach you?"

"No. I'll call you tomorrow, same time, ten o'clock. Answer the phone if you want them. I have other customers."

When he heard the click signalling the closing of the elevator doors, Glen placed a call to Chris at Vibratim.

"He came, Chris. He was either one of the thieves or an associate, introducing himself as Nick Weaver of North York. He showed me the pictures of two of our famous cups. He wants two hundred thousand. He'll call me tomorrow. If I agree on the price, he'll come with the two cups."

"Can you describe him?"

"Yes and no. About 5' 6", maybe a little less. Medium build. Grey hair. He wore shoes for clubfeet. He looked 40 or 45, but his voice told me he was younger."

"Fine. I'll inform Mr. Villard. He'll call you and let you know what to do." He paused. "Thanks, Glen. I hope all this isn't too much trouble."

"Trouble? I enjoyed playing detective. Don't worry about me. Talk to you later." He closed his phone, got a can of iced tea and turned on the TV. He was about to sit in front of it when the telephone rang. It was Villard.

"Mr. Sandcroft told me you've been successful," he started. "Good fingerprints?"

"Unfortunately, none. I offered him a cup of coffee, then a beer, but he refused, and he took the pictures of the cups with him."

"The door?"

"Yes, he opened it going out, and he pushed the button for the elevator."

"No luck with the second, too many people will have touched it before my man arrives. Can you give us a description?"

"Not really. I took a good look at him, paying attention to the few things that cannot be disguised, as you told me: the height, the build...no luck with the eyes, since he wore sunglasses."

"Not much to go by then. You may be followed, so you should play tourist, go to a museum, for instance. He'll call back tomorrow, Mr. Sandcroft told me."

"Yes. I'll be in my room at the hotel. I'll sleep here."

"He may want to take you to a place of his choice. In that case, gain time. Agree in principle but tell him you have to check with your wife, and then that you need time to gather the money. Don't show that you're eager to conclude the transaction. And try to keep him on the phone for at least five minutes. Your phone number is already in our system, so we have one side of the equation; we'll try to find out what his phone number is. He's probably using a stolen cell phone, but sometimes people get careless. That's when we get lucky and can trace the call to the phone's real owner."

"Fine. I'll follow instructions."

"Great. The police artist will be there in about an hour. He'll have a couple of amphorae with him, peeking out of a bag. We need to keep up your image of being an eager collector in case our thief is still on the premises."

*　*　*

Once at home, Chagrain fixed himself a tuna sandwich and patiently waited for Nozemni to return. Mr. Fort had seemed genuinely interested in the cups, or in any other art object for that matter. Two large framed pictures stood askew against one of the walls and another man had asked for him at the hotel reception desk and then gone up to his room. However, something was troubling Chagrain. It was Fort's accent. He couldn't place it, but it didn't sound like an Australian accent. *Maybe New Zealand?* He sat on a stool at the kitchen counter and bit into his sandwich. He was still worried.

Finally, Nozemni arrived and immediately slumped into the only upholstered chair in the kitchen. Drops of perspiration raked his face.

"The Fort man can walk, I tell you. Am I tired. I followed him to the Art Gallery, then to Yonge Street. He browsed in two shops but he didn't buy anything."

"And then?"

"At 4:30 he descended into a subway station...at Bloor, I believe. It was busy. I lost him in the crowd. Do you think he's our buyer?"

"Hmm...I don't know. Maybe. I have to think about it." The shriek of brakes suddenly made Chagrain jump off his stool. He neared the window and looked out. "Oh, he's here. Give me a hand, Nozemni. There's work to do."

"I'm tired," Nozemni said, still sprawled on the padded chair.

"From what? From having followed an old man around town? Don't give me that shit. Move. We have to load the cases that are in the corridor and the living room. And be careful—they're glass." He went to open the door, followed by a cranky Nozemni.

"Why do you need me? The truck driver can help."

Chagrain ignored his remark. "Load all the stuff, and as fast as possible. I don't want anyone to have a chance to see what we're doing." He lifted one of the cases and gave it to Nozemni. "Hurry up. Henry, the driver, has already lowered the ramp at the back of the truck."

"What do you have in those cases?" Nozemni asked as he carried the case outside.

"My stock of liquor, bought at the Indian reserve. Load them, then go to the basement and get all the others. They're light; it's tobacco."

"And what will *you* do?"

"I'll settle the business with the driver." He gestured for Henry to come into the kitchen and sit down. "I expected you yesterday."

Henry shook his head. "It wasn't possible. We've only got one truck and the boss was using it."

Chagrain offered him a beer. "I see. It's 2,850. Your boss said you'd bring the money with you."

Between one sip and the next Henry nodded. He then gave Chagrain a roll of bills kept together by a rubber band.

"Anything for me?" he asked. "Something extra? I'm short of money."

"Yeah, yeah, I know. It's the same old story every time you drive here."

Henry was an old man, his face battered by age, weather, and alcohol, his clothes rumpled and dirty. Chagrain hauled some loose change from his pocket and counted out five loonies. He slid the coins toward the driver.

"Don't drink it all at once."

"No, I won't," he said, his smile saying the opposite. "Do you have a new man working for you?"

"No, he's passing through. He should be gone pretty soon."

The driver finished his beer and rose. "Next load in two months, right?"

"Maybe. I'll call you." Chagrain followed him outside and watched him drive away.

"You didn't tell me about this side of your business," Nozemni remarked as they walked inside together.

"Normally I don't do business with these people. Henry's boss is a small operator and doesn't pay as well as the others. But with all the money I've spent for the cups' operation, I find myself short of cash. We need money to keep the dwarf quiet." He moved into the sitting room and sat on the sofa, his forehead covered with creases. "Now, how do we get the money to Poitr or to the dwarf?"

PART 6

Bureaucracy at Work

CHAPTER 51

Toronto, December 2005

As soon as the Airbus A300 lifted into the air, Chagrain slipped a roll of American dollars into Nozemni's coat pocket.

"What is it?"

"Shush," Chagrain whispered. "Not so loud, and speak our dialect only, so nobody can understand what we're saying. I gave you the money for the dwarf." He repeated the operation with another roll and he then continued, speaking in Croatian, "The other one is Canadian dollars. It's for Poitr." He showed Nozemni a sheet of paper. "Take the Radics to this address, and don't accept them saying they don't want to go. They have to leave Dubrovnik at once."

Nozemni glanced at the piece of paper. "Where is this village?"

"Near the border of Albania, where I grew up. My mother still lives there. I already called her and explained that she'll have to take care of some people for a while. Take the Radics there, no matter how much they might complain or threaten you. It's too dangerous for them to stick around." He paused, and then lowered his voice to a whisper. "Are you still sure you don't want to blow the whistle to the police in Dubrovnik? It'd save us money."

"No. I told you already that I don't want the Radics hurt. I don't give a damn for Poitr—he's an SOB—but Helena is the one who felt sorry for me. If one goes to jail, the other follows, there is no escape." Nozemni sighed. "A mine exploded when a friend of mine and I were playing soccer in an old army field. My friend was killed, and my face got half smashed. Below my eyes, fortunately." His voice broke with emotion. "When I came back from the hospital, my family took me to the Radics' orphanage. My father—he was high in the Party—wanted to unload me, and he didn't want me to carry his name anymore. Poitr didn't want me either, but Helena convinced him to take me in. I was a strong boy, she said, and I could be of help in the years to come. Finally they adopted me and sent me to school. She treated me as a son. She's the one I feel sorry for."

"A soft-hearted criminal—you won't go far." Chagrain lowered the back of his seat and stretched out. "As I said, the American money is for Jos. The man has been useful more than once and he still could be. He can gather information like nobody else, but his price is getting too high. Tell him that if he asks the Radics for one more penny he's a dead man. Tell him *I* said so— he'll shit in his pants." He gave his traveling companion a serious look. "Got it?"

"Yes. Anything else?"

"You have a return ticket from Zagreb to Toronto via Frankfurt. Remember that I got these tickets because of my connection with Skytrotter, the travel agency I used to work for, and for which I still do sometimes. You must return in five days. Don't miss your flight." He paused. "One more thing. Your passport—that is, Mirko Grogan's passport—expires in a week. You don't want to spend time in an office at the border. They'd ask you a ton of questions, and you wouldn't know what to answer. Got that?"

"Yes. But when will my other passport, the Croatian one, be ready?"

"When I'm back. It's my insurance that you won't take off with the cups or any of my valuables."

Silence dropped between them like a dividing drape.

"How are you going to find Mirko?" Nozemni asked after a while.

"Through the fellow who rescued him. I already found out where his boat is moored on the Adriatic coast. It's at *La Scarpetta*. Once I'm there, I'll get his address. It'll be a breeze to find Mirko. As far as I can gather, the man isn't too alert, so I'll be able to approach him without raising suspicion and take him with me." He laughed in a sinister way Nozemni had not heard before. "If I can, I'll make it look like suicide."

"If you think it's necessary to get rid of him—"

"It is." Chagrain got some gum out of his pocket and began chewing. "Now, I have some instructions for you in case I'm not back in time to call Mr. Alain Fort, the guy from Australia. I have a feeling that he's gathered the money to buy our two cups." He gave Nozemni a note. "Call this number and set up an appointment at your old motel, the Altavista. If the deal goes through, don't forget to count the money carefully. It must add up to $200,000, not one dollar less."

Nozemni took the note and stashed it in his pocket. "Don't worry. I'm interested in the sale as much as you are."

Chagrain handed his partner a worn card. "This is my contact in Italy. I always let him know where I am when I travel there. In case of an emergency, leave a message with him." As Nozemni shot him a puzzled look, he added, "Emergency only. Understood?"

* * *

Rome, Italy

Immediately after deplaning at the airport in Fiumicino, Chagrain slipped into a cab and waved a piece of paper near the driver's shoulder.

"Take me here," he said.

The cab driver, an older man with a mane of grey hair, looked at the address and turned around to face Chagrain.

"Are you sure you want to go there? It's the worst neighbourhood south of Rome."

"Yes."

The man shrugged and put the car in gear. "Okay, but remember that I warned you."

Forty minutes later they stopped at a dilapidated one-story structure where the stucco on the walls was falling apart.

"Thirty euros," the cab driver said.

"What? How come that much?"

"That's the fee. Gasoline is expensive around here. One euro and 30 cents a litre. Look at the display. It shows the price."

Chagrain paid, then waited for the cab to disappear before knocking at the door. The door silently opened.

"Finally you're here," a voice from inside said.

Chagrain entered the building and stood in a large room with four windows protected by thick drapes.

"The plane was late, two hours," he said.

A man in a blue coverall locked the door and walked behind a small counter cluttered with an ancient cash register, a telephone, and a computer.

"Do you also need an international driver's license?" he asked. "It's required these days for foreigners."

"No, I have my own. I just need the car—five days max—and the other thing."

"It's 5,000 deposit, 1,000 for the five-day drive and 1,000 for the extra. Euros, of course."

"That much?"

"Take it or leave it."

"My friend at the Skytrotter told me he had arranged the deal for 6,000 euros altogether."

"That was a week ago. The price went up."

Chagrain had just set the last hundred euros on the counter when the man grabbed the money and pocketed it. He extracted a parcel from underneath the counter and removed it from its plastic folder.

"Beretta. That's what you ordered, right?"

Chagrain took the pistol and examined it. "Ammo?"

"In the car, underneath the driver's seat."

Clearly the man hadn't taken any chances. Chagrain dropped the gun into his backpack. "Let's go to the car, then," Chagrain said.

Together they exited through the back door and walked into a yard fenced off by tall brick walls. Motorcycles, motor scooters and old pickups, mixed with farming equipment and lawn mowers, covered most of the ground.

"That's your car." The man pointed to a Fiat Grande Punto. "The tank is full."

Chagrain circled the car and then slipped inside. His hand searched underneath the seat. He found a magazine and checked that it fitted the Beretta. He dropped both into his right coat pocket and started the car.

An iron gate reinforced by steel bars opened in front of him. Chagrain took off without saying another word. This enterprise was going to cost him a bundle. He could only hope that it would be successful.

After a brief stop for lunch, he followed the signs leading to Freeway A1.

He was worried. The sky was darkening by the minute, and he knew the drive would be long and challenging as the road wound through the Apennines. He would encounter several climbs and turns to fit the contours of the mountainous terrain. The tunnels, designed to shorten the way from one valley to another, would present a sudden lateral wind at the exit.

Exhausted, but safe, six hours later Chagrain eased into SS16, the road that, coasting the Adriatic Sea, would take him to his destination. Thirty kilometres from the outskirts of Brindisi, the sky released its burden of rain. With visibility further reduced by the night, Chagrain felt he should stop. Daylight would give him a better advantage to search for the little marina where *Il Corsaro Rosso* was anchored. He took a room at a small hotel off the road; the hotel's sole advertisement was the nondescript sign *Hotel*.

The room was small, with two single beds, a night table and a common bathroom down the corridor. Splashes of rain ran down the window, washing away the bird droppings that covered the windowsill. *It'll do for tonight,* Chagrain reasoned, and without a second thought he lay on the bed to recover from a long and tiring day.

When he woke up at nine o'clock the next morning the rain had ended, but the wind was still strong and the clouds low. He got going on the road again and soon reached *La Scarpetta*, the bay where *Il Corsaro Rosso* was moored. A couple dozen boats covered by tarps of different colour, fabric and size, swayed in the water. The marina was fenced off, and nobody was in the booth at the entrance. *Damn! What do I do now?* He didn't want to attract much attention, yet he had no choice but to make some inquiries. He drove back and stopped at a coffee shop; he hoped the owner would mumble a few words of English. He did, so Chagrain sat down and ordered a cappuccino with a croissant.

"Not much activity at the marina," Chagrain said.

"None this time of year, for sure." The owner fidgeted with the espresso machine. His white apron contrasted sharply with his dark trousers and black, long-sleeved shirt. He lifted the door of the glass cabinet built into the counter, removed a croissant and set it on a dish. When the cappuccino was ready, he brought both items to Chagrain's table.

"Looking to buy a boat?" he asked.

This is a good pretext to find out what I want, Chagrain thought. "As a matter of fact, yes, I'm interested in a boat. I was told *Il Corsaro Rosso* was for sale."

"That boat? *Oh, no, non ci credo!*" He shook his head. "Mr. Anzieri would never sell *that* boat."

"But he isn't using it."

"Well, no, not now."

"How come?"

"It's a long story. I see you don't know. He rescued a young man who almost drowned, then took him to a house in the country." He stopped and searched for words. *"Per farlo guarire."*

"Where did he take him?" Things were going better than he expected.

"To Molino di Sant'Anna," the owner said, and quickly turned around as the door opened and a customer stepped in. *"Oh, ciao, Carmelo! Qui c'è un Tizio che vuole comperare una barca. Vieni, vieni."* He took the customer by his sleeve and introduced him to Chagrain. "This is my brother, Carmelo Squinteri. *Lui* sells boats." He pointed to himself. *"Io sono Antenore."*

Oh, oh…I'm getting too much exposure, Chagrain thought as he shook Carmelo's sweaty outstretched hand. "I'm interested in *Il Corsaro Rosso.* I was told it was for sale."

Carmelo turned to face the shop's owner. *"Cosa vuole, Il Corsaro?"*

"Sì, ha sentito che è in vendita. Ci deve essere uno sbaglio," Antenore said.

"Di sicuro," Carmelo replied.

Chagrain didn't understand what was being said. It was better to take off. He looked at the bill and left three euros on the table.

"Wait, wait," Antenore said.

"For what?" He looked sternly at the two interlocutors. "I'm interested in the address or the phone number of this Mr. Anzieri, who owns the boat. Since you can't help me, I'll be going." He wanted to get out. The situation was becoming too complicated. He moved toward the door.

"Wait," the shop owner said. "I'll give you the number Mr. Anzieri gave me. It's a strange number because it's for a satellite phone. It's for his boat. He can use it anywhere, he told me."

The man rushed behind the counter and copied a number onto a piece of paper from a little booklet. "Here, take it." His smile was ingratiating. "If Mr.

Anzieri doesn't want to sell his boat, come back here. Carmelo and I will find a boat that suits you, fine looking and good price."

Carmelo promptly proffered a greasy business card and placed it in Chagrain's hand. "For you," he said.

Chagrain nodded, thanked him and strode off.

Back in the car, Chagrain tossed the card and the note with the phone number onto the passenger seat and started the engine. He had seen the sign for Molino di Sant'Anna when he had driven to the marina, so he had no problem finding the little town.

It was noon when he reached the centre of the village. Old houses, some still built entirely in natural stone, surrounded a small square, where a church took up one side. There were five vehicles parked near what looked like a store. Chagrain stopped on the opposite side and stepped out of the car.

He sauntered into what appeared to be a grocery shop, which contained a counter with sandwiches for sale. A crowd talked animatedly, and Chagrain, feigning interest in some items, tried to grab a few words. They all spoke at the same time, and for a while he couldn't make sense of their dialogue.

"Let's go home," one man finally said to another in clear English. "The police are stationed in front of the house and send away anybody that gets too close to the gate. We can't interview Mirko, and Anzieri refuses to talk."

With a decisive stride the two men left and drove away.

Chagrain lingered a little longer. When he saw all the other people—he assumed them to be reporters—leave the shop, he quickly followed them. He returned to his car and pondered the situation. He was in the right place, but clearly he would have difficulty entering the house where Mirko was stashed away. He needed a diversion, but first he would take stock of Mirko's hideout.

*   *   *

Molino di Sant'Anna, Southern Italy

At ten o'clock that night Gabriele's cell phone rang, interrupting the game of Scrabble that Sean, Mirko and he were playing.

"There's a fire at the marina," a voice said. "All the boats are at risk." Then there was a click.

Gabriele jumped from his chair. "Who is this?" he shouted into the phone.

"What is it?" Sean asked.

"A fire at the marina."

Without losing time, Gabriele called Antenore Squintieri, whom he had put in charge of looking after *Il Corsaro Rosso* while he was away. There was no answer, so Gabriele punched in the number of the local police station.

Sean rose. "I'll go talk to the police outside."

When he was put on hold for more than a minute, Gabriele dialled 112, the emergency number. Once he had given his location, name, phone number and the reason for calling, he was put on hold once more.

Sean stepped back into the house. "No cruiser outside. They left for the night, I guess."

Gabriele grew more impatient by the minute; Sean and Mirko stared at him.

"Mirko, can you handle the phone?" He slid it across the table, skilfully avoiding the Scrabble board. "Sean and I will be driving to the marina."

"Sure, I speak a bit of Italian. I'll tell them you went down to see to the boat." He smiled. "Finally I can do something for you."

Sean had already left to start the car.

Gabriele grabbed a coat, waved goodbye to Mirko and joined Sean.

Half a kilometre from the marina, Gabriele spotted the lights of a fire truck. As he approached the shoreline, the police stopped him and asked him to park his car beside the road. He and Sean proceeded on foot. A fire truck stood on the ramp going into the water; the truck's hoses stretched to the maximum to reach three of the boats and its powerful lights shone on them. He glanced at *Il Corsaro*; its tarp had been yanked off, and Antenore Squinteri was on the gangplank.

"I'll go talk to Antenore," Gabriele said to Sean. "Stay here. See if you can find out what happened."

Thirty minutes later Gabriele was back.

"A sad story, but Antenore thinks my boat is going to be okay. His wife saw a strange light through the bedroom window. He slipped out and saw flames coming from the marina. He called the fire department, then rushed over here." The wind blew smoke his way, and Gabriele coughed hard. "Antenore was very quick and brave. He boarded the boat from the stern, took a couple pails of water and threw them onto the hooks that held the tarp in place. Then he unhooked the tarp and threw it into the water so my boat never caught fire." He could always count on Antenore. He was vigilant and spared no energy to take care of *Il Corsaro*. Gabriele continued. "Meanwhile the fire had spread to the awning of the nearest boat, and from there to several others." He coughed again. "Did you find out anything?"

"Plenty. I heard the chief of police saying it was arson. A hole neatly cut into the fence and traces of gasoline. He was very upset. He said he'd get the delinquent who did it even if he has to work over the Christmas holiday and all the holidays he has before retiring. This is a resort area that lives on the tourism brought in by the yachts, he said, and it's always been a safe place. He wants it to remain that way."

Gabriele patted him on the shoulder. "I hope so. Let's go have a drink with Antenore. He's waiting over there."

CHAPTER 52

In Santavecchia's country house Mirko made himself a cup of coffee and stored away the Scrabble board and its tiles. He checked on the cellular and realized that the connection with the emergency number had been lost. He clipped the phone to his leather belt hoping to soon hear from Gabriele. He browsed through the stack of CDs Gabriele had brought with him, uncertain what to choose. He loved music, and so did Gabriele, who often used his portable CD player in the backyard. Mirko finally opted for *Il Trovatore*. As Verdi's popular overture filled the house with its harmony, Mirko went into the bedroom and picked up his diary. He sat at the kitchen table and took a pen. Dr. Santavecchia had recommended he write down all the fragments of recollection that came to him, no matter how insignificant they appeared to be.

He had worked at a grocery store; unfortunately he could dredge up no memory of the shop's name; he had frequented the Athletic Club, where he exercised for hours on the rowing machine. Nervously twirling his pen, Mirko forced himself to probe further into his memory. He needed clues and links to bring to the Canadian consulate so he could go home.

As a glimmer of sunlight filtered through the sheers over the kitchen window Mirko realized morning had arrived and he had not heard from Gabriele. *No use going to bed,* he thought. He would stay up until his friend returned. As he walked to the counter to brew himself another cup of coffee, he heard a knock at the door. Through the pinhole he saw a stranger, a friendly smile on his face, and a car parked outside the white fence.

"I'm Nick Weaver, a friend of Gabriele's." There was urgency in his voice. "He sent me to pick you up and take you to the marina." The man paused, and Mirko opened the door. "Gabriele said he needs all the help he can get."

Mirko extended his hand. "Mirko Grogan. What happened?"

The man shook his hand. "The entire marina is ablaze. Get your coat and come with me." As Mirko showed some hesitation, he added, "They need a lot of people to help extinguish the fire."

Mirko nodded. "Sure. Anything to help Gabriele." He grabbed his windbreaker and followed the man outside.

*   *   *

Of course he knew how Mirko looked, yet Chagrain couldn't recover from the surprise. He didn't expect him to be so tall, healthy-looking and alert. As they started to climb the cliff, he also noted how agile he was. After a few steps, Mirko was already well ahead of him. Thank God he had stuffed the Beretta in his backpack. He might have to abandon the idea of simulating a suicide and go for a straight kill.

Still in motion, Mirko turned his head. "How far is the seashore?"

Between one puff and the next, Chagrain replied, "Once we're on top of this cliff we can see the beach." He stopped and took a deep breath. "Then we have to walk half a kilometre south, pass a bay, and there is the marina."

"Oh…wouldn't it have been better to take the car? That's what Gabriele did."

Chagrain didn't reply and inched up closer to Mirko. "Maybe," he whispered. He laid his backpack on the ground, exhausted.

With one resolute move Mirko snatched the backpack. "Let me carry this. You'll walk lighter. We're almost on top of the cliff. Going down will be easier."

"No!" Chagrain howled, but Mirko was already five steps ahead. He mentally cursed. *I need my weapon or everything will be lost.*

Once on top of the cliff, Mirko stopped and stood, scrutinizing the sky. "I don't see any flames—not even a glare. Are you sure this is the right way?"

"The bay is more inland," Chagrain said. "Give me my backpack. I need my pills." He pulled on the straps forcefully, in the motion stripping Mirko of his windbreaker. He needed to act, or Mirko would be soon out of reach.

Mirko picked up the windbreaker that had fallen onto the ground and wrapped it around his waist. He began the descent toward the shoreline, often leaping from one rock to the next. Then the phone chirped and Mirko stopped. He tried to get at the phone he had pinned on his waistband, but the windbreaker was in the way. He quickly unclipped his leather belt, hung it around his neck, and freed the phone.

"Is it you, Gabriele? Your friend and I will be there in minutes." He paused and listened. "What? What are you saying?" He turned to face Chagrain.

Chagrain wasted no time. Mirko's silhouette, looming partially against the sky and partially against the sea, made the perfect target. He was lining up his pistol when Mirko got hold of his belt, bent as low as he could and rushed him, brandishing the belt.

One powerful sweep and the Beretta tumbled down the slope. A hit on the legs knocked Chagrain to his knees, and a third, lashed around his shoulders, made Chagrain burst out.

"Stop it! Stop it!" Chagrain held his arms forward, protecting his face.

"Who are you?" Mirko asked.

"Nobody! I'm a nobody to you."

"Your name," Mirko said, keeping at a safe distance. "And it'd better be the real one."

"Jim…Jim Chagrain." His voice was a mere whisper.

"Why did you want to kill me?"

Chagrain didn't utter a sound.

"No problem. You'll talk later, I'm sure." Mirko walked behind the man, wrapped the belt around Chagrain's body and pushed his arms inside the loop he had created, then tightened the loop and dragged him so that he could fetch the phone he had dropped a few steps away. "Are you still there, Gabriele?" He listened. "No. I'm okay. There's a jerk here who tried to kill me. I'm taking him back the way we came. You'd better call the police. His gun rolled down toward the shore. I'm not going to rescue it. Since I'm holding him by my belt, I'd like to take him home right away and put a solid rope around him. See you there."

And with that Mirko began pulling Chagrain down the cliff.

"I can't make it. You run too fast, I might fall."

"You don't have to make it, and I don't care if you fall. I can drag you all the way down, but it will be a bumpy ride for your old bones."

*   *   *

A car from the local police and one from the *Carabinieri* were parked in front of Santavecchia's country house. They searched Chagrain's rental and one officer made a list, item by item, of what they removed.

Gabriele ran to meet Mirko as a policeman took Chagrain into custody.

"In his car they found a canister for gasoline and pliers to cut heavy wire. His fingerprints will tell the rest," Gabriele said. "Come inside." He opened the gate and gently guided Mirko into the front yard. "It must have been scary having a gun pointed at you."

Mirko threw his arms up. "Why did he want to kill me? I don't understand. I don't know the fellow—Jim Chagrain is his name, he said—and I don't think he knew me either." Mirko slumped in a chair and slowly sipped the steaming cup of instant coffee Gabriele had made for him.

"His name is indeed Jim Chagrain, and he's from Toronto. At least, let's say, he has an international driver's license with that name. We found it in his briefcase, together with maps and flyers." Gabriele took two frozen waffles from the freezer and inserted them into the toaster. "Let's have breakfast. The police are busy recovering the gun. It'll take a while before they come to see you." He put maple syrup on the table, along with two dishes and the silverware.

"I forgot to ask—your yacht? A lot of damage?"

"Almost nothing. I was one of the lucky ones. The person in charge of my boat when I'm away was right there and took care of it. Six others were almost completely destroyed." The waffles popped up and Gabriele put one on each plate. "Let's eat." He invited Mirko to help himself to the syrup. "So Chagrain came to pick you up with the excuse of joining Sean and me at the marina?"

Mirko finished chewing. "Yes. He said he was your friend. I can't understand why he wanted to kill me." As Gabriele remained silent, Mirko added, "Maybe because I'm a Don, a big boss from the mafia." Mirko laughed and gave Gabriele an innocent, genuine smile. "I can't remember anything of the sort, but as our doctor repeats all the time, people have a selective memory. They tend to bury the things they aren't proud of."

Gabriele dismissed the issue. "I can't believe you've done anything wrong in your life. You're too much of a gentle soul for that."

Mirko raised his eyebrows. "Actually, when I used the belt to fight my attacker, I remembered I'd used it as a weapon before. When and why, I can't recall."

With a brief knock at the door, a police officer stepped in. "I need to take your deposition," he said to Mirko. He took off his uniform cap, hung it on the pommel of one of the rustic chairs and sat at the table beside Mirko.

Chapter 53

Harrisville, December 2005

Conspiracy hovered in the air as the Howards and Chris sipped on a cup of herbal tea. They had convened for a quick gathering in the furnished apartment Glen had rented on Queen Street after making sure no one had followed them.

"Glen, what do you make of Nick Weaver's last call? I mean, what do you make of the idea of his postponing the meeting to the end of the month?" Chris asked.

"Not much. I can only hypothesize. One, I didn't show enough interest in the cups—but how could I, with only photographs? It would have raised suspicion. Two, he found another prospective buyer. Or three, what he told me, that he had to go see his dying father, is true."

"It's Christmas next week, so being with family makes sense," Elisabeth said.

"He didn't look much like a family man," Glen mumbled.

Vivian rose and refilled their cups. "So what are we going to do?"

"Wait for his call," Glen said. "He told me he'd give me a ring around the end of the month. I already checked out of the Four Seasons—that's an expensive hotel. I left, as a forwarding address, our home in Edinburgh—without my real name, of course, and booked a room for the 30th."

"Well, then we can make plans for Christmas." Vivian wiggled in her chair, looking happy that, for the time being, business was set aside.

Chris looked at her. "What do you want to do? I hope it isn't a trip into the wilderness."

"No. Mother and I would like to take care of Christmas. Get a sumptuous tree, decorate the interior of the house, and put gifts all around the tree." She looked at Chris and tapped on his hand. "All you have to do is take me to buy a tree—nothing else. Mother and I will also be in charge of the cooking. You'll just relax and take care of your father."

"How is he?" Glen asked. "Has he talked again about going back to Italy?"

"Not in the last few days. I rehired Lillian. You should have seen how happy he was. Five days a week, four hours a day. Lucio didn't comment on it, but I think he was happy about the new arrangement." Chris paused, his thoughts clearly focused on his father. "I think the imminence of Christmas gives him a sense of family closeness, something he knows he wouldn't find in the old country."

"You think it may not last?" Elisabeth asked.

"Difficult to say. I don't know whether the crisis he had when he came back from the hospital was temporary or was something that's simmered for some time."

"Did you tell him about the theft?" Glen asked.

"Yes. I had to take him upstairs so he could scout around to determine which pictures were missing. The thieves took stuff only from the second floor. Most of those paintings were from Mother's collection. I explained to him what they were, and in some cases he remembered having given them to her as presents. Their disappearance didn't convey much emotional loss to him. It would've been much worse if the pictures we'd brought with us recently had been stolen."

"What about the young man lost at sea and rescued by the Italian yachter? Mirko is his name, right?"

"I didn't mention it to him. I'd prefer to get more information about the entire situation." Chris took a cookie from the tray Vivian had put on the coffee table and then continued. "Did I tell you I managed to talk to Mr. Anzieri, the owner of the yacht?"

"No. I knew you were going to call him, since I didn't get anywhere with that rude reporter. So what did you find out?"

"Not much."

"Were you able to talk to him?"

"No, he'd disappeared. The police were out looking for him."

Silence reigned undisturbed, except for the little noise made by the splitting and the munching of the cookies.

THE RED MANOR

"Do you plan to call Anzieri again?" Vivian asked.

"Yes, but not before Christmas. We all need some quiet time. If Mirko is my twin brother, he'll still be my brother after Christmas. Meanwhile, other facts might surface that can clarify the entire state of affairs."

Christmas Day

As agreed upon, Chris got up early and went directly to his father's room to help him get ready. Lucio was a meticulous dresser, and when Chris finally thought everything was in order, Lucio, for the third time, undid and redid his tie.

"You look great," said Chris, growing impatient. Lucio had lost weight, and he'd had a new suit made for the festivities. "That tie looks great with your brown suit." It was pale-yellow silk with brown speckles.

Lucio turned around in front of the full-size mirror. "Not bad for a poor cripple," he murmured.

"Stop feeling sorry for yourself." Chris dragged a chair close to him and opened a jewellery box. "Here, make yourself useful."

"Oh?"

"Help me choose a ring for Vivian. There isn't one with a stone as big as the one the Texan offered her, but I think she'll be happy with any of these. Grandfather kept them in the safe at Vibratim and I never looked at them before yesterday when I brought the box home. Some of the pieces are fantastic."

Lucio's eyes sparkled. "Are you going to—?"

"Yes. I always liked Vivian and I've finally had time to get to know her. I don't think I could find a better partner, and we're in love, which is a great plus for a lasting relationship."

"It sure is." Lucio picked up one jewel after another, and in no time he had a hand full. He frowned. "I don't want you to give her any of these: I bought them for your mother. They're bad luck."

"But those are the most beautiful."

Lucio kept shaking his head. "Buy her a new one. You have to make a woman feel special, unique."

"That's what I'd have done, except that I had no time. There *was* no time, I should say, with all that's happened in the last weeks."

261

From the ornate wooden box Lucio chose an emerald flanked by two marquis-cut diamonds and dropped it into Chris' opened hand. "This was my mother's ring." His eyes twinkled. "Not bad for a temporary engagement ring." He looked at Chris, his eyes moist. "I wish you all the happiness in the world, *Son*."

Chris bent to kiss his father on the forehead. "Thank you, *Father*."

As Lucio wheeled into the kitchen for a quick coffee, Chris ran upstairs and shoved the jewellery box underneath his bed. He would hang the ring on the top of the humongous Christmas tree, which Vivian and Elisabeth had decorated with garlands, artificial flickering candles and other sparkling ornaments.

Chris descended to the first floor and entered the family room.

Bertha was sitting among the boxes, most of which were broken open, and was happily chewing on a pair of slippers.

"Bertha!" Chris shouted. The dog stood, more still than a statue. "Come here!" The dog didn't budge, so Chris reached for her collar, opened the patio door and shoved her outside. "Stay!"

Lucio had come in, attracted by the noise. "Oh my God, what a mess!"

"You can say that again." Chris slumped in a chair, circling the emerald ring on his index finger. "What do we do now?" Bertha began whining because of the exclusion, but also for the cold. "Look at her. Look. She's wagging her tail and looking at me with those eyes that make me feel like a monster. I'm not going to look at her." He turned to face his father. "Tell me, what are we going to do?"

Lucio was examining the damage, using his reaching tool to separate the broken boxes from their contents. "She didn't damage much. She just had fun pulling on the wrapping paper and chewing on the boxes. She was probably here all night."

"Probably." The Wilsons had gone to their children's place for the holiday and Lillian had just left for a cruise and wouldn't be back until after New Year. Bertha emitted a long howl this time, her tone pleading for mercy. Chris used to spend time with her, walking with her and training her to obey his commands. He couldn't remember the last time he'd done it. He sighed, realizing how wearisome the past few months had been and how much he had neglected the poor lab. He rose, let Bertha in and, holding her by the collar, led her to a corner of the room.

"Sit." He glared at the dog. "Sit, I said."

Her head down, Bertha finally complied.

"Let's get to work; the Howards will be here soon." Chris grabbed a chair, stood on it, and hung the emerald ring on top of the Christmas star. "That's for Vivian to find. What do you think?"

"That she'll spot it immediately. Women have a sixth sense when it comes to jewellery…rings in particular."

All of a sudden the chimes spread their song through the house. "They're already here," Chris and Lucio said together.

Chris strode over to the main door, opened it, and found a wall of legs and boxes—only Glen's face was partially visible.

"Come on in. And Merry Christmas, whoever you are." Chris took the cartons from Vivian and Elisabeth. He stepped into the kitchen, followed by Vivian. "There's enough food for an army."

Vivian shook off her coat, revealing a bright red outfit in tune with the season. "Everything okay?" she inquired, looking at Chris' jeans and T-shirt.

"Not quite." He pulled her to him and kissed her, then indulged in caressing her neck. "*Now* things are okay."

"Oh, good. Mother and I have packed brunch in those boxes, as we agreed, but also dinner. So we'll be able to enjoy our time together without having to do any work." From the pile of boxes she took a few packages wrapped in shining red and green paper. "These don't contain food; they're gifts. I'm going to set them underneath the tree."

"Wait," Chris said, but Vivian had already entered the family room where Lucio was explaining to Elisabeth and Glen what had happened.

Chris pointed at Bertha, who was sprawled in the corner of the den, her muzzle between her front paws.

"That's all her fault. She'd been working on the presents all night long."

"It's a mess, but so what? We'll have fun guessing which gift is for whom," Lucio said, and moved toward the CD player. "Let's play some Christmas carols."

Vivian stared at the top of the pine tree. "There's a shiny little thing on top of the star." She turned to smile at Chris. "I wonder if that could be for me."

CHAPTER 54

Harrisville, December 30, 2005

Seated on the edge of the bed in Room 211 of the Altavista Motel, Nozemni mulled over recent events. His trip to Dubrovnik had been successful. He had found the dwarf gagged and tied to a chair inside the Radics' hideout. He had no problem convincing the Radics to get in the ancient Mercedes he had rented at the airport and leave Dubrovnik at once. Both Poitr and Helena were in poor health and scared they would finish their lives in prison. The dwarf's opinion was neither asked for nor given. Loaded into the car's trunk, he had made the trip to Chagrain's hometown quietly if not comfortably.

The return to Harrisville, however, had proved cumbersome as Nozemni had experienced one delay after another. When he finally entered Chagrain's house, he found no trace of the man. He began to fret, thinking of the upcoming meeting with the Australian customer. Chagrain could have been delayed—but why hadn't he left a message on his answering machine? Where was he? What had happened to him?

Nozemni knew he was now in charge of selling the cups. He would follow his friend's instructions. After he had ascertained that Mr. Alain Fort had checked in at the Four Seasons Hotel, he called him and explained that Nick Weaver had been detained abroad due to urgent business. He, Nick's partner, was now in charge of the sale. On the other end of the phone line there was at first reluctance, then hesitation, but finally Mr. Fort agreed to meet him at the Altavista at nine o'clock that evening

It was now past ten o'clock, yet there was no sign of Mr. Fort. Nozemni's anxiety grew by the minute. He was in a foreign country, and Chagrain was the sole connection he had established in Canada, and Chagrain seemed to have vanished. He had little money of his own and doubted he could get a job as Mirko Grogan. What should he do? He could stay at Chagrain's house for a while, but that would hardly be a permanent solution. He regretted he hadn't stayed in Croatia. No matter how gloomy things were there, he had grown up in that country and he had plenty of contacts there. Stealing the cups had been a simple operation, and working with Chagrain looked like a great idea as Chagrain was a successful operator with an expensive house. He thought associating with Chagrain would help him make a quick buck so he could go back to his country with money and prestige. But now his future was uncertain.

His hands shook as he picked up the phone and placed a call to Mr. Fort. There was no answer. He opened the last beer in the fridge and turned on the television. Images paraded in front of him, but they appeared as disconnected visions. He could hardly understand what was going on. At midnight he called the Four Seasons Hotel again and asked about Mr. Fort. He was immediately connected to his room, and Mr. Fort came on the line.

The tone of his voice was very apologetic. "Oh, you can't believe what happened. The cab driver insisted on taking a shortcut to come to Harrisville, but in the end, we toured half the city and never found a sign on how to reach your motel. Finally, when I saw the fifty dollar fare, I told him to take me back to my hotel." He paused. "I'm exhausted."

Hmm…Nozemni was not convinced by the explanation. "Are you still interested in buying the cups?" he asked, hoping with all his heart that the man would call the deal off.

"Of course. I can try tomorrow morning. I talked to the manager here at the hotel, and they'll provide me with a private car and a chauffeur." Mr. Fort paused. "Or else we could meet at my hotel. The Four Seasons is easy to find."

Nozemni was tempted to accept the offer, but he didn't dare defy Chagrain's instructions. If Chagrain wanted the deal to take place in a shabby motel, he had his reasons. "No," he answered. He repeated, word by word, the sentence Chagrain had made him memorize. "The cups are held in custody here. What time tomorrow morning?"

"Let me think. I want to have a good night's sleep. Let's say eleven o'clock?"

"Fine. Eleven o'clock. Altavista Motel, Room 211."

"Do you have a phone where I can reach you? You know, just in case?"

"No." Nozemni said. "If you don't show up tomorrow morning, the deal is off."

Glen Howard wiped away the beads of perspiration raking his forehead. "How was my Australian inflection?"

"Good," said Acting Chief Villard, who had been listening to the conversation on another phone. "But I don't think our man could notice it. Too bad we can't get at the other person, the one who made the initial contact. Nick Weaver was his name? I wonder what happened to him. It'd be good to get them both at the same time."

Villard had orchestrated the operation and had instructed Glen Howard to delay the meeting, hoping Nick Weaver would make the next contact.

"Tomorrow morning a limo will pick you up. The Altavista is under surveillance right now. We could find an excuse for entering Room 211, but we want to catch our thief with the stolen goods in his possession." Villard paused. "For tomorrow I see two possibilities. The transaction occurs directly at the motel. In that case you don't have much to do, Mr. Howard. Just let him show you the cups."

"Should I ask whether he has other items for sale?"

Villard became pensive. "If things go really smoothly, you might. But only if that's the case."

"Ah, good point. I understand...the man could be armed."

"Yes. It's likely that he carries a piece. But one of our men will enter the room through the bathroom window at the back. We won't give him time to draw a gun."

Glen showed his satisfaction for the well thought-out plan. "The other possibility?"

"He'll try to get you into his car and take you to another place." Villard's voice became grave. "You must refuse, since in this circumstance we won't be able to protect you."

"Would he kill me?" Glen asked.

Villard hesitated. "He might. Look at things from *his* point of view. He could get your money and keep the cups." He paused. "Do we agree that you won't follow him no matter what he says or does?"

"Yes." Glen smiled. "Life is precious to me, Mr. Villard. I have no intention of defying your...your recommendation." He slumped in the ample armchair nearby, picked up a bottle of mineral water from the coffee table, and took a sip. "I've lost 20 pounds since the television show went on the air. Not much time for eating or drinking and a lot of moving around. By the way, I forgot to offer you a drink. The little fridge is well stocked with soft drinks."

"Oh no. I'm heading home. It's late. Have a good night's sleep, Mr. Howard. See you tomorrow."

Villard had just closed the door behind him when Glen placed a call to his wife, Elisabeth, reassuring her that everything was under control. Then he called Chris, whom, he knew, wouldn't go to bed before being informed of the delay tactic's outcome.

"Do you want me to go to the motel with you, tomorrow?" Chris asked.

"No, it'll be a breeze. An officer is stationed at the motel right now—he'll follow the suspect if he leaves and tomorrow there will be other police there. I just have to play the part of the interested collector and let him show his merchandise. The police will take over from there."

"Sure?"

"Yes, Chris. The show is set for eleven o'clock tomorrow morning. I'll call you as soon as I have news."

CHAPTER 55

With secure strides Glen Howard left the black limo and rounded the Altavista Motel's premises to reach the staircase leading to Room 211. He knocked and waited.

"Come in," a low voice from behind the door said. "Don't turn around. Go straight to the bed."

Glen, disguised in the same manner as when he had met with Nick Waiver, took a few steps inside. Only a slit of light sifted in.

"Drop the briefcase," the voice said. "The cups are on the bed. And don't turn around."

Glen let go of the briefcase. It contained only a top layer of real twenties. The rest was counterfeit. As his eyes slowly adjusted to the dim light, Glen spotted the silhouette of two cups lying on the bedspread. Behind him, he heard the closet door open.

"I can't see," he said. "I need some light. I want to examine the cups, just as you want to count the money."

"Open the curtains…just a bit!"

"I thought this was going to be a friendly meeting," Glen said as he parted the curtains. He noticed the bathroom door was ajar and saw movement behind it.

"You were late, almost an hour," the voice said.

"Oh, these cabs and limos. Who in the world gives them a license? They don't know the layout of the city, not to mention that they don't understand English." Glen retreated to the middle of the room and neared the bed. He could hear the shuffling of paper behind him. "These cups are fantastic." He took one and went close to the window. "Look at the handles, how nicely they're crafted. They probably date to 1600? Do you know?"

"No. My partner is the expert."

"Where is he? I had a nice chat with Nick. I don't really feel comfortable with you. You seem not to trust me."

"That's how I do business."

"I see. Well, I'm happy with what I've got. By any chance, do you have any other items of artistic value?" He heard steps approaching the door to the hallway. "I understand you may not have anything comparable to these two beauties, but maybe you have some other items for sale?"

"In fact I do, oil paintings, mostly. But they aren't here. I keep them in a safe place."

Glen looked at his wristwatch. "I'm supposed to have lunch with a friend of mine. After that, I'm free." Clearly the man was ready to leave, so Glen hastened to say, "I'm very interested in looking at what else you might have." He paused. "I'm a compulsive art collector, you know. It's my hobby. I don't have any other interests. I'm not going back to Sydney until well after the New Year." He wanted to give the man time and room to manoeuvre. "Would you let me have a look at the other stuff? I can come anywhere you want and anytime. As early as this afternoon or as late as next week."

He heard the door open, but Glen didn't budge. He hoped greed would prevail.

"Toronto, 17 Metcalfe Boulevard. It's a big house, yellow brick, with a tall birch on one side and thick shrubs on the other. You can't miss it." He was already out the door, when he hollered, "Two o'clock this afternoon. Be on time."

Glen waited until the Buick was out of sight, then walked toward the unmarked police car that was stationed on the other side of the Altavista Motel and got in.

Villard put his car in motion. "Well done, Mr. Howard. I'll take you home. Queen Street, right?"

"Oh no. This fellow wants to show me some stuff he's stashed in a house. I got the address. 17 Metcalfe Boulevard. I should be there at two o'clock."

"Out of the question, Mr. Howard. My men are following the Buick, waiting for the most appropriate moment to make an arrest on possession of stolen goods and fencing. We want to wait in case our suspect takes us to his accomplice or accomplices. Fencing involving art objects is very popular in this area. There could be more than one man in the house."

"But I could help."

Villard shook his head. "This operation is becoming too complex. I'm thankful for your cooperation, but that's as far it goes. We have the situation under control. We can get a court order to search the place you just mentioned."

Glen wiggled in his seat. "I'd begun to like playing the part."

Villard shot him a quick smile. "I can see that, but this operation is not for amateurs, Mr. Howard. Leave it to us."

* * *

Nozemni felt exhilarated, almost in a trance over the ease with which the transaction had occurred, a big difference from the problems Chagrain had experienced at the airport. He had given Mr. Fort an appointment at Chagrain's house. Now he should attempt to sell as many goods as he could—the silver Madonna to start with, or the oil paintings? Or should he try to unload the remaining two cups? *No, too much money. Better offer a few different items, and let Mr. Fort choose.*

Nozemni stopped at a Take-out he spotted along the way and ordered a burger with French fries and a large Coke. He moved to the far end of the parking lot and began eating in big bites. Life felt pretty good. He had money and the opportunity to make even more money.

Of course, there was the problem of what to do next. Should he try to leave the country? Mirko Grogan's passport had expired. Would they really check the date at the airport? Would it be easy to apply for a new one under Grogan's name?

He finished his meal. Maybe he should go to the Skytrotter and ask to speak with Chagrain's friend, Norton. He had gathered that Norton was the man in charge of providing him with a Croatian passport under his real name, Nozemni Radic. He was about to start the engine when he remembered that the Skytrotter was in Scarborough. He quickly got a city map out of the glove compartment and unfolded it over the passenger's seat. Hmm…it would take him a good 40 minutes to reach Skytrotter and another 30 minutes to go to Chagrain's house for the appointment with Mr. Fort. He glanced at his wristwatch. He had no time for that.

He should go to Chagrain's house and see if he could make another profitable sale.

* * *

Toronto Police Service had taken over the operation as soon as the white Buick had entered the city limits, inconspicuously following the suspect until he had turned into Metcalfe Boulevard. Immediately after, the siren on and the lights flashing, a police car had signalled the Buick to stop. As the warrant for searching the premises wasn't yet in their possession, the police wanted to act before the car disappeared into the safety of the garage.

Nozemni stopped and lowered the driver's window, looking blankly at the policeman who was standing beside his car.

"Driver's licence, please, and registration."

Unhurried Nozemni took Mirko Grogan's licence out of his wallet and handed it to the officer. Then he bent sideways to reach into the glove compartment for the registration. He noticed that a second policeman was standing on the curb, one hand on the gun fastened on his belt. Nozemni's hands were shaking when he finally palmed the plastic folder with the document. He extracted it and gave it to the first officer.

"Do you live around here?"

"No, I was just visiting a friend of mine. He's the one who lives here."

"And your friend would be…?"

"Jim Chagrain," Nozemni spat out in a hurry, as if that name would protect him.

"Step out of the car, please."

It was then that Nozemni understood he was only one step away from being arrested. Something—he didn't know what—had gone drastically wrong.

He put the car in gear and took off.

The tires squealed; he reached the end of the boulevard before the cruiser began the pursuit. He turned left, then right into a narrow street, and rounded a park where fireworks were in preparation for New Year's celebrations. A crowd of musicians and cheerers, chanting and waving nondescript flags, crossed the street behind him, allowing Nozemni to put a fair distance between the cruiser and himself.

He had made it.

The way to the Skytrotter appeared in his mind as clear as it had been on the map an hour earlier. He disengaged himself from the holiday traffic, and half an hour later he stopped in front of Skytrotter, the tourist office. He took his backpack and entered the building, where last-minute vacationers were booking their trips. He asked for Jim Chagrain's friend, Norton, and was directed to the back room.

Norton put down the phone, looking exhausted. "Hi," he said. "Don't tell me you just decided to go on a cruise or go skiing in the Rockies or something crazy like that!"

"No," Nozemni said, and took a seat in front of Norton's desk. "I'm here to get the passport for Nozemni Radic. Jim Chagrain told me it would be ready by now."

"Oh, *that* passport." Norton went to a file cabinet and got out a manila envelope. He looked inside. "Two thousand and fifty dollars." He slid the envelope across the desk close to Nozemni.

Nozemni opened the envelope and leafed through the first pages, checking the data carefully. Out of his jacket pocket he hauled out the cash he had previously stashed and tossed it on Norton's desk. "The price was $2,000," he said and scowled.

"Chagrain said to rush the order. We used a courier."

Nozemni didn't know what to do. Surely he didn't want to show he had extra money in his backpack. It was too dangerous. "I don't have the fifty."

Norton gave him a strange look. "Your leather coat then, it's not the greatest but it'll do."

"My coat? Eh, man, it's cold outside."

"Your problem. If I push the button underneath my desk you don't get out of here with the passport."

Better forget about the coat and leave the premises—clearly he was dealing with a crook. Nozemni slipped off the coat and threw it on the desk. He strode off. Laboriously he pushed his way through the crowd still waiting to book their vacations and reached for the door. A man stepped in front of him, opened the door and yelled, "Elisa! Elisa!"

A Hyundai was parked near the entrance curb, the motor running. A woman lowered the window.

"Yes?" she said.

"Come in. You have to sign, too." He held the door open, waiting for her. Elisa got out of the car and joined her husband.

Nozemni made up his mind very quickly. He waited until the man and wife were inside the tourist office, then entered the Hyundai and put it in gear, slowly guiding the car out of the driveway and into the main traffic.

He had lost his coat but he had managed to ditch the Buick and get another car with a tank full of gas.

Now he had to think about his next move.

CHAPTER 56

Would the police be on his tail? A recurrent, nagging feeling that he was still in deep trouble flickered on and off in Nozemni's mind. He called the emergency number Chagrain had given him and found a message for him to come to Rome at once. That was perfect since he wanted to get out of Toronto as soon as possible. He headed for Pearson International Airport. On the Departing Flights screen he saw two flights scheduled for Rome, one close to the other. He assumed that the first, now boarding, had been delayed. It had probably picked up passengers who were scheduled to fly with the second but were eager to arrive early at their destination. After all, it was New Year Eve. He approached the first class counter.

"I just closed up my shop and decided to take a vacation." He flashed his brilliant smile to the young woman behind the counter. "I wonder if there is a seat available for Rome."

"Oh yes, we had plenty of cancellations for the second flight."

"Fantastic."

The young woman struck a few keys on her computer terminal and smiled flirtatiously. "Window? Return?"

"Yes to both." *Better let her believe I'm coming back,* he thought. He exhibited his passport. "I have only cash. I took all the money with me that I made today. No time to go to the bank."

The young woman printed out a ticket and a boarding pass. "Maybe *we'll* take all your money. It's $6,025." Nozemni didn't flinch, and she took the packets of twenties Nozemni lined up on the counter. "Wait here a second. We have a machine for counting bills. Be right back."

With anxiety Nozemni noted that two airport guards were approaching, one with a dog on a leash. He hoped the raincoat and the leather briefcase he had bought before coming to the airport would give him some distinction.

The guards passed by the counter and never looked in his direction.

The young woman was back. "Everything's in order, sir. I wish you a wonderful vacation." She returned his passport together with his ticket and boarding pass.

*   *   *

Rome, Italy

What he had feared as nearly impossible—fleeing the country—had been easy. But now, three days later, he was still in Rome, cooped up in the little apartment of Chagrain's contact, Primo. Primo—he hadn't been able to grasp his last name—didn't speak a single word of Croatian and expressed himself using a few words of English, an amazing number of gestures and a few sketches. Nozemni was lingering in the improvised bed made out of an old sofa when he heard Primo's motorbike take off. He sprang up, walked to the window and looked down on the street. Primo was speeding away, the exhaust fumes from his old muffler leaving a dark wake. *Ne seri*, he screamed aloud. He wouldn't take it anymore. He would find a way to reach Dubrovnik, his hometown, and forget about Chagrain. After all, the money he had with him was his due share.

He was going to wash up and dress.

Steps resounded on the landing and a key turned in the lock. Nozemni snatched a kitchen knife and flattened himself against the wall of the corridor.

The door opened and a bag skittered across the floor.

"Nozemni? It's me, Jim…Jim Chagrain."

"Jim? Oh, my God. What happened to you?"

"They caught me. I was in jail. Primo came down yesterday and bailed me out."

"They arrested you? For what?"

Chagrain shrugged. "They tried to pin a charge on me for attempted murder, but it didn't stick. There's still one pending for arson, but the trial is months and months away, according to my lawyer."

"Did you get Mirko?"

They both stepped into the kitchen and Nozemni slipped the knife he had grabbed for defence into the open drawer.

"No. That's why I told you to come down. You have to help me. We have to eliminate the man. It's in your interest, too. By the way, have you seen any of the recent Canadian newspapers?"

"No, I didn't have to. I'm wanted. I know that much already."

"Yes, but listen to the best part of the story: it's *Mirko Grogan* who is wanted for fencing and assault on Lillian Carrigan, not Nozemni Radic, and I'm only suspected of receiving stolen goods." He paused, ran a glass of water from the tap and drank it in one gulp. "Finally I understood what you had been doing the first time you went to the Sandcroft's house. You didn't look for the cups—you went after that woman. You're the biggest fucking idiot I've ever met. Rule number one is *never* mix pleasure with work."

"Well…she was there, half-naked when I entered the room. She didn't react at first, so I thought—" He paused, looking sheepish. "Doesn't matter. What's done is done."

"I've never had a more stupid partner."

"Go easy, will you? Who's the one who got caught? *You*, not me! I managed well, and all by myself in a strange country."

"You have the money for the cups with you?"

"Yes, less the air fare and a bit of clothing."

"How did you manage to go through all the check points with your old passport?"

Nozemni wasn't going to tell him he had gotten the new one at the Skytrotter. Chagrain would ask right away for compensation. "I used my charm," he said, and winked.

Chagrain shrugged off his coat and sat at the kitchen table.

"Hmm…we need a plan," he said. "And it'd better be good since Mirko and the people around him will be on guard now and probably armed."

* * *

"Are you sure it's going to work? I mean, shortening a shotgun to make it a handgun?" Nozemni asked Chagrain, looking at the two semi-automatic Brownings lying on the bench. Each was about 125 centimetres long.

The two men were in a hut that housed all the tools of a blacksmith. It was one of the useful hideouts that Primo, Chagrain's Italian contact, had made available to them.

Chagrain rolled his eyes. "It's the only chance we have. We can't enter Mirko's house with a shotgun on our shoulders. We can't even walk around with one."

"We could say we're hunters."

"In the middle of winter? Oh, shit. What a fucking partner I got myself. One that would turn on a light in the middle of a robbery."

Yesterday afternoon they had managed to break in at the *Club dei Cacciatori* and find a way into the underground room where the members' guns were stored—a set of six guns in each of the elegant wood cabinets that covered the walls. Disengaging the locks of one cabinet had been easy, and in 10 minutes Chagrain and Nozemni were in possession of two splendid old Brownings. As they were about to leave, the reception room came to life, with a dozen waiters coming and going to set the tables: it was party time. With dismay, they also saw three guards taking a stand around the building. Chagrain and Nozemni had to wait until the celebration was over. It was in the middle of the night when the club's main hall was plunged into total darkness and the cars began leaving. Disoriented and with no flashlights, Nozemni had almost turned on a light switch, but Chagrain had slapped his arm in midair.

Chagrain got angry at the memory. "Why did I ever listen to you and your ideas? You've been nothing but trouble."

"Oh, forget about the incident with the light switch." He tapped on the guns. "I still think the cutting will make the guns useless."

"When I was in jail they listened carefully to my predicament. They told me this was the only way to get two handguns in a short time."

Chagrain took one of the Brownings and, using a steel-cutting blade, chopped about 60 centimetres off the barrel. When he was finished he sawed about 20 centimetres off the end of the stock. "Do the same, don't stand there like a statue. Get busy," Chagrain shouted, pearls of perspiration raking his face. "It's hard work."

From a toolbox Chagrain extracted a measuring tape. Only about 45 centimetres remained of what once was a beautiful shotgun. But those centimetres held the two indispensable firing tools: the barrel and the chamber.

"How is it going to work?" Nozemni asked as he slowly replicated Chagrain's steps.

"One shell will sit in the barrel. Fired at close range it can easily kill a man. From the chamber two other shells can be reloaded." He stopped to blow dust off his newly-altered weapon. "Hidden underneath a coat, this gun will be hard to spot." He took a dozen shells from a box and dropped them in his pocket. "Six shots each. More than enough to kill a man if we manage to enter the house where Mirko is hiding."

* * *

Molino di Sant' Anna, Southern Italy

The rain showers that had battered the Adriatic coast for the past day had given way to a pale January sun, which appeared and disappeared behind the last few clouds.

Gabriele was on the phone with his lawyer, who was trying to put together the fragments of Chagrain's deposition, hoping that some of the related information would help Mirko's case in returning to Toronto.

"What do you mean Jim Chagrain contested the facts?" Gabriel asked. "Uh…huh. Hmm. Okay. Thanks for calling."

Gabriele shut off the phone.

"You can't believe what this Chagrain or his lawyer came up with, Mirko," he said. "He denies knowing you, and he denies having tried to kill you. Since the fingerprints on the gun were too patchy to be worth testing, the charge of illegal possession of firearms has been dropped." Gabriele paused. "Then he filed a complaint: that the police had taken for valid the deposition made by a person not sound of mind—that is, you. Chagrain said he never intended to kill you; that the attempted murder you're accusing him of is a figment of your imagination."

Mirko remained silent for a moment, then laughed. "Jim Chagrain has a good lawyer. Maybe we should hire *him* for my case!"

Gabriele smiled. "You never lose your sense of humour. That's what makes you so special."

The cat rubbed against Mirko's ankles, then wound around his legs and mewed. Mirko grabbed it, set it in his lap and began petting it.

"My journal is now full of facts, names and addresses," Mirko said. "I want to go back to the Consulate and talk with them as soon as the holidays are over, that is, after the Epiphany. I'm sure I can go home."

"That's true, but the fact remains that somebody tried to kill you. Chagrain has a Canadian passport. If they set him free there's no guarantee he won't try again."

"Would they drop the charges for arson also? The evidence was pretty strong, the chief of police said."

"No, that stands, and there is another factor to consider. Europol will pass the documentation to the RCMP and probably also directly to the Toronto Police Service, which may have something on file about the man."

Mirko looked at him, full of admiration. "Where did you learn so much about the Canadian system?"

"It comes from Sean. He was bored, so he bought a laptop and learned to surf the Internet. All my knowledge is second-hand." He paused. "Are you very anxious to go home?"

"I want to go back where I belong. I also want to pay you for the expenses I caused you. I remember that I lived in a house, my own, and that it was enormous. It should be worth something." As he read disappointment on Gabriele's face, he said, "This doesn't mean I don't like it here; you've been generous and kind with me, Gabriele, and I hope one day I'll find a way to show you my gratitude."

CHAPTER 57

Harrisville, January 3, 2006

Normally the Harrisville Dispatch arrived at the Sandcroft's at eight o'clock in the morning. Gideon would glance at the headlines; Kathy would read the local news during her lunch break, and then the newspaper would find its way to the family room. But with the Wilsons being away, the newspaper lay on the cement porch in front of the house until Father Paul arrived for a visit that evening. He picked up the newspaper and took it to the family room, where Lucio was waiting for him. He laid it on a coffee table and greeted Lucio.

"Two reasons for my visit," Father Paul said as he sat close to him. "First, to wish you a Happy New Year, and second, to give you some fresh news."

Lucio thanked him and reciprocated the wishes. "So what's the big news?"

"I'll be going to Brazil for two months, together with two of our priests, newly ordained. Leaving as early as February."

Lucio remained silent and picked up the newspaper from the nearby table. "I wish you the best," he said. He kept silent for a long moment, then muttered, "Two months is a long time for people my age."

"Don't be so negative. You're surrounded by people who love you, who really care about you, Lucio. That's what counts most in life."

Ignoring the priest, Lucio took a pair of eyeglasses out of his pocket. He removed the newspaper from its plastic sleeve and unfolded it on his knees.

One quarter of the first page carried a picture of Mirko Grogan, wanted for stealing, fencing and sexual assault. Next to the article, which described the police action that had taken place with the cooperation of Glen Howard, was the picture of Jim Chagrain, wanted for fencing and possession of stolen goods.

Lucio read avidly, often uttering words without sound. Then, "That's him. That's my other son, coming to bring harm to the family. He's here. He's the cause of all this."

Father Paul craned his neck to look at the paper, then pulled it away from Lucio so he could read it.

"It can't be," he said. "But this Mirko surely looks like Chris." He glanced at Lucio, who had reclined his head over his chest, his eyes closed. "Lucio. Lucio," he called aloud, shaking his shoulder.

"It's the prophecy. I knew it was going to happen." He opened his eyes only to look sidelong at the priest. "There is no escape, my friend…no escape at all."

"Bullshit. Excuse my language. The prophecy, the curse, whatever you call it, is pure bullshit."

Lucio stretched his arm to tap on the front page. "It's all here. My poor Chris will have a fit when he sees this picture."

Attracted by the commotion, Chris entered the family room, Bertha bounding at his side.

"I heard voices, shouting," he said. "What's wrong?"

Bertha moved close to Lucio and wagged her tail, hoping for a petting that didn't come.

"Look. Look at that picture." Lucio pointed at the newspaper. "Rick is alive. He's a criminal wanted by the police."

Chris grabbed the paper and began reading. Minutes ticked by, the only noise being the rustle of the Harrisville Dispatch pages being turned.

Quietly Father Paul went to the kitchen to fetch a glass of water. He set it on the coffee table close to Lucio, who nodded in thanks and sipped it, his hand shaking.

Chris finished the reading, tossed the newspaper on the chesterfield, then went to the bar in the corner of the room and poured himself a large whisky. He sat on the sofa twirling the ice cubes around.

"I don't like it that a criminal looks like me, but it's not my fault Mirko Grogan has my facial features." He paused. "Mirko? Is that his name?" He looked at the newspaper for confirmation. *Oh my God…*Chris' grey cells entered into a feverish state. *Two Mirkos, and Mirko isn't even a common name. There is one stranded in Italy who has no documents and keeps* *mentioning the Red Manor; then there is a Mirko Grogan who broke into my house and who can't be my brother, since the DNA of the man who raped Lillian is different from mine. Oh no! No! This Mirko Grogan could have stolen my brother's identity!"* Chris jumped up, hitting the corner of the ottoman close to him and making it spin. "Oh my God," he said, and scuttled off.

"Maybe you should go see what Chris is up to," Lucio said. "I've never seen him so upset."

"You okay?"

"I'll be fine. Don't worry about me." He petted Bertha. "This friend of mine will keep me company."

Father Paul left the family room and followed the noise he heard coming from the kitchen.

Chris put down the phone and turned to face the priest. "Can you take care of Lucio until I come back? The Wilsons are still away and the Howards, all three of them, are down with the flu." He pointed to the wall phone. "Call our family doctor if Lucio gets too upset, depressed or sick. The number is in the memory; just press *Doctor*. She makes house calls. I'm going to see a lawyer." Chris stroked his hair in a compulsive gesture, as he did whenever he was under pressure. "Maybe you can explain to Lucio that the Mirko Grogan who is in the newspaper *cannot* be his son. The DNA of Lillian's rapist is different from mine, and Rick and I have the same." As Father Paul looked at him a bit puzzled, he added, "Use any hocus-pocus you can think of—all churches have a bag of it—but keep Lucio calm. Convince him he doesn't have to worry about *that* Mirko Grogan."

"But then why are *you* so troubled?"

"Because there is another Mirko wandering around in Italy and talking about a Red Manor. If that is my brother and the one featured in the Harrisville Dispatch is an impostor, Rick's life is in danger."

CHAPTER 58

His heart in turmoil, Chris drove to Jeremy Weldon's residence. With his business closed for the holiday, Chris had looked forward to spending time with Vivian and making plans for their future together. They had gotten formally engaged on New Year's Eve, and for a day Lucio had become lively, joking and laughing as he had before the heart attack. It had been a marvellous time, Chris acknowledged, as he revelled in the idea of having Vivian around all the time. She had brightened his life, her cheerfulness and *joie de vivre* were contagious. The times when he dreaded going home to an empty house were over. Vivian would be there to make it a home and fill it with action and laughter. She was unpretentious, and her desire for him was at least as strong as his for her. Both were concerned about Lucio's poor health, so they had set the wedding date for March 25, the earliest date that would give friends and relatives time to plan their participation.

So much for the week of fun and pleasure I had in mind, Chris thought as he reached Weldon's old house. It was located in the centre of Aurora, its Victorian style uncorrupted by the passing years.

Dressed in brown corduroy trousers and a polo shirt, the lawyer received Chris in his office on the main floor. A tray with two tumblers, an ice bucket, a bottle of Crown Royal and two cans of ginger ale lay on the side table.

"Thank you for receiving me so late," Chris said.

"No problem. I hadn't anything scheduled tonight." He sat in one of the leather armchairs. "Sit down, Chris, and help yourself to a drink. Last week Glen mentioned the possibility of your brother Rick being alive. It's a curious story, complicated by the fact that Rick or Mirko, whoever he is, couldn't remember much after the accident he had at sea."

Chris nodded as he poured a glass of ginger ale. "At first I was suspicious, thinking of an impostor trying to take advantage of my father's weakness when it comes to his lost son, somebody probably aware of de' Vigentinis' wealth."

"Lucio still has money in Italy?"

"Oh, yes. He still owns several parcels of land, mainly uncultivated, spread all over the region. We're trying to unload them. They're worth a few million dollars."

Jeremy poured himself a whisky. "I also know you talked to the person with whom Mirko was staying, but you couldn't talk to Mirko himself."

"Right. That added an element of suspicion, together with the fact that the name Mirko is a slave name. Another thing: today there was a news report that a man named Mirko Grogan had been charged with stealing the famous cups and suspected of being the person who assaulted Lillian Carrigan. He was spotted in Toronto and is currently being sought by police."

"I know." He paused. "I can see the predicament. If this Grogan in Canada is an impostor, he'd have a serious interest in eliminating your brother in Italy, to cover up the identity theft."

"Exactly."

"And you came for advice?"

"If you have any." As the lawyer remained silent, Chris said, "I was thinking of flying to see Mirko-Rick and talk to him."

"That could be a good idea."

"Right. And there's something else…something extremely disturbing. First, the shipwreck—it could have been a fatality—then the fact that the Croatian police couldn't trace where Mirko-Rick was staying or when he'd arrived in Dubrovnik, and then the lack of documents. Too much of a coincidence, I'd say."

Jeremy nodded. "Going to Italy and verifying things in person might be helpful." He gave Chris a concerned look. "However, if somebody wants to eliminate Mirko-Rick he won't stop just because you're around. Your life could be in danger, too." He paused. "Tell you what, Chris. I have connections abroad, since my father was an ambassador in a couple of Europe's capitals. I can make a few calls and see whether I can get somebody detached from one of our embassies to escort you."

"Escort me? What do you mean?" As Jeremy remained silent, Chris asked, "A bodyguard?" He couldn't refrain from chuckling.

"Not really, just somebody who's alert, knowledgeable of the difficulties you may encounter and—" A grin appeared on his face. "And yes, somebody who can fire a gun, if necessary."

Chris raked his hair. "Hmm, wouldn't that be too much trouble?"

"Not to worry, I'll charge you for it."

Chris laughed. "Fair enough. I also wanted to ask if you could act as my brother's lawyer—just in case."

"Right now there isn't much to go on, but sure, if he needs a lawyer, I'll be available. The case intrigues me." Jeremy quietly finished his whisky. "Meanwhile, I could see whether Mirko Grogan ever owned property. A search through the cadastre will give us the answer; then we'd have a reference for carrying out other searches."

"That'd be great." Chris rose. "I'm going to book a flight to Rome for tomorrow night."

"Will you stay in Rome?"

"No. I plan to call Mr. Anzieri and then drive directly to his house—if Mirko is still with Anzieri."

The lawyer rose too. "That doesn't give me much time to arrange for—" He winked at Chris and finished off, "For your personal assistant." He saw Chris to the door. "Give me a call tomorrow before you leave."

It was one o'clock in the morning when Chris tiptoed into his father's bedroom. The lamp on the nightstand spread a discreet light throughout. Lucio was asleep, his breathing steady, and Bertha was sprawled on the bed beside him. At the sight of Chris, the dog lifted her muzzle and rhythmically wagged her tail. She lay there, clearly comfortable, despite being trained not to go on any of the furniture.

Chris gave her a look of reproach and wiggled his index finger.

In response Bertha lowered her muzzle to the bed and stretched her paws even more. Clearly Bertha had found another master, one who was around to take care of her. He should accept the fact that Bertha was now Lucio's pet, and, clearly, his father allowed her to sleep with him. Definitely a minor disappointment in the midst of all his troubles. Chris petted the dog, compensated by a warm licking of his hand. He then retraced his steps and entered the family room.

Father Paul was stretched out on the chesterfield, sound asleep, a small pillow under his head.

"Father?" Chris called softly. He tapped on the priest's shoulder. "Father? I'm home."

Father Paul rubbed his eyes and sat up straight. "Oh, where have you been?"

"To see Mr. Weldon." He quickly reported on the conversation he had with the lawyer. "I want to go to Italy and find out what the story of a second Mirko is all about."

"It might be a good idea." Father Paul looked at his wristwatch and rose. "I talked to Lucio for quite a while. I believe he's at peace now. He's convinced that the man accused of rape is not his other son."

"I knew you could get through to him, Father. Thanks for everything."

"Anytime, Chris. I should be going now. Don't move. I know the way. You need all the rest you can get."

Chris watched Father Paul disappear into the corridor, then quickly climbed upstairs and walked into his bedroom. His laptop lay on the dresser. He hooked up to the Internet and logged onto *expedia.ca*. Within 20 minutes he had booked a flight to Rome and printed out his boarding pass.

CHAPTER 59

The shower felt good, refreshing Chris' body and mind. He dried himself, then searched the closet for a pair of jeans and a sport shirt. He dressed quickly, as it was already nine o'clock. From the outside came the noise of the snowplough—Gideon was back to work. Relieved, he descended to the main floor and heard Kathy chatting with Lucio. His father was having breakfast. He skirted the kitchen and walked directly into the family room where he kept the booklet with his personal phone numbers, then placed a call to Gabriele Anzieri.

"This is Chris Sandcroft from Canada. I—"

"Oh, my! Am I happy you called." Gabriele said. "You can't believe how hard I've tried to contact you. I have news, *big* news. Mirko, the man who almost drowned last summer, finally mentioned a castle with a tower standing at the front, the Red Manor. That answers the question you asked me last time you called, right?" Gabriele stopped and tried to catch his breath.

"Yes, it does. Mr. Anzieri, I've booked a flight to Rome and would like to meet with you and Mirko, if possible."

"Sure. Mirko is staying with me, here, in Molino di Sant'Anna. He's out for a walk right now. When do you plan to arrive?"

"Tomorrow morning, seven o'clock. Leonardo da Vinci Airport."

"I'll be there."

"Oh no. No need to come. I've already rented a car at Avis. I know the region well and I'll enjoy a nice drive."

"Are you sure?"

"Yes. Just give me the directions on how to reach your place."

Gabriele did so, and explained that it was Dr. Santavecchia's house, in case Chris had to make some inquiries. "It's on a side road off the main drag, which is Road SS605. The address is *Via dei Santimbanchi 4*." He paused to give Chris time to write that information down. "Since you don't need me at the airport, Mirko and I will take the little trip we've already planned. We should be back by seven o'clock."

"Fine. I'll take it easy then, maybe stop for lunch."

"Mr. Sandcroft?" Gabriele paused. "Who are you? I mean, why are you interested in Mirko?"

Chris hesitated. The entire affair needed to be checked out before letting out that Mirko could be his once-lost brother. "I believe Mirko and I knew each other…when we were kids."

"Oh, that's interesting," said Gabriele, his tone expressing relief. "I'm looking forward to meeting you. Goodbye, Mr. Sandcroft."

"See you soon," Chris answered, and clicked off.

Satisfied to have established a direct contact with the man who had saved Mirko's life, Chris left the family room and walked into the kitchen.

Kathy neared him and wished him a belated Happy New Year.

"I made some waffles for your father," she said. "Would you like some?"

"Of course. I love waffles." He plunked into a chair opposite Lucio. "Good Morning, Father. How are you today?"

"Not bad, though at times I can hardly breathe."

"Is the new spray effective?" The doctor had given him a new drug for his lungs.

"Yes, it is. But don't worry about me. I was shocked when I saw that newspaper, but now I understand the situation." He paused, smiled at Chris and sipped his hot chocolate. "Father Paul talked to me last night. He explained that the villain on the front page of the Harrisville Dispatch can't be my little Rick." He wiped up all the syrup on his plate with the last piece of waffle.

Chris wondered whether it was the right moment to tell him about the reason for his upcoming trip. Lucio had gone through a lot of turmoil in the recent months. *What if I raise his hopes, and then it turns out that the Mirko in Italy is just an impostor? Maybe I'd better wait.*

With an even voice he said, "I'm going to be away for a few days. Between Kathy and Lillian you'll have all the assistance you might need." With hurried bites he ate the waffles Kathy had placed in front of him, and took a last swallow of his coffee. "I must go," he said, and rose. "I have to organize a few things before I leave." He leaned over his father and kissed him on his thin hair. "Take care, Lucio."

CHAPTER 60

Molino di Sant' Anna, Southern Italy, January 2006

Sleeping in a pickup truck with the guns underneath their bodies had been a practical, though not a comfortable solution. Chagrain and Nozemni had bought the old vehicle instead of stealing it, thinking it would be one of the last occasions they had to use the Master Card that had been issued to Mirko Grogan the year before.

Alternating at the wheel, they drove mostly in silence, careful to abide by the road signs and never exceed any of the speed limits.

A few kilometres before reaching Molino di Sant'Anna they left the main road and entered an old cornfield. They would wait until dusk and then quietly proceed on foot to the house where Mirko was supposed to be staying. They reviewed their plan of action.

"How are you going to be sure Mirko is still in the house?" Nozemni asked.

"I'm not. I just hope. We'll make our move around suppertime. Whoever is in the house will probably be sitting at the kitchen table. We can easily count them since the two side windows have sheers, not real curtains, as I noticed the first time I was there. We'll surprise them as they're peacefully savouring their meal. You come in from the back, and I'll come in through the front door."

Nozemni opened a bag and filled his mouth with a handful of almond cookies.

"That may not be wise," he said as he chewed. "Once I heard that when you carry out a raid, one group should enter from the front and the other from the side, in order to avoid shooting at each other."

"So what do you suggest? That we call in a construction company to alter the house plan? You sure make stupid remarks." He grabbed a few cookies and began munching too. "Remember, if you hear any noise, anything at all—a dog barking, a car approaching, a person's voice—we regroup at the back of the house and wait. Clear?"

Nozemni nodded. "What happens once everything is over?"

"Before the police have time to swarm the place, we walk through the woods and come back here, jump into our truck and follow the road that will take us down to the coast. A fishing boat will pick us up. It's all arranged. By morning we'll be on the other side of the sea, perfectly safe."

* * *

At the Leonardo da Vinci Airport, Chris had a surprise: the escort Jeremy Weldon had promised him was waiting for him at end of the jetway. "My name is Karl Steiner. I'll be traveling with you." He extended his hand and gave Chris' a strong shake.

About 5'7" in height, Karl wore a dark blue suit topped by a windbreaker he kept open at the front.

"I've already signed up for your rental, a Mercedes," he said. "We can be on our way, if you're ready." He grinned. "Wherever you go, I go. I'm your personal assistant."

Chris nodded, as he recalled the conversation he had had with Jeremy Weldon. The lawyer had done some research and pondered the situation the two Mirkos were posing. He had suggested it would be wiser for Chris to wait a few days before embarking on a trip that clearly presented several unknowns, some of which could endanger his life. Chris had listened carefully, but in the end he had told Jeremy he was anxious to meet with the person who could be his brother.

Without delay, Chris and Karl climbed into the car. Steiner was not a man inclined to conversation. After a preliminary exchange of information about the goal of Chris's trip and the people Chris planned to meet, Karl had gone through all the newspapers Chris had brought with him. Then he had begun punching keys on his Blackberry 8700, insensitive to the turns and bends Chris had to negotiate to follow the hilly terrain.

Chris glanced at the phone. "I thought that gadget didn't work around here because of different standards."

"I had an add-on attached to it. It works. The Internet does also."

He didn't offer any more information and then he asked some questions related to the circumstances of Chris' brother being lost at sea 27 years ago.

A few hours later Karl looked up from his Blackberry.

"I couldn't get much off the Internet, except a brief bio on Mr. Anzieri and his picture." Karl paused. "The man has circumnavigated the globe. He retired at 42, and now he scouts the Mediterranean up and down on a super luxury yacht." He held up his Blackberry. "That's what he looks like."

Chris glanced at the image. "A friendly face for sure. I'm anxious to meet him."

It was late in the afternoon when Chris saw the road sign for Molino di Sant'Anna. He slowed down, then entered and exited the downtown area. *Via dei Saltimbanchi* branched off a few kilometres ahead.

"That's the place," Chris said, as Santavecchia's house drifted into sight. He turned off the engine. "We're early. Probably nobody is home yet."

They opened the little gate and approached the main door, Karl in front of Chris. They rang the bell once, then again. There was no answer.

Karl put a finger to his lips and then his ear against the door. Finally he said, loudly, "Nobody's home. Let's go. We'll come back tomorrow." He repeated the message in Italian. "*Non c'è nessuno. Andiamocene, torniamo qui domani.*" He grabbed Chris' arm and together they went back to the car.

"What was that all about?" Chris asked.

"I could hear noise, people moving around, whispering."

Chris gave him his full attention. "How many?"

"At least two."

"An ambush?"

"Could be. Let's move out of here. We'll park out of sight and come back on foot. How many people do you expect to meet with?"

"My presumed brother and the man who saved his life, Mr. Gabriele Anzieri. They took a trip together this afternoon."

Chris turned the car around and drove it to a spot where it couldn't be seen from the house.

"We have to be careful," Karl said. "This place is fairly isolated and there are evergreens and trees all around. Do you carry a gun?"

"Me? No. It'd be totally useless in my hand. I've never fired a shot in my life. Besides, I have terrible aim."

As by magic a Walther P38 appeared in Karl's lap.

"This model is old, but simple to use."

Chris glanced at the handgun as Karl loaded it and lowered the hammer using the de-cocking lever.

"Keep the hammer down. When you pull the trigger you fire the first shot. A fresh round is then reloaded into the chamber." He proffered it to Chris. "At close range it's impossible to miss." As Chris hesitated, he added, "Take it for security—just in case."

With reluctance Chris accepted it and shoved it into his coat pocket. He got out of the car and locked the doors, then followed Karl, who was already well ahead of him. They walked along the woods until they reached Santavecchia's house. Together they approached the closest lateral window. Somebody was moving a penlight up and down inside a cupboard. Another silhouette sat at the table, nibbling a sandwich.

Karl pulled on Chris' sleeve, gesturing him to retreat in the bushes.

"Any idea of who they might be?" Karl asked.

"Not the faintest. They seem to be waiting for Mr. Anzieri, though. For what? Kidnapping? Extortion?"

Karl remained pensive for a few seconds. "I'm afraid it might be something worse." They moved a few more steps away from the house. "If you don't mind me telling you what to do, I'd suggest you go get us a couple of flashlights. There's still a bit of light and the moon's coming up, but it's getting cloudy. We may need them. I'll stay here and keep an eye on things."

"Sure," Chris said, and strode off in the direction of the parked Mercedes.

Soon afterward a car stopped near the gate. Karl rushed toward the driver and whispered, "Mr. Gabriele Anzieri?"

"Yes, I am he. And you are—"

"Karl Steiner, Mr. Sandcroft's assistant. Mr. Sandcroft went to buy a couple of flashlights."

Gabriele got out and extended his hand. "Pleased to meet you."

Karl shook his hand and positioned himself in front of Gabriele, almost barring his way. "Two men are hiding in your house. You have to be careful."

"Oh, no," said Mirko. "Now that the police aren't keeping an eye on the house they've come back." He paused, then addressed Karl. "You can't believe what happened! A month ago somebody tried to kill me. Why, nobody knows. Maybe these are friends of his."

"Somebody tried to kill you?" Karl asked.

Gabriele answered for Mirko. "Oh yes, it was a fellow who went under the name of Jim Chagrain. Mirko got the best of him and delivered him into the hands of the authorities."

"Did they charge him?"

"Yes, for arson—he also set some boats on fire down at the marina—but not for attempted murder."

"That's strange. I want to hear more about it, but later. I believe you shouldn't enter the house. It's too dangerous." From underneath his coat Karl freed a Glock 20 from the holster and checked the cartridge clip. "I propose to take some direct action. Do you mind if your door gets smashed?"

"My door? Actually it isn't my—no, what do you have in mind?"

"To sneak up on the two fellows who are in the house and have a nice, friendly chat."

"Are you sure you have the training to—"

"Oh, yes. I'm *that* kind of assistant," Karl said, and quickly moved toward the house.

"I want to help," Mirko said, following him.

Karl grabbed his arm. "Do you carry a piece?"

"You mean a gun? No."

"Then don't come in. I'll give you another job. Guard the corner of the house." He pushed him to his left. "I know it's getting dark, but try to see whether anybody takes off for the woods. It'd be the easiest way to escape, once I bust in."

"Got it," Mirko said, and flattened himself against the wall, craning his neck to keep one side of the house under surveillance.

With one powerful kick Karl freed the wooden door from its hinges, sending it skidding into the house. "Come out or I come in!"

Three shots answered him.

Karl extended his arm through the breach and discharged his clip. There was a cry of pain and then a hurried stomping. Quickly Karl reloaded his gun and went inside.

"Drop your weapons," he said.

Nozemni dropped his gun, but Chagrain fired more shots, one of which hit Karl. "They're going out the back door," Karl shouted as he recovered one of the shortened Brownings and then retraced his steps. He stood in front of the house. "They got me in the leg. It isn't bad, but I'm afraid I can't be of much help. Watch out. One man is still armed."

In his rental, Chris was just a few hundred metres from Santavecchia's house when he heard Karl's last words, followed by Mirko's shout. "They're getting away! I can see their shadows moving through the birches." Chris kept going, as his direction was the same as that of the two fugitives.

Mirko, neglecting Karl's warning, ran after them.

As Chagrain and Nozemni cut across the road to reach their pickup, which was parked in the cornfield, Chris made a wild turn and stopped his car between the fugitives and their vehicle. He lowered the window on his side and fired his Walther into the pickup's tires. Then he got out of the car and took cover behind it.

"You can't go anywhere," he said. "If you come closer, I'll shoot."

Nozemni raised his arms. "I'm hit! I'm bleeding! I have no gun! Don't shoot!"

Chagrain stood for a second, then darted for the pickup. It was then that Mirko, breathing heavily from the long run, caught up with him, brandishing his leather belt. With one hit he propelled the man's gun into the air. With the second, lashed powerfully at Chagrain's knees, he knocked the man to the ground.

"Don't move or I'll smash your face," he said.

Chagrain remained still.

The noise of a car engine broke through the air. It was Gabriele with Karl at the wheel. The Fiat Stilo stopped a few metres away from Chagrain.

"Well, look who we have here," Gabriele said, the car's headlights shining on Chagrain's face. "I thought you were in jail in that model prison we have in Brindisi. How did you escape?"

"I did *not* escape. I was bailed out."

"Oh, I see. Mirko? I have some rope in the trunk of my car. Not very strong, but good enough to do the job. Tie this fellow's hands and ankles. Make sure you make tight loops." Turning to Chagrain he said, "Maybe they'll keep you in jail a bit longer this time…if the police arrive in time to find you alive."

"What do you mean?"

"Well, you tried to kill Mirko twice, right? So maybe it's our turn to do the same to you, just once?"

"What? That would be murder!"

"Yes," Gabriele said. "It certainly would be."

"I want to be taken to a hospital." Nozemni grunted, and fell onto the ground. "It's my right."

"Sure, sure," Mirko muttered, and repeated the tying operation on Nozemni. "I can't believe what's happening," he said. "Coming a long way to kill me. The two of you have a lot of explaining to do."

"I suggest we take these two gentlemen to the house for a chat." With Mirko's help Gabriele picked Nozemni up and shoved him into the back seat of his car. "I don't think he'll give you any problems," Gabriele said to Karl, who hadn't moved from the driver's seat.

"No, he looks pretty tame to me," Karl replied.

Gabriele waved him away. "You can go ahead. We'll see you at the house."

Chris had been silently following the action, his attention focused on Mirko, whose facial features and gestures were at times illuminated by the cars' headlights and at times obscured by the people moving in front of him. It was a strange sensation to see a replica of himself in front of him. Mirko was more muscular than he had ever been, and Mirko's long, curly hair had made him look like an angel of vengeance when he had subdued his opponent. But what had eliminated the last doubt about their brotherhood was Mirko's voice. It was the same as he had been told his was—assertive yet melodic.

Suddenly Chris wanted to be with him, talk to him, hear what he had to say. Unfortunately the situation was not suitable for a family reunion.

As if he had guessed Chris' innermost thoughts, Gabriele came to his rescue.

"I assume you're Chris Sandcroft," he said as he made Chagrain hop toward Chris' rental and pushed him inside. "Do you mind if I take your car?"

He didn't wait for an answer. He tossed a flashlight to Chris. "I believe you may want to walk to the house with Mirko."

The taillights of the Mercedes disappeared into darkness, leaving Chris and Mirko physically close to each other—though far apart emotionally.

Chris wasn't prepared to meet his brother in a circumstance like this. Memories that had been buried in his subconscious for years suddenly surfaced: Rick riding his tricycle, Rick challenging him to jump off the turrets of the castle, Rick wearing a red-and-yellow hat at their fifth birthday...It was like those images, statically stored, were magically coming to life. Chris sighed, painfully aware that he had to think of something to break the impasse.

He flickered the light beam toward his brother, who stood silently in front of him. He then lowered the light to the ground. "You'd better pick up your belt and put it back in your trousers or you'll risk losing your pants."

"Yeah, sure. Like to boss me around, eh?"

"If I can. I lost a few good years of that."

"You were a hard brother. You never let me ride your tricycle, no matter how much I begged you."

"Why should I? You smashed yours coming down the huge staircase in the castle. That was two floors high."

"It was an experiment."

"Yeah, you were good at experimenting."

They began walking, their steps synchronized by an invisible clock.

"Sorry...I know what you mean," Mirko said. The silence stretched for a few moments, then Mirko continued, "Gabriele took me to the Red Manor. It helped me remember a few things. When I saw that huge, double staircase leading up to the living quarters I remembered tumbling down it with my tricycle."

Chris stopped. "You went to the Red Manor?"

"Oh, yes, just a few days ago, and this afternoon again." He paused, making an effort to remember. "The first floor is fenced off for repairs, but the museum in the old dungeon is open to the public. We found a volume with a complete, updated history of the castle and its people. I read about the accident—you know which one—and that my mother took you away because of that. At the end I was given up for dead." Mirko paused. "Our father never wanted that story included in the archives. The new curator put it in, just recently."

Chris felt relieved he didn't have much explaining to do. It would be too painful to speak of their mother's sorrow and the anguish that had afflicted their father for so many years.

"So, what should I call you: Mirko or Rick?"

"I guess Rick, even if I may not be quick to respond when I hear that name."

"You were never quick anyway, so Rick it will be."

Mirko-Rick stopped and said, "Watch your tongue. I'm stronger than you are."

Chris turned the flashlight off. "You can't see where I am. I have control of the situation."

They both stumbled on an old branch.

"We'll have plenty of time to bicker," Chris said. "Let's get out of here."

They quietly moved out of the cornfield and onto the road, the flashlight beam making a round splash ahead of them.

"How come you live in Canada? This is a beautiful country."

"That's where I was raised most of my life. I came here for holidays, but only after Mother died." Chris paused. "My work is there. My entire life is there."

"Are you married?"

"No, but I'll soon be." Chris paused as his thoughts went back to Lucio. "Father isn't too well so Vivian—Vivian is my woman—and I decided to get married soon." He paused and grinned, patting Mirko on the shoulder. "Since you're such a good boy, we'll squeeze you into the wedding party."

Mirko stopped walking. "My father," he whispered, his voice wavering. "Is he mad at me?"

"Oh no. Lucio blames himself for what happened, together with the curse, of course."

They resumed walking, and Mirko continued. "You call father by his first name?"

"Yes, for the longest time. He didn't want to be called *Father* after you…disappeared. He felt he wasn't worthy of that name anymore."

"Oh, I'm sorry about that."

"Don't worry. You'll make him the happiest man on earth when you show up. It's just that…see, his health isn't too good…we'll have to break the news carefully."

They had reached Santavecchia's house, and they could hear shouting and screaming. Chris stopped.

"You know what?" he said to Mirko. "Why don't we take my car and go celebrate?"

"I was thinking the same thing. I'll go in and tell Gabriele."

CHAPTER 61

"When are the police coming?" Chagrain asked for the third time, the dark crescents below his eyes deepening by the minute. He glanced at Nozemni who, sprawled on the only sofa of the house, had fallen asleep, probably because of the considerable number of painkillers he had eagerly swallowed.

"The police? Oh, we called them, but we told them it was nothing urgent," Gabriele said. He rose and grabbed the two shortened Brownings. "They'll also be interested in these guns. There was a break-in at one of the nearby hunting clubs. They were looking for them."

Chagrain shrugged and remained silent.

For the last hour Karl and Gabriele had been trying to find out what Chagrain and Nozemni were doing in Santavecchia's house, all to no avail. Nozemni had admitted to some wrongdoing, but Chagrain hadn't budged. Karl gave it another try.

"Why was your friend carrying three credit cards issued to Mirko Grogan, one Canadian passport—"

"One expired Canadian passport," said Gabriele, who was leafing through the documents.

"And another passport as Nozemni Radic?" Silence greeted him, so Karl continued. "We also found an undetermined number of bank notes—twenties and fifties. They're mostly fake, so we didn't bother counting them."

"Fake? *Counterfeit?*" Chagrain screamed. "You *must* be kidding!"

Nozemni opened his eyes for a second, looked around, shook his head, then dropped his head over his chest.

"Now let's hear your story," Karl said. "Your friend here, Nozemni Radic, told us you helped him steal some objects from the Sandcroft house, and that you got Mirko's money out of the bank. We believe him, but that doesn't explain why you two came here."

"My friend is injured and sick. He doesn't know what he's talking about. He should be in a hospital."

"We've called for an ambulance, but things are slow around here," Gabriele said.

"I have a lawyer in Brindisi. I want to call him."

"What about the money you guys were carrying?" Karl asked. "Where did it come from?"

"I don't have to answer any of your fucking questions," Chagrain said.

Whistling its way through the night, an ambulance stopped by the house. Two female nurses came out quickly, carrying a stretcher. They couldn't lift Nozemni from the sofa. He was over a hundred kilograms of dead weight.

When Gabriele went to their rescue by grabbing Nozemni underneath the shoulders, Chagrain made his move. He jumped from his chair and raced through the door.

With effort Karl rose to his feet and, even in pain and limping, dashed after Chagrain just in time to see him hopping over the fence on the left side of the house. Blinded by the many lights of the ambulance, Karl soon lost sight of the fugitive. Where had he gone? Was he hiding behind the bushes or among the birches? Though deprived of leaves, the trees still provided good cover.

Finally the ambulance took off, leaving darkness behind. Karl couldn't spot any trace of Chagrain. He took a few tentative steps left and right, then returned to the house to get a flashlight.

A TIR truck advanced at sustained speed, its huge mass taking up half the road.

Chagrain came out of the bushes and ran in front of the truck, waving his arms in a signal to stop.

The screech of brakes filled the air as the truck swayed left and right in an effort to avoid the man. Finally it leaned sideways, skidded along the fence of Santavecchia's house, and came to a stop. Chagrain's body, tossed high in the air, fell hard on the tarmac.

"Oh my God," said Gabriele, who lingered on the threshold.

"Oh my God," echoed Karl. "How insane can you be to force a heavy truck to stop." He moved to check on Chagrain, who lay a few metres away in a pool of blood. He stayed with him, moving the flashlight over him to assess his condition.

Gabriele cautiously approached the truck and helped the driver open the jammed cabin door.

Shaking his head, Karl shouted to Gabriele.

"Call for another two ambulances, but I don't think there's any hope for Chagrain."

*   *   *

At the Bellavista Restaurant where Chris and Mirko had drained two bottles of champagne and savoured the restaurant's famous pastry, it was closing time. They had talked and laughed together and, in a couple of instances, even remembered together. Anxious to know about Mirko's life, Chris had asked most of the questions, appalled at what his brother's life had been at the mercy of unscrupulous people. Mirko had described in detail the beatings and the starving he had suffered in the orphanage, and the lying and cheating he had to practice almost daily in order to comply with the Radics' requests.

Mirko, intrigued by Chris' work, wanted to know about his company and the seismographers he was building.

When the waiter tactfully slid the tray with the bill near his hands, Chris realized that he had spent more than four hours chatting with his brother. It had been a marvellous time, and a reunion he had never dreamed could happen. He laid his credit card on top of the bill, anxious to prolong the encounter for a few minutes. He wanted to stop time and carve in his memory the image of his brother as he talked about his life, in the old Yugoslavia first, and in Toronto afterwards, often stopping to excuse himself when his memory failed him.

"I still have plenty of empty spots—lacunas, I believe they're called—but my recollection of events gets better by the day," he would say, smiling. "Sometimes I can't link things together or say for sure that one happened before the other."

What surprised Chris the most was the way Mirko described his past, with sadness at times, but never with resentment. The physical and emotional abuse he had suffered and the solitude that had enveloped him in an invisible web had not left scars on his heart. It was a miracle. He was still full of enthusiasm, open to people and ready to enjoy life. *Is it real?* Chris felt the need to prod his brother's inner feelings.

"Don't you want to go after the people who caused you so much pain?"

Mirko rocked the empty glass between his fingers before answering. "What for? It wouldn't undo the past, and it would bring back more bad memories. When I took the trip to Dubrovnik last year, I wanted to find my roots. I wanted to know why I never felt at home…no matter where I was. That was my goal." His smile was a child's smile, innocent and sweet. "And see? I got what I was desperately looking for. I'm at peace with the world."

For a moment Chris was without words. Mirko had survived a terrible tragedy and managed to shake off all the hurt from his life as if it were mere dust. *He's a living miracle.*

Mirko rose and walked to the large window that stretched from wall to wall.

"What a marvellous view. One can see the harbour and all its lights for a long stretch." He turned toward Chris. "Of course, there are many beautiful places like this around here."

"I gather you like this country," Chris said as he pocketed his credit card, which had just been returned by the waiter.

"Oh, yes. You know what? I've been here only six months, but Italy has me bewitched."

CHAPTER 62

When Chris and Mirko reached Santavecchia's house, two tow-trucks were at work trying to pull up the TIR truck.

"What the heck?" Chris said as he went past the house and parked his rental along the road.

"A serious accident there?" Mirko asked. "Where the road is perfectly straight? That's strange."

As the main door was held in place by pieces of wood, and duct tape filled the biggest cracks around the doorframe, Mirko suggested using the back entrance. He walked into the house and quietly looked inside the two bedrooms.

"Gabriele and Sean are asleep."

He moved into the kitchen area, followed by Chris.

"Sean? Who's Sean?"

"The skipper of *Il Corsaro Rosso*. He'd been supervising some changes Gabriele ordered for his yacht. Probably Gabriele called him back."

Karl, who was stretched out on the sofa, woke up.

"You won't believe what happened around here," he said.

"We could tell there was a serious accident," Chris said. "Anybody hurt?"

"Yes. The man who went under the name of Jim Chagrain jumped in front of the truck. The driver tried to avoid him, but he didn't make it. Chagrain was dead when the ambulance arrived."

"The truck driver?" Mirko asked.

"Apparently he suffered only minor injuries, although he'll have to undergo some tests."

"And the other fellow?" Chris asked. "What happened to him?"

"An ambulance took him to a hospital in Brindisi. He admitted to some wrongdoing. He claimed to be Nozemni Radic, although he carried several documents with the name of Mirko Grogan."

"Radic?" Mirko asked. "That's the name of the people who ran the orphanage. Now I'm starting to see a connection. They didn't want me around to spill the beans about the orphanage and all their crimes."

Karl sat up straight and kicked off the blanket he had over his feet, showing a bandage covering half of his leg. "I think you're right. I tried to make some sense of what was happening, on the basis of the newspaper clips that Chris gave me earlier." He hopped on one leg and sat at the table. "I believe that when Mirko got lost at sea, they decided to steal his identity, along with all his belongings. My guess is that Nozemni got cosmetic surgery to look like Mirko. He has several scars to prove it. At a couple metres' distance the man looks just like you two. His frame is heavier, but even in height the match is pretty close."

"By the way, why aren't *you* in the hospital?" Chris asked.

"The paramedics came, looked at my wound and patched it up. It'll do for the time being. Tomorrow I'll go to see a doctor."

Meanwhile Mirko was leafing through the papers spread on the table.

"Look here. This is my passport!" He waved it proudly in the air. "I can go back. I can go back. I don't need to go to the Canadian embassy."

"Oh no you don't," said Chris. "While using your identity, Nozemni committed several crimes for which he's wanted by the Canadian police. If you ever got near a counter asking for a flight to Canada, you'd be arrested." Chris turned to Karl. "Where do you keep the newspaper I gave you?"

"In my windbreaker, inside pocket." He responded to Chris's astonished look. "Yes, I do have an inside pocket in the windbreaker."

Chris fetched the paper. He pointed at the front page. "Read here." The article explained that Mirko Grogan was wanted for rape, robbery and fencing.

Mirko-Rick glanced at the newspaper and then sat down, distraught.

"But then I won't ever be able to go anywhere."

"Cheer up, little brother. We'll find a way. You just have to be patient." As Mirko-Rick looked at him, totally flustered, Chris added, "Just be a bit more patient. I know you've waited years, but now it's only a question of days. I've already retained a lawyer, since I suspected there might be problems with your coming home."

"Is it going to work?"

"Absolutely." Chris turned to Karl. "Did you find bank notes in any of the fellows' bags?"

"Yes. About one hundred and eighty thousand dollars, mainly counterfeit. The police took all of it."

"Good. Those notes were part of a trap set up to catch the perpetrators of a robbery. They travelled a long way, but in the end they'll serve their purpose. It's the evidence that Nozemni was involved in selling stolen goods."

Karl's cell phone rang. He covered the mouthpiece and whispered to Chris, "Jeremy Weldon." Karl listened attentively, then said, "He's here." He handed the phone to Chris.

Chris paled as he listened. "I'll be on the first flight available." He paused. "Jeremy? The person you're talking about is indeed my twin brother. I need your help to get him back. Karl Steiner will explain the situation. It's complicated, but I think we can sort it out." He gave the phone back to Karl, who moved away from the table.

"Lucio, our father, collapsed onto the floor," Chris said, looking at his brother. "They took him to the hospital. I have to go back." He pulled out his wallet and extracted a business card that he slid toward Mirko-Rick. "My home phone number." He looked into his wallet. "I have only Canadian dollars. Here are a few hundreds—I'm sure you can exchange them at any bank." He hugged his brother and left.

PART 7

Reunited at Last

CHAPTER 63

Harrisville, January 2006

With one stop in London and another in Montreal to change flights, Chris managed to fly across the Atlantic and land in Toronto in under 16 hours. Vivian welcomed him with a silent, long hug.

"Sorry about Lucio," she said. "At the moment they can't do much for him. Just oxygen to help him breathe."

Chris nodded and took her hand, and together they walked to the parking lot.

"I knew Lucio's heart was in bad shape from what the doctor said and the fact that he never mentioned surgery. The lung problem was a terrible aggravation." He paused, pensive. "Now that we finally found my brother, my only wish is that he survives long enough to see Rick, touch him, and realize that he's alive and well."

"Is he really okay?"

"Physically, yes, he's stronger than I am, and he looks good. Emotionally…hmm…the man went through a lot, and he still suffers from retrograde amnesia."

"After he talked to Karl—whoever Karl is—Jeremy Weldon told my father a long story, one of abuse and misery, culminating with the stripping of your brother's identity and possessions."

"His possessions, too?"

"Yes. Jeremy just found out. Mirko Grogan's house was sold and his bank account closed months ago while your brother lay semi-conscious in a hospital in Italy. That's why they had to eliminate him."

"Well, the important thing is that Rick's alive; the man who threatened his life is dead and his accomplice is behind bars. He'll have nothing to fear from now on." They had reached the Lexus and Chris threw his carry-on into the back seat. "Nice to have a driver," he said, and sat in the passenger seat. "Are you taking me to Victoria's?"

"Yes. The doctor will be there when you tell Lucio about Mirko…or Rick…whatever name you want to use."

"Before I left I wanted to tell him that there was a chance Rick was alive, though stranded in Italy. I didn't. I was afraid of what might happen if I raised his hopes and then it turned out that Mirko wasn't his son. So I decided to wait, go there and see for myself." Chris sighed as if to release a big weight he carried inside. "Sometimes I can't make it right no matter how hard I try."

"You did a lot for Lucio," Vivian said, and patted him on the shoulder. "Once he told my father that the time he spent with you was the best he'd had since your brother disappeared."

*   *   *

Chris and Vivian crept into the hospital room and looked around.

A large ceramic container, bursting with silk flowers and leaves, stood in the middle of the windowsill, flanked, on each side, by small packages wrapped in colourful paper.

Lucio lay in bed, propped up on pillows; two tubes carried oxygen into his nostrils. He opened his eyes, and his mouth creased into a tiny smile.

"Chris, you're here." He lifted his arm to take Chris' hand. Chris shook it while bending to kiss his father. "And Vivian." Lucio stretched out his other hand to greet the young woman. "Nice to see you both."

Chris dragged a chair close to the bed as Vivian went looking for the doctor.

"How do you feel?" Chris asked.

Lucio was pale but his eyes were alert as ever. "Weak, but without pain. Ready to go home."

"Home?" Chris feared that he meant his home country.

"Yes, home. Don't I live on the first floor of your house? Isn't that my home now?"

Chris squeezed his hand. "It sure is."

Vivian was back, the doctor in tow, and both stood opposite Chris.

Chris' gaze shifted from Lucio to the doctor. He raised his eyebrows and the doctor nodded.

"Father, I have wonderful news." Chris looked at his father and paused, afraid to continue. He measured his next words. "The news you've being longing to hear."

"Rick?" Lucio's eyes brimmed with excitement, his frail body tense with repressed energy.

"Yes. Your other son is alive and well." Chris stopped, gauging his father's reaction.

"Where is he? Can I see him?" Lucio pushed the button to lift the headrest.

"Not yet, I'm afraid. He's in Italy, and he's among friends."

"Why can't he come here? Unfortunately, there's no way I can go there anymore."

"You remember that fellow in the Harrisville Dispatch—that Mirko Grogan who looked like Rick but wasn't?"

Lucio's brown eyes doubled in size, anxiety overshadowing his joy.

"Well, that guy stole Rick's identity. Rick went under the name of Mirko Grogan. The man stole his cards, ID, everything he had, and passed himself off as Rick while Rick lay in a hospital in Brindisi, the victim of an accident that left him in a semi-catatonic state."

Tears flew onto Lucio's face in rivulets that couldn't be stopped. "My little Rick," he said, his voice broken by emotion. "Is he really okay?"

"*He is*, Father. We have to work out a way to bring him here. The Canadian police are treating Mirko Grogan as a criminal, so there's plenty of explaining to do. Our lawyer, Jeremy Weldon, is looking into the matter."

Lucio tried to shake off the cotton blanket. "I have to go home."

"Why?"

"Because it's important, that's why. *È urgente!*"

"Oh no. You don't move. You *tell me* what's so important."

"Don't you see? I have all the documents for Riccardo de' Vigentini and the police in Italy collected a lot of facts and data about him when the big search was launched: strands of hair—Deborah, your mother, kept a strand of hair from the first time you two had a haircut—blood type, etc. I took everything with me and stored it in the first drawer of my dresser. Rick can get a passport as my son. He doesn't need Jeremy Weldon."

"Hmm…it's an interesting angle. We should explore it."

"I need to call Arcibaldo Cortesi. Take me home. I want to tell him about the documents I have and see whether they're enough to get him a passport." Lucio tried to rise, but he didn't make it.

The doctor put a hand on Lucio's shoulder. "You can't go, Mr. de Vigentini. Not yet. Maybe the day after tomorrow, but that isn't a promise."

Vivian bent over Lucio and kissed him on the cheek. "We should go home now. I'll help Chris gather all the papers about Rick." She joined Chris on the other side of the bed.

"Keep up your spirits." Chris glimpsed at his wristwatch. "It's too late to call Arcibaldo Cortesi tonight. I'll call him first thing in the morning and let you know how far we got."

Lucio rolled his eyes and screwed his lip up in disappointment. "Three against one," he murmured. "It isn't fair."

Chris and Vivian were a couple of hundred metres from the Sandcroft property when they heard an insistent barking, which became louder and louder as they proceeded toward the house.

"What the heck's up with Bertha?" Chris asked. As they drove under the archway, he could see lights. "Oh no. Reporters."

"Do you want to turn around? They probably haven't found out where I live." Vivian slowed almost to a halt.

"No, keep going. I'll face them. This is an occasion to tell the truth. It may take some time and I'm very, very tired, but Mirko-Rick's story, once printed and reprinted, can get the authorities from both countries to move and help my brother come home."

Two cars were parked in front of the house and four vehicles were stationed along the wall near the patio. Holding Bertha by the collar with one hand and a phone in the other, Gideon stood on guard at the threshold of the main entrance. Kathy, wearing a long leather coat with a fury hood, patrolled the side of the house. Two photographers ran toward the Lexus and began shooting before Vivian had brought it to a full stop.

"What do I do?" Vivian asked, intimidated by the crowd.

"Smile, and, if they ask questions, talk about your father's shop in Edinburgh."

312

Chris got out of the car and approached Gideon. "Take Bertha in the kitchen and be sure she doesn't come out. Tell Kathy to go home. It's freezing, for heaven's sake. I'll invite the reporters in and talk to them." He motioned for the reporters to follow.

As Gideon opened the door, a couple of photographers went ahead of Chris, shooting pictures of him and Vivian first, then of the stairway, the paintings hanging on the wall, and the marble floor.

Chris moved onto the second step of the staircase and raised his right hand.

"Ladies and gentlemen, please stop whatever you're doing for a minute and listen to me," he said. "I haven't had a good sleep in 48 hours and the only thing I'd like to do is go to bed. But I understand that you want to know if the rumour that several media have reported is true. Yes, it's true. My twin brother, who was lost at sea 27 years ago, is alive and well."

"Where is he?" a reporter asked.

"At the moment he's in Italy, but we hope to bring him home soon."

"What's his name?"

"Riccardo de' Vigentini."

"Is he the man who suffered aphasia and memory loss?"

"Yes."

"What happened to him?"

"Apparently he couldn't stay away from the water and got lost at sea a second time."

"Is Riccardo's father—your father—Lucio Maria de' Vigentini, the Lord of the famous Red Manor?" a woman inquired.

"Yes, and he's quite ill. That's why my priority is to bring my brother home, so he can be reunited with Lucio." He stopped and raked his hair in a compulsive gesture. "And now, ladies and gentlemen, I'll kindly ask you to leave the premises." With authoritative gestures he encouraged people to move toward the main door.

"Is this lovely woman your wife?" the same woman asked.

"Not yet, but she's my fiancée, Vivian Howard."

One flash after another almost blinded both Vivian and Chris.

"Please," Chris said. "Have a heart and let me have some rest."

Finally the door closed after the last reporter left.

Chris took Vivian by the hand and together they entered the family room. "For the time being we're safe," he said. "They knew the story already. The Italian newspapers have been out for almost 20 hours. They just wanted a few direct words they can quote, and some pictures to brighten their morning edition." He sat on the chesterfield, followed by Vivian. "Let's have a drink and then call it a night."

CHAPTER 64

When he woke up, Chris found himself clinging to the back of the chesterfield with both hands. He shook his head to get his bearings. He had experienced a frightful dream where he was lost in the wilderness; a river flowed fast down in the valley, and he was desperately trying to avoid falling by clinging to a huge rock. But the rock had no protrusions or indentations he could hang on to. It was a frightening situation, and that fear had jolted him awake. He wondered about the dream, whether it had any connection with the reality he was living. Hmm…he knew of rivers and rapids, but he had never attempted to climb a mountain.

The rustling of paper made Chris turn his head. Vivian was seated at the desk, wearing one of his pyjama tops and her reading glasses.

"Hi, Sweetheart," Chris said. "You look homey, cozy. I like it."

"Oh, you woke up. Good, I'll go make some coffee." She stood, her well-shaped legs stemming out of her top.

"Nice outfit you have on. It doesn't show much at the top, but plenty at the bottom." He rubbed his eyes, got up and followed her. When he was in the kitchen he wrapped his arms around her. "Coffee could wait," he whispered in her ear.

Vivian turned to face him, grinning. "Coffee could wait, but Lucio can't. He already called twice."

"Good point." He placed a long kiss on her neck.

"I took everything out of the drawer that Lucio mentioned yesterday. I found a birth certificate for Riccardo, a strand of hair—actually two…there's one of yours, too—a hospital certificate with the blood type, several photos, and a huge amount of correspondence and newspaper articles."

"I see. I'll go shave, then, and get dressed."

"Omelette okay?" Vivian called after him.

"Yes. Plenty of toast, too. I'm hungry like a bear."

Dressed in chinos and a casual, long-sleeved shirt, Chris was back half an hour later.

"What happened to your outfit? I kind of liked the one-piece pyjamas."

"Too revealing," said Vivian, now wearing suede pants and a red cashmere sweater. "We have to work, and I thought I'd better not distract you from the job."

"But we've been separated for almost a week," lamented Chris.

Vivian stood before him, her hands on her hips, her head cocked to one side. "Did you forget last night?"

"That was just a quickie." With resignation, Chris sat at the table in front of an omelette that filled his entire plate.

"Do you think getting an Italian passport is going to work?" Vivian asked.

"I don't have a clue."

In no time breakfast was over and they both sat at the desk, leafing through the documents that concerned Riccardo de' Vigentini.

"Well," Chris said, perplexed. "I don't know what to think of this material, if there's anything useful to the cause. I'd better call Arcibaldo."

"Lucio's lawyer?"

"Yes, and long-time friend. Let's see what he says about requesting an Italian passport."

After having exchanged a few words with the lawyer's secretary, Chris made contact with Arcibaldo Cortesi.

"Oh, Chris, you can't imagine the trouble I've had. I couldn't spring loose from a certain gentleman, Gabriele Anzieri. He was so persistent. He brought Riccardo—Rick, I mean—in here once again. He wants me to get Rick a passport as Riccardo de' Vigentini." The lawyer paused, and cleared his throat. "I couldn't make him understand the situation. You see—" He coughed again, and Chris knew he was in for a long explanation. "According to Italian law, once an individual is missing for more than 10 years, he's declared dead. If he ever reappears, he's entitled to all the rights he had before, including any wealth and inheritance he may have accumulated during his disappearance." Arcibaldo laughed softly. "If there's any left. As Rick had been missing for more than 20 years, we need two people who have known him for the last 10 years to testify that he is, indeed, who he claims to be."

Oops! Chris thought. *I got the answer before even asking the question. What the government wants is justified, but it doesn't help Rick's case.*

Arcibaldo continued. "You understand, right? Rick didn't lose any of his birthrights; they only have to be reinstated." He paused. "Keep in mind, Chris, that I have no doubt that the man who came to see me is your brother. He's your copy. But what I think has no legal bearing."

"Oh, I understand. Lucio thought the procedure would be quick and simple since we have with us Rick's birth certificate and a strand of his hair."

Arcibaldo paused for a long moment. "His hair? If the follicles are still active, that strand can be used for a DNA test: that would definitely link your brother to the identity of Riccardo de' Vigentini. But it'll take a long time to go that route." The old lawyer sounded tired. "From what I know, he lived in Canada for a long time, so there must be a way to get him back on the grounds that he is a Canadian citizen."

"Sure we can, but the name he's carrying as an adopted child, Mirko Grogan, is associated with three crimes—crimes, of course, that he didn't commit." Chris felt queasiness in the pit of his stomach. Lucio was in bad shape and might not survive long enough to meet with Rick. "Mr. Cortesi, thank you for your time," Chris finally said. "If you think of anything that can help Rick, anything at all, please let me know."

"Sure thing, Chris." The lawyer rang off.

"Well, let me call Jeremy Weldon," Chris said.

A glance at the clock hanging on the wall made Vivian spring to her feet. "I have to leave. Mother and I have to go through the invitations for the wedding. 'Bye, love. See you tonight."

The wedding! He had forgotten about it. It was good that Elisabeth and Glen loved to organize parties. The only thing he'd probably have to do was show up on time. He looked outside, where a thin layer of snow made the patio look neat and pleasant. Glen had the extravagant idea of holding the ceremony outside under a heated tent and having the altar supported by the four original cups—upside down and reinforced, of course—and Vivian had approved wholeheartedly.

The idea of performing the ceremony in a tent had sent Father Paul into objectionable mumbling, but the donation that Lucio had offered shortly afterward for his seminary had made him smile from ear to ear. Chris remembered how well organized the television programme was. Glen would set up a grand, elegant show for the wedding of his only child.

Chris' only worry was his father's health. His brother might not be able to see Lucio alive.

The call to Jeremy Weldon was put on hold, and Chris ruminated about the bureaucracy that often engulfed personal rights into procedural matters. Finally, Jeremy came on the phone.

"Hi Chris. I talked to Karl at length and he told me that your brother and Mr. Anzieri have tried to get a temporary permit from the Italian Government. It didn't work, so they were both very disappointed."

"I know. I think we'll have to work it out from this side."

"Well, I did a preliminary study of the case." That rang money in Chris' ears, but on the other hand, he was in the lawyer's hands. "It's complicated. I found one employee of the grocery store where your brother worked part-time and the owner of the construction company that remodelled his house, which, by the way, isn't his anymore. They're both willing to testify on his behalf. And his doctor, Bernard Alvinski, would be his guarantor. So once your brother is here, there would be no problem getting him new documents."

Of course not. Chris was growing impatient. Jeremy was working around the issue, not *on* the issue. The problem was repatriating his brother. He patiently waited for the lawyer to continue.

"Regarding the possibility of re-entering Canada, we have to make a petition, and that petition has to go to court."

Chris had scientific training; although patient, he was accustomed to shooting at the problem without pussyfooting around it. Jeremy sounded as if he wanted to continue.

"Time frame?" Chris asked.

"Five weeks if they buy into the compassionate angle, three to six months otherwise. However, if you can find a way to make Rick touch Canadian soil, we can bring the witnesses directly to the port-of-entry and identify him. Then—"

"How could I bring him in? Put him on a balloon and hope it flies across the Atlantic?" He paused, trying to regain his cool. "Go for the petition while I think of an alternative. My father won't last that long."

Let things cool down, Chris advised himself as he drove to Vibratim. He hoped that the requests for equipment had slackened off. Once he arrived, he settled in his office. He looked at the tray with the incoming mail and made a few notes on some letters to indicate how they should be answered. He then reviewed carefully the draft of a contract for three new magnetometers. As Vibratim was behind in production, he changed the delivery date.

Once he had dealt with urgent business matters, Chris' thoughts returned to Rick's predicament and its impact on his father's condition. He couldn't believe it was so difficult to get Rick back promptly where he belonged. Why was there no way to help the victim of an identity scam? Something in the system was wrong. Rules were made to serve the citizens, not to hinder them. For a moment he relished the thought of a shortcut. He could ask his brother to get a good haircut and send him an air ticket with his own passport; then Rick would come back smoothly. After all, his weight, looks, and nationality were a perfect match. He was so upset that the temptation to use that trick grew larger by the minute. Then his telephone rang.

The call was from Gabriele Anzieri.

"Hope I'm not bothering you. I heard of the difficulties you were having in your country—not as bad as the ones here, but still nerve-wracking—and I have an idea how to get your brother into Canada. Before I talk to him, however, I'd like to run it past you."

"I have an idea too," Chris said. "But mine isn't too…lawful."

"Oh, mine is, Chris. It's just going to be very expensive, and dangerous on two counts."

Chris wiggled in his chair, ready to listen. "Shoot…money won't be a problem."

"Take Mirko—I mean Rick—in my boat and cross the Atlantic." Gabriele paused. "A quarter million dollars, less if we get reasonable weather and don't have to fight gale-strength winds."

"Can your boat make it? What kind of vessel do you have?"

"It's custom made. Very similar in performance to the Mediterraneé 50, with a fuel tank of almost two thousand litres. We'll refuel in the Azores, then shoot for the maritime coast. It should take about a week."

"What about icebergs? Don't some slip down in the winter?"

"No, not normally. In wintertime, the polar cap is a pretty solid block of ice. In any case, our expert in naval communications will keep in contact with the Canadian Ice Service. They issue daily reports and they're pretty accurate. They use aerial observation and RADARSAT-1 imaging."

"Have you done anything similar before? Who else would be aboard?"

"Not on a leisure vessel, no, only on cargo ships and those are not easily frightened by waves or wind. My skipper, Sean Despin, will be with me. We'll alternate at the helm."

Chris couldn't believe what he was hearing. "The concerns?"

"First, Rick. Would he take such a long trip after all that happened to him before? He might get too scared and suffer a regression. My friend, Dr. Santavecchia, advises against it."

"The second?"

"The weather. We might encounter a severe storm and have to be rescued. If we're close to the Canadian coast there'll be no problem. Rick will end up on Canadian soil. If we're in the middle of the ocean, well...the situation can be serious. We may end up elsewhere or be brought back to where we started." As Chris remained silent, Gabriele asked, "What do you think? Karl is so fired up at the idea that he'll come with us for nothing, and I know of a young man, Cesare Porta, who's anxious to go on a journey like this. He works at the communication centre of the Brindisi harbour."

"Dangerous and expensive, you're telling me, but feasible." Chris paused. "Would your insurance pay if your boat got smashed?"

"I'd have to pay an extra premium, but that cost is part of the sum I mentioned."

"Hmm...we're risking lives here, Gabriele. Let's me think about it. But thank you for the thought. Rick was very lucky to find you." He paused. "Can I call you tomorrow morning? I think better at night."

"Sure. Call anytime."

Crossing the Atlantic in mid-winter in a leisure boat? Is it wise? No, it's crazy. Chris sat in the darkness of the family room, weighing the risks that such an operation posed. Gabriele sounded at ease about the journey. He seemed more concerned about Rick's reaction to being at sea than anything else. Chris helped himself to a whisky, hoping to relax. It had been a long, strenuous day. He paced the room, looking at the photographs that had mysteriously appeared on top of a console after his father had arrived: a wedding picture of his parents, Rick and himself as they opened Christmas presents, the two brothers standing on top of the Red Manor tower, and Chris sitting in a red Lamborghini. He sipped his drink slowly, savouring each drop. *Am I risking my brother's life to brighten the last moments of our father's?* Suddenly, everything became clear. *I'll leave the decision to Rick. He's sound enough in mind to make it.* He picked up the phone and called Gabriele.

CHAPTER 65

Aboard Il Corsaro Rosso

Mirko was listening to the second act of Puccini's *Turandot*, where Prince Calaf solves all three riddles that will give him the right to wed Turandot. *Music is great, but action is much more exciting.*

Carrying a crew of four—Gabriele, Sean, Cesare and Karl—*Il Corsaro Rosso*, with the Italian flag fluttering at its stern, had moved smoothly from *La Scarpetta*, the marina on the Adriatic Sea, into open waters. Then, after crossing the Strait of Gibraltar, it headed for the Azores.

Mirko had been drowsy for some time, as Santavecchia had given him pills to relax and for seasickness. One condition Gabriele had posed before starting the voyage was that Mirko would stay in his stateroom and come out only for meals. Mirko had agreed, not only because it was a *sine-qua-non* condition but also because he was afraid of his own reactions. After all, boats had brought him plenty of bad luck. However, he was excited at the idea of rejoining his family and felt confident thanks to the support that Gabriele and his friends had given him for months. Now, Mirko wanted to be an active part of this unique adventure—crossing an ocean aboard a leisure boat while defying adverse conditions of all kinds.

He leafed through the vast collection of CDs Gabriele had stored in his stateroom, then paused. He was tired of listening to music. He paced the room, fretting to be active. He was curious to see how Cesare, the communications expert, kept in contact with the rest of the world. He wanted to find out how the radar equipment worked. There was so much occurring and he was cooped up in a room. Karl had been so intrigued by the trip that he was spending vacation time aboard the yacht. Sean had come alive at the idea of being at sea in the biggest voyage of all. Things were happening all around him, and what was he doing? Nothing.

Enough nonsense, Mirko thought. He opened the door, and poked his head out.

"Gabriele," he called out.

Dressed in a dark blue uniform, Gabriele appeared at the threshold, a worried look on his face.

"You okay?" he asked.

Mirko nodded. "Come in, Gabriele. I want to talk to you."

Uncertain, Gabriele moved in.

"I'm feeling well, Gabriele—great actually—and I'd like to have something to do." As Gabriele remained silent, he added, "I'd like to be part of the crew."

Gabriele cocked his head to one side and then the other, as if to analyze the person he was talking to. "We have an agreement, Mirko," he said in a stern voice. "I have enough on my plate now that the most challenging part of the trip has begun."

"I understand, and yes, we have an agreement." He paused. "You've been very good to me, Gabriele, and I'm sorry I can't be good to you the way you'd like."

Gabriele waved off the issue. "I came to terms with that—no need to bring it up. Certain issues are better left unspoken." He placed a hand on Mirko's shoulder. "I care about you, and I always will. You're very special to me and I hope we'll remain friends for life. However—" He stopped and removed his hand. "However, I engineered this trip knowing that it could be critical for you to be at sea. That's why you had to promise to stay down here. Just for another three or four days. That's all."

"But don't you see? I'm okay. My memory is almost all back, and I have no problem talking. I've improved a lot. I'm my old self, and that person wants to live, Gabriele, not vegetate."

Gabriele took off his captain's hat, raked his hair and put the hat back in place. "I'm the boss around here, Mirko, do you understand? What I say *goes.*"

Mirko gave him a suave smile. "I know. That why I'm addressing my petition to you."

"Hmm….Just out of curiosity—and I'm not saying I agree—what would you like to do?"

"Anything, anything at all. I can cook, or maybe assist Cesare or Karl in their jobs. I promise one thing: I won't go on deck."

Gabriele mumbled, "Problems, problems...I seem to have a special talent for finding them. Okay. Go to the kitchen and see what you can do there. After all, we could all use a decent meal. As for assisting Karl and Cesare, you wait until one of them comes down and takes you up. Understood?"

Mirko sprang up and performed a military salute. "Yes, sir. Yes, *Captain.*"

It was only early afternoon, yet the sky remained dark as more clouds closed in. Up on deck, Gabriele scrutinized the immense mass of water that extended before him. *So far so good,* he thought. They were on schedule and had just hooked up to the last extra tank they had loaded—the extra fuel making up for the passengers that *Il Corsaro Rosso*, built to carry 14, didn't have aboard.

Sean approached Gabriele. He chewed tobacco, a habit he had acquired after he quit smoking his beloved pipe.

"They want you downstairs," he said.

"Problems?"

"Yes. A storm is closing in. They think we should change course, five points south."

Gabriele descended the staircase and stepped into the little room, which contained a variety of navigation instruments. In the middle of the table lay a map with ocean currents painted in different colours and a tack marking the actual coordinates of the yacht. Mirko stood in a corner, watching; Cesare bent over the map, one long ruler between his fingers; Karl, a sheet in his hand, read information to Cesare.

Cesare Porta, who held a diploma in computer networking and radar navigation, had worked in the communications office of the Brindisi harbour for the last seven years. He had immediately bonded with Sean, absorbing all of the sailors' stories that Sean enjoyed telling. With Karl things had been different, as Karl would answer hardly any questions regarding his life or his job.

"What's new?" Gabriele asked.

Karl read from the sheet he held in his hands. "Storm warning: strength eight. Developing about twenty nautical miles northwest of us." He pointed at a dotted line. "It's moving fast in this direction."

"It doesn't pose a threat if it keeps that direction," Cesare said. "It'll miss us, but not by much. However, there's always the chance of small variations."

"The Champlain, the tanker ahead of us, has changed its course to the south," Karl said. "Five points."

Gabriele shifted the map around to look at the trajectories head on. "Cesare, when will we reach the Champlain?"

Cesare made some calculations. "If the wind stays the same, we can be there in three hours and 20 minutes."

"Change course to intercept the tanker. Once we get close, keep in touch with them."

"How much are we going south?" Karl asked. "Won't we enter American waters?"

"No." Cesare moved close to Gabriele and changed the ruler from the previous course to the new one. "At worst we'll end up at Clark's Harbour, south of Halifax. Not a great detour."

"Once we're near the tanker we'll reduce our speed to match theirs," Gabriele said. "Probably down to five knots."

Cesare punched a few more numbers into his hand calculator. "At that speed we'll be in territorial waters late tomorrow morning."

"Depends," Gabriele said. "If the storm goes by us quickly, we can resume our normal speed or even go up a notch, since we have plenty of fuel left."

*   *   *

For five long hours the navigation of the vessel relied almost exclusively on instrumentation—the skipper's eyes only witnessing the prow follow the swales in a roller coaster. Pitch, combined with roll, at times replaced by yaw, gave each member of the crew the feeling of coiling like rattlesnakes.

When finally it became clear that the storm had moved east of them, jubilation filled *Il Corsaro Rosso.*

"I'd like to propose a toast," Gabriele shouted from his post of command, "but I can't do it on two counts: we don't have anything to toast with and our stomachs need to settle down."

He veered to the northwest and stepped up the speed, bringing it to 20 knots. He actually wanted to cruise at the maximum of 30, but the haze that had replaced the clouds made him adjust speed to visibility. He had been at the wheel for the last five hours, determined to bring his yacht to its destination.

Finally Mirko would be reunited with his family.

Gabriele glanced at the GPS-based instrument at his side and realized that they were only 10 nautical miles off the coast of Nova Scotia. He adjusted their direction to point directly to the Halifax harbour. In the far distance he heard a horn, meaning that fog could soon replace the current haze.

To his surprise, Sean moved up next to him, a serious look on his face. "You'd better go see Mirko."

"Why? Is he sick? He shouldn't be. He was the only one lying in a hammock." As Sean didn't reply, he added, "So, what's the problem?" Approaching a harbour with reduced visibility was always a critical manoeuvre. *I should stay at the helm.*

"Mirko wants to jump off the boat to avoid going through the checkpoints." Sean coughed slightly. "I felt like belting him one."

"Why didn't you?" Gabriele set the motor to a minimum and proceeded cautiously, gliding toward the harbour like a ghost.

"He's too big and too strong. Karl tried to reason with him, but there was no way. Mirko is very determined. I've never seen him like that." He took the wheel from Gabriele's hands. "We all feel that only you can dissuade him."

Gabriele glanced around. "Be extra careful. Banks of fog spear at you all at once." Taking two steps at a time, Gabriele descended the stairs.

Engulfed in a leather coat and with a ski hat that covered his ears and forehead, Mirko was checking the contents of his pockets.

"Hi, Gabriele. I was going to come up and say *arrivederci* to you. See you at my brother's place in a day or so."

"What do you think you're doing?" Gabriele's voice was tight.

Mirko gave him a broad smile. "Going ashore. I'm home, Gabriele. *Home!*"

"If they catch you without documents you're going to have big problems. This isn't the smartest thing to do."

"No? And why not? I've been very patient and followed all the avenues to convince the authorities that I am Mirko Grogan. And what happened? Nothing. I'm not going to spend another minute talking to a bunch of bureaucrats or waiting for people to witness my identity here, in the middle of nowhere." He quickly counted the money Chris had given him and put it back in his pocket.

Gabriele set a hand on Mirko's shoulder, putting pressure on it. "We've made it, Mirko. We've made it. Don't blow everything now."

"I'm not blowing anything, my friend. Canada is my rightful home. If somebody wants to challenge my identity, the burden of proof falls on that somebody. Let *them* find people to swear in court that I'm *not* Mirko Grogan—*the real Mirko Grogan.*"

A scraping sound made their heads jerk. The boat tilted. Immediately after, there was a thud. Gabriele and Mirko rushed to deck while the motor went idle.

The prow of *Il Corsaro Rosso* was wedged between two rocks.

Mirko lost no time. He ran to port and hopped ashore. In the small moments that elapsed between one wave retreating and the next surging to lick the boat side, he tried to assess the damage. It took him several minutes.

"It isn't too bad," he shouted. "Nothing to worry about. The damage looks superficial. You shouldn't take water."

As Gabriele took the wheel, Sean unwound the rope used for docking and jumped ashore. He made it, but slid on a wet rock and let go of the rope. Before the rope could fall into the water, Mirko stepped on it, and then helped Sean stand up.

"I think I can disengage the boat by myself," Mirko said. "Keep the rope in your hands and be ready to jump back if I make it."

Mirko moved in front of the prow and climbed onto the two rocks, setting one foot on each. He gave Gabriele the sign to back up, then braced the prow with both arms. With one powerful lift he freed it and then, calling upon all his strength, pushed the boat back into the sea—a humongous splash washing over him.

Sean leaped in the direction of the boat as Karl and Cesare pulled on the rope to shorten the distance. He barely managed to take hold of the rail.

Karl lifted him inside the boat.

"Bon voyage," Mirko called out. But *Il Corsaro Rosso* had already disappeared in the fog.

CHAPTER 66

Harrisville, Chris' home

The Sandcrofts spared no money or effort in welcoming the crew of *Il Corsaro*.

Lucio, informed that Rick would come later, put up a brave face in spite of his great disappointment. Rick intended to reach Harrisville by land, Chris had explained to him, and that would take a couple of days.

Lucio had come home from the hospital a week ago, and had enjoyed speaking to his once lost son on the phone. When *Il Corsaro* was at sea, in fact, a daily call informed Chris and Lucio of the activities taking place aboard the ship, and on the boat's distance from the Canadian coast. Lucio had treasured the few minutes he could hear the voice of his beloved Rick. Those calls had been a balm for Lucio's old emotional scars, and the expectation of seeing Rick had raised his spirits.

The first night, Gabriele Anzieri, the guest of honour seated at one end of the table between Chris and Lucio, had entertained his hosts and the Howards with a description of the recent voyage. Sean often interrupted to add colourful details. Cesare, seated to the left of Lucio, kept asking him questions about the Red Manor and his new life in Harrisville. Karl, in a chair between Vivian and Elisabeth, had dropped his distant attitude, refilling the women's glasses and his own with unusual solicitude.

The second night the atmosphere was still convivial, but Rick's absence had become palpable. Glen had succeeded in engaging everybody's attention by talking about the new shop he was planning to open in Toronto.

"The request for art objects and replicas of the famous cups keeps rising, and they come mostly from this side of the Atlantic," Glen said. "My shop in Edinburgh can't keep up. It'll be after the wedding, however, since now we're all very busy." He stopped, and then explained at length the history of the cups, the success of the reality show, and the idea of using those precious items as supports for the altar during the nuptial celebration.

It was then that Gabriele roared with laughter.

"You mean to tell me that with all the history and artistic heritage the Red Manor has, the wedding is going to be celebrated in a tent with a make-do-altar?" Gabriele turned to Lucio. "Signor de' Vigentini, why don't you say anything?"

A smile crept across Lucio's lips, and he opened his arms in surrender. "I don't interfere with my son's decisions. If he's happy, I'm happy. And let me tell you something, he is so happy to marry Vivian that he would do so at the North Pole while standing on an iceberg. Does it sound awkward—a modern idea together with a touch of the old stuff? Maybe, but Glen knows how to set up a show, I guarantee you. You'll see it, since you're all invited."

Glen wiggled in his chair, clearly pleased. He looked at Vivian. "You like it, right?"

"It's a terrific idea," Vivian said, her eyes glowing with excitement. "Mother and I've already found the right furniture to rent. It'll be a blast."

Gabriele seemed appeased. "I'm looking forward to seeing it."

Glen looked at Chris. "By the way, where are the cups? The real ones, I mean?"

"Hidden in a safe spot."

"But where?"

"Well, I don't know if I should tell."

"We need to know. The altar is going to be custom-made."

"You can use the fake ones. They've been returned with all the other art objects."

"Come on, Chris, you can tell," Glen said. "You've made me curious all this time."

"Well…they're inside the fountain." He turned to the other guests. "They were too big to fit in a safe, so I locked them inside the bronze base of the fountain. I thought…well, it was a wild guess, but I thought that a thief in search of the cups would use a metal detector and would blame the bronze when his sensor rang a bell."

The third night, all the efforts that Chris, the Howards, and the crew of *Il*

Corsaro Rosso made to keep any form of conversation alive had failed. Nobody said a word about the worry they all shared. Where was Rick? Had he been arrested? Was he sick and suffering in some obscure corner of the country?

Immediately after the main course Lucio excused himself and retired to his room.

"When did you say you plan to leave?" Chris asked Karl.

"In three days. My vacation will be over by then." He paused. "I booked a flight—the latest I could. I still hope to see Rick before leaving."

Chris went to the kitchen and came back with dessert, a chocolate pudding. "Skimpy supper tonight," he said, trying to look cheerful. "Kathy had the day off." He filled the china cups with perked coffee.

The conversation faltered and a chill floated in the air. With its formal, ornate style, the Chippendale furniture contributed to the cold atmosphere reigning among the diners.

Soon after, the Howards stood up and so did Gabriele, Sean, Karl and Cesare.

"Maybe tomorrow night you folks should be our guests, for a change of scenery." Gabriele turned to Chris, a concerned look on his face. "Too bad I had no time to give Mirko my cell phone."

Chris waved off the comment. "There are plenty of ways to make a call. I'm not worried yet. My brother is a big boy."

The words Chris had pronounced in front of his guests had been mere sound, a soothing invitation to stay calm. Inside, however, he was filled with anguish. While in the hospital, his father had lost weight and he looked very frail. His pulmonary disease was getting worse by the day. Chris wondered whether Lucio would live to see his beloved Rick.

No reason to go to bed, Chris thought. He wouldn't be able to sleep.

He walked to the entrance hall where Bertha lay placidly asleep and woke the dog up. They had already jogged twice and the dog dragged her feet as Chris called her outside. The night was clear with temperatures hovering just above zero. He found the fresh air invigorating. He tapped the phone tucked into his belt, as if that would make it ring. Then he made one last round to the pond and back.

At three o'clock in the morning he finally re-entered the house and moved upstairs to take a shower. He would go to bed and snatch what sleep he could.

The rumbling of a motor entering the premises broke the stillness of the night. Already showered and in his pyjamas Chris descended to the first floor, tiptoed to the main door and looked through the peephole.

His brother, a wool hat covering most of his hair, was paying the cab driver. In his bare feet Chris ran outside toward Rick.

"You made it, Rick! Oh God! You can't believe how much I've worried!"

Rick embraced him tightly. "Thank you, *Brother*. Thank you for agreeing on the trip and for sending that pile of money. I owe you for life."

Skirting Bertha who had followed him outside, Chris dragged Rick into the house.

"Let me go put a bottle of champagne in the fridge," he said. "Come on in. What happened to you after you jumped ashore? We expected you two days ago!"

Rick looked sheepishly at his brother and sat at the kitchen table. "When I started walking I realized I was wet from head to toe. I could hear the water squeezing out of my shoes every time I took a step. And cold? You can't believe how cold. I walked to the nearest hotel and took a room. I laid my clothes on the heat register and slumped into bed. I woke up some twelve hours later."

Chris got a box of cookies from a cupboard and deposited it on the table.

Rick dug into it. "When I pushed the boat back into the sea, everything got wet. The money—I mean the notes you gave me—were not damaged, but the card with your phone number was; the water had wiped out the ink. When I tried 411, I found out your number was unlisted."

"Oh, yes. Sorry about that," Chris said, and went to fetch two flutes. "So what did you do?"

"I went to a bus station, but there was nothing leaving at that hour. I had to wait for the next day. Can you believe it? All together 14 hours to reach Montreal. Here I took a train to Toronto, then a cab to Harrisville. I didn't have your address either. The cab driver contacted the local cab service and found out where the Sandcrofts lived." Rick munched with delight on a few more cookies.

"Want something more substantial to eat?"

"No. I'm just waiting for that champagne. We had no frills on the boat, only the essentials. All the extra weight we could carry was taken up by tanks of fuel." He paused. "How is Father?"

Chris frowned. "On borrowed time."

"His voice always sounded remote, kind of feeble, when I talked to him on the phone."

"He's weak. I hope seeing you will put his mind and body at ease. Do you want me to wake him up?"

"Up to you. I don't want to cause him any distress by appearing in the middle of the night." He looked at Chris and chuckled. "I've done enough of that, I believe."

"Maybe we'd better wait till morning, then."

Rick looked around. "What about that champagne? It should be chilled by now."

Chris uncorked the bottle and filled two glasses, then raised one. "To you, Brother. To your courage and your faith in life."

"To us," Rick replied, clinking glasses. "And to our father."

"How did you feel, spending a full week at sea? Was it rough?"

"Nice weather the first two days. Then it became windy and the sea was raging."

"Were you sick?"

Rick leaned against his chair. "Not really. The first day they gave me pills. I was sleepy, but never frightened or sick." He paused. "Then I told them I wanted to be like everybody else. I wanted *to become* like everybody else. Gabriele hesitated, but in the end the pills disappeared and they gave me chores to do. I had to prepare the meals and clean up afterwards. I sat close to Karl and Cesare for hours. They were in charge of the navigation and checking meteorological conditions." He paused. "You may not believe this, but I had the best time of my life. I learned a lot travelling in the company of those extraordinary people." He laughed. "Once in a while I looked out of a porthole, but the view never changed—only water."

"Incredible! The trip, the jumping ashore…everything's incredible!" Chris moved behind Rick's chair and hugged his brother around the shoulders. "It's nice to touch you and feel that you're real, not a vague image lost in the darkness of time." He hugged him again, stronger this time.

A slight noise made both brothers turned their heads. The kitchen door swung open and Lucio appeared, a red housecoat over his pyjamas, the wheelchair way too big for his small body. He looked at Chris, then at Rick.

"Oh my God! It's *you*!"

Rick rose and knelt in front of him. "I'm here, Dad. It's me, Rick."

Lucio patted his long hair and kissed it. "My dear son, *ti ho ritrovato, finalmente*! At last I see you!" He kept Rick's head between his hands and then tilted it up to look at his face. He fingered his nose, the contour of his eyes, his long eyelashes and his lips. "My little Rick, you don't know how much I've missed you all these years." He dried a tear with the back of his hand, but more came; he couldn't stop sobbing.

Rick stood and looked for a box of tissues. He knelt again and gave one to Lucio.

"I thought you'd be happy to see me," Rick said. "Instead you cry." As Lucio attempted to laugh, Rick crossed his heart. "I promise I won't be any trouble. I'll be a good boy from now on."

With a tremor, Lucio gestured for Chris to come close. He embraced them both.

"There's nothing else I'd want on this earth," he said. "God granted me my deepest wish: seeing my sons together and in good health. Thank you, Lord."

CHAPTER 67

Under the February sun the snow glistened. *Still very cold,* Chris surmised as he retreated from the window and finished dressing. He descended the stairs, knowing very well where the joyful voices came from. He opened the kitchen door and took a seat at the table, close to Rick.

"I hope you left something for me to eat," he said as he watched Rick, Lucio, Lillian, Kathy and Gideon eating, chatting and laughing. For the last couple of weeks Lucio had invited Lillian and the Wilsons to have breakfast with him. He wanted Rick to get to know the people who surrounded him.

Kathy rose to pour coffee for Chris. "I came to your bedroom, but you were sound asleep so I didn't dare wake you up."

"You came home late," said Lucio.

Chris took a slice of French toast and nodded. "At the lab we had to do one last test before getting our shipment ready. It was one o'clock in the morning when I finally left. Was it cold. Fifteen below, I believe, and more of the same for tonight, I heard."

"Fifteen? Brrr," Lucio said. "It's great I don't have to go outside. It's warm and cozy here."

Both Cesare and Karl had flown back home, but Gabriele and Sean were still around, enjoying short trips in the country by day, and scouting for good restaurants by night. There was always an open invitation for the Howards and the de' Vigentinis to join them for supper, but most of the times Chris and Rick declined the offer.

Chris sipped his coffee, taking stock of the people around him.

Rick seemed to treasure every bit of the attention his father gave him. Settled in the guest room for the time being, he was thrilled to be with his family. He wasn't a bit worried about the length of the legal process necessary to provide him with new documents. He definitely looked happy.

Lillian, who had been reserved at first, even uneasy every time he was around, had finally gone back to being her old self, and showed how much she appreciated having been rehired to take care of Lucio.

Gideon was looking after the house maintenance with his usual efficiency, and Kathy had surpassed herself with superb cooking, no matter how many guests arrived unexpectedly.

"You're quiet. Still worried about your work?" Lucio asked.

"No. I met the deadline. Everything's okay. Time to relax."

"Going out with Vivian?" Rick asked.

"Nope. She's busy with preparations for the wedding."

"Right. The big day is only a month away," Lucio said, and pushed away his plate, the French toast almost untouched.

"So you have nothing planned for the day?" Rick asked.

"Not really." Chris looked at his brother. "Something you'd like to do?"

"There are a lot of things I'd like to do." Rick grinned.

"I can understand that. Catching up for the time spent in the hospital. For the moment tell me two things you'd like to do, one long-term and one short-term," Chris said.

"Well, one day I'd like to go back to Brindisi to see a girl; Daniela is her name. She's be-au-ti-ful, I tell you. Blue eyes and long, curly hair." He paused, uncertain whether to continue. "Nice legs too."

"Weren't you supposed to be sick at the hospital?" Chris asked.

"Yes, but she helped me get better."

"Well, that's long-term all right. Something you'd like to do today, with your older brother?"

"Hmm…Let me think. We could wander through downtown Toronto. Look at the shops on Yonge, go to a show…nothing specific, just let our spirits guide us."

"Fine," Chris said. "Get one of my heavy coats. You may need it today."

"Okay if we take off?" Rick asked Lucio.

Lucio had followed the exchange of words in silence, his eyes, still vivid and alert, absorbing the view of his sons. "Of course. Just give me a hug before you leave."

The two brothers leaned over the wheelchair, one on each side, and delicately embraced their father.

Lucio patted them on the shoulder. "Don't get into trouble," he said, and smiled. Then he pulled them closer, hiding his face between their shirts. "God bless you both, my children."

*   *   *

They laughed and sang and joked. They watched a horror movie, bought DVDs and books and then identical baseball caps that made them look like exactly what they were: twins.

It was late when Chris and Rick returned home.

"It's been a fun evening," Rick said, as Chris parked his Camaro in the garage. "And I'm not tired yet. What a life."

"Keep quiet. Lillian is probably sleeping on the sofa. She doesn't leave until I get home."

"So? You have to wake her up anyway."

"Well, maybe, and maybe not. Actually I should let her sleep. She's been very busy with Lucio lately." He got rid of his coat. "Get a drink ready while I go to say goodnight to Lucio. There's a light on in his room. He's probably reading. Sometimes he can't go to sleep for a long stretch of the night."

Chris tiptoed into Lucio's room and leaned over the bed.

Lucio lay immobile, his eyes closed, his arms bent, a family album sprawled on his chest, his hands in the pretence of holding it. Chris turned on the central light and felt for Lucio's pulse at the neck.

There wasn't any.

For a few minutes Chris was unable to move. Then he gently freed the album from Lucio's hands. They were still warm. He bent to kiss his father on the forehead and on the cheeks.

"Good night, Lucio," he murmured, and fell to his knees in prayer.

He didn't hear Rick until he knelt close to him. "He's dead, isn't he?"

"Yes. He died in his sleep."

"What should we do?"

"Nothing any more for Lucio. He's home."

"Did you expect him to…to…so soon?"

"Oh yes. I was happy he had some time with you. I believe the thought of seeing you first, and your presence later, kept him alive this long."

Chris rose. "I'll go wake up Lillian and tell the others. Then I'll call the doctor."

*   *   *

For two days one flake after another fell, morbidly but incessantly, creating a thick carpet of snow. The third day an abrupt plunge in temperature gripped Harrisville in an excruciating mantle of cold and wind.

Lucio's funeral was being celebrated in the chapel of the Don Bosco Seminary, which barely contained all the people who had come to pay their last respects to Chris' and Rick's father, the Lord of the Red Manor.

The hymns had been carefully selected by Father Paul. *The Lord is my Shepherd* and *I Go Before You,* sung in unison by over twenty ordinands, filled the chapel with melody and Chris' heart with emotion. He had buried his grandfather and his mother, and now he was saying farewell to his father. Never before, as in this precise moment, was Chris so thankful to have his brother close to him.

He only vaguely followed the eulogies delivered by Glen Howard and Father Paul. His mind went back to the year before, when he had questioned himself about the wisdom of bringing Lucio to Canada. That doubt had tormented him then, as it had many times in the last year.

As the mourners gathered at the cemetery where Deborah Sandcroft had been interred, Chris felt the inner laceration that severing the last earthly bond provokes.

When Father Paul pronounced the ritual words *dust to dust, ashes to ashes*, Chris wondered whether he had, unwillingly or unconsciously, shortened Lucio's life. He had meant to brighten it, give his father comfort, make him part of his own life. But when Chris thought he had finally achieved that, a series of events had conspired to worsen Lucio's precarious health. Chris sighed, loud enough to attract Vivian's attention.

She squeezed his arm. "You okay?"

Chris nodded, but his mind still mulled over his own doubts and the last events that had occurred in Lucio's life. Was there anything he could have done differently after Lucio had come to stay with him? Should he have taken Lucio back to Italy when he became homesick?

It was then that Rick patted him on the shoulder.

"I had no chance to get to know my father," Rick whispered. "But I believe that he loved his children so much he'd have given his own life for them." He paused for his turn to lay the red carnation he held in his hand on Lucio's coffin. Then he came back and stood close to Chris again. "Father told me you've been the best son anyone could hope for."

To hide his tears, Chris moved quickly to lay his carnation on the draped coffin. He looped around and took a few steps away from the crowd while the coffin was lowered into the ground.

Slowly the mourners began to leave the cemetery and headed for their cars. Rick had not moved, and neither had Vivian. She stretched the collar of her long tweed coat as high as she could to protect her face from the biting wind.

Chris drew near her. "Maybe you should go wait in the car. It's very cold here."

Vivian shook her head and linked arms with him. For a few minutes they remained in prayer near the tomb, their heads down. Then Chris took her hand and moved away, followed by Rick.

"Chris?" Vivian asked. "I was wondering if you might want to postpone the wedding."

"Do you want to?"

"It's *your* father we're mourning. It should be *your* decision."

For a moment Chris didn't utter a sound. "Let's go ahead then. Lucio was immensely happy to see us getting married." He shot Vivian a little smile and winked. "Let's not disappoint him."

The End

BY THE SAME AUTHOR

The Jungfrau Watch

The collapse of the Soviet Union leaves two prominent members of the Red Brigades without funds, without a job and without a cause. They both find asylum, under false identities, in Canada. One continues in his criminal activities, the other wants to make a break from his past. Years later their paths cross again. When the prototype of the Jungfrau Watch is stolen, Alesh Stefanich is hired to establish a fake laboratory based on the production of efficient fuel cells. Soon after a project is stolen from the lab, providing a major breakthrough.

But the Red Brigades aren't dead. Alesh Sinkovich will have to adopt drastic measures to save what's very dear to him.

Available at www.PublishAmerica.com

Operation Woman in Black

Nothing and nobody seem to penetrate the criminal ring that plagues the town of Varlee, Ontario. When Varlee's Chief of Police, frustrated by five years of unsuccessful attempts, resigns, Conrad Miguel Tormez becomes in charge of the investigation. Aware of the potential that *Pappa-Pappa,* a new speech emulation system, offers, Conrad Tormez engineers a daring operation: he'll replace the Woman in Black, a recently deceased member of the criminal ring, with Savina Thompson, an ex-agent and amateur performer.

But *Operation Woman in Black* isn't the only challenge Conrad Tormez has to face. For the last year he has been searching for Isabel, his teenage mentally impaired daughter. Then one day he finds her—living in a log cabin in the Rocky Mountains, together with a baby and a wolf. A loving father yet a cunning detective, Conrad Tormez has to balance every minute of the day between parenting and police work.

As *Operation Woman in Black* progresses Conrad Tormez realizes that the mastermind of the criminal ring is a formidable opponent—his deadly tentacles can reach anybody, anywhere, anytime.

Available at www.PublishAmerica.com

The Collage

A cleverly masterminded plot entraps young heiress Allison Summer in a web of deceit and violence—slowly but without mercy. Even if surrounded by a multitude of people, beautiful Allison is alone in her struggle, not knowing whom to trust: not her father, not her husband, not even the handsome man who pledges his love to her…

A nosy reporter makes Allison's life difficult, a mysterious fire destroys her home, a killer seemingly coming from nowhere knocks on her door, while an accusation of murder hangs over her head.

Overcome by guilt and disheartened by the loss of loved ones, Allison suffers in solitude, hoping for better times. But when the life of the man she loves becomes at stake, Allison musters her strength and takes control of her destiny. And she will not stop until the innocent is free and the guilty secured behind bars.

Cross of Sapphires

Chief Steve Carlton seems to have successfully carried out his mission—he has finally managed to take fugitive Livia White aboard his aircraft.

Shortly after take off, however, Steve's plane crashes in the wildest region of Venezuela. Severely injured, he is nursed back to health by an attentive and caring Livia. For five long weeks Steve tries to picture her as a killer. To no avail. Her limpid blue eyes, her rare but genuine smile, and her kindness capture his heart.

But when Steve returns to New Brunswick he discovers that the evidence accumulated against Livia is staggering. The law being his one and only creed, Steve battles his feelings as the life of accused Livia White unfolds before his eyes.

Follow Steve in his struggle and his adventures, where the stakes are high and the rewards none too sure.

Mountains of Dawn

Pack and Leave are the words that Tanya Caldwell, orphaned at the age of six, heard many times over as she wandered from foster home to foster home. She hears them again from Malcolm Clark, the head of the prestigious agency *Invicta*, after she narrowly escapes two murder attempts.

On Malcolm's advice, she retires to the hills of the Riviera.

The Mediterranean shores offer endless inspiration to Tanya the artist. Here she meets Kevin Matwin, a publisher of arts books, and a friend of his, Luigi Amedeo, Count of Monteturro. The count's dignified manners and daredevil enterprises hide more than one secret.

Accidents similar to Tanya's also occur to Brian, Malcolm's brother. Because Tanya's and Brian's misfortunes have a common denominator in a...

For more information, see the author's Web site: www.vermeil.biz

Also available from PublishAmerica

SHINE AND INSPIRATIONS

by Tiffiney Rochelle Bradley

Shine and Inspirations is a text designed to teach humanity the purpose and role of prayer in everyday life. This book seeks to deepen believers' insights and understanding of how a continual prayer life will serve to strengthen the soul of believers and equip them in remaining encouraged while in the midst of life's stormiest situations.

Another book, entitled *Inspirations*, a collection of Christian testimonies, is included. Many of these touching testimonies explain how prayer served to stabilize and/or uplift those who testified out of situations such as HIV, severe physical illnesses, single parenthood, and hunger. Read, enjoy, and forever be inspired as you connect with the Spirit of Christ, which will enable you to Shine.

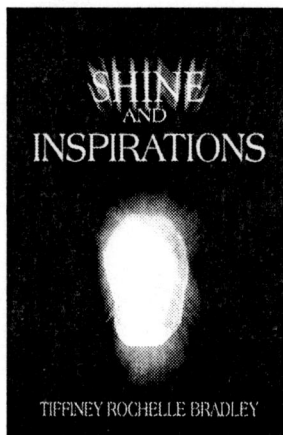

Paperback, 198 pages
6" x 9"
ISBN 1-4241-8489-4

About the author:

Shine and Inspirations came to life out of my call to serve the Lord, and my passion to help people. Prayer is having an intimate conversation with God. Having a Master's degree in Communications and having served in the field of education has been quite fulfilling, but publishing *Shine and Inspirations* has also been fulfilling, if not more so. What could be more exciting for a communicator and a servant of the Lord than helping others experience a dimension in Christ that I have already experienced.

Available to all bookstores nationwide.
www.publishamerica.com

THE GIRL IN THE PICTURE

by Charles E. Merkel II

Everything is going great for 18-year-old Brian Kitzmiller, who is assigned to a non-combat unit in 1967 Vietnam. His responsibilities include being the outfit's mail clerk, and he soon becomes a welcome face to everyone.

He carries a picture, which he has enlarged then placed above his bunk, of a girl from his hometown whom he really does not know but passes off as his girlfriend. As time goes on, the gorgeous girl becomes the most famous lady in the whole unit and the juicy stories abound. Brian does nothing to stifle this ever-growing myth. In fact, he enjoys his "legendary" status as he has never known anything but loneliness and obscurity back home.

Paperback, 266 pages
6" x 9"
ISBN 1-4241-3047-6

The lid blows off when a cruel skeptic from the same town arrives and Brian's life unravels. Wracked by relentless humiliation and scorn, his decisions from that point become reckless.

About the author:

Charles E. Merkel II grew up in Louisville and Indianapolis, the son of a state engineer inspector and an elementary school teacher. A graduate of the Indiana University School of Journalism and a Vietnam veteran, he has been published in various literary magazines nine times. He has worked as a regional sales manager in the RV industry for twenty-five years.

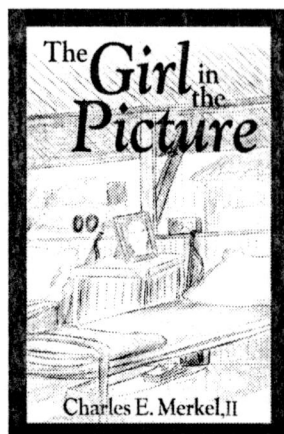